HOUSE of DESTINY

JANET LEIGH
HOUSE OF DESTINY

MIRA BOOKS

MIRA

ISBN 1-55166-125-X

HOUSE OF DESTINY

Copyright © 1995 by Janet Leigh

First Edition

MIRA and the star colophon are trademarks of MIRA Books.

Printed in U.S.A.

To my husband Bob, my children Jamie and Kelly,
my grandchild Annie—
you are my life.

To Lillian Burns Sidney—without your
encouragement, belief and guidance, I would never
have had the courage to meet this challenge.

My grateful acknowledgment to:

Laura Archila
Marty Arrougé
Loretta Barrett
Betsy Barrymore
Roberta McKurcher
Dianne Moggy
Dr. Lew Morrill
Les Outzs
Mary Outzs
Robbie Pierson
Lillian Sidney
J. R. Simplot Company
Gloria Sorensen
Ada Tesar
Laura Van Wormer
and
MIRA Books

"No two men differ so much as one man
differs from his prior self."
—Pascal

Prologue

Friday, March 16, 1990

Seventy-year-old Jude Abavas walked mechanically down the long hall. He was six feet two inches tall, weighed a trim, hard hundred and eighty-five pounds. His hair was almost all completely gray, but full and thick. Dark eyebrows topped dark eyes and a generous, sensual mouth. He was ruggedly handsome.

He was flanked by men in uniforms, three on each side, the seven sets of shoes echoing eerily as they marched over the concrete floor.

His steps were strong and regular but his reflections wandered erratically. He envisioned the onlookers. Penelope's beautiful face would show anguish, her big brown eyes filled with tears. The two young men standing beside her would give her strength and support, but their guts would be churning.

Who thought it would have ended like this? Had Penelope? John? Matthew? Polly? Revel? Vincent? Had Noah? Willamina? Wade? Thelma? Keane? Luke? Madge?

Was it a shock? Or had it been expected? A sardonic smile crossed his lips. Too late now. The seeds had been sown too long ago. Jude remembered what his father had said to him when he was almost eight. "I give you a caution. There is a craving in you that must be controlled."

Jude had a craving, all right—a craving to get the hell out of there.

Why did this walk have to be so damn long? Again the jaundiced grin. He couldn't help comparing the situation to a scene in a bad movie. Any merciful person would have made it quicker. But what the hell did anyone care about the agonizing—the fear, the dry mouth, the jelly legs, the pounding heart. Cruel. But soon—soon—it would be over.

Armed police officers pulled open the heavy metal doors.

This was it. No reprieve now.

I

1

Hailey, Idaho
January 1936

Sixteen-year-old Jude Abavas was ready! Ready to kick butt! His body tingled with anticipation. How he wanted to be victorious! And if, in that process, he beat John, his twin— Well, that would just be icing on his cake.

"Jude," Tom McCruger called. "Did ya hear the news?"

"What news?" Jude asked, harnessing one of Mr. Wangler's horses. "You're late!"

"Sorry. But listen! Some fancy dude's in Ketchum, wantin' to build a swell hotel. Wouldn't that be great?"

"Well, yeah, guess so, but now you'd better get your rig set up if you wanna be my partner. John is hooked up with Clyde Warhas and they'll be tough. Damn, it's colder than a cow's tit!"

The boys were preparing for Hailey's monthly Sunday race. They were set to compete in the day's big event, the relay, where a skier was pulled by a cantering horse one block and then, when he crossed the line, his teammate shot back to the start. It was difficult enough for a skier to balance behind the irregular gait of a canter; managing it while dodging other galloping horses and skiers was downright perilous. And the skis, which were generally homemade wooden slats about twelve feet long, bent with steam and then grooved, were almost impossible to turn. On an incline, the skier could only point downhill and go. Sometimes, on a steeper hill, a long sapling pole was straddled, offering a stingy bit of maneuverability.

The relay always caused the biggest stir because there were spills and thrills aplenty. This Sunday there were four teams, the street scarcely broad enough to contain them, and the spectators crowded the walkway so as not to get trampled. Tom was first up; Jude was the anchorman. John started for his team with Clyde taking the return lap.

Tom and John were neck and neck at the onset. But then Tom's horse nipped the animal next to him, who clearly didn't think that was neighborly and bit right back. Both racers used all their resources to avoid a collision, but Tom lost valuable time against John, who came in ahead, yelling to Jude, "*Ye-ow!* We're gonna beat ya!"

Jude was ready when Tom crossed the line, and lashing his horse with the reins, he took off after Clyde at a full gallop. His horse kicked so much snow in his face Jude couldn't see where he was going or where his opponent was. He just kept driving the horse and trying to stay upright, but finally the pace was too much to handle, his skis hit a rough spot and he lost control, tumbling and rolling in a flurry of snow. He stopped in a heap and caught his breath, gingerly moving each part of his body to check for damage. Jude was lucky. Very lucky. Nothing was broken except the heavy wooden skis.

"We won! *Ya-hoo!* We won! You caught 'im and crossed the finish just when you fell!" an excited Tom shouted, running to help his hero.

Jude just grinned. He liked to win, and there was nothing better than beating his brother, John.

The twins' father, Noah, smiled proudly as friends and family gathered to congratulate Jude and Tom.

Suddenly a completely frustrated John pushed his way through the crowd, knocked Jude away from Tom and started pummeling his brother with his fists. It took Jude a few seconds to realize what was happening, and then he started fighting back. They were big strong boys and blood quickly spilled.

Noah, livid at the display, rushed in to separate his sons. "You shame me," he hissed to them once he had finally managed to put some distance between them. "Get your things and go home. I speak there."

Noah was pacing in front of the fireplace when Jude and John entered the room. They looked a mess, dried blood under their noses, numerous facial and hand cuts, bruises starting to swell.

Their clothes were worn, their eyes were puffed and full of apprehension.

Noah turned away to control the compassion that swept over him. He understood sibling rivalry, and he knew the anguish of defeat. But it was his duty to try and stop this jealousy between the boys.

"Why? Why do you brawl in street like you be bums? You be brothers! We be citizens and live by the law! We be children of God and act in love and peace!"

"He started it!" Jude blurted. "Durned if I'm not gonna hit him back!"

John's discontent erupted again. "He thinks he's so high and mighty. I'm as good as he is. He's just lucky, he fell over the finish line, we coulda won. Why him, Papa? Why always him?"

It seemed the fracas was going to start again. "Enough!" thundered Noah. "I do not know the answer to your 'why,' John. But I know you cannot question God's will. If you do your best, you can ask for no more. If you do not, blame yourself, not your brother."

Noah paused and turned to Jude. "I do not fault you for defending yourself, but I do fault you for continuing the fight. You always need to win, you may become blind to needs of others and cause them pain. You may cause yourself pain."

He sighed heavily. "I love you both. But do not betray my trust again. Now go clean yourselves and apologize to your mama."

Noah sat alone for a long time thinking about the complexities of humanity and life. He remembered his difficulties with his brother and father. He had only been a year older than Jude and John when he had bid his family goodbye. Was it twenty-one years already?

The Basque Provincia of Alava
Spanish Pyrenees, March 1915

Noah Abavas didn't dare look back. He marched resolutely forward, his wooden shoes clattering over the cobblestone road.

He barely noticed when the austere mountains began to give way to the misty hills of the lowlands and the rural stone houses to the festive red and green homes of the villages. In each ham-

let women were doing their laundry at a dependable spring,
rubbing and slamming their wash on stone slabs and then rins-
ing farther upstream. He passed the beloved and inevitable
handball court and prayed there would also be such things where
he was going. The reality of his position was gradually hitting
him. He knew *nothing,* absolutely *nothing* about his destination, except that it was in America, in a country called Idaho.
The enormity of his voyage was staggering to him now.

The following morning Jude had concluded it was of no use
to fret about his plight—the decision had been made and there
was no alternative. Tickets and money were securely hidden in a
pouch around his waist.

His father had designated Noah's older brother as his heir.
Noah's future had been settled when a cousin, who was already
in America, wrote to say that Mr. Horace B. Wangler in Idaho
needed sheepherders and would pay their transportation expenses. Noah's father ruled this was the proper course for his
second son to take.

At seventeen, Noah simply decided he would accept the challenge, conquer this Mr. Wangler and Idaho, come home a rich
man and marry Willamina.

Oh, but, Willamina! How he would miss her. Willamina, with
her flashing blue eyes and flowing black hair, her defiant chin
thrust forward. He savored again their farewell—the forbidden
kiss and embrace, her firm breasts pressed into his chest, her
arms holding him tight, as if to keep him with her always. Passion and desperation had flared and almost overcome them. He
was to relive that moment for many, many months.

Upon reaching Cartagena on the Mediterranean coast, Noah
was introduced to another Mr. Horace B. Wangler recruit, Antonio Navassa. Noah and Antonio surmised that Mr. Wangler
had to be a very wealthy land baron to have need for two sheepherders. And then, as if to confirm their suspicions, before their
ship sailed they met eight more young men with the same destination.

The teenagers gazed at the receding coastline of their homeland, fearful of the unknown before them, yet jubilant with anticipation.

The old steamer glided through the Straits of Gibraltar into the
Atlantic Ocean, and finally, into New York Harbor under the

protection symbolized by the great lady of hope, the Statue of Liberty. Still entranced by The Lady's spell, they were hustled off the ship at Ellis Island and then thrust into a teeming mass of humanity who all wanted the same thing—to enter the United States.

The boys were ushered through the portals of a redbrick building that to them resembled a palace. When it was their turn, the board of immigration authorities stamped their visas with a simple "Spanish" title. After processing, which was expedient because of the prearranged employment, they were ferried to the island of Manhattan and then bused to the railroad yards.

Their glimpse of New York City left a lasting impression—tall buildings, asphalt streets, sidewalks for pedestrians, hundreds of automobiles and the continuous din of horns, whistles and voices. And the language! Nary a word of Basque, and only an occasional hint of Spanish. Noah vowed he would learn this strange tongue called English as soon as he could.

The boys were befriended on the long journey west by the train's conductor and a family traveling to California. The parents, who were schoolteachers, had noticed Noah's avid interest in the lessons they taught their children. Using sign language and a smattering of Spanish to communicate, they began to tutor Noah.

At Shoshone, Idaho, the recruits had to change to a branch line of Union Pacific to reach Hailey, Idaho, their final destination. As a parting gift, Noah's train family presented him with two precious books to continue his education. He could not express his gratitude—the books were his treasured companions in the ensuing months.

Noah's cousin, Jose Abavas, met the weary group and bundled them into a wagon for yet another journey, this one to the main ranch near Fairfield, about twenty miles to the south.

Mr. Horace B. Wangler was there to greet them. An imposing figure, he was well over six feet—taller with his high-crown cowboy hat—with a hardy build, demanding eyes and wide mustache twirling upward on either side. He was a self-made man, dedicated to his work, and fair and compassionate toward his hands. Fortunately, he was fluent in Spanish and understood some Basque.

The new recruits were assigned to experienced herders—Noah joined Jose, and began the arduous task of learning the rou-

tine. In the spring each team would take their band of two thousand sheep north, moving slowly to Ketchum, at the base of Bald
Mountain, and then toward Challis National Forest heading into
Copper Basin. At the end of the summer, the migration returned to winter headquarters in Bliss or Hagerman or Fairfield.

The loneliness and isolation took its toll on many, but Noah
filled the time with his two textbooks, his struggle to learn English, and his dreams of some day showing his Willamina this
magnificent country.

As time went by, Mr. Wangler noted Noah's interest in books
and allowed him access to his personal library. Noah had progressed so well and had handled several emergency situations
with such sense and strength, that he had been entrusted with
Mr. Wangler's finest band of sheep. And Mr. Wangler's plans
for Noah had not ended there!

In July of 1918, Noah's presence was requested at the main
ranch.

"Ah, Noah." Mr. Wangler beamed. "Sorry to drag you back.
I have someone I want you to meet."

He led Noah to the dark parlor, and coming from the bright
sunshine, Noah could barely make out a dim outline of a figure. It was a female—in a long black skirt, high-necked blouse,
a silk scarf rolled and arranged like a little cap on her black hair.
He faltered. This apparition had taken on the appearance of his
Willamina. He was fearful his dreams had begun to rule his
senses.

"Actually, Noah, I think you already know this young lady,"
Mr. Wangler said.

The two moved haltingly toward each other. Trembling, they
reached their hands out and touched.

It was reality. It was truth. It was warm flesh and blood. It was
Willamina.

Noah looked at Mr. Wangler, eyes brimming with tears.

"I wanted to surprise you," Mr. Wangler said, "I'm afraid I
didn't realize how much of a shock it would be." He paused.
"This is my way of saying thank you, Noah. None of my men
have advanced so quickly.

"There's a vacant cabin on the grounds that can be yours,
Noah. And you won't have to return to the mountains until next
week." With a twinkle, he added, "*After* the wedding."

On June 4, 1919, Noah and Willamina became the proud parents of twin sons—Jude William Abavas and John William Abavas. On December 1, 1920, the couple's third son, Luke Noah Abavas, was born. Shortly afterward, Noah was promoted to foreman, reporting directly to Mr. Wangler. The family moved to Hailey. And on July 7, 1925, Matthew William Abavas greeted the world and his three brothers.

The house of Noah was faring well.

Hailey, Idaho
January 1936

By the end of January, all of Blaine County, Idaho, knew about the prospective resort-hotel to be built near Ketchum. The "fancy dude" behind the development was Count Felix Schaffgotsch, an Austrian amateur skier and resort developer who had been asked by Mr. Averell Harriman, the young chairman of the board of Union Pacific Railroad, to survey sites in Union Pacific territory suitable for a winter sports center. Harriman wanted to generate industry in the West, which in turn would promote traffic for the railroad. He had noted the popularity of skiing in Europe and in the eastern United States and believed promoting the sport would be a worthwhile venture for the West. The count knew the prerequisites: a high mountain with powder snow and room for open slopes, and scenic peaks to provide some protection from wind and sun.

Union Pacific railroad men showed the count many possibilities in various states, but none were suitable. He'd been about to give up, when a Boise employee realized the men had neglected to take the count to Ketchum, Idaho. Union Pacific spent more money on snow removal for the branch of railroad running from Shoshone to Ketchum than on any other in the system.

A telegram was dispatched to the count who was then in Denver and he agreed to return to Idaho. He arrived in Ketchum in a foul humor: his train had been forced to follow a snowplow from Shoshone in the midst of a savage storm. He also believed, from his initial observations, that "This valley is too wide, too wide."

What he couldn't see until the next day was that the valley narrowed in Ketchum, and that just to the northeast, towering mountains surrounding a snug basin came into view. And Idaho welcomed the count with a breathtakingly beautiful scene. The snow shimmered like a jeweled carpet, the trees were illuminated with the gleaming white. From the top of Dollar Mountain, the count looked down at the level floor that ran into Trail Creek. Foothills perfect for ski slopes rose before him, while higher peaks loomed behind him. To the north, Trail Creek Canyon, Trail Creek Summit and the Pioneer Range. To the southeast, Bald Mountain.

After three days of intense study, the count wired Mr. Harriman that he had found the ideal spot.

Mr. and Mrs. Averell Harriman, with guests William S. Paley—the equally young chairman of Columbia Broadcasting Systems—and his wife, arrived by private railroad car in early February. Union Pacific's land and tax men came soon after. March 26 brought the announcement that the 3,888-acre Brass Ranch had been purchased. At the end of March, the count also brought Charlie Proctor, renowned skier and member of the 1928 United States Olympic ski team, and Steve Hannagan, New York public relations whiz, to Ketchum. Mr. Proctor was a natural choice to select the sites for ski runs, but Mr. Hannagan was hardly suited for his assignment, since he abhorred cold weather and thought people who voluntarily lashed boards to their feet and hurtled down mountains on them were crazy. But, as it turned out, his was an inspired appointment. His memorandums regarding the promotional campaign for the new resort became the basis for establishing its special appeal. He battled for and won the right to name the area Sun Valley. He pushed for and got the resort a bowling alley, a movie house, an ice rink, hot mineral water pools, sleigh rides to appealing restaurants, and perhaps most important, "a mechanical device to take people to the top of the mountain."

"When you get to Sun Valley," he said, "your eyes should pop open. And after you have spent a few hours there, you should say, 'Well, I'll be damned. They've certainly done this place well. There isn't a single thing I could wish for that hasn't been provided.' Imagine that!" His wish was to out-elite the elite.

On June 11, 1936, construction began. So, from the roaring mining days, to the sleepier sheep-raising ones, the community of Ketchum suddenly found itself the center of a building boom. The locals marveled at how those "city folk" managed to transform ideas into reality in only six months. The face of Ketchum and the entire Wood River Valley was irrevocably changed. And so were the lives of its citizens.

As soon as school was out in June, Jude applied for a position with the construction crew building the resort. At seventeen he didn't have an appetite for farming or working with livestock, despite the fact that his father now owned some land and bands of sheep of his own. This wasn't the life Jude had in mind. His twin brother, John, could have it all. Jude was after bigger game.

Nor was Jude interested in his mother's flourishing business—Willamina had opened a home restaurant. After all, she "be the best cook around."

Jude was hired and he and his friend Tom McCruger shared room and board in Ketchum. The two boys looked forward to a family-free and profitable summer.

The two seventeen-year-olds were in hog heaven. They had ample dates and were making more money than they had ever imagined, which allowed them to visit the cribs on River Street whenever they felt the urge for wine, women and song. They thrived on the stimulation of new people and a new kind of work.

Jude was particularly intrigued with the project called Operation Chair Lift. Since Steve Hannagan's announcement that rope tows and J-bars were not dignified enough for the guests of Sun Valley, Union Pacific engineers had used every ounce of their genius to develop a better way to transport people to the top of the ski runs. It was Jim Curran, a relative unknown in the ranks, who revolutionized skiing by designing the world's first chair lift. The concept was astonishingly simple. Curran, who had helped build equipment to load bananas in the tropics, substituted a person for a bunch of bananas and replaced the hooks with chairs. There was opposition from the chief engineer. "It is too dangerous," he said, but Charlie Proctor was a believer and took Curran's plans straight to Mr. Harriman. With one look, the railroad executive said, "Develop the chair lift!"

Jude immediately recognized the benefits of this new invention: a greater loading capacity, which meant added revenue from ticket sales; the enticement for skiers to make more runs during a day; and the appeal to less hardy skiers who dreaded the climb up, or the timid souls who feared the ruts of a rope tow or J-bar.

As construction on the resort progressed, Jude, ever-ambitious and never bashful, voiced his opinions to the foreman.

"You really shouldn't install the Dollar and Proctor mountain lifts in the valleys—the best skiing is *in* the valleys. Put 'em on the ridges," he urged. "And make sure there's enough room under the lifts for the winter snow buildup."

The foreman thanked Jude for his ideas, promptly dismissed them and proceeded as planned. Regardless of the mistakes he thought were being made, Jude didn't hesitate to volunteer to take the first test ride. He wanted to have the experience before anyone else. It was wonderful!

Later, when the lifts were actually in operation, Jude's calculations were proven correct. The estimated four feet from the ground was too low and crews were forced to plow wide furrows so the chairs could get through the snow. And, as he'd predicted, everyone soon discovered that the valleys were the best places to ski, but the stanchions of the lifts were constantly in the way. And so, when a third chair lift was built the following year on Rudd Mountain, complete with a forty-meter ski jump and judging stand, the lift went up on the ridge and was high enough to clear the deepest snow.

Jude and his buddy Tom were working construction that summer of 1936 on the mammoth Sun Valley Lodge. The unique hotel was to be built entirely of reinforced concrete. Pilasters, outside stairways and trimming would be made of native Idaho stone, quarried from the Magic Reservoir between Ketchum and Shoshone. The lodge would be three stories high and have four wings spreading in the shape of a double Y. Each of the two hundred-plus rooms would have a window with a view. No detail was overlooked, no cost was spared, to make the resort as fine a hotel as any in the United States. Every amenity Steve Hannagan insisted on was included, even a Saks Fifth Avenue ski shop.

When school resumed in September, Jude and Tom had to leave. But they had earned the reputation of being hard workers, and had been promised weekend work as the pressure to finish the project increased, and the chance for jobs during Christmas break and for the grand opening.

The friends returned to Hailey reluctantly, their ordinary regimen a bore after a summer of liberation. Jude hated waiting tables in his mother's restaurant, hated doing dishes and hated doing homework—in that order. Recognizing the value of education, however, he concentrated on his studies and alleviated the tedium by playing on the school's ragtag football team until ice hockey season started, which was more to his liking.

Things weren't any better with twin brother John, who had developed a smug attitude because he was working with Noah. Luke, who stayed close to Willamina, seemed distant, as well. It was only with eleven-year-old Matthew that Jude felt any sort of rapport.

Jude and Tom started working at the lodge site on weekends. On Saturday nights, they went out on the town. They were big boys and no one ever questioned their age, so it was easy to get a mite sloshed and then head for a crib.

His mounting anticipation for the grand opening of Sun Valley made time move excruciatingly slow for Jude. Advance publicity was already in full swing. Pictures of a handsome young man stripped to the waist on skis told the world how warm and wonderful it was to ski at Sun Valley. *Life* magazine committed to a cover story during the inaugural week. High society, Hollywood celebrities and major political figures were vying for invitations to the opening. Preparations were pushed to a frantic pace. Painters worked round-the-clock, with steam heat on to dry the paint, while carpet layers waited in the wings. Workmen were literally going out the back door as guests were coming in the front.

When the lodge was finished, Jude and Tom weighed the job possibilities. The hotel or the mountain? Hans Hauser, the Austrian champion, was going to head the Sun Valley ski school and bring instructors from Europe, but some locals were going to be used as guides, lift operators and for ski patrol. Tom opted for the mountain. But as much as Jude loved the outdoors, he felt he could get such a job anytime. He chose, instead, to take one of the bellman positions at the hotel, hoping to meet the celebrities and be in line for the promised gratuities.

Jude's instincts turned out to be on target once again. When it became apparent that no significant snowfall would occur before the grand opening, Averell Harriman sent a wire to the guests. *"No snow here. If you are a good gambler, come on out and be our guests till it arrives."* No one could refuse that offer, and the wealthy guests, usually generous tippers, anyway, were even more magnanimous. Jude almost made enough for a down payment on a car!

On Monday evening, December 21, 1936, a gala dinner officially put Sun Valley on the map as the "newest winter playground of the rich and famous." Over three hundred formally attired guests filed into the spacious, tastefully appointed dining room. A wide flight of corner stairs permitted each couple to make an entrance as they descended to their table on the lower floor. Mr. and Mrs. Harriman, the Union Pacific establishment and the parties responsible for Sun Valley were very much in evidence. Idaho statesmen mixed with national politicians. Blue book socialites, like Lydia Du Pont of the Delaware Du Ponts, J. J. Studebaker III, Margaret Emerson McKim Vanderbilt, Baker Amory, Gloria Baker, Mr. and Mrs. Earle Prickler and son, Wayland Colby Prickler, smiled for photographers and were rivaled only by Hollywood's nobility—Claudette Colbert, Joan Bennett, Madeleine Carroll, Constance Bennett, Lili Damitra, and David O. Selznick. Added to this pantheon was a crush of beautiful Hollywood starlets praying to get photographed with anyone. The scene was a press agent's dream.

Even a slight altercation was used by Steve Hannagan to garner national press headlines. "Charles Gore of Chicago joined the table of Mr. and Mrs. Selznick, Gene Markey and his wife, Joan Bennett, Dr. Joel Pressman and his wife, Claudette Colbert, uninvited, and asked one of the film stars to dance." One newspaper ran "Mr. Selznick promptly knocked Gore flat." The lead read "Sun Valley Opens With A Bang!"

The menu was superb. Each course was carefully recorded for the newspapers, despite the fact that few postdepression readers would understand what brioche au caviar, beef tea des wiveurs, pailettes dorées, suprême of sole au champagne, tournedos sauté chatelaine were. Music was provided by Carl Smith's New York Orchestra, the broadcast given over to KSL from the club room, and guests danced until an early hour.

Nothing was sacred to the media. Jude quickly discovered this when a reporter pulled him aside at the opening. "How would you like to make some extra dough?" he asked.

Jude was wary. "Who do I have to kill?"

"No, no, nothin' like that! You're around all the time. Just keep your eyes and ears open. Keep track of who's doin' what to who, who's mad at who, you know!"

"Sure, I know," Jude answered. "Go sit on a pole, you creep."

Jude relished being involved, albeit on the fringes, carrying luggage and running errands. He knew he could learn from the guests. Their world was on another planet, a distant, exotic place he couldn't visit . . . yet. He wanted a ticket to that world, he wanted space on that planet, and these were the people who could point him in the right direction to get there. He would watch and listen carefully—how they talked, what they talked about, how they dressed, how they reacted. He would extend himself beyond expected duties, make himself available for any and all demands. He would try to anticipate their needs, make himself indispensable.

And he would be on the alert for their weaknesses. A slip, or a sign, anything that would give him an edge, an advantage, perhaps something that could put them in his debt.

Jude walked dogs, made hot chocolate in the middle of the night, fixed sandwiches after room service had closed, roused a Ketchum doctor for a sick wife, helped the emergency repairman with stuck doors, frozen toilets and broken doorknobs. Anything and everything was his motto. Well, almost. One hungry lady had an appetite for more than just food. Jude had no urge to deal with a jealous husband at this point in his life and so he was always in a rush when she asked for a delivery in the middle of the night. "I've noticed you work hard to keep our guests happy. But you're smart not to make them *that* happy," the front-desk manager told Jude.

"Thank you, sir." Then Jude grinned and added, "She's not my type, anyway."

2

The most popular socialite at the Sun Valley opening was Wayland Colby Prickler, born in 1914 to Elizabeth Colby and Earle
Thomas Prickler. His childhood was spent in a Hancock Park
mansion, an elite Los Angeles neighborhood. Grandfather
Prickler had amassed an empire of real estate in Southern California, a tradition continued by Wayland's father. Mile after
mile of open fields and orange groves stretching in all directions
from the heart of Los Angeles fell under the Prickler banner.
And as the immature city spread, developers were forced to deal
with the Pricklers, resulting in the family's growing fortune. The
Pricklers would never know a financial worry.

Wayland was groomed for the future at the "right" private
schools where he associated with the "right" privileged children. He tolerated the "right" social amenities, such as dancing
school, where he wore a velvet suit and learned to guide frilly
white-gloved little girls around the floor in a two-step or waltz.
He excelled in tennis and skiing. His equestrian skills put him on
the polo team. His shooting ability put him in skeet competi-
tions. While his life was perfectly orchestrated, there was still one
flaw: Wayland had no desire to be a member of the business
community. None! He had the intellect, but not the inclination,
and consequently his grade-point average ruled out admission to
another family tradition, Harvard. He did, however, manage to
be accepted in the University of Southern California.

Tall and well proportioned, Wayland was a very handsome
young man with dark brown sun-streaked hair and bright blue
eyes. He was an unorthodox individual who reveled in speed,
sports and pleasure, possessed an ingenuous delightful person-

ality and was so charming even his parents couldn't remain annoyed with him for long.

Not unexpectedly, he was popular on campus, where he led his fraternity brothers on many a wild escapade. His sharp eye noticed most of the pretty coeds majoring in liberal arts, which promptly became his major. Astonishingly, he found many classes engrossing, particularly literature. It was this discovery that led him to drama, which in turn led him to performing. No one was more amazed than Wayland himself that he would ever seriously consider acting as a profession. But he was a natural: he had a distinct flair. He incorporated all the desirable elements—a boyish zest for life mixed with suave sophistication, a spicy wit that did not mask the complete sincerity of his emotions, an adventuresome spirit fraught with virility, a graceful agility and a capacity to project all of these qualities with effortless honesty.

Toward the end of his senior year in 1936, Wayland played a major role in the university's production of George Kaufman and Moss Hart's *Once in a Lifetime*. A scout from the Charles Feldman Agency who routinely covered amateur productions in hopes of discovering raw talent, saw an answer to his prayers in Wayland. He was immediately impressed by the charisma Wayland radiated to the audience, how women responded to his aura of sexuality and how men identified with his masculinity. It was the best of both worlds, an agent's dream.

"If this kid can come across on the screen like he does here, I've found a damned gold mine," Max Goldbloom muttered to himself, pushing his way through the throng of well-wishers backstage. He presented his card at the dressing-room entrance, but had to wait outside since Wayland was one of no less than five occupants using the cubbyhole.

"You want to do what?" a surprised Wayland asked the agent.

"Like I said, I want to represent you. Take you to a studio. Get a screen test. I think you got what it takes, and if I'm right, we're in clover. Whatta ya say?"

"What if you are wrong?"

"Whatta ya got to lose?"

"That's true," Wayland reflected aloud. He hadn't, as yet, contemplated a definite career course, but in a short while he would be graduating and he had to do something with his life. He could go to graduate school, but perhaps he should find out now if film held a future for him. The man was right—what did he have to lose!

So the wheels were set in motion. Max Goldbloom approached the newly merged Twentieth Century Fox Studios first because he knew the head of the talent department there quite well. Wayland impressed this shrewd lady just as Max had hoped. A screen test was arranged, two scenes were chosen, one from *The Thin Man* which had starred William Powell and Myrna Loy, and one from *Anna Karenina* with Greta Garbo and Fredric March. One was a contemporary comedy/mystery, one a period drama. The two scenes would provide a visual gauge for the studio executives to grade the young actor's range, ability and appearance.

Nothing seemed to daunt Wayland's confidence or concentration, not the unfamiliar camera, not the strict exactness of position, not the jolting cry of the director's "Action!" and not the extreme differences between the two roles. He was completely at ease. He was doing what he liked to do. The whole experiment was a lark.

Everyone was flabbergasted at his composure. Usually, untrained aspirants were nervous, self-conscious, simply scared out of their wits. This one was unique. What they had no way of knowing was that unlike other hopefuls, Wayland's bread and butter did not depend on this opportunity. He was filthy rich and had been exposed to a wide spectrum of extraordinary experiences since birth. Competition did not panic him in the slightest, either.

Within the day, the studio bosses were salivating. What a find! A cocky Max Goldbloom negotiated the deal in their swank offices. He knew the going rate for a stock contract player was fifty dollars a week, forty weeks of the year, but he felt their enthusiasm and so he asked for two hundred dollars a week with yearly increments. They settled for one hundred and fifty a week.

Max proudly informed Wayland of the deal.

"But that is not acceptable. I do not wish to be paid when I don't work, only when I do," Wayland told his stunned agent. No matter how Max sputtered and spewed, Wayland would not be dissuaded.

A hasty meeting with the brass was called. Wayland was the only person in the room who was unruffled.

"You see, gentlemen, I value my free time. I have no objection to the exclusivity clause—I certainly have no desire to align myself with another company. And I have every intention to labor industriously in your assignments. But when my presence is not required, I want my days to be my own. If I was on salary, that would not be possible, correct?"

"But it could be weeks—months maybe—before we have a part for you!" They were sure they had powerful ammunition with that statement.

"Then that is ideal!" Wayland exclaimed. "After graduation, I had planned on a vacation. In addition, it is going to take me a while to broach the subject of this new development with my family. It must be done delicately. There has never been a thespian in our ancestry." He smiled. "Now then, when I do begin, would two hundred and fifty dollars a week be fair? When I'm actually employed?"

The group sat in disordered silence. Never had they encountered the likes of this one. Wayland discreetly excused himself under the pretext of having to make a phone call, allowing them a chance to mull over his offer. He was pleased the screen test had been received so well, and the prospect of making films did excite him. On the other hand, he did not fancy losing his independence, or being confined to base. His plan seemed perfectly logical for all sides. Wayland had assimilated enough of his father's business acumen to understand that if a commodity sold too cheaply, it lost value to the buyer.

Meanwhile, back in the office, the studio heads were in a quandary. The cash-register part of their heads quickly figured this idea of Wayland's would save them money. They were worried about setting a precedent, however. But then, how many performers could afford *not* to have a guarantee? How could *he* afford it? And then, suddenly, it dawned on them.

"Prickler. My God, could Wayland be one of *those* Pricklers?"

No wonder he could waive a sustenance warranty. Now it made sense. They all agreed to agree, only they would counteroffer with two hundred a week, commencing with preproduction activity, and increasing substantially with each yearly option exercised on a seven-year commitment. Everyone, including Max, knew contracts could be renegotiated later. But one hurdle remained. How could they tell Wayland the name Prickler had to go! They shuddered at what the press would do with the name, the jokes that could be disastrous.

Clumsily they tried to explain the need for a change to Wayland. Too long for the marquee. Prickler not catchy enough.

Wayland smiled again. "No problem. It could work to my benefit in appeasing the family, as a matter of fact. Let's see..." After a few moments, he thought of his mother's maiden name, "How about Colby? Ah, Wade Colby?"

"Good! I like that! Nice sound to it!" Nods of agreement around the room. "Well then, welcome to your new Twentieth Century Fox family, Wade Colby."

Sun Valley, Idaho
January 1937

Wade's celebration at the Sun Valley opening was interrupted when a bellman brought a telegram to his room.

"Hope it's good news, Mr. Prickler," the young man said, beaming.

"The good news came in the form of snow, right? But thank you. What's your name?"

"Jude, sir. Jude Abavas."

"Pleasure meeting you. I'm sure I'll see you around." Wade slipped him a dollar.

The telegram asked Wade to return to Los Angeles as soon as possible. The studio had decided on his first project. All details would be explained when he arrived.

"Rather a suspicious way of conducting business," grumbled his father, Earle Prickler, who harbored a Victorian prejudice against show business.

"Now, now, Earle," soothed his wife, Elizabeth. "Wayland must do as he sees fit. We discussed this thoroughly months ago. Just remember, the Prickler name will not be tarnished. And Mother and Father Colby—God rest their souls—will never know. I doubt our friends will ever make the connection, so there is no cause for concern, Earle. Besides, some of...*those* people were quite respectable, I thought. Miss Colbert was especially enchanting.''

His mother was so naive, Wade thought. But he was not about to enlighten her. He knew if he was to succeed as an actor, there would be no way of maintaining the family's anonymity.

Henry King, some years earlier, had directed Gary Cooper's first major role in *The Winning of Barbara Worth,* and Cooper had become a star. The year before, Mr. King had directed Tyrone Power in *Lloyds of London* and Power had become a household name. Twentieth was counting on this veteran director to work the same magic with Wade Colby.

The film was to unite the team of Tyrone Power and Madeleine Carroll, with Wade playing the second male lead. It was an eighteenth-century swashbuckler titled *The Mystical Castle.* Fencing lessons began immediately, with an instructor, and with Tyrone Power. Both pupils learned quickly and well. Wade found that Tyrone, or Ty as he told Wade to call him when they were introduced, was a kindred spirit. Both enjoyed wine, women and adventure, much like the romantic rogues they portrayed in the script. And both enjoyed their work. Their chemistry exploded on screen and the daily rushes sent studio toppers home dreaming of dollar signs.

The gorgeous Madeleine Carroll chided Wade gently on the set one day. "You are a naughty boy! Why didn't you tell me you were Wade Colby when we met in Sun Valley?"

"If I had even suspected I was to have the good fortune of appearing with you, my lady, indeed I would have done so," Wade gallantly replied.

Yes, Wade was everyone's favorite. Word of the captivating newcomer spread rapidly in the smallish kingdom of Hollywood. It wasn't long before Wade knew the entire roster of stars, directors and producers at Twentieth. And not too much time elapsed before hostesses from every studio hierarchy were clamoring for his presence at their gala soirees. Handsome, eligible bachelors were always in demand.

The public relations machine was put in high gear for Wade Colby's screen debut. He was kept very busy during and after the film with interviews and photo sessions, which he handled with his usual aplomb. He absolutely bewitched the feared columnists Louella Parsons and Hedda Hopper.

Wade was rushed into another feature, *Lovely Little Lady,* starring the studio's biggest box office attraction, Shirley Temple, and longtime favorite Alice Faye. A sweet, sentimental and modern story, the film allowed the studio to show off the versatility of their protégé.

3

Sun Valley, Idaho
February 1937

Another victory for Steve Hannagan during the resort's first season: Paramount Pictures decided to use Sun Valley as the location for the film *I Met Him In Paris,* starring Claudette Colbert, Robert Young and Melvyn Douglas. North Fork Canyon, just north of Sun Valley, doubled for a Tyrolean retreat in the Alps.

This was a coup for Jude, too. His friend, the front-desk manager, recommended Jude to one of the assistant directors who was casting local talent.

"Can you skate?" he asked Jude.

"Oh, yes, sir!"

"Good. You're hired."

Jude had been working Friday nights through Sunday because he had to attend school during the week, but for this experience he took two weeks off. He was fascinated by the proceedings and impressed with each department's specialized skills. A quaint village had been created, complete with hotel, hillside church, chalets, sleighs and skating rink with snow-topped gazebo and ice bar. Jude was to play one of the skating waiters. A featured player was the head waiter and a modest routine on ice was designed around him. Jude was very comfortable on skates and was thoroughly relaxed, enjoying the whole experience and, as always, observing and learning.

Jude sensed the nervousness of the actor playing the head waiter. He was probably unsure of his abilities compared to those of the locals who were so obviously skating experts. The actor kept making mistakes, and the company was getting edgy; too much time was being spent on a relatively minor scene. Finally, he actually fell. Jude quickly tripped deliberately to land on the ice near him.

"Damn ice is sticky!" Jude said so everyone could hear.

The actor flashed him a grateful look, and agreed. The next try at the scene was flawless. Jude had helped restore the actor's confidence by letting him know the locals were with him.

The production manager pulled Jude aside afterward. "Good thinking, Abavas. You saved us time, which means you saved us money. There'll be a little extra in your envelope this week. I could use your kind of savvy back home."

The filming of the movie in Sun Valley left its mark on the area in many ways, one of which would be visible for years to come. Averell Harriman had plans to build another hotel, a homey, less expensive one for people who could not afford the lodge. He wanted to call it the Challenger Inn, the name tying in nicely with Union Pacific's new streamlined economical sit-up trains called the Challengers. Harriman had admired the ersatz movie village and decided to pattern the new hotel complex after its Tyrolean style. In the summer of 1937, the inn, a theater, the Opera House, a third lift and a large cottage for the Harrimans were built.

When occupancy was slow at the lodge, Jude worked on construction, but otherwise he preferred to be around the resort, pursuing his one-on-one theory with visitors. In the summer, guests came to fish, hike and go horseback riding, and later, in the fall, to hunt. Jude saw these as ideal situations to get inside a guest's head. Sharing nature's glories and sporting thrills had a way of breaking down barriers, of stripping away masks and veneers: most people, humbled by the majesty of creation, allowed themselves to become vulnerable. Jude was an ideal guide, charming and personable, to be sure. At lunch or during a break, he entertained guests with the old Basque folk songs he played on his father's ancient guitar, and with the stories passed down to him by Noah and Willamina of the mountains and streams and back country of northern Spain.

Jude and John graduated from high school in June. Unlike the previous year, when a measles epidemic hit Hailey and caused the cancellation of the senior ball, senior breakfast and the baccalaureate exercises, the ceremonies went on without a hitch. John now saw Jude as less of a threat, and graduation was one of the happier family occasions. As they received their diplomas, both twins were aware of the pride stamped on the faces of Noah and Willamina. The boys symbolized the rewards of all their years of toil: their firstborn sons were standing as equals with their peers.

Willamina closed the restaurant and prepared a Basque feast for some of the graduates and their families and friends. Even the Wanglers came. Noah ensured the evening's success by concentrating on offering great food, music and dancing. He had no desire for any games or contests that might reopen old wounds between his eldest sons. This was too pleasant, too special a time not to protect.

Noah welcomed John into his ever-growing operation and acknowledged Jude's need to pursue a different field. He knew Jude was slowly infiltrating the Sun Valley organization and didn't doubt he would do well. Noah actually confided to Willamina that he felt the Union Pacific's project had probably saved them many heartaches. The thought of day-to-day confrontations between Jude and John in his business made him shudder. God worked in wondrous ways!

And so, with his parents' blessings, Jude moved to Ketchum on a permanent basis. He bought a used Ford V8 and was, in his eyes, emancipated. No sheepherder jokes for him, thank you! No sheep for him, period!

Over the summer, Luke was off with Noah and John tending sheep, so Willamina reluctantly permitted Matthew to spend time with Jude in Ketchum. She knew Matthew adored his older brother Jude and was lonely for him, but she worried about Jude's "fast" life-style. Her misgivings were groundless, for Jude behaved impeccably when Matthew was there. Absolutely no hanky-panky. He arranged for Matthew to be a part-time pinsetter in the lodge's bowling alley, and he took Matthew along as his helper on some camping trips he guided. They made a beguiling duo for his clients. At twelve, Matthew was an immature replica of Jude—the same thick black hair, the same piercing black eyes and the same generous sensual mouth, with the promise of the same height and strength to come.

"He's going to be a heartbreaker" was the usual comment made to Jude. It was often followed by "And what about you? I bet you've broken many a girl's heart. Anyone have her hooks in you yet?" "Nope," Jude always replied. "I date once in a while, sure, but nothing steady for me. Too many things I want to do, too many places I want to go." That was, of course, a perfect segue to discuss the guest's business, goals and life. Jude never missed an opening to learn, observe and store more information.

Word spread, in that rarefied atmosphere of the privileged, about this impressive young man. Guests were assured of a trophy fish or a massive elk rack for mounting with Jude as their guide. They would see virgin country, enjoy lively conversation and delight in unique fireside music. When reservations were made for lodge accommodations, people began to request Jude's services.

Sun Valley, Idaho
1937

In August, Wade Colby squeezed a few days' rest in Sun Valley between projects. His fishing guide turned out to be the bellman who had delivered the telegram to him during the grand opening in January.

"Will you please call me Wayland, Jude? Or better yet, my *new* first name—Wade?" He liked this boy, who, he discovered, was five years younger than he to the day—they shared the same birthday, June 4. Wade told Jude about the contents of that telegram in January and what had resulted. "The jury's still out, though," he finished. "The public has the final say."

"I just know you'll be wonderful, Mr. Pri—Way—ah, Wade. I can't wait to see the picture," Jude said. And then he told Wade about his brief acting experience while *I Met Him in Paris* was being filmed in Sun Valley.

"You really did save the day. That was quick thinking!" Wade praised after hearing the story of Jude's deliberate fall to help the actor.

Jude cut him off. "Be ready, Wade—one's lookin'. Remember, don't jerk or yank—*feel* 'em take the fly and then set the hook, gently. *Now!*"

"I have him! I have him!" Wade yelled. "Oh, boy, Jude, you're making my day, that's for sure. Oh, this one is big—look at him jump." With Jude's coaching, Wade let the trout take the line while keeping his rod high. He played the fish for about fifteen minutes, slowly reeling in the slack when possible, until Jude was close enough to scoop the prize into the net.

"He's a beauty," Jude said, panting. "Brownie—male—'bout twenty-four inches, and I'd say around five pounds. Good goin'! Where's your camera? I'll take a picture."

Wade happily posed with his fish and then asked, "But can we put him back?"

Jude looked at him with new respect. Here was a man who didn't need a trophy for his wall to prove how good he was. And he certainly didn't need food for his table. Jude liked that.

Jude quickly put down the camera, removed the hook from the fish, lowered him into the water and massaged the tired trout until he could wiggle away on his own—a safe but wiser fish.

"What fun! We'll have to do this every year," Wade promised.

4

Hollywood
December 1937

The Mystical Castle was released to critical acclaim and with terrific box office, and the rough cut on *Lovely Little Lady* indicated a winner. Wade Colby's future in movies was firmly established and Max Goldbloom wasted no time in having Wade's contract rewritten to their lucrative advantage, with little or no opposition from the studio executives.

Elizabeth and Earle Prickler were completely unprepared for the reaction once their friends realized Wade Colby was none other than Wayland Prickler! They had underestimated the power of the movies and the lure of the glamorous and the famous. Their circle was fascinated with the idea that one of their own was a bona fide movie star. Wade was relieved; despite his need for independence, he loved his family and had not wanted to inflict unhappiness or embarrassment on them. And so, for the moment, gratefully, he hadn't.

With the onset of winter in Sun Valley, Jude had to determine which way to go again. A ski instructor would have the personal contact he wanted, but the Austrians held most of those positions. The other mountain jobs were too detached from the visitors, so Jude accepted the job offer of head bellman for the season.

When the luxury train *City of Los Angeles* pulled into Ketchum in December carrying the Harriman party and a load of holiday revelers, it was greeted by a band, dog teams with sleds, horse- and reindeer-drawn sleighs, buses, the lodge manager and

Jude and his bellman crew. He helped the Harrimans move into their newly completed cottage; he worked with the room clerk to switch Darryl Zanuck to a more acceptable suite; he tracked down misplaced luggage and rerouted bags to the proper rooms; he double-checked to see that the right pairs of skis were in the right slots for the right guests. Zanuck pulled him aside, slipped him a twenty, and said, "You're great, kid. If you're ever in Hollywood, look me up!"

Christmas Eve was a continuous cycle of parties for both adults and children. One reindeer pulled a sleigh with Santa Claus and his sack of gifts to the clock tower at the Inn. A couple who had brought their two young children to the lodge wanted to attend a cocktail reception, so Jude volunteered to take their little ones to see Santa. He didn't consider this a chore because he loved children. Their eyes were wide with wonder at the beautiful scene. The lights of the Christmas tree glowed through snowy branches as Santa jumped from his sleigh. But the reindeer, known to be a fairly mean critter, decided he had had enough of Christmas cheer, lowered his antlers and charged at Santa's baggy rear end, chasing him round and round the tree. Everyone shrieked with laughter, and then with fright when it suddenly looked as though Santa might get hurt. Jude put his young wards in a safe place and then on one of the laps grabbed the reindeer's horns and stopped the reign of terror. The tots were still giggling as Jude delivered them to the hotel baby-sitter.

Early Christmas morning, Jude drove to Hailey to bring his family presents and spend a few hours with them. Good humor abounded and there was talk and gossip aplenty. They had not seen Jude for a while.

"Lila Baker's growin' into a beauty."

"Luke's doin' good in school, specially with figures. Might work for Mr. Wangler when he graduates."

"Papa's workin' so hard, but John's a big help."

Matthew couldn't hold his juicy bit any longer. "John's got a girlfriend! John's got a girlfriend," he sang.

"Matthew!" warned Willamina.

"And who is this lucky gal?" Jude asked.

"Shut up, Matt," John muttered, embarrassed. "Can't anyone do anythin' round here without you snitchin'?"

"You took Thelma Warhas to the movies, didn't ya? And I betcha held her hand—and even kissed her!" Matthew blurted out. "You're sweet on her!"

"That's enough!" Noah said, ending that exchange.

Jude would have liked the teasing to continue. Baiting John used to be one of his favorite pastimes. He wondered if John even knew what to do with a girl. He was almost willing to bet that his brother was still a damn virgin.

New Year's Eve at the lodge was a madhouse. Everyone wanted something. Hostesses needed more decorations, primping ladies needed accessories, men called in a panic about forgotten garters. The staff was pulled in so many directions, they all needed aspirin.

Miraculously, almost all of the celebrations were under way on time, the guests were fully clothed and the lodge personnel functioning at full throttle. At midnight, the funny hats appeared and the horns tooted and everybody was well on their way to a dandy hangover.

Leaning on the bell stand in the lobby, Jude watched out of the corner of his eye as Mrs. Arnold Pummer, a voluptuous young blonde, slipped upstairs with Adolph, a ski instructor.

A little later, Mr. Pummer, a tipsy older man, rushed up to Jude.

"Have you seen my wife—Mrs. Pummer? I seem to have lost her."

"Ah, yes, sir," Jude answered, "I believe I saw your wife going in the direction of the—ah—ladies' room. Why don't you go back to your dinner, and I'll tell Mrs. Pummer you're looking for her?"

"Thank you, young man. Thank you, indeed." The little man wove away.

Jude knew he had to try to prevent the scandal that would result if Mr. Pummer found his wife in bed with a ski instructor. He hurriedly checked the room number, dashed up the stairs and knocked quietly on their door. "Mrs. Pummer, are you all right? Mr. Pummer was asking about you," Jude said through the door. "I told him I thought you were in the ladies' room."

Silence. Then a weak voice said, "Thank you. I did feel a bit faint. Would you wait a few minutes and then be kind enough to tell my husband I am in our room—ill? And you are...?"

"Jude, ma'am. Jude Abavas. And I will see to it that he receives that message in a few minutes."

Jude stifled a chuckle as he visualized Adolph hopping around trying to find his pants. He waited five minutes and then found Mr. Pummer to relay Mrs. Pummer's message.

After the Pummers left Sun Valley, an envelope with fifty dollars and a note was waiting at the bell desk for Jude.

> My husband is a very wealthy and influential man in Los Angeles, should you ever decide to relocate. Perhaps you and I can discuss this further on our next visit.
>
> Mrs. Arnold Pummer

Gambling, though not officially declared legal, had been part of Ketchum and Hailey for a very long time. Miners, farmers and cowboys would come to town and try their luck at poker or faro. The sounds of clinking glasses, tinny piano music, laughter and loud voices could be heard all hours of the day and night. Things didn't change when the wild old Ketchum Kamp was purchased and renamed The Casino, except that the patrons began to include royalty, millionaires, Hollywood celebrities and film crews.

Thelma Warhas had been working at The Casino all season, and she spotted Jude's group as soon as they arrived. They weren't at her station, though. Despite the fact that she had been keeping company with John Abavas and knew he fancied her, she had always had a hankering for Jude and right now wanted *him* to notice her.

"Guess who?" Thelma said, coming from behind to put her hands over Jude's eyes.

Jude was already well in his cups—the holiday season was finally over and it was his first night off in weeks. "Uh, let's see— well, who could this be?" He reached his arms around the back of his chair and grabbed at her crotch.

She was so startled, she jumped back and Jude toppled backward in his chair to the floor. He looked up from his prone position, almost directly up her dress, and with his vision blurred, still didn't recognize her.

"Who is it?"

"Thelma Warhas, silly!"

"Sure—Thelma!" Why was that name familiar? he wondered. He couldn't remember. "Sit down, ah... Thelma. Soon as I can get up, I'll order you a beer."

"I can't until I finish my shift. But then I will."

Thelma called her brother Clyde and told him not to pick her up after work. Jude Abavas, she told him, would see her home.

Thelma was pretty, though not spectacular by any means, but in Jude's state she looked perfect. "Why don't I drive you home?" he whispered, brushing his lips across her ear.

"I'd like that," Thelma said, thrilled that her plan was working.

While she was gathering her boots and coat from the back Jude finally remembered who Thelma was—she was John's girlfriend. Not that she could be much of a girlfriend if she wanted him to take her out. He clearly had much to teach his brother about women.

Jude winked at the boys as he escorted Thelma out of The Casino and toward his Ford.

"So where do ya live? Oops—don't slip!" Jude cautioned. Actually, it was debatable who was helping who; Thelma was giving as much support on the city street as she was receiving.

"Near Hailey. I hope that's all right," she apologized.

"Sure. Pretty night for a drive," he said as they reached the car. "We'll just take it nice and slow. This baby's not scared of slick roads," and he patted the hood affectionately.

It was a beautiful night. Cold and clear, the moon illuminating the snow-covered trees, the stars twinkling fiercely. Jude pulled over to follow a side road to the bank of the East Fork Big Wood River. After he stopped the car, the only sound was the water rushing through the ice. He put his arm around Thelma and leaned to kiss her. She responded. Thus encouraged, he repeated the kiss, again and again. Their mouths opened and tentative tongues found each other. Her arms wrapped around his broad muscular shoulders. His hand gradually found the hem of her sweater and crept under and then slowly to her bosom. She shuddered at his touch. He maneuvered them into the back seat where necking turned to intense petting. He fondled her breasts and felt the mound of hair under her panties. He freed his throbbing organ from his pants and lay on top of her. There were more sounds now—heavy breathing, hoarse mumblings, grunts of passion. He went beyond the point of control and forced himself into her. She struggled at first, protesting, but his lust was not to be denied. She cried out when his thrusts broke her hymen, but his need drowned out any awareness. He climaxed quickly and slumped over her.

"I'm sorry, I couldn't wait," he said drunkenly. "I'll do better next time. Hey, why're you cryin'?"

As his mind began to clear, he realized he had just deflowered a virgin. He had not intended to go so far—he had always sought relief with professionals, never with a real girlfriend. He just hadn't been able to stop himself. The least he could do, he reasoned, now that the damage was done, was to give her an equally gratifying experience.

He soothed and comforted her and eased her anxiety, all the while stroking and massaging her entire torso with his fingers, with his lips, and then finally, with his tongue. Until all resistance subsided. Until he could feel her body start to quiver and her moans of pleasure grow louder. This time when he entered her, she was wet and receptive, her body lunging up to meet his rhythm. Together with abandon, they fused into final satisfaction.

Their good-nights at her door were brief. It was late and Jude was hung over already and exhausted. All he wanted to do was go to sleep, and he still had to drive back to Ketchum. He promised to see her soon, gave her a peck on the cheek and was off.

In the beginning, Jude had had every notion of keeping his promise. But as his work load increased, there were more exciting demands on his time. David Niven arrived in Sun Valley at the invitation of the Count Felix Schaffgotsch and had elected to stay in the more relaxed atmosphere of the Challenger Inn. The management asked Jude to take on a stint at the Inn to ensure the smooth operation of services there. The debonair and completely charming David Niven took a liking to Jude and followed his suggestions that he might enjoy the merriment at the Ram Bar versus the more elegant Duchin Room at the lodge, named for Averell Harriman's friend, Eddie. The actor learned to dance the hokey-pokey to the Ram Trio, and he enjoyed listening to Heinie, the ski instructor, playing the accordion. Jude also introduced Mr. Niven to the colorful characters and gambling found at The Casino in Ketchum. He did think of Thelma when he sent Mr. Niven's party down in the taxi. Jude knew she'd be thrilled to see this handsome movie idol, and he hoped she would get to wait on his table.

Mr. Niven couldn't understand why Jude couldn't come skiing with him one afternoon. Jude tried to explain about the jurisdiction of the Austrian instructors, but Mr. Niven refused to take no for an answer. "My dear boy, the mountain belongs to everyone. I don't want you to teach me, just to ski with me—as my guest."

Of course Jude was given the few hours off to ski with Mr. David Niven. The power of stardom!

In early March, Jude stopped in at The Casino to have a fast beer after work. He had dropped by a few times in February to explain to Thelma about his busy schedule. She seemed to understand completely but in all honesty, he didn't really care whether she understood or not. She didn't own him—they had no real commitment.

But this night she pulled him into a corner and said, "I have to talk to ya, Jude. I've been waitin' for you to come in. I woulda called you tomorrow."

There was an urgency in her voice he could not ignore, so he said on a sigh, "Okay, I'll drive you home. But hurry up, I'm beat." He had no intention of repeating the events of their last drive—he had a big day tomorrow—and he certainly wasn't planning on having any type of relationship discussion.

Thelma was silent and withdrawn in the car. Finally, Jude, exasperated, bellowed, "Well, what do you want? What was so important?"

"I'm pregnant!" she blurted out, dissolving into tears. "And I'm sorry. I knew you'd be mad. I di—didn't want to tell you! But I didn't know what t'do. I'm—so—so scared, Jude!"

Jude swung the car over to the shoulder of the road and slammed on the brakes. He was genuinely shocked.

"What do ya mean you're pregnant? How do ya know? An why are ya tellin' me if ya are? How do ya know it's mine?" But even as he assailed her, he knew in his heart she was telling the truth, that she had been with no one else, that he had been the first. He was just *so* frustrated! And he could feel a new emotion welling inside him—fear. Fear because he didn't know what to do, either. Fear because in the dark recesses of his mind lurked one solution he knew he really couldn't contemplate. Fear because that single sentence of hers may have doomed all his dreams for tomorrow.

A merry-go-round of thoughts whirled in his head. Maybe one of those operations. How much would it cost, though, and would she agree? Who could he go to for help? Noah. Surely Noah would know what to do.

He had been so absorbed in his own thoughts, he forgot Thelma was beside him. Her sobs finally pierced his preoccupation. Her eyes were filled with terror and misery and something he couldn't bear to acknowledge—love. Love for him.

Awkwardly, he took her hand and stammered, "I—I'll think of something. I'm sorry, I didn't mean to blow up. I just—well—it was a jolt, I guess." He simply could not say what she wanted to hear.

During the sleepless night, in between the tossing and turning, an old saying popped into his head. "Why be poor and stupid all your life when you can buy a pint and be rich and smart in half an hour?" Booze, that's what got him into this mess, but what was going to get him out?

In the morning, for the first time ever, Jude called in sick and drove to Hailey. Willamina was glad to see him, but also surprised and curious. But she kept her silence and told Jude where he could find Noah working that day.

As Jude approached the old Fairfield Ranch, the place where he had been born, he thought about how complex life had suddenly become. He reminisced about the carefree days of wandering with Mama and Papa in the hills, even with John and then later with Luke and finally Matthew. He remembered when his mind need only concentrate on how to win a game or race and when his closest friends were Basa and Orey. Jude had named his two dogs, who were the offspring of a black furry "sort of" puli sheepdog and a German shepherd, after the Basque words for deer, *basauns* and *orein*. Although he hated to be apart from them, he'd had to leave them at the ranch when he moved to Ketchum. Each of the dogs had recently fathered a litter. But fatherhood wasn't for Jude—he had too many places to go and too many people to see.

Noah knew something was wrong the instant he saw Jude walking toward him. This wasn't his confident, jaunty son. As soon as the greetings were out of the way, Noah quietly asked, "What is it, Jude?"

And Jude told him everything. "What am I gonna *do,* Papa?" he finished. "I thought you might know of—a doctor—or a woman who could—well, you know...take care of it."

"Never!" Noah yelled. "God forbids—"

Suddenly, an unhuman howl of rage and pain interrupted Noah and a body hurled through the air at Jude. "Ahh! I'll kill ya—you bastard!"

John knocked Jude to the ground and went for Jude's throat. "Take everything, don't ya! Care 'bout no one, don't ya! Had to have my girl just cause ya knew I liked her. You son of a bitch—*I'll kill ya!"*

Jude's normal automatic reaction would be to fight back, seize the advantage, but this time he didn't. He just lay there, resigned almost, and allowed John to give him the physical punishment he couldn't give himself.

"No more! Gonna make sure *no more!"* John growled, pounding Jude's head into the ground with each word. "You—don't—deserve—to live!" His fury made his fingers tight, like steel clamps.

Jude began to fade in and out, and his body went limp, but John continued his death grip.

Noah crawled on his knees and squeezed himself between them, pushing his back upward, forcing John to release his hold on Jude's neck.

John rolled over in the dirt, his energy dissolved, his terrible anguish pouring out in sobs. "Oh, God! No! Why? Why Thelma? Why Jude? Why—always—Jude! Oh, my Thelma!" He lay crumpled, moaning.

Noah was able to revive Jude. There were angry red marks on his throat and he groggily held his battered head. The three of them just sat there on the ground in silence, struggling for breath.

Jude's apathetic defense was a sign to Noah that Jude felt oblivion offered the solution he sought. But Noah could not have this, for either son.

Finally, Noah was able to speak, praying for an effective way to penetrate their troubled souls.

"Today could have been a tragedy—one our family could never, never, be over. A grave sin. God forgive, maybe, but we?

We be spared. Thelma choose Jude, not you, John. You cannot tell Thelma's head and heart what to do. Your action today not answer to problem.''

Noah turned to Jude, wrenching with each word. "I once warn you about this need, this force in you, and that you must rule it before it rule you. Now you must face what this need do to others. You must do right thing."

His tone darkened as he continued, "You shame me when you think of—" He couldn't bring himself to voice Jude's question about a doctor. "You will listen to me. You will marry Thelma."

Both Jude and John winced at the words, and shrunk closer to the ground.

"*At once!* And you will be good to her. She be welcomed to our family." To John he continued, "She be Jude's wife. Nothing to be said of today. To no person. Not even Mama. Understand?"

Noah waited, thanking God for his gift of composure, giving his sons time to absorb his edict. Then, "You be same blood, but blood run different. Different be all right, but spoiled blood or spilled blood not be all right."

Noah scrambled to his feet. "John, go back to work. Soon as you feel able, Jude, go and do what you must do."

Jude drove slowly. His head ached and his throat was so sore he could barely swallow. But his thoughts hurt the most.

The more he searched for other alternatives to this crisis the more he realized there were none. He had no choice. He had to obey Noah's command. He had to do the honorable thing. He had to make the supreme sacrifice. He was trapped.

5

Hailey, Idaho
April 1, 1938

Thelma Warhas and Jude William Abavas were married in his parents' home on April 1, 1938. Ironic date to choose, for Jude already felt a complete fool—not quite nineteen and here he was saddled with a pregnant wife. John would not have been pleased whatever the date. The antagonism between the two brothers still smoldered, but both struggled to suppress it as Noah had ordered.

The family and friends who gathered for the wedding gave no indication that they were celebrating anything but the joyful union of two young people. Lila Baker was Thelma's maid of honor and Matthew Abavas proudly served as Jude's best man. Thelma wore a simple, but pretty, white dress and looked blissfully happy. Jude wore his Sunday suit and looked almost acceptably expectant.

Jude, thankfully, had not been subjected to the usual bantering aimed at a prospective groom, or to the customary stag brawl. Instinctively, his buddies had sensed this was not a typical betrothal. But they were all there to see their friend fall from the ranks of single men. Thelma's friends, on the other hand, while happy for her, were also jealous and upset that she had managed to snag the catch of the town.

There were modest wedding gifts from family and friends. Mr. and Mrs. Wangler presented the couple with U.S. savings bonds and the Sun Valley Lodge gave Jude and Thelma dinner and a suite for their one-night honeymoon.

Despite the fact that Jude had vowed never to drink again, he decided the situation warranted reconsideration. He needed fortification. The die was cast. He couldn't get in any more trouble, and he hoped a little firewater would put some juice in his equipment. He certainly hadn't experienced any great surges of passion recently; his mental obsession with his forced marriage had precluded that. And his pride wouldn't permit him not to perform well in the nuptial bed, whatever the reason for being there.

So he had wine at the reception, which eased his spirits somewhat. He began to rationalize about his options. After all, he was now married, he couldn't change that. He wasn't in love with Thelma, but he could try to make the best of it, since he was stuck, anyway, and she wasn't distasteful to him. On the contrary, as memories of that night in the car had surfaced, he remembered he had been quite satisfied by her. His mood started to shift a tad toward the positive side.

Noah, for his part, was relieved. He had been plagued with the fear that Jude or John or both would misbehave in some way, maybe disclose the reason for the hasty ceremony, either purposely or by accident. He thanked God no one had marred this day. He also sent Willamina waves of love from across the room, as she tended to the guests. She had not asked one question since he'd first announced the news, nor had she raised an eyebrow in his direction. That she knew or guessed the truth he was certain. Quite a woman was his beautiful Willamina.

Thelma and Jude shared more wine in their suite at the lodge. Both were trying to allay their private qualms. Abruptly, Thelma knelt in front of Jude and, fervently claimed, "I love you, Jude. I love ya so much I hurt. I've always loved ya. I'll make ya a good wife, I promise. I'll work hard, I'll take good care of ya, I'll cook 'n clean 'n wash 'n iron, I'll be thrifty, won't cost ya much and I'll love ya till the day I die."

Jude was touched. He pulled her tenderly into his lap and cradled her like a little girl. She started to cry softly. "I know ya married me cause of the—the baby. Please don't hate me. Please don't be sorry."

"Shh, shh, we'll be just fine," Jude murmured. "Don't cry. And don't worry. We'll be fine." Maybe theirs wouldn't be a storybook romance, but now that the deed was done, he intended to honor his commitment. He would be a man of his word. He would treat Thelma well and make her as happy as he was able. Berating themselves would be a waste of time. They had a life to get on with.

And to make sure that they did just that, he carried her to bed to make love as husband and wife.

John moved to the Fairfield Ranch, assuming more of Noah's responsibilities in that branch of the Wangler empire. Luke soon joined him and so the newlyweds had their own little two-room apartment in the Abavas home in Hailey. Thelma plunged into a heavy work load, determined to prove her worth to the family. She helped Willamina in all aspects of the restaurant—cooking, cleaning and waitressing—and soon won her mother-in-law's heart. She also kept her vow to do everything for Jude.

"You spoil him!" was Willamina's opinion. And Thelma, eyes glowing with pride, answered, "I want to. I love him so."

It was a longer commute to Sun Valley for Jude, but he was satisfied that living with his parents was the right arrangement; he worked very long hours and didn't want Thelma to be alone. And if he wanted to have a beer with the boys once in a while, he didn't feel pressured to hurry straight home. If he had a short turnaround in his shifts, he could bunk in the help's quarters at the Challenger Inn. Thelma never interrogated him about how he spent his time away from home, so his freedom didn't seem entirely suspended.

At home, Thelma was extremely giving and always available to Jude. She was never too tired, never told him she had a headache, two excuses he had been warned about by fellow husbands. All in all, he was fairly happy with his life.

In May, Thelma told Willamina she was pregnant. She couldn't wait any longer because she was filling out rapidly. Willamina was properly surprised and thrilled. When Thelma's stomach ballooned out of proportion with her "recent" pregnancy, Willamina merely remarked, "Must be boy. I pop out quick, too. A big boy!"

Young Matthew liked his sister-in-law, and not just because her presence assured him of seeing Jude more frequently. And he liked the idea of a baby. Now he wouldn't be the youngest and the brunt of all the teasing. On his thirteenth birthday in July, Thelma and Willamina had a party for him. Noah, John and Luke came in from the hills and Jude planned his schedule so he could also be there.

There was still considerable tension when Jude and John were in the same room. Thelma had invited Lila Baker to Matthew's party as a sort of date for John. She didn't know about the brothers' battle before her engagement, but she couldn't help sensing that there wasn't a lot of love lost between them. She thought Lila could ease the strain by entertaining John. The strategy was successful to a degree and the twins were civil to each other, turning Matthew's birthday celebration into a pleasant memory.

Jude was much in demand that summer and fall as a guide. It paid extremely well, so he was quite content to simply work the bell desk between bookings. And often, as during the previous years, he brought Matthew along as a helper. The two of them were camped up north near the Salmon River with a group when Thelma went into labor. Noah and Luke were away checking sheep at one of the ranches, and so only Willamina and John were at the Hailey house. John had just come to town on bank business and had stopped by to see his mother. Willamina could have handled a simple delivery, but she knew something wasn't right. Thelma's water had broken, the contractions were close and severe, but the baby simply wasn't coming. Willamina was furious at herself for not learning how to drive an automobile, but knew God had saved the day by sending John to her.

I'll be damned! he thought. *First Jude steals my girl, then gets her pregnant, and who ends up having to drive her to the hospital? Me! Dumb ol' me!*

But he put aside his self-pity because he could not bear to see Thelma's suffering. He was as gentle as he could be, and waited with Willamina until a baby boy was born, breech delivery, at 10:30 p.m., October 15, 1938. He weighed eight pounds six ounces, and measured twenty inches. Not bad for a "premature" baby!

In spite of himself, John was moved to tears when he saw the little guy with Thelma. *That lucky son of a bitch,* he thought as he drove Willamina home. *I wonder if he expects me to hand out the cigars for him, too?*

Two days later, a smelly, dirty Jude Abavas burst through the hospital door to see his son nursing at Thelma's breast. For once in his life, he was speechless. He could only gaze, spellbound, at the scene before him. This hungry little tiger was finally satiated and Thelma handed the precious bundle to his father. Curly black hair, sapphire eyes, and no doubt an irresistible personality confronted Jude.

"He's—he's just great!" Jude managed to say after a while. "Keen! That's what he is!"

Thelma, overflowing with gratitude and relief at Jude's obvious elation, suggested, "Then why don't we name him Keane? Keane William Abavas! Do ya like that, honey?" She had never used a term of endearment with Jude before. She still felt on precarious ground with him and wasn't sure how he would respond to the word. But under these conditions, she'd braved it.

He didn't seem to notice anything different at all. "Yeah! Yeah, that's good! Keane—hello, Keane! Look! He likes it! And he knows me! I can tell!"

Thelma had never been so happy, so full, so deeply grateful. It was as if she had died and gone to heaven. All of her dreams had come true. Jude did love her. Jude wasn't upset about the baby. Jude loved the baby. What a glorious day!

In short time, Keane William Abavas took over the household. Jude was utterly bowled over by this miracle called his son and surprised himself and everyone else by becoming a doting father. Willamina and Noah were typical grandparents, eager to help, and eager to offer their superior knowledge. Especially Grandma.

"No! No! Let him be. I never pick up mine 'cause they cry."

"If this be colic—rub back. No! Lower! And firm! Don't pittypat! In a circle."

"Don't feed so much. But feed when be needed."

"Jude! He not rag doll. You too rough. Be gentle."

Thelma, and Jude when he was home, patiently listened to the older woman, attempted to comply and then, when they were alone, like all young parents, did exactly what they wanted to do.

The 1938-39 winter season was busier than ever. Sun Valley was attracting world-famous skiers and adventurers. These plucky souls would venture farther than Proctor and Dollar mountains. Twelve miles or so north was Durrance Mountain, and people like Gretchen Junigk, who would go on to win a gold medal in the slalom in the 1948 winter games, and Don Frazer, who would be on the 1946 Olympic team, would walk up the mountain and then ski down the virgin terrain. Jude was still not permitted to instruct in the ski school, which was fine with him since his position was steadier. But as the real "mountain man," he was allowed to take these unusual outings.

He needed no prompting for these trips. The gratuities were substantial, but the environment renewed his thirst for life. Each time he was a part of those vast mountains, he would experience new sensations, behold new beauty. He could hardly wait to show Keane his discoveries: the ice frozen on the trees in shapes—a bird in flight, a giraffe stretching its long neck, a pudgy bear—all resembling glass figurines. There was the paisley pattern of white and darkness, and the alpenglow of sunsets. *Hurry up and grow, little fella. There's so much I have to show you.*

6

Los Angeles, California
1938

After completing another movie and enjoying a late-summer sojourn in Sun Valley, Wade returned to Los Angeles to decide where he wanted to permanently live. Numerous Sunday gatherings at the beach homes of Marion Davies and Louis B. Mayer, among others, led him to finally opt for Santa Monica. Over the fall, he supervised the remodeling of his very first house, and after spending the Christmas holidays with his family at Sun Valley, he moved in.

The first order of business in the new year and in his new home was to organize a lavish ball. He intended to be adventurous with the guest list, to brave the unknown by mixing the world of make-believe with the world of high finance. His experiment fared surprisingly well. There was some hesitancy at the start of the evening, but as the champagne flowed, the barriers gradually relaxed, and by the end of the night's festivities real-estate tycoons were dancing with film queens and movie moguls were gliding across the floor with the wives of bankers.

There were a few mishaps, of course. After the Chateaubriand sauce béarnaise course had been passed at dinner, the head of a stock brokerage firm, who had had too much of the bubbly, insisted he had not been served.

"But, *monsieur,* I came to you myself, and placed it right on your plate," the bewildered waiter explained.

"Do you shee it? Where ish it if you put it there?" the broker complained drunkenly. He made a great show of looking all around the top of the table and beneath, on his chair and under it. His dinner partners joined in the search. All anyone found was the man's wallet.

"Oh, yesh! I was putting this lovely lady's number in that," he said. "Musta dropped it. Never mind, jush bring me another steak." The waiter hurried to obey. "Can't get good help nowadays," the drunk lamented to no one in particular, trying to get his wallet into his inner coat pocket. But it wouldn't fit, the space was already occupied. He frowned, reached in and pulled out a dripping slice of Chateaubriand sauce béarnaise, which he had pocketed instead of his wallet. "Shee! I told you it wasn't on my plate." He dangled the evidence for all to see.

The other side of the guest list had its moments, too. The wife of a department-store magnate was absolutely dazzled when she found herself seated next to Jay Brant, the idolized star of musical extravaganzas. She could hardly wait to be in his strong arms, whirling gracefully around the floor, her full skirt billowing with the movement, all female eyes fixed enviously upon the two of them. When the orchestra started, she swayed slightly in her seat and murmured, "Oh, I just love to dance."

"Shall we?" the actor asked and he led his bewitched fan from the table. He was remarkable. She was rapturous. The tempo increased, he really got into it. Other couples gave way to watch the master at work. The lady's dream was being realized. That is, until that last gulped-down glass of champagne hit Jay. In the middle of a fast spin, dizziness overwhelmed him and down they went to the floor, sliding on their derrieres into the crowd, dragging a few unfortunate souls along for the ride. There was an undignified tangle of limbs and tuxedos and satins and beads and chiffon. Luckily, no damage was done, except for a few shattered illusions and minor nicks to their pride.

Wade was pleased with his debut as a host.

Newspapers and magazines constantly linked Wade romantically with one beauty or another. Mothers of available girls continuously tried to snare this elusive catch. But Wade had no intention of being caught. He was enjoying life to the fullest. Why should he make waves? He was a considerate, amiable and generous escort, simply not a permanent one.

Having been a quasirebel in a relatively tame environment most of his life, Wade was intrigued by the life-styles of some of his new actor friends. Errol Flynn and David Niven corented a house at 601 North Linden Drive in Beverly Hills that could only be described as the quintessential bachelor pad. It was there that Wade met the legendary John Barrymore. He was mesmerized by this fading giant with the flashing eyes, flamboyant gestures and booming voice. And he was positively wide-eyed by Errol Flynn and his prowess with, and appetite for, women. While Wade admired Barrymore and Flynn, it was David Niven whom he wished to emulate. To Wade, Niven epitomized the dapper, sophisticated, educated, witty and genuine gentleman. The two became good friends.

Each had arrived at celebrity status by different routes. David had gone through the obstacle course of the struggling actor. He had been broke and hungry. He had been an extra. He had done bit parts. He had finally landed a contract with Goldwyn, and from that had come pictures for Selznick, and only then was it onward and upward. David just shook his head when he heard of Wade's fairy tale path, not begrudgingly, just in amazement.

"I knew I was damned fortunate," Wade explained apologetically. "But I guess I didn't know how fortunate until I spent time around the studio—this profession is a battleground for some. I've watched actors stuff themselves at lunch on location so they wouldn't have to buy dinner. God only knows where or how they live. I've seen the glazed look of lost dreams on the faces of the older ones, and the yearning and hope in the eyes of the young. It was a jolt, I can tell you. I never meant to be blasé, and I certainly was never ungrateful. But I have come to realize that I have been blessed."

"Dear boy, we don't deal life's cards, do we? It's how we play the hand that counts," David assured him.

During their many evenings of conversation, Sun Valley and their mutual attraction to skiing was often discussed. They also spoke of Jude Abavas and how much they liked the young man.

Flynn and Niven went their separate ways early in 1939, and David took a small house near Wade's in Santa Monica until he left at the end of the year for duty in the British forces. One of David's going-away parties was held at Romanoff's in Beverly Hills. "His Imperial Highness Prince Michael Alexandrovich Dmitri Obolensky Romanoff," the beloved impostor, gave David an amazing send-off. Not many of the happy revelers, however, remembered the night very well—they assumed that a good time was had by the size of their hangovers.

When Wade left Romanoff's that night, he carefully made his way to his shiny black Cadillac. "Must get a new car," he mumbled, fishing in his wallet for the doorman's tip. "I can't see the damned thing at night—too dark." The doorman solemnly nodded in agreement, especially with the five dollars in his hand.

"You drive safe now, Mr. Colby, sir!"

"Absolutely! Not to worry, my man!" And Wade chugged over the curb, missing the driveway completely.

As he wound his intoxicated course westward on Sunset Boulevard, his mind filled with sentimental thoughts of how much he was going to miss his buddy, leaving no room to concentrate on steering his automobile or heeding the speed limit. The sound of a siren interrupted his drunken melancholy, and he saw the red light whirling on a black and white in his rearview mirror. He pulled over and rolled down his window.

"Yes, Officer, what may I do for you?" Wade asked in the most innocent, sober-sounding voice he could muster.

Apparently, the policeman was not a moviegoer. "Well, mister, you can start by getting out of the car—real slow like. And then you can bend over the hood with your arms out. Atta boy." Wade did not resist as he was frisked, hoping to lull the officer with passiveness before using his persuasive powers.

"There must be some mistake. Perhaps you are searching for someone who looks like me. You see, I—"

The man was not cooperating. "Not lookin' for anybody. Now come over here and walk this straight line I'm puttin' down between our vehicles. You weren't drivin' straight, so I doubt you can walk straight. It's either a drunk-driving charge or speedin'—gotcha either way."

Before Wade was forced into a test he could never have passed, they heard the screech of brakes and a crash—an accident in the eastbound side of the four-lane boulevard.

"Stay where you are—don't move!" barked the policeman to Wade, as he ran across the road. It turned out to be a fender bender, nothing serious and no injuries, but it did cause a mass of commotion and traffic congestion the officer had to handle on his own.

In his foggy state of mind, Wade decided to take advantage of this twist of fate. He got into his car and sped off, knowing the officer had not had time to see his license or even get his license-plate number. He did have sense enough to drive slowly and cautiously the rest of the way home, congratulating himself on his cleverness all the while.

The door chimes echoed through the house and awakened Wade. The clock read 4:00 a.m. He heard his houseman and unfamiliar muffled voices. Then there were hurried footsteps coming toward his bedroom and a knock on the door.

"Mr. Colby, Mr. Colby, come quick. Policemans. Come quick, Mr. Colby!" the houseman said, his pitch rising higher and higher. "In the courtyard!"

"Calm down, Chang. I'll be right there. Everything is just fine," Wade assured him, wishing he could believe it himself.

Damn, the cop must have seen my license plate, Wade reasoned. *But he has no proof, must remember that, just his word against mine. Play the role of the wrongly accused citizen, and don't panic,* he instructed himself.

As Wade approached the courtyard, he saw two policemen in uniform. One was the same officer who had stopped him.

"Gentlemen! What seems to be the trouble? Has there been a robbery, or something?" Wade asked anxiously. "I haven't heard any unusual noises—have you, Chang? Of course, I retired early, and I am a heavy sleeper."

"No, no, nothing like that, Mr. Prickler. Wayland C. Prickler, isn't it?" the officer said, and Wade nodded, wondering how he knew his real name.

"Could you tell me, please, where you were around 1:00 a.m. this morning?" asked the policeman who knew exactly where he'd been.

"I have no idea what is going on here," Wade sputtered. "But of course I can tell you. I was asleep!" Which wasn't a total lie, considering his condition at the time.

"Me sleep, too! Me sleep, too!" chanted Chang, who didn't understand anything except his fear of the lawmen.

"I see. You were here, you say. Then you would have no objection if we had a look in your garage."

"Absolutely none! Chang, why don't you return to your room and I'll show these gentlemen the garage myself." The little man was overjoyed to be dismissed.

"Now, if you'll come with me." They followed Wade, who continued to talk, "I must say, I am rather shocked at this intrusion. Four o'clock in the morning is an ungodly hour to be barging into someone's—" Wade's voice dwindled to silence as soon as he opened the garage door. For there, in all its glory, was a black-and-white police car. He was dumbfounded. He had, obviously, driven off in the wrong car—and hadn't even known the difference! And what could he do? The evidence was staring him in the face.

What he didn't know was that the policeman was in as much hot water as Wade was if this got out. An officer must never leave the keys in the ignition when he steps out of his vehicle, no matter what: one, to prevent theft, and two, to insure that no one stole the shotgun in the trunk.

Without going into details, the policemen told Wade they had decided to be magnanimous and forget the whole incident, that the episode had become so complex, it was just better to let bygones be bygones. And if they could just exchange the cars, they would be on their way—with the understanding that Mr. Prickler was not to discuss this matter with *anyone,* and that in the future, Mr. Prickler would never drive while under the influence.

Mr. Prickler was so relieved by his reprieve, he would have promised them anything.

After the car swap, the second officer said, "You know, Mr. Prickler? You're a dead ringer for that actor Wade Colby. Did anyone ever tell you that?"

Wade quickly discovered that when a person lives at the beach, he quickly wants to do what the beach dwellers do. And so Wade became a surfer. It was a difficult sport, but the harder it was the better it suited Wade's nature to try to master it.

Many of the young men he met surfing couldn't afford a car and took the more economical route by driving motorcycles. Naturally, Wade had to have one, too. He decided on the very powerful British 4 Stroke Triumph 650. He loved the speed, the wind whipping at his face—and most of all, the danger.

The day after a heavy spring rain, Wade took his bike for a spin, north toward the sparsely developed Trancas beach. He opened up full throttle on the deserted expanse and flew over the flat surface.

Without warning, the motorcycle was suddenly tossed into the air, completely out of control, and in seconds Wade lay bleeding and unconscious beside the twisted mass of metal. A flash flood from the mountains had caused a trenchlike gully to form on the beach. A gully filled with rocks and debris. The gully where Wade had landed.

The cold water from the encroaching tide revived him. He looked around in bewilderment, not sure where he was or what had happened. He spit sand and salt water out of his mouth, and when he touched his aching head, his hand came away sticky with blood. Only one thing was clear, he had to get out of there and he had to find help. Somehow he mustered the strength to pull himself upright and begin the laborious trek across the beach. He fought off swells of giddiness and finally staggered to the road. Weakly he tried to flag down oncoming traffic.

His appearance was so frightening that several motorists sped by, not wanting to become involved in a situation that obviously meant trouble. Fortunately for Wade, one Good Samaritan at last screeched to a halt, bundled Wade into the car, wrapped a rag around his head to stop the bleeding and rushed him to Santa Monica Hospital.

Wade awakened later and saw anxious, but somewhat relieved faces peering down at him. His left arm was hooked up to an intravenous line, and with his right arm he gingerly felt his bandaged skull.

"Yes, it's still there," said Dr. Lawrence Morrow, smiling. "Although you nearly succeeded in demolishing it." Dr. Lawrence Morrow, the Pricklers' physician, had been called immediately by Wade's parents when the hospital superintendent had notified them of Wade's admittance.

All hell broke loose when news of the accident became known. Wade's family, studio representatives, Max Goldbloom, reporters and photographers all descended upon the hospital en masse. Once it was established that Wade Colby would survive, the media pressed for details. How? When? Where? Would there be permanent scarring? Was there brain damage? Was he disabled? Was foul play involved?

To quell rumors and present a factual report, Dr. Morrow, with the help of the studio's public relations department, held a press conference. He explained the extent of Wade's injury. Mr.

Colby had received a severe piercing cut to the head from the force of the fall, which in turn, had caused a piece of bone to separate. There would be no visible scarring from the wound, no lasting effect either physically or emotionally.

The production head of Twentieth Century Fox, Darryl Zanuck, made the decision to postpone Wade's scheduled feature until the actor had fully recovered. Mr. Zanuck grumbled a lot about the evils of those "damn bicycles with motors," but he was a bit more understanding than expected, probably due to the success and acclaim of the studio's latest release, *The Grapes of Wrath*.

In the entertainment world there was nothing quite like a hit to improve everyone's disposition.

7

Idaho
Summer 1939

The summer of 1939 brought more expansion to Sun Valley. Ski lifts were built on Bald Mountain, which had been nicknamed Baldy because of its treeless top. Ample runs were cut for every level of skier—beginner, intermediate and expert. Some still preferred to ski on Dollar Mountain, however. The movie idol, Van Johnson, later explained it this way: "I would rather be a lion on Dollar than a mouse on Baldy."

The summer also brought expansion for Jude's family. Jude and some of his old construction friends built a house on the lot behind his parents' home in Hailey. This afforded the couple privacy, more room for Keane to grow and space for the puppy Jude insisted Keane have. Keane was going to be an active one. Already was, in fact, and not even a year old. The proximity of their new house to Jude's parents' home also made it convenient for Thelma to continue working with Willamina in the restaurant.

Both Basa and Orey had died of old age, but not before Basa left his legacy in one last litter. The puppy Jude chose for his son reminded Jude so much of Basa that he named the irrepressible little black ball of fur Basa, Jr. Jude only wished that Orey had been more amorous!

Keane and young Basa became inseparable. Keane wouldn't go to sleep unless Basa was with him. And when Keane was crawling and then staggering around, Basa was always by his side, and would bark if he thought the baby was in trouble. Jude was already anticipating a small sled and harness. Just to be ready, he bought them for Christmas.

There were several surprises at Christmas. Willamina timidly informed her husband—who was absolutely delighted—and family—who were shocked—that *she* was pregnant. A premenopause jolt, as it were. The boys were shaken the most, apparently unable to accept the idea that their parents actually indulged in sex. That act was reserved for them.

Thelma giggled to Jude. "We'll be givin' your mama our baby's ol' things. You were smart, honey, to build this house." "Honey" came a lot easier to Thelma now.

John dropped the next bombshell at Christmas dinner. He and Lila Baker were engaged, the date set for next June. The family all rushed to congratulate him. Jude was the last to slowly stand up. All eyes darted back and forth between the two brothers. Jude's walk was deliberate as he approached John. They looked at each other long and hard. Then Jude extended his hand and John finally took it. The relief was apparent in a number of audible sighs. Thank God! was the unspoken message sent above.

John, however begrudgingly, had to acknowledge the change in Jude's attitude and behavior in the past year. And because Lila had returned his love, and his work efforts had been recognized by his father and family, John's own sense of worth had improved.

Jude, for his part, had forgiven John for his attack the year before and for his constantly antagonistic disposition. The adoration for his son, the comfortableness of his marriage and the rewards of his work had filled his life. There was no space left in his heart for malice.

Wade Colby arrived at Sun Valley early in the spring of 1940 to continue his recuperation from his motorcycle accident. The Pricklers' ten acres fronted the Big Wood River, five miles to the north. It was a beautiful tranquil spot, just what the doctor ordered. Wade rested, relaxed, read a great deal and hiked the gentle trails. When he was up to it, he called Jude to guide—not for overnight camping—just for a few hours during the day. Jude and his guitar were soothing to Wade's fragile head. Wade heard about Jude's new house, the antics of Keane and Basa and was amused by Jude's reaction to his mother's unexpected pregnancy. Wade had to admit he'd probably feel the same way if it were Elizabeth Colby Prickler who was enceinte.

One day they made the trip to Silver Creek. There was the long walk to the water, even more burdensome because of their heavy fishing waders with steel clamp soles. Then there was the trudge through the muddy marshes. The fish in the conservancy were famous for their size, and notorious for their selectivity. The natural hatch was usually so prevalent, they had no appetite for the man-made fly. Even so, Wade had enjoyed the hard work it took just to get to the spot.

Wade was tiring but was too excited to call a halt. He had had a couple of strikes and was sure he was due to reel in a monster. It was becoming increasingly difficult for him to lift each leg out of the clinging mud, so he shuffled both feet along the bottom. Then, suddenly the base dropped away and he was up to his neck in a hole. When he struggled, he sank lower into the ooze.

Jude, who was ahead, heard the soggy splash and rushed toward Wade. He braced himself as well as he could against the bank and then reached out. Wade was like deadweight. Jude used every ounce of his reserve strength to inch Wade upward. The insatiable muck sucked at its prey and Jude's shoulder sockets groaned from the pressure of pulling. Jude gave one final heave and dragged Wade free. Both flopped in the grass, Wade ashen with fatigue, Jude flushed from exertion. After a while, Wade gasped, "I just didn't have it. I wouldn't have been able to get out of the hole." He looked at Jude—a long look that spoke more than words. Then, "Thank you. Thank you, my friend."

After a moment, Wade continued, "First the motorcycle accident, now this. I guess I better behave myself. That was number two. Three strikes and I'm out, right?"

Just the idea or intimation of death, even in jest, was unsettling to Jude. "Naw! You coulda climbed up the side. Maybe not as fast, that's all." Jude noticed that Wade was shivering. "The sun's hot, but the water's like ice. You're soaked. Here, put on these dry duds."

Jude pulled off his companion's waders and helped him get out of his wet jeans and sweater. Jude always carried a spare set of clothes and a pair of tennis shoes in case any of his clients took a tumble in a creek. He also had an extra jacket should the weather take a turn, as it often did in the mountains. When he sensed that Wade was calmer and had regained enough strength, he picked up Wade's gear and led them back to the car.

Both were quiet on the ride home. The incident had left its imprint.

In that summer of 1940, John Abavas married Lila Baker on June 15—with everyone's blessings.

And Luke Abavas became engaged to Ethel Wangler, grand-daughter of Mr. Horace Wangler, the wedding to be in the fall. Also with everyone's blessings.

Matthew was regularly employed over the summer by the Sun Valley management as a caddy on the golf course, or, when needed, as Jude's assistant.

Jude had become progressively more valuable to Sun Valley. He was now, almost exclusively, hired out as a guide. And for the coming winter the position of mountain manager would very probably be his.

Willamina and Noah Abavas became parents of a baby girl on August 15, 1940. Revel, short for Revelations—Willamina still believed in using the Bible for names—looked like no other in her family; she had auburn hair, a fair complexion and hazel eyes. Noah remembered there were some people with this coloring in his homeland, but it certainly wasn't the norm. He and Willamina would soon discover their daughter would not follow the Basque tradition in many ways.

Thelma had taken over the restaurant during the last two months of Willamina's pregnancy, and for the three months after Revel's birth. It had not been an easy experience for Willamina and she'd needed rest.

Noah continued to buy land from Mr. Wangler. His mentor was too old and feeble to run all his holdings now and Horace, Jr., simply wasn't interested in developing the estate. The old man knew Noah and his two sons, John and Luke, cared so he gladly sold Noah whatever acreage he could afford.

Jude was promoted to mountain manager at Sun Valley. At the invitation of the Union Pacific Railroad, Ernest Heming-way and wife-to-be, Marty, had arrived for the first time at Sun Valley the previous fall. It was the start of the writer's love af-fair with Wood River Valley. Now in the fall of 1940, Heming-way and "Ol Podner," movie legend Gary Cooper, planned their annual hunting expedition. Jude desperately wanted to be their scout, but the established ranchers and his supervisors prevailed. He did, however, have brief encounters with these two giants creating yet more treasured memories.

Jude's new position allowed him more free evenings. This Christmas Eve he had his two-year-old son perched on his shoulders to see Santa Claus at the Inn and receive a goody. Keane's squeals of delight were the best Christmas present Jude had ever received.

Then it was on to Dollar Road with Keane and Thelma to watch the torchlight parade. At 6:00 p.m., the single ski instructors assembled at the top of Dollar Mountain, lighted their torches and wound a snakelike path down the ridge in the dark—looking like magical fireflies in the night. A thrilling sight, to be sure, but not necessarily a thrilling night for the skiers. Picking a path in the blackness was not easy, to say nothing of coping with the sparks flying in everyone's faces. The biggest problem, however, was the result of the length of time the instructors had spent at the Ram Bar before their performance. The number of schnapps consumed could determine who made it down the mountain and who didn't. Jude chuckled as he saw one firefly stray from the serpentine configuration. Then another. And another. He tried to remember their assigned order so he could congratulate the wayward ones on their solo performances the next day.

But the night was not over yet. The three of them met the horse-drawn sleigh at the Challenger Inn, and with other holiday revelers, boarded for the ride to Trail Creek Cabin and dinner. Tucked under warm lap robes, they sang Christmas carols and watched gentle snowflakes fill the air. Keane couldn't sing the words yet—he sort of created his own interpretive melody—but he was clearly enchanted—and enchanting. On the way back, snuggled against Jude, content, eyes fluttering shut, he mumbled, "'Ank 'ou, Dada." Jude wouldn't have traded that moment for a whole bank.

On December 26, Jude continued his holiday spree and took Keane, Thelma and Matthew to the Liberty Theater to see Cecil B. deMille's *Northwest Mounted Police*. He had always enjoyed movies but had been too busy to indulge often in the past couple of years. He didn't want to miss this one, though, because it starred his "almost" friend, Gary Cooper. Keane fell asleep—too much celebrating for his little body, Jude reckoned—clutching the free Eskimo doll handed out to all the children in the audience.

Wade reported for work in late 1940, as good as new. There was a great deal of hoopla when he finally started the long-delayed film, and there was still much written about his narrow escape from death. He never talked about the second incident. His lifestyle resumed, the epitome of a bachelor's dream. He did make one alteration in his domestic situation—he exchanged Chang for a respectable married couple, Anna and Eric Olsen, a move that pleased his mother and was his one token step toward convention. Also, he decided not to buy another motorcycle. Not right away at least. Elizabeth and Earle Prickler convinced themselves their twenty-six-year-old renegade was on the brink of conformity.

The 1940 Olympics had been canceled because Russia invaded the host country of the games, Finland, but beyond that, there was not a great deal of talk or apprehension in Idaho about the war in Europe. There was, however, one concerned citizen connected to Sun Valley. Averell Harriman was well aware of the menace in Europe and had agreed to travel to Russia as head of President Roosevelt's lend-lease program.

But the 1940-41 winter season in Sun Valley continued as if nothing was happening. Partying took place everywhere—at the Christiana Club in Ketchum, the Duchin Room at the lodge, at the Ram Bar, the Trail Creek Cabin and at the Round House on top of Baldy Mountain! This nighttime social scene was riotous fun for everyone but the Sun Valley employees. It wasn't the work Jude minded, it was the safety factor. Sending food, cases of liquor and guests up on the lift wasn't a problem. But getting the guests *down* the mountain after those cases of spirits had been depleted, *was* a problem. At times, partygoers would have to be tied into the chairlift. When an individual was put on the lift at the Round House, the number of that chair was phoned to the bottom. If the chair was empty when it came down, Jude and the ski patrol would go searching for the "misplaced" person. Fortunately, perhaps because these people were so "relaxed," no one was ever seriously hurt.

During this heyday period, female visitors, of all shapes and sizes, came on to Jude. He still thought it unwise to mix business with pleasure, and with his new family at home, he really wasn't tempted. Of course, he always tried to handle these incidents delicately. He had his own little rules, too. If the lady in question happened to be a beauty, he would not have one drink, not even a beer with her—just in case. He remembered his past weakness. His cohorts kidded him about being henpecked, afraid of his wife. Jude just smiled.

Bumping along in a borrowed truck in early June, on the way to the Sawtooth wilderness area, Jude rambled on to his attentive audience, which consisted of Thelma, Keane and their dog, Basa. His brother Matthew had elected not to accompany them on this ten-day vacation. At almost sixteen, Matthew had discovered girls. The mountains were where he *worked* with Jude— what kind of vacation was that!

"Never too soon, you know, to start Keane appreciatin' this country," Jude was saying. "Next year, maybe, we'll go way up north, to the big lakes, like Pend Oreille, Coeur D'Alene and Priest. Trout there can weigh forty pounds or more. See a lot more moose and deer and grizzly bear up there, too. Pretty country."

"Deer an-ee-mal," Keane announced.

"We saw a deer the other day, out by Warm Springs," Thelma explained.

"Well, good for you, little guy!"

"Me big! No lil."

"He thinks you mean, little, like Revel," interpreted Thelma, referring to Noah and Willamina's one-year-old daughter.

"That's right, li—ah—son. You saw a deer. And the elk is bigger than the deer. And the moose is bigger than the elk. And a bear, well, that's *really* big. Whoops!" Jude swerved to miss a large rock in the road.

"Has he seen an eagle yet?" Jude asked Thelma.

"Yeah, but I don't think it meant much then."

"Well, he'll see one this trip for sure. You know where else I'd like to go sometime? East to the Tetons—Wyoming. I hear those mountains are really somethin'. After all, in French *teton* means—ah—a woman's—well, titty. The peaks reminded some

Frenchman of a woman's boob. Isn't that a kick? Hey, how about the Grand Teton? That must mean *big* tit.''

"Tit!" mimicked Keane.

"Now see what ya done," Thelma admonished.

"Ah, hell! Better he hear it from us than someone else. You know, a fella told me he was over in Driggs—the Idaho side of the Tetons—fishin' the Snake River. Said he saw two osprey fight off two bald eagles away from their nest, just like those fighter airplanes we see in the newsreels at the movies. Can you beat that? I thought eagles were the most ornery critters around. They sure cause a ruckus with sheep, I can tell you that!''

As if on cue, they began seeing sheep on the hillsides. The density increased and soon they were forced to stop—sheep blocked the road. Darting dogs and harried herders attempted to clear a passageway for the truck.

"Look at that, Keane," Jude said, pointing. "Grandpa used to do that. Even Grandma. And Daddy helped, too. Quiet, Basa!" Basa was barking furiously, obviously angry at being trapped inside the truck when he should have been out there in the midst of the action with the sheep and the dogs. Keane looked captivated by the scene before him and made his displeasure known when their truck finally inched away.

Jude was silent over the next few miles. The sheep had triggered thoughts about the early years: how hard his mama and papa had worked; how they, despite this labor, always made sure the family was happy. A pang of regret and guilt gripped him. He remembered putting down their way of life and their locale; he had deliberately wandered from their path. He involuntarily shuddered as he recalled his initial reaction to the news of Thelma's pregnancy. Now, here he was extolling the virtues of Mama and Papa's land to a son he had almost denied. His right hand sought and found Keane's little hand and squeezed hard. *I'm sorry, little fella. I didn't know. But I do now. I love you and will forever. I will protect you with my life.*

Jude and his family crammed an aeon into those ten days of vacation. Hiking around Boulder Basin they caught a glimpse of a shaggy, bearded Rocky Mountain goat. Jude showed Keane the results of the diligent beavers' toil, their dams. Waiting patiently at a marshy pond off the Big Wood River, they actually saw a beaver swimming, its rich brown fur barely visible, until it gave a slap at the water with its broad flat tail and changed directions. Alpine Lake was still iced in, even with summer advancing. At Frog Lake in the White Cloud Mountains, they gazed at the towering Castle Peak while reeling in their trout for breakfast. On North Fork, Payette River, they saw an otter catching a fish for its meal. Keane learned the value of silence, or the "an-ee-mals" could be scared away.

And Keane learned about fear. At Redfish Lake late one night, Jude was awakened by something thrashing about outside the tent, somewhere near the coals of the campfire. He grabbed his rifle and peered out the flap. A bear or a mountain lion could be out there, just curious. Or they could be hungry and mean, especially if their cubs were near. And where was Basa? Before Jude's eyes adjusted to the dark, Basa came charging in from somewhere behind the tent barking at whatever was there. Keane woke up screaming, obviously sensing the unknown danger. Jude yelled for Basa to come, knowing the dog would be no match for a bear or mountain lion. All the commotion was too much for the unsuspecting buck who had come to visit, and he took off into the forest. But there was no more sleep. Jude and Thelma comforted Keane until the spectacular sunrise returned his thoughts to the beauty and wonder of nature.

Jude was sorry Keane's guileless world had been breached, but he regretfully acknowledged the good it would do his son in the future.

On another occasion, while lolling around in a Sawtooth meadow of parry primrose, Indian paintbrush, glacier lilies and countless other wildflowers, Keane succeeded in capturing his first buzzing insect—a bee. And he paid the price. He howled and held up his "hurt" for Mommy and Daddy to "make better." As they packed his hand with mud, Jude and Thelma tried to explain how it was all right to observe nature's creatures, but how it was better not to interfere. How, with some, the "hurt" could be a lot worse than a bee sting.

They spent their last night on the shores of Pettit Lake. Keane looked spellbound as Jude strummed Grandpa Noah's guitar and sang songs. Jude didn't want this idyll to end, this interlude of sharing togetherness. With Keane nestled between them, Jude put his arm around Thelma and whispered magic words in her ear.

"What do ya think? When we get home, how about goin' for another baby? I mean, shouldn't Keane have a little brother or sister?"

II

8

Idaho
December 7, 1941

War! Suddenly, the apathetic retreat was bursting with patriotism. There was speculation that the first line of defense against a Japanese attack would be the Rocky Mountains. And because Sun Valley had worldwide recognition, there was always the remote possibility it would be singled out as a target. A defense meeting was called by the Legionnaires and civilian defense procedures were taught. A Ketchum home guard unit was formed, soon followed by the Sun Valley Commandos. Countywide blackout drills were practiced. And then the FBI moved in, with rumors running rampant—spies, saboteurs, secret shortwave radios. The fact that Count Felix Schaffgotsch, the site finder of Sun Valley, had returned to Germany to fight for the führer only fueled paranoia. Several Austrian ski instructors were arrested and taken into custody as enemy aliens.

Although Jude had always been a bit jealous of the Austrians for monopolizing the ranks of ski instructors, he didn't believe they were involved in anything treasonable. So he was glad to hear, later, after they were released, that some had enlisted in the United States forces and distinguished themselves for bravery.

Wade Colby managed to sneak in a few days at Sun Valley over the holidays. He confessed to Jude that he was hopelessly frustrated. He had tried to enlist in every branch of the armed services and had been refused. "All because of that damned motorcycle accident!"

As disappointed as Wade was with his predicament, the Pricklers were equally grateful. And the studio was thrilled. One by one Hollywood was sending off its young male stars to serve their country, and now Twentieth's cupboard would not be completely bare. Wade was kept before the cameras constantly and joined the ranks of the highest paid, most popular actors of the time.

Wade dolefully remarked to Jude, "I guess I'll have to satisfy my patriotic zeal by buying war bonds, making war bond tours and visiting hospitals."

Jude knew his friend would do just that and do it with absolute dedication.

Despite the war, Sun Valley operated in a relatively normal manner. Both the lodge and inn were at capacity, complete with a full quota of celebrities: Claudette Colbert, Norma Shearer, Ann Sothern, the Gary Coopers, the Ray Millands, the Henry Hathaways, the Darryl Zanucks and, briefly, Wade Colby. There was one change to the usual agenda. Instead of just taking afternoon tea and socializing in the Redwood Room, guests and employees gathered together to knit for the troops. Thelma joined this endeavor to do her part and received an unexpected bonus.

"Honey," she cried to Jude. "Ya can't imagine who I sat two chairs away from—Norma Shearer! An' I even talked to her! Well, she asked me what I was makin', said it looked really bright and cheerful, and I said, 'a sweater,' just like that! She is *soooo* pretty. I couldn't believe I was that close to her. And Keane! Her son's older, but she just thought Keane was the cutest!" And Thelma gushed on and on to Jude, to Willamina, and to anyone who would listen.

The Abavas clan carefully mapped out its own security strategies. In the event of an air raid, they would head for the deep mine tunnels at the nearby Triumph Mine. An emergency kit of provisions and other necessities was packed and kept close at hand for a quick escape. Guns and ammunition were also in readiness. Noah joined the home guard along with others too old for the draft. The group's only weakness was its thumbs-down attitude about training. No young whippersnapper was going to come in and tell them about guns and horses and stalking!

John and Luke were eligible for the draft, but the consensus was they would be deferred because of the contribution their agricultural careers made to the war effort. To do their bit, they became members of the home guard, relieving Lila and Ethel's anxiety just a little. John and Luke grumbled—largely for effect, though, because they were truthfully not upset about missing the adventure of war. Matthew was only sixteen, so he was safe, at least until his eighteenth birthday.

Jude was another matter. He certainly was a candidate for the draft. Since the army didn't appeal to him, he planned to enlist in the marines before he was called up, but after he got his family settled.

When the ski season officially ended in April 1942, the writing was on the wall—Sun Valley would not reopen the next winter. Gas rationing was inevitable, and the resort was losing most of its key personnel to the war effort.

Thelma was filled with dread at the prospect of Jude's leaving, and was despondent because she hadn't conceived another baby. She couldn't reconcile that she had become pregnant so readily the first time with the fact that she hadn't conceived this time despite several months of trying. She should have gone to a doctor, she berated herself. He might have told her what was wrong. Jude, however, believed it was just as well. Now that he had finally enlisted, who knew what was going to happen? But Thelma kept praying, wanting and needing something more of Jude to remain with her while she waited for him to come home from overseas.

There had been several heavy wet snowfalls that year, unusual for late April. Finally, a bright, warm sunny day arrived, and Jude took Thelma and Keane and Basa for a picnic. His departure date was closing in on them and time together was precious. Jude drove his family out Warm Springs Road, past the ski access, to an old abandoned hot springs at the foot of Baldy Mountain. They romped and played, throwing sticks for Basa to retrieve, rolling a ball around—which drove Basa crazy because it was too big to put in his mouth—laughing at Thelma's attempts to catch Jude when she was "it" at tag.

Jude kept his eyes on Keane, savoring each image, drinking in his son's presence, hoping to absorb enough to tide him over until he returned. Damn war! he thought. Damn Japs! Damn Germans! Don't they have kids they want to be with?

"Ya better start the fire so we can put the potatoes in," Thelma suggested about three-thirty in the afternoon. "Keane's goin' to get hungry pretty soon. I'll take him for a little hike—maybe we'll see some "an-ee-mals," and pick up some more wood. Come on, sweetie." Basa raced ahead of them, barking at an imaginary squirrel, and Thelma and Keane, hand in hand, trotted off after him.

Jude began collecting rocks for the circle and logs for the fire. A dissonant sound started filtering through the familiar noises. At first, Jude thought it might be ice breaking up downstream. But when he paused and listened intently, what registered sent horror tearing through his heart. It was the groan of loosening snow—the telltale rumble of an avalanche.

"Oh, my God—no! Keane! Thelma! Come back!" Jude yelled as he ran in the direction they had taken—the direction of the thundering. He stumbled through the underbrush, the deep snow making progress slow, screaming for them to stop, to answer, to give a sign of their location, for Basa to come! Farther ahead and above came the full gathering fury of the onrushing snow. Before the roar became overpowering, he heard a few muffled distorted screams. But where?

In a matter of seconds, which seemed like an eternity to frantic Jude, the attacking hurtling white death had spent its venom and lay spread in front of him, a huge sheet shielding its own destruction. Eerie quiet hung in the air. Dustlike powder still floated, then settled as a lid on the newly formed snowfield. Rocks and uprooted trees protruded from their snowy grave. Jude stared at the vastness. There wasn't a human sound. And the sound that came from Jude then was not human. He went berserk. He started digging with his hands—clawing—trying to penetrate the slowly hardening surface. Crying, cursing, bellowing like a wounded animal, he dug. In one place—then another—not sure where to try next. He didn't know his hands were bleeding, he just kept digging, aware that time was of the essence and agonizingly frustrated by the extensive area he needed to search. He took off his boots and used them as scoops. Minutes, then hours elapsed; evening approached, and still he dug. Relentless cold ice gnawed at the blood vessels in his face. His mouth was frozen shut, he couldn't yell anymore even if someone had been there to answer. His extremities were strangers for he had long since lost any feeling. And still he dug.

* * *

Willamina peeked out the window in Revel's room at the small house in back. No lights yet. She didn't approve of Thelma and Jude's keeping Keane out so late. But then she sighed and forgave, remembering how little time was left to her boy before he marched off to war. She shuddered at this thought and prayed for his safety. How many mothers, she wondered, were experiencing the same fear? And how many would have to be told, in the days and weeks and months to come, that their sons had perished on the battlefield? How many young widows and infants would be left behind? Willamina prayed for them all.

Satisfied that Revel was sleeping quietly, she returned downstairs, wondering what was more difficult: being a man and enduring the dangers of combat, or being a woman and suffering the pain of isolation and the constant worry of death.

Noah's entrance ended her meditation. "Sorry I be late," he apologized. "It seems more work, less time to do, than ever before."

"No matter," Willamina replied, and she called Matthew to come for dinner.

"Navassa tell me there be avalanche today," Noah said. "He say he knew would happen. That man always know everything 'bout everything—much snow too late, too-hot day, too-cold night triggered slide. Good thing no houses in its way—was by Old Geyer Hot Springs off Warm Springs Road. Big he say. What be wrong?"

The platter Willamina had been carrying clattered to the floor, smashing to smithereens.

"That where they go! And they be late. Oh, Noah!" she gasped.

"That is where *who* went, Mama? What are you talking about?" Matthew asked as he entered the room.

"Jude! And Thelma and Keane. Make picnic—said go to Warm Springs."

Noah sprang into action. "Matthew, ring John and Luke. Meet us at turnoff to Warm Springs. Not worry, my Willamina. Probably all be well, we just make sure. We go by Navassa's—get more people."

Noah and Matthew grabbed shovels, lanterns, picks, gloves, coats and were off. Willamina sat and began her vigil—alone.

The landslide had traveled across the access road to Warm Springs, blocking one section of it, so Noah was forced to go back and rouse the county road-maintenance department for their snowplowing vehicle. Everyone knew everyone in these parts, and all red tape was bypassed. The motor procession crept along behind the snowplow until, abruptly, the lane was clear. About fifty yards farther, they saw Jude's car. Grimly they organized equipment and headed straight in toward the mountain, planning to spread back into the slip area, depending on what they did—or did not—find. Very soon they came upon the remnants of the aborted outing: unopened food basket, soft-drink cooler, small pile of logs for the fire, strewn jackets and odd pieces of clothing. Noah's guitar was lying there, ready for the evening's concert. John stooped and picked up a bright object. Keane's ball. Matthew lost control and in desperation started to run forward, but Noah stopped him.

"No! Not alone. We go together," he ordered hoarsely. "We walk carefully—one next to other—that way, we not miss anything, and no one else becomes lost."

The rescue party fanned out, holding lanterns high, slowly making their way through the blackness. A high-pitched wail pierced the darkness. They couldn't determine whether its source was human or nonhuman, but they quickened their pace toward the sound.

The lamps threw their beams and showed a howling, shivering Basa sitting beside an unconscious Jude, his stocking feet burrowed in for support, his blood-clotted hands in his boots, still in the position to dig. The lanterns' rays relinquished no other information.

Noah and John gently pried Jude's body from its prison and Luke and Navassa began the laborious trek to the car, Matthew following with the terrified and confused Basa. Noah, John, Clyde Warhas and the others, encouraged that at least Jude was alive, continued onward, hopeful the snow would release more hostages. They plodded on until they reached the opposite side of the slide, then reversed at a slightly higher elevation. Back and forth, back and forth. Exhausted, haggard, they would not give up the search. Word spread and by dawn relief troops appeared, led by Matthew, Luke and Navassa. The new volunteers took over, allowing the original searchers a brief rest and some hot coffee. But not for long. Each passing moment diminished the odds of finding Thelma and Keane alive. With daylight, they could use tools to prod beneath the surface; they had been too dangerous to use in the dark. Back and forth, back and forth.

In trying to reconstruct the scene, they reasoned that Basa must have been far enough in front of Thelma and Keane so that only the fringe of the landslide caught him, tossing him about, but allowing him to escape. If Thelma and Keane were trapped in the middle, they still could have swum with the flow and could be close to the top. Unless, in their tumbling, they struck a rock or tree. Knocked out, offering no resistance, they would have been at the mercy of the onslaught, and could be buried anywhere.

The anguish of ebbing faith was reflected in the faces of the rescuers as the day wore on. The tempo accelerated, draining everyone's last ounce of effort, as dusk came closer. They strove to search and search—every inch. Until they could see no more. Until fatigue and failure had them slumped over their picks and shovels. Until the finality engulfed and devoured them.

Thelma and Keane were lost to them forever.

Silently, they filed away, too spent to utter a word. Only Noah and John remained behind. John sank to his knees and at last unleashed his suppressed sobs. Noah cradled him like a baby. Because Noah understood.

9

Jude fought two battles in the hospital. One for the body and one for the mind. Physically, he was combating exposure, frost-bite, severe lacerations. Mentally, he was still in a duel with the elements for Thelma and Keane. One battle was not helping the other. He would lapse in and out of consciousness, and when awake, start flailing his arms, trying to pull his two loved ones to safety, yelling through his swollen and blistered lips for his family to hang on. The doctor was obliged to place restraining straps on the bed so he wouldn't further damage his wounds.

Thelma's parents were in seclusion, her brother, Clyde, caring for them. Willamina and Matthew rotated the bedside watch. John's wife, Lila, cared for little Revel. Noah, John and Luke came to the hospital when work allowed. Each had trepidations that Jude would become fully conscious while they were there, and that they would have to be the one to tell him the awful truth. The task fell on John. He was alone in the room when Jude's eyes focused, and seemed alert for the first time in days. Jude weakly tried to shift his position, but he was pinned down by the binding strips. John quickly undid them and Jude turned slightly in John's direction. John opened his mouth to speak several times, but nothing came out. Jude just kept staring at him, quietly, waiting.

"How do ya feel?" asked John lamely.

Jude nodded feebly. "Okay" came the barely audible reply. His expression was begging John to tell him what he wanted to hear.

"You're gonna be all right, Jude. Take a while, but you'll be okay. The doc says—" John wasn't sure how much he should reveal about Jude's condition. Two toes on his right foot had been amputated, and it wasn't certain that would be the extent of the frostbite damage. His hands—the hands that had dug until they dripped red on the white tomb of snow, until the flesh had turned to raw meat—had fared better, for his boots had, in the end, acted as buffers as well as makeshift scoops. John inwardly pleaded with the Lord not to have Jude ask the question. But he did.

"Wanna—wanna—see—" Jude began struggling hard to make his sedated senses work.

"Where's b-baby? Wanna see K-Keane an'—an' Thelma." The effort drained Jude, but still there was no response.

After an eternity, John said, "Oh, Jude—we dug and we dug—and we dug—and we tried. Oh, God, we tried." John could not say the words. He lowered his head; he couldn't even look at Jude, the tears dripped down his cheeks and over his chin unchecked.

Jude watched his twin's grief through a clouded murky haze, dispassionate, detached. For his mind was already denying what John had intimated.

He drifted into comfortable oblivion.

The next time, Noah was sitting beside Jude, with Willamina and Matthew in the background. After John's experience the family had decided that no one should have to assume the dreaded responsibility alone.

Jude's eyes searched the room for more faces, and then returned to question Noah. Noah gently took his son's bandaged hands and said simply, "The ones you seek are not here. They be with the Lord." And then he embraced and comforted his son. Because Noah understood!

The next weeks were torturous. Jude fought acceptance that Keane and Thelma were dead. That he would never again see his angelic son. That he would never again hear his joyful laughter. That he would never again feel those trusting little arms around him. That he would never again know the complete and unselfish love of his wife. How could that be? How could such life and vibrancy just cease to exist? How could that flow of energy just be snuffed out?

When the fact that they were dead *was* fully realized, a flood of emotions scourged his mind. *Resentment! Rage! Despair!*

Blame! He had failed to rescue them. He hadn't been able to keep his silent promise to Keane—something *had* taken his boy. He knew John blamed him. Would Thelma still be alive and happy with John if he hadn't interfered with her? Was God to blame?

Vengeance! Toward himself. Toward God.

Questions with no answers. Why? Why them? Why not him? Was this God's punishment? Punishment because he hadn't loved Thelma enough? Punishment because Keane was conceived before marriage? Why them? Why not him?

The questions came relentlessly. They never stopped. He heard their voices pleading for him to save them. He imagined the terror they must have felt, the suffering they must have endured. He cried out to God to exchange him for them. He didn't want to live.

God did not heed Jude's request. Jude survived. Until he could learn to adjust and compensate, the loss of the two toes on his right foot caused a slight limp and difficulty balancing. The other loss caused a constant, dull, aching void, interrupted only when an overt encounter caused a lightning flash of acute pain.

Willamina had wanted to remove Thelma's and Keane's things before Jude's return home from the hospital, but Noah had not agreed. He was convinced Jude would be better served if he assumed this responsibility himself. Jude would be allowed to privately vent his grief with each reminding possession. Then Noah prayed Jude would release that grief, bringing him closer to releasing Keane and Thelma.

Basa gingerly approached Jude upon his return; the dog wasn't secure about anyone or anything at this point. He had refused to leave the little house, and had barely touched the food brought to him daily. His bumps and bruises had healed, but his psyche was demoralized. He pined for Keane. Jude knelt and gathered the pitiful sight in his arms. Together they rocked back and forth, clinging to each other in need. At least Jude could cry.

Jude, with Basa at his side, eventually braved facing the contents of the house. Jude lovingly fondled every toy. He polished the slightly used sled; cleaned the well-worn tricycle; dusted and looked at each book—reliving the nights he had read them to Keane. Carefully, he folded every small article of clothing.

Tucked away under Keane's Levi's jeans he found a cigar box filled with a little boy's treasures. A lucky marble. A pretty rock from last summer's excursion to the mountains. A dented sheriff's tin badge. A tiny whistle from a box of Cracker Jacks. A paper ring off a cigar.

Sometimes, like right then, he would choke, he was so full, and he would have to bail out. Then, he and Basa would head toward the river and roam the banks until the suffocation subsided.

Thelma's cache of riches was neatly stored in a cardboard gift box in the bottom bureau drawer. Jude sifted through the treasures, his throat closed, his eyes brimming. Keane's lost tooth—oh, how he remembered that day. Keane had slipped on some ice and fallen on his face! A couple of stitches, a knocked-out tooth, Keane soothed with an ice-cream cone and Thelma consoled by the fact it was only a baby tooth. A lock of hair from Keane's first haircut. Every greeting card Jude had ever given her—another guilt spasm when he thought of the occasions he had forgotten. The inexpensive engagement ring he had quickly bought and which she had only worn at special times. A locket, a Christmas present from Willamina and Noah, with a picture of Keane on one side and Jude on the other. The "something blue" garter from their wedding—he visualized that night, the room in the lodge, and heard again her ardent pledge of love and loyalty. She had kept her promise.

The family left him in seclusion, respecting his need for solitariness and catharsis. Willamina brought supplies and quietly put them in the kitchen. She longed to venture farther, but yielded to Noah's judgment of distance, at least for the present. Their sorrow could be shared with Jude when he was ready.

But he was not ready yet as he wandered the house searching for the essence of his lost loved ones. Jude lingered over each snapshot on every page of the photo album that chronicled the four years of their marriage, and the three years and seven months of Keane's existence. He studied the faces staring out at him, faces that reflected happiness, contentment, serenity—even his. Had he brought as much to their lives as they had brought to his? He doubted it. Had he told them, had they understood, how much they meant to him? He doubted that, too.

The first few pages of the album had been devoted to Jude's young life, photos scavenged by Thelma from Willamina's small collection. He compared the before and after and saw two completely different people. Which was he really? He didn't know.

Thelma's Bible was next to the album, with a marker at Psalm 23. As he read, he marveled at the tenacity of her faith. And that of his parents. Why couldn't he find solace instead of fault with the Lord? Prophetically perhaps, his eyes drifted to Psalm 22 and he asked again why his God had forsaken him.

Jude knocked on the screen door of Willamina's kitchen. "Can I come for dinner, Mama?"

She walked slowly toward him, eyes brimming, heart grateful, and hugged him tightly. "You be always welcome, my son." Because Willamina also understood. Because Willamina had always known the complexities of her firstborns; what each one was, and what each one was not.

In the following days, she assisted Jude in gathering the useful clothing and playthings to donate to the needy. A gesture that, Jude thought, Thelma would have liked.

Jude asked Matthew if he would like to move in with him. Matthew had been shattered first by the tragedy and then by Jude's distance, although he had tried to understand. The invitation came as a sign that Jude wanted to reestablish their bond. Although Matthew had just turned seventeen, he realized Jude would still have his dark periods. He believed he was not only strong enough to weather Jude's expected black moods, but that he might even be able to help his brother survive them.

Jude tried to adjust to the textures and rhythms of family life once more. Some situations were more delicate than others. The first night, at dinner, seeing the almost two-year-old Revel sitting in her high chair had sent Jude and Basa disappearing off on one of their purging walks. He anticipated he would have this searing emotional surge with each child he saw. Would the degree of pain ever lessen?

The first family dinner including John and his pregnant wife, Lila, and Luke and Ethel, was extremely stressful for everyone. No one knew exactly what to say, or more important, what not to say. Or how to act. Should they just behave normally, ignoring what had happened? Or be openly sympathetic and compassionate? Somehow, they bungled through the evening, but not without a covert exit by Jude and Basa.

The likelihood of Jude's going off to war, where he could forget his sorrows, was now impossible. He had been reclassified 4F.

In August, he was asked to take a fishing party, and he tried—he really tried. But the group comprised people he had guided before and he couldn't cope with their well-intentioned condolences. And the mountains, which had always represented freedom, now seemed almost claustrophobic with memories. Sun Valley was closed for the duration of the war, and seemed closed for Jude, as well.

In the fall, Jude volunteered to help Noah. Autumn and spring were Noah's hectic seasons with bands of sheep coming in or going out, and harvesting or planting to be done. Things were even busier now that Noah had his own lands to manage in addition to those of the Wangler estate. The extra hands were much appreciated.

Basa had a romping good time, but not Jude. For the first time in his life, he wanted—and needed—a sense of family cohesion. But something blocked his entrance into that safe haven—"Noah & Sons." He hungered to follow Noah's lead, to experience the same soul-gratifying satisfaction from this business that Noah did, to become one of the Noah & Sons collaboration. But he couldn't. Even the past months hadn't mellowed his gut feeling of being a stranger in his own family. John and Luke were firmly entrenched, by choice. So why not him? He was of the same blood—why couldn't he belong? Why did one part of him thirst for conformity, and the other part refuse to comply? Why was he damned with being different?

John was not the sole reason. Oh, Jude knew John's proximity would always present a problem. How could the two of them—conceived at the same moment from love and passion—be so diabolically opposite? Yes, he knew accepting orders from John as the foreman would be difficult. Their personalities would be at war, sooner rather than later. And yes, he knew the memory of Thelma would always loom large between them. Yet there was something more, something else that made him feel so alien.

No, this interlude was exactly that—an intermission between the acts of his life. If he was to have a life, he had to acknowledge that this could not be the location for it. This land belonged to Noah and John and Luke. He decided he would have to leave.

10

John Abavas, Jr., was born on January 23, 1943, to proud parents, John and Lila. Jude was perfunctorily pleased for them and for the healthy little boy. But the baby's arrival only cemented his decision to move on.

The opportunity came in an unexpected way. Matthew had been accepted for the Navy V-12 Officer Training Program, and after graduation in June was to report to the University of Washington to begin the summer semester. Jude seized the opening. He would drive Matthew to Seattle, help him get settled, be with him on his eighteenth birthday and maybe even scout the shipyards for employment so he could stay in the vicinity. Finally, he had a reason to leave Hailey.

Jude sold his house and furniture to John and Lila. He traded in the old Ford V8—and its stinging memories—for a 1941 four-door Chevrolet. He would only bring a minimum of personal belongings, the remainder would be stored with Willamina. Noah furnished him with extra gas stamps, since rationing was more generous for farmers.

Shortly before Jude's scheduled departure, Mr. Horace B. Wangler's giving heart stopped beating for the last time. He was eighty years old. Provisions in his will stipulated that Noah was to remain as manager of his estate, with an increase in salary. And if the heirs should desire to sell any of their holdings, Noah was to have the first option to buy. No blood relative lamented Mr. Wangler's passing more than Noah. And Willamina. From the onset, this man had provided the foundation for their lives. They gave thanks he had not suffered, that he had led a long and rewarding life and that his accomplishments would be a legacy unto themselves.

Jude could not go to the funeral services. It was too soon. He mourned the loss of Mr. Wangler at home. Alone, with Basa.

The car was packed, the basket of food and cooler of drinks conveniently placed. The boys were ready to say their good-byes. Willamina and Noah asked for strength from above; they didn't want to show their sadness. True, Matthew would come home during the first break. And they were fortunate he was going to college instead of straight to a war, but still, he was leaving the nest and they knew life would never be the same again. And Jude—they both had a premonition that much time would pass before he returned. Yet, when they were young, they had left their families, too. This was evolution. This was the ordained process of growth and change. They must be willing to accept, and with acceptance, understand.

Matthew and Jude each held little Revel high in the air and then hugged her in their arms. She carried the doll they had given her as an early third birthday present. Matthew squeezed and kissed his mom, hugged his dad, promised to write regularly, and ran for the car before his dam burst. Basa was already inside, barking for the trip to begin. Jude looked long into Willamina's and Noah's eyes. No words were uttered, none were necessary. He drew his parents close to him. And then he was gone.

Noah and Willamina reached for each other, calling out their blessing as the Chevy pulled away. "Go with God!"

Jude and Matthew traded time at the wheel. There was little conversation in the beginning—each had too much to sort out. The enormity of their adventure settled heavily on their minds; the future was a complete question mark. They drove at a leisurely pace. There was no reason for rushing to the unknown. The traffic was light, and because of rationing, most of the vehicles they encountered were military. Neither had ever been this far north before, and as they neared the big lakes, Jude felt a shiver of pain. This was the region he had hoped to one day show Keane and Thelma. Would he ever be able to handle their loss?

The second day of their journey, they crossed the border into Washington State. The farmland in this eastern part of the state spurred Matthew to share his thoughts with Jude.

"Ya know, I don't wanna be a farmer. Or a land and live-stock man like Papa, or John and Luke. I'm, well, I'm not sure what I want to be or do, but I know it's not going to be that! Is that okay?''

"Course it's okay!" Jude grunted, remembering that he'd voiced the same concern.

"I was thinkin'," Matthew continued. "What do you think about me being a pilot? A navy pilot? I mean—if I could? I don't know if I could even qualify, but what do you think about me tryin'? I'd like to. I don't know about my chances, but do you think Papa and Mama would be upset? It's no more dangerous than anything else in the service. Is it? And then maybe I could be a pilot after the war. I mean, if I made it through the war—"

"Don't talk like that!" Jude barked. He couldn't contemplate another loss. "You'll make it. Crappy war better be over before you get out of school, anyway. And if you want to be a flier, then be one. Just think of it! You're the first in the family to go to college. What an opportunity! Nothin' you can't do if you put your mind to it, so work hard and fight for it. Don't matter what Papa and Mama want—it's what *you* want that counts. It's your life! They know that!"

Jude realized he had been wallowing in his own dilemma, focusing on himself so long, he hadn't given any consideration to Matthew's uncertainty about the future. Since Jude had been refused the right to serve his country, he had tried to ignore the war, brushing it aside as if it were a minor nuisance. He had completely shut out the concerns of a young man on the brink of realizing his independence, yet understandably confused and fearful about the future. He loved Matthew and was appalled by his own selfishness. He had to put aside his private grievances and concentrate on Matthew. At least for now.

Jude devoted the rest of the trip to hammering into Matthew's head that it was not disloyal to pursue one's own goal, and that he had to build the confidence to reach for his dreams.

Seattle was a beautiful city, grander than they had imagined. But it was the size of the University of Washington that surprised them most.

After many inquiries and sets of directions, they finally located the correct building for Matthew to present his papers. His orders were duly noted and the complicated processing procedure began. A mountain of forms had to be filled out. Curriculum to be decided—yes, courses could be added that would lead to a career in aviation. Quarters to be assigned. Uniforms to be issued. Medical examinations to be endured. Rules and regulations to be learned. A map of the campus to be studied.

The initial days were a whirlwind of activities. Matthew's head was spinning, but his eyes were bright with excitement and expectation. Jude found a nearby motel and was available whenever Matthew was free. The university wasn't an actual military base—many regular students were also enrolled—so civilians were able to roam the designated areas of the campus. Navy and marine cadets had restrictions and curfews, with separate procedures to sign in and out of dorms, the library, classes and mess hall. They also had rigid academic requirements, which, if not met, would result in their disqualification and immediate reassignment to active duty.

"Well, how do I look?" Matthew paraded before Jude in his navy uniform and new haircut. "I borrowed a camera from my roommate so you could take a picture to send to Mama and Papa. Dennis—Dennis Tesar, that's my roommate—hated when they cut his hair and he thinks these white hats are silly. I kinda like them. Oh, by the way, they call me Matt."

"Hold still!" Jude ordered. "How can I snap this thing if you're prancing around like a peacock? Mama and Papa are going to be surprised when they see this! You've grown up."

Jude investigated the docks and shipyards. He didn't feel comfortable there. Loading and unloading or building ships simply did not appeal to him. The lumber industry didn't interest him, either—it reminded him of Idaho. What was he searching for? He still could manage with the money he had, so he decided to push on. Maybe if he kept moving, something would reach out and hold him, some place would beckon irresistibly.

Jude had no compunction about leaving Matthew now. Matthew—or rather, Matt—was well situated. He had adjusted quickly and his work was cut out for him. He had to study and study and study! He didn't need a baby-sitter hovering over him any longer. He had taken the first few steps of his own journey.

After celebrating Matthew's birthday on July 7, Jude headed south with Basa. South had seemed as good a direction as any.

"Ya know what, Basa?" he asked his dog. "I think I was more bothered about us drivin' on than Matt was. His head is so full—he's gonna be one smart cookie when he gets out of there. He's set and he's not gonna miss us. But we'll miss him, won't we? We're the ones up the creek without a paddle."

Basa whined sympathetically and licked Jude's face.

"Hold on there! I gotta drive, ya know. I'll tell you somethin' else, Basa, somethin' I wouldn't tell another l-living soul— why do I stammer when I say living?"

Jude rubbed Basa's ears before continuing.

"I would go crazy if you weren't with me. I couldn't stand being so alone. Jesus, somebody hear me talkin' to you like this, they'd think I was already batty. But I don't care. I don't care what somebody thinks. Somebody hasn't done a damn thing for me lately. And you have! So fuck somebody."

The pair aimlessly meandered down the state past Mount Rainier, and later, Mount Saint Helens. The foliage was denser and greener than it was in Idaho, the air wetter.

"Guess it's true what they say about the rainfall 'round here. At least it's not coming down now. We'll stop for the night first likely spot I see."

Jude had replenished his provisions and had decided camping out was better than getting in a hassle with a motel manager who wouldn't allow animals—he'd been through that in Seattle. Anyway, it was cheaper, and it made sense to conserve his resources. He hadn't realized before how fast the miles and cost of fuel added up. Noah's gas stamps made the trip possible, but he still had to pay the price of the gasoline.

They veered west, toward the coast, across the Columbia River, into Oregon, through Portland, until, finally, they reached the Pacific Ocean.

"I wish—ah, hell! You know what I wish. I wish Keane and Thelma were here to see this, too!"

Jude had concentrated on Matthew's fears while they were together. But now that his brother was settled, Jude's own plight again held sway.

As they made their way down the curving coastline, some of the names of the scenic locales ominously reflected Jude's inner turmoil: Boiler Bay, Devil's Churn, Devil's Elbow. He watched with fascination the angry clouds, those teasing temptresses that promised blue skies and airy fluffs, but held the trump card of storm and violence to ward off complacency. It was like life, Jude thought.

He did not feel comfortable in this landscape. The innocent smoke that came out of a chimney mixed with mist and fog, enveloping Jude in what appeared to him to be evilness. He felt dwarfed by the height of the spray and the size and force and power of the relentlessly pounding ocean, its overwhelming mass a reminder it could not be mastered. Again, like life. Jude immediately recognized he would never be at ease in this environment. So, where was he going? And when he arrived what was he going to do?

He attempted to reconstruct his life, searching for clues. His mind worked like a projector, throwing up images of earlier days. *Stop! Look!* It was fairly obvious that that boy had known who he was and what he wanted. Had he pushed aside his twin, so he could emerge first? That boy's objective had always been to be number one, the best in everything! So what had happened?

The pictures flashed again. *Stop! Look!* Now that young family man had a new sense of well-being, a new goal. He didn't have to prove he was a champ, his son and wife already believed that unequivocally. He still worked tirelessly, but for all of them, not just himself.

For the last picture, he only had to look in the mirror.

Winning had been all-important. And he had always won. Until now. He had suffered the worst defeat possible. He had lost his family. He had lost what had fulfilled his life. He couldn't appeal the judgment, it was irrevocable.

Now he was alone once more. He couldn't replace the loss and wouldn't—he would never expose himself to such vulnerability again. As he had when a child, he would only survive if he outdid, outplayed, outrivaled, outthought, outworked any and all opponents. He had to win again. He had to succeed again. No matter what the cost. That would be his salvation.

"And I think I know where we're heading, Basa," he said, scratching his dog's ear. "How would you like warm weather, palm trees and a beach? We're on our way to Los Angeles—Hollywood, Basa! I'm goin' to look up some of those people who told me to look them up. Yes, that's exactly what I'm gonna do. There's an old saying, 'When you're sitting downstairs, you never know where anyone in the balcony will spit.' Well, watch out, everybody, because if anybody's gonna be doing any spitting, it's gonna be me!''

For the first time in over a year, there was a spark—a small one, but still it was there in Jude's eyes.

And so on July 20, 1943, Jude William Abavas arrived in Los Angeles, California. He was twenty-four years old.

11

Los Angeles, California
July 23, 1943

The guard at the entrance gate of Twentieth Century Fox Studios hung up the telephone and strolled back to Jude, who was standing by his Chevy.

"Just as I thought, Mr. Zanuck's office never heard of ya," he snarled at Jude. "Better be on your way, you're blocking the road!"

"That's not true! He—"

"Are you calling the secretary of Mr. Darryl Zanuck, vice president in charge of production, a *liar?*"

"You're callin' me a liar, and I don't like it, not one bit!" Jude warned. Their tones were menacing—a scuffle was imminent.

Jude was primed for battle. After the initial culture shock and excitement of seeing the huge metropolis of Los Angeles, events had not gone well. He had driven from place to place looking for lodging and not one would accept pets. So he'd spent the first night in the car. There was no place to camp out in this concrete jungle, and no creek or lake in sight where he could take a dip and freshen up. A gas-station rest room had had to do as a substitute.

The next day, stiff and cranky, he had finally managed to locate Gower Street and Melrose Avenue and Marathon Way, which dead-ended at the gates of Paramount Pictures. He had intended to flush out the production manager he'd met on *I Met Him in Paris*—the movie that had been shot at Sun Valley—and offer his savvy for hire. That gentleman, as it turned out, had moved on to greener pastures, and no one else in that depart-

ment had wanted to talk to him. Jude was still undaunted—
dented maybe, but not about to give up. Consulting his newly
acquired map, he sought out some of the tourist highlights in
that same area: Columbia Studios, R.K.O. Studios, Hollywood
and Vine, Sunset and Vine Streets. The Brown Derby restaurant. Grauman's Chinese Theater. He had been properly awed
by the grandeur and the glitz. And wistfully he had thought of
Thelma and how she would have reacted, how thrilled she would
have been to have seen all this. Keane would not have been impressed, except perhaps by the bright neon lights. Jude tried to
look harder, more intently, absorb enough for all three of them.
How he missed them!

"Oh, Basa, this is a different world," Jude said as he drove
along the street. "Matt thought Seattle was big—wait till he sees
this! Even I can't believe it. We're out of our class here, boy. But
who says we can't learn. I can lick you, Hollywood!" Jude suddenly shouted out the window.

That night, Jude was determined to sleep in a bed and enjoy a
shower. He registered at a small, inconspicuous motel and
smuggled Basa inside. The deception was successful until a
loudmouthed couple checked into the room next door and Basa
started barking at the intruders.

The night clerk banged on Jude's door. "You got a dog in
there?" he shouted.

"No! I always sound this way when I cough!"

"Don't get shitty with me—ya have ta leave!"

"What's the matter with this place?" Jude demanded, opening the door. "You let some drunken numbskulls in here but you
won't let a dog stay. He's smarter'n they'll ever be—and better
mannered!"

"Them's the rules. You gonna go—or do I call the cops?"

"Stick it in your ear, asshole!" But Jude didn't want to risk
trouble with the police, so he threw his stuff in the car and took
off.

Later that same day, with his resolution shaken but still intact, he painstakingly found the route to Culver City. There he
steered past the Metro-Goldwyn-Mayer studio—what a giant
fortresslike complex—and continued east on Washington Boulevard to the more modest headquarters of David O. Selznick. A
sign, simple but elegant, announced Selznick International. Be-

yond the expansive green lawn was a large white colonial structure.

Jude parked on the street. He put on the jacket that he had carefully hung on the hook in the back seat so it wouldn't wrinkle. He had worn his wedding suit because he thought it looked more businesslike. He wasn't sure what people wore in studios, but he recalled that the men from Hollywood had dressed formally every night in Sun Valley, so he couldn't be too wrong in a suit.

"May I help you?" asked a pretty young woman at the reception desk, eyeing this good-looking stranger with interest.

"Well, yes. I would like to see Mr. Selznick—please." The way she looked at him embarrassed him.

"Do you have an appointment?"

"Ah . . . no."

"Are you a friend of Mr. Selznick's?"

"Oh, not exactly. I met him—saw him—a couple of times in Sun Valley, Idaho."

"Your name?"

"Jude Abavas, ma'am."

She dialed a number, spoke softly into the mouthpiece, replaced the phone in the cradle, and delivered the verdict.

"Mr. Selznick is out of the city for several weeks. His secretary did not find your name on any of his lists, so she will not schedule a future appointment. If you care to leave an address and telephone number, perhaps Mr. Selznick will contact you when he returns. Now, is there anything *I* can do for you?"

"No! I mean—I don't think so. I'll come back later. Thank you, ma'am," and with that, Jude beat a hasty retreat.

While Jude was changing back into his regular clothes in the now-familiar Standard Station men's room—he didn't want to mess up his suit—a sudden inspiration swept over his disappointment. *David Niven!* Of course! Of all the guests, David Niven had been the most forthright, the friendliest, the nicest. Except, of course, for Wayland Prickler a.k.a. Wade Colby. But he didn't want to contact Wade yet, not this way. Wade was too good of a friend. Jude wanted to get a job on his own first.

After hanging his suit on the hook in the car, he took a walk and came across a park—Los Angeles evidently had a few public parks—and while Basa was fertilizing the grass, Jude racked his brain for ways of getting in touch with Mr. Niven. A discarded newspaper's headline caught his attention: U.S. 7th Army Captures Palermo. The damn war again! And that was when he remembered that David Niven had returned home to his native England to fight for his country.

So much for that idea.

That evening, Jude and Basa munched their dinner in the parking lot of one of the numerous drive-ins in Los Angeles, a big-city innovation he was really coming to appreciate. "Tomorrow we tackle Zanuck, Basa! That's gotta work. I'll be damned if I'm gonna call that blond bitch Mrs.—what was her name?—oh, yeah, Mrs. Arnold Pummer. That would really be the last resort. We'd just get the hell out of Los Angeles before that. We could go somewhere else. Don't you worry, Basa, ol' friend, we'll make out!"

So by the time he found Twentieth Century Fox at Pico Boulevard and Motor Avenue, in yet another section of Los Angeles, he was not in the mood to take no for an answer and be verbally abused by a guard in the process.

It did cross Jude's mind that he might dirty his suit in the course of a fight, but to give vent to three days of frustration by punching this obnoxious guard's face in might be worth it. He was ready.

"Jude? Jude Abavas!" a voice called from behind him. "What in the hell are you doing here?" It was Wade Colby, sitting in a white Lincoln Continental convertible on the exit side of the gate. "What is going on here, officer?"

"Oh, Mr. Colby, sir. You know this . . . person? He wanted to see Mr. Zanuck, and Mr. Zanuck couldn't see him, and well..." The guard sounded flustered; he obviously didn't want to get on the wrong side of the studio's superstar.

"Hello, Wade," Jude said. He turned to the guard. "I'm sorry I lost my temper. I'll be goin' now." He felt embarrassed and awkward and just wanted out of there.

Wade sized up the situation quickly. His parents had told him about the tragedy of Jude's wife and son—now Jude was here in Los Angeles. Wade assumed this meant Jude had fled memory-ridden Idaho. But what did he want with Zanuck? Wade saw the desperation and panic on Jude's face and decided to simply plunge in and take charge.

"We'll forget this episode!" Wade told the anxious guard. "Come on, Jude, hop in your car and follow me a few blocks out Pico to a bar I know, and we'll do some catching up."

Jude didn't protest, he almost welcomed being told what to do. He kept his car close behind the gleaming, open white convertible. Several people honked their horns and shouted greetings of recognition at Wade, who always waved in response.

"How nice to see you, Mr. Colby," cooed the headwaiter, ushering them inside the dimly lit, Polynesian-decorated lounge. "Right this way. Your favorite table is waiting." Wade ordered for them both from a waitress dressed in a skimpy flowered bra and grass skirt. Jude could only stare.

"I damn near didn't know you in a suit," Wade said, breaking the ice. "Why were you trying to see Zanuck? And why didn't you call me? How long have you been in town? And how long will you be around? Doesn't matter, I want you to stay with me. Now, I want to hear what is going on."

Wade's obvious enthusiasm about seeing Jude made it a lot easier for Jude to try to explain, to talk, in general.

"I've been here three days. I was gonna call, but not until... well...see, I'm here lookin' for something to do. A job. Zanuck and some of the other guys always said there might be something for me here. I couldn't ask you—the others aren't friends, I don't really know them, so it doesn't matter what they think of me. I would have called you soon as I got work. You understand, don't you?"

Wade nodded. He understood this man only too well, which made him like Jude all the more.

"To tell you the truth, Wade, I couldn't stay in Sun Valley any longer. I couldn't work there—" Once Jude started talking, the floodgates opened and he poured his guts out to his friend. He was finally able to verbalize the details of that wrenching, harrowing afternoon of his wife's and son's deaths, to tell about the days and nights of suffering in the aftermath, to explain the random lack of direction he was now experiencing. Until now there had been no need to talk. Everyone around him already knew what had happened and had assumed how he felt. Wade encouraged his confidences, without judgment or comment.

A few hours and several drinks later, Jude was still talking. "So, anyway, that's what I was doing at that gate." A pause.

"Jesus, I've been bendin' your ear long enough. I'd better be on my way. And poor Basa, I forgot all about him. Thanks, Wade. Thanks for—"

"Just a minute" Wade said, grabbing his arm. "I listened to you, now you listen to me. I'll forgive you for not calling me, but only on one condition. You and Basa stay in my guest cottage. Don't interrupt!" Jude had opened his mouth, obviously to object. "I employ a couple—Swedish man and wife—who live in the apartment over the garage. They run the house—and me, I might add—and, they would welcome someone else around. They thrive on taking care of wayward souls like us. I also have a dog, Floozy, so named because that is exactly what she is. Flounced up to the door one day and decided to move in—spoiled rotten, of course. Perhaps Basa will be able to show her a real master. Who knows? Maybe they'll make beautiful music together."

Wade looked intently at Jude. "One more thing before we leave. I am your friend. Trust that. Accept that. And true friends are there for each other. I would never hesitate to seek your help, because I know you would give it willingly. You already did. So allow me the same privilege."

Wade quickly paid the check and led a solemn and quiet Jude out into the glare and heat of the July afternoon sun. He didn't allow any opportunity for discussion; he kept up a stream of optimistic chatter while they waited for a grateful Basa to sniff around the parking lot. "That water will hit the spot. It's several degrees cooler at the beach, you know. Did you remember I live at the beach? Or did I ever mention that in Sun Valley? There is quite a colony of film folk in Santa Monica—Norma Shearer and her husband, Marti Arrougé, are at 707 Ocean Front—did you know Marti when he was a ski instructor?" Wade only permitted Jude time to nod before continuing.

"Really nice chap. In the Navy Air Corps now, I believe. He's Basque, too, isn't he? French Basque, right? And Mr. and Mrs. Louis B. Mayer have a home at 625 Ocean Front. How long he'll remain at those premises is a question for debate, however. Rumor has it that he is about to fly the coop. Ah, I see Basa is ready. I'll finish the neighbor list and wrap up the gossip later. It's not too far—stay close behind me."

And with that, Wade hopped in his car and took off. Jude had no choice but to do the same.

What am I doing, Jude wondered as he drove. *I can't let him do this. It's too much—it's—just not right. It's exactly why I didn't call him in the first place. But he's right! He really is my friend. And I'm his. If he wanted the moon and it was mine to give—he'd have it!—my friend!*

Jude continued to think as he guided the Chevy through the traffic, tailing the white Lincoln Continental. For a moment, he felt a pang of guilt. Was he putting Wade ahead of his own flesh and blood? He would do anything for Matthew and Papa and Mama! And meet any needs of his brothers and sister. He respected his family. And his own family—well, he didn't have to analyze how he had loved and loved Keane and Thelma.

No, this was different. Friendship was different. A stranger, a contemporary comes into one's life, and for whatever reason, a bond is formed, an empathy established, a relationship nurtured to maturity. The commitment is voluntary.

With that guilt dissipated, another took its place. Was he too prideful? Was that why he was finding it difficult to accept Wade's offer? And why hadn't he contacted Wade when he first arrived? Noah's warning came to mind—was this protective pride a part of that "force" that haunted him?

Or was he afraid of not being in control? Afraid of showing weakness? Afraid of being vulnerable? Afraid to trust again?

"Basa," Jude said, "let's just see the lay of the land. If we're not in his or anyone's way, if we're not causing too much trouble by being at Wade's, then maybe we'll stay a night or two—until we get settled, or move on. Maybe we can pay—like in a motel. Now, that's an idea!"

Basa barked in agreement.

The Pacific shimmered in the sunlight. Mild whitecaps broke against the shore while tanned young bodies frolicked in the surf. Volleyball nets were strung intermittently up and down the expansive public beach and heated games were in progress. Ahead, Wade signaled right on Ocean Front. A few blocks north, he pointed to a residence on the left and motioned for Jude to pull ahead of him into the parking area in front. A large door magically opened and Wade drove his whale of a car into the garage. Before Jude could get out of the Chevy, Wade bounded from a door in the high brick wall that encased and harbored the property.

"Don't bother with your things—Eric will bring them in. Just hold on to Basa. You don't want him dashing into the street. The traffic is deadly—once we're inside, he can run free. I can't wait until Floozy sets eyes on him. Eric! Anna!" Wade led his guests into the courtyard. A profusion of multicolored flowers and forest green plants surrounded the tended lawn and tiled patio. A tall, Nordic man appeared, who Jude assumed was Eric. And charging from another direction rushed a barking Floozy. White, looking as if she was part poodle, she was haughtily suspicious of the intruders, especially Basa. Ignoring Jude momentarily, Floozy thoroughly inspected Basa. Basa was patient at first, then gave a warning growl; he had had enough, it was his turn.

"Aha! See that, Eric? Floozy has met her match!" exulted Wade. "Eric, this is Mr. Abavas. He, and Basa over there, will be staying with us. Anna—hello!—you'll be delighted to know I brought a good friend home who, I promise, will do justice to your exquisite cuisine." Anna's blond head bowed in greeting, but not before Jude caught her pleased smile.

Jude looked on in wonderment as Wade continued to act as tour guide for a visiting VIP.

To the north side of the central enclosure was the garage and upstairs apartment where Eric and Anna lived, kitchen, pantry and utility room. To the south side, the self-sufficient guest quarters with separate entrance, where Eric was already depositing Jude's belongings. And straight ahead, through large sliding glass doors, was the main part of the house. Jude was ushered into a mammoth room with a dining space on the far right, and sunken bar on the far left. There was sand-colored oversize furniture on terrazzo floors, huge soft pillows, well-placed area rugs and bold modern canvases with great splashes of color. Hidden behind one of the paintings was a screen, and on the opposite wall, another picture camouflaged a movie projector. Beyond yet another set of sliding glass doors was a covered lanai flowing to an Olympic-size swimming pool. A tinted wrought-iron fence and gate adjoined the brick wall, allowing visibility and access, while maintaining a degree of privacy. And beyond was the beach and the Pacific. Wade's wing was an impressive appendage on the north side of the house that opened onto the extended lanai with a full ocean view.

"When I bought the house, the master suite was where the guest quarters are. But it seemed to me the purpose of living out here was to see and hear the ocean. So I indulged myself and built this rather elaborate new addition. I may have gone a bit overboard with the dimensions. But should I ever marry and have—'' Wade caught himself as he saw the involuntary shudder that passed through Jude's body. Like an astringent brushing a raw wound.

Hastily, Wade went on. "Well, let's just say, there is ample room. Are you ready for a dip in the big pond?"

As each went to change into bathing trunks, Jude surveyed his own more than comfortable accommodations: a spacious room, fitted as a sitting room—with a portable kitchen and bar—and two baths with adjoining dressing rooms. The decor was simple and tasteful. This was a far cry from the houses Jude was used to in Idaho. But, oddly, he felt at ease. He did not feel intimidated or out of place. For the most part, that had to be thanks to Wade, he concluded. Wade was so unassuming, so unaffected, so genuine, one couldn't help but be relaxed around him. His home reflected this same wreath of unpretentiousness, even if the wreath was woven with elegance.

Floozy and Basa joined their masters for a long romp in the Pacific. Jude could feel the salt water drain away his tensions. But the calm he felt couldn't be attributed to the water alone. He hadn't been at all embarrassed by exposing his slightly deformed right foot for the first time, which surprised him. He heard his own laughter, which had been silent for so long. He was feeling a surge of exhilaration again, and for the moment, at least, he had no misgivings—about staying, about work. He was—*yes*—he was enjoying himself!

Wade had discreetly canceled his appointment for the evening so he could have dinner with Jude. He had formulated a plan—such an ideal solution that it was difficult to contain. But he knew he couldn't unveil it too quickly, the timing had to be right. He recognized that Jude had been walking an emotional tightrope and had to be approached gently. Hopefully, by tomorrow Jude would be receptive. Because Wade also knew Jude was not one to linger or be inactive for any length of time.

They watched the sunset while enjoying cocktails. Over supper, as two good friends should, they reminisced—and savored the food. Anna lived up to her advance publicity.

Jude finally yielded to his tiredness. He slipped between the cool sheets, Basa contentedly cuddled beside him. He thought about the events of the day and wondered what he had ever done right in his life to deserve such a friend as Wade Colby. Before succumbing completely to a blissful sleep, he decided that God definitely worked in mysterious ways. The coincidences of Wade's coming to Sun Valley, of Wade's coming out of the studio at that precise moment today. Maybe only in America could this happen. Yes, definitely. Because only in America was there no rigid caste system to prevent their friendship.

But Jude could only wonder what had really prompted two such diverse people to become friends.

12

Jude awakened with a start. He looked around the room, wondering where he was, what city he was in. Basa opened one lazy eye, apparently wanting to know what was going on, but clearly hoping it wasn't important enough to disturb his rest.

Then Jude remembered, and patted Basa reassuringly. "It's okay, Basa, I just kind of forgot for a minute there. We really conked out, didn't we? Well, yesterday was a pretty big day for us. Almost getting in a fight with that guard, Wade saving my ass—and then Wade taking us in like he did. Isn't he something? I still can't get over how you and me can be lucky enough to have him as a friend. Come on, sleepyhead, let's go find Wade and Floozy!"

When Jude entered the main room, he was dazzled by the panorama of light patterns dancing on the surface of the ocean. It had been a long time since he had allowed himself to appreciate nature's beauty.

After an invigorating swim, Jude and Wade were finishing breakfast, when a call came for Wade.

"Damn!" he cried into the phone. "I had no idea he was such a bad one. What in the hell am I going to *do!*" Wade slammed down the receiver in exasperation.

"What's the matter? Can I help?" Jude asked anxiously.

"Oh, it's nothing. I'm sorry, Jude. I didn't mean to ruin our day, but I am just so—*frustrated*—and disappointed!"

"Please, tell me. I probably can't do much, anyway, but I'd sure feel good if I could try. Anything, just name it!"

"Well, you're right, of course. If I'm going to bitch, who is there better to listen to my complaints than my friend." Wade proceeded carefully—so far, his plan was working. "So, here's my tale of woe. Two days ago, I had to dismiss my stand-in. A stand-in is the person who takes an actor's place while the cameramen and electricians are setting up for the next scene. This way, the actor's energy is conserved, and it allows him time to study dialogue or rehearse or—"

Jude interrupted. "But aren't there a lot of guys who could do that for you? I remember a little from when they shot that picture in Sun Valley."

"Not just anyone would do," Wade explained. "For one thing, the stand-in has to be relatively the same size and have similar coloring, for lighting and framing purposes. In addition, very often—and this was my case—a stand-in acts as a double. For long shots of a potentially dangerous scene, the studio prefers not to use the actor, but rather his double. It has to do with risk and insurance and all that nonsense. Then they zero in on the actor for the close-ups. But I'm sure you know that already." Wade was watching Jude's expression intently as he talked.

"And, this chap I had was also my informal secretary. He would take messages, make phone calls and appointments, coordinate my schedule at home and at work, and so on. This latter responsibility, I found out, was his Achilles' heel. People began to recognize him as a representative of mine, and he began taking advantage of the association. He would tell the assistant director that I wanted this young lady or that young man to work in my film, and, as a favor "to me," the A.D. would hire the person. And then this scoundrel would take a fee from these poor kids for getting them the job."

"What scum!" Jude was starting to boil.

"That's not all! It seems he also conducted 'couch interviews' with girls on my behalf. Can you imagine? Screening my potential bed partners! Quite an insult—I do very well on my own in that department, thank you very much."

Both shared a chuckle on that one.

"Thank heavens some people started to complain and word came back to me before the damage was irreparable. And now, I was just informed that he ran up considerable personal charges on my account." Wade sighed. "It seems there is no one I can trust."

"That bastard!" Jude muttered. "I'd like to get my hands on him and teach him a few old-fashioned Idaho lessons."

"He isn't worth the effort. But thanks, anyway—it's nice to know someone is in your corner. The shame of it is, I considered him sort of a pal, a companion, a confidant. I'll miss that." Wade looked sadly at Jude.

"I wish—shit, I wish I knew this place!" Jude was adamant. "I wish I knew how to find you someone."

"That wouldn't be easy, even if you were a native Californian. No, I'm afraid there aren't many people like you around. People who are loyal and dependable and honest and bright are hard to come by. If only..." Wade's voice trailed off and then he stared at Jude as if struck by a sudden idea.

"If only what?" Jude asked.

"Oh—nothing. For a minute there, I had this wild notion that you might— But no, I couldn't expect—it would be such a perfect solution, though. But I couldn't impose—"

"Expect what? Impose what? What'n the hell are you talking about?" Jude demanded.

Wade answered reluctantly, as if Jude were dragging this from him. "Well...if you insist. When I was describing the qualities I would look for in someone, I realized I was describing you. And I—well—call it wishful thinking, but I thought how wonderful it would be if we could work together. But then I thought how selfish it was of me—to even imply such a thing—to interfere with your—"

"Me!" Jude was dumbfounded. "I don't know beans about your business."

"Come now! Don't underestimate yourself. You had some exposure on Claudette's film. And there were reasons why those people suggested you come to Los Angeles. *They* obviously perceived you could be valuable. Your reactions are quick and instinctively correct. You work diligently. You're innovative, and most important, you care about what you do. No, your ability is not the question here at all. The question is, what right do I have to see a resolution to my problem without considering your plans."

Wade waited quietly, hoping he had not pushed too hard or too fast. Everything he had said was true—he *had* fired his conniving stand-in, he *had* been interviewing to fill that position,

Jude *would* be ideal and was definitely qualified. His only act of misrepresentation was arranging for this morning's phone call. He had already known about the misuse of funds, but he had needed a catalyst to get Jude involved. The outcome hinged on Jude's believing that he, Wade, needed him.

"I don't know. I just don't know," Jude pondered aloud. "No bull, Wade, I don't have any plans. I want a job. I need a job. But I feel kind of funny taking a job from you—my friend. A job I don't know! Like charity or—"

"No, Jude," Wade said quickly, "that is not the case. I will have to choose someone, and soon. I begin another feature in a few weeks. The timing of your arrival almost seems like an omen. Especially since you are not yet situated. All the pieces fall into place. This is the truth."

Jude wanted to believe Wade. But he found all this difficult to reconcile—it was just too good to be true. He couldn't make himself accept that he deserved this favorable turn of events, that he was up to the job. The old plague of pride—mixed with self-doubt—was resurfacing. But at the same time, Jude knew he had to start trusting someone.

And then Jude thought of one more obstacle. "What about the studio? Don't they pick who they want, too? They don't know me."

Wade tried not to show too much excitement. Because that question indicated Jude was near to saying yes. "When it comes to a stand-in/double for a—if you will pardon the expression—star, the star has complete autonomy. The studio is really quite fair—they feel their performer should be comfortable with the person who will work so closely with him, so they don't interfere."

"I was reading one time—about a union? What if I can't get in?"

Wade took that hurdle easily. "You're absolutely right. We have the Screen Actor's Guild—I think it was fully recognized back in 1937. But there is no problem in joining, provided you have a guaranteed contract waiting. I know it's odd, but you cannot work without being a member, and you cannot be a member if you haven't worked. Glad I don't have to figure that out."

"Well, then, if you're sure I can do it—and if you're sure you need me—I guess I'll try," Jude said. "But you have to promise you'll level with me if I'm doing somethin' wrong."

"Absolutely," Wade swore. "Jude, I am so pleased. And so relieved. I know this is going to be a rewarding liaison, I feel it in my bones, and good for the two of us. This is a beginning, leading to who knows where. I am thrilled."

Basa and Floozy bounced up, obviously sensing something unusual in the air. Wade picked up Floozy and danced around the table with her. "Oh, Floozy, the most wonderful news. Basa will now be here permanently to keep you in line, my little vixen!"

"Whoa there!" Jude exclaimed. "We can't stay here!"

Wade stopped. "Why not?"

"Because it's not right. I'll be your employee, and employees don't live in their employer's house."

"You'll also be my right hand, and right hands do live with their employer if the circumstances permit. Don't you see how advantageous it could be? You could drive me to the studio while I studied the upcoming scenes. And we would have an opportunity to discuss the day's agenda before the frenzy on the set started. We would have the time to talk about matters in general, to and from the studio. I intend to pick your brains, you realize, utilize your natural talent, take advantage of your energy. In other words, I intend to work your butt off, mentally as well as physically. I wouldn't dream of it with anyone else, but with you, it's a model arrangement. It's what I've craved since I've been in this business. There is such temptation to fall into the trap of insulation, of isolation—you would keep me in touch with reality. And God knows, there is room enough here for privacy when desired. I wouldn't expect you, or want you, to baby-sit me all the time. Every man must have his moment, so to speak. Now, what do you say?"

Jude could see the validity of everything Wade had said. And he was startled at how highly Wade regarded him. But still . . .

"I don't know if I can meet your expectations, but I'm grateful to you for thinking it, anyway. I'll sure do my best. But how 'bout I pay room and board for Basa and me? That's really the only way I can stay. And we put this whole idea on a trial basis—to see if it really works."

Wade readily agreed. He didn't want to fight over minor points since he had already won the war. Besides, he endorsed Jude's stand for independence. Wade could see in Jude something more than Jude was able to see. A spiritual gift, really—of faith, of caring, of believing so much in someone else, they could begin to believe in themselves, too.

The next few days were busy with preparations. The studio was notified and Jude was put on salary. "You receive the usual amount for a stand-in—extra when you double—and I pay for the secretarial services. Don't say a word. It's the same amount I paid that idiot, no more or no less—you may look at the ledger if you want. The only difference is you will deserve it!''

Jude joined the Screen Actor's Guild, but he swallowed hard when he saw the initiation cost. "I guess you do have to spend money to make money," he observed to Wade.

Jude's orientation included a tour of Wade's address book. "These are the people you'll more than likely be contacting—my agent, business manager, banker, broker, tailor, restaurants, family, friends, studio personnel and so on. It won't take you long to discern which telephone calls are legitimate and which are crank. The daily calendar is your domain, as well, to ensure I'm not double-booked at any point and that I adhere to the program. Also, I would really like you to read the scripts I'm sent. That way, you will know what is going on, and I will have the benefit of your input. How do you like it so far? Have I frightened you away?''

Jude's eyes sparkled. "No siree! But I haven't done anything yet.''

Jude accompanied Wade on every appointment. The first reaction to secretaries or assistants was usually wariness. Would this one be on the take? How much influence would he have on their star, their bread and butter? Jude's disposition didn't invite instant communication, either. He preferred to sit back, digest the surroundings, size up the person in question. He remembered his introductory year as a bellman at Sun Valley. How he had pledged to watch and listen and learn from the guests. How he had endeavored to do more than any of the other boys. How he had been on the alert for any telltale signs of weakness, which he could take advantage of by being there to help. He intended to recapture that concept. And so he remained an enigma to Hollywood regulars for some time. They kept their distance, not sure what to make of this Jude Abavas, intuitively knowing he was not someone to fool with.

The third day driving through the studio's gate, Jude saw the conspicuous unease of the guard who had turned him away. When Wade was settled in the wardrobe fitting room, he excused himself and walked back to the gate.

"Look, I'm sorry about the other day," Jude said to the guard. "You were doing your job, and I was a frustrated jackass. It looks like I'll be coming here a lot with Mr. Colby, and so I think it's dumb for us to be carrying a grudge. What do you say?" Jude held out his hand, and the surprised guard grabbed it and pumped it heartily.

"Much obliged, Mr.—"

"Jude Abavas."

"Much obliged, Mr. Abavas. No one's ever done that before." And Jude had a champion for life.

He had telephoned Willamina and Noah as soon as he'd reached the decision to work for Wade. They were overjoyed—and such a position! They hadn't heard that ring in his voice since—well—for a long time. He promised to call regularly to give them a progress report. Everything was status quo in Ketchum, except that Noah was working harder than ever with the increase in government orders. Jude might have suffered some guilt, but he knew he wouldn't have been of much use to his papa. John and Luke were there for Noah, and for themselves. Jude smiled, thinking how John must be reveling in his importance.

Then he called Matthew. Matthew was thrilled. "You're Mr. Colby's *what?* You get to go into the studio anytime you want? Wow! When I get leave, if I ever do, can I come and visit?"

Jude thought that might be possible. "If I'm still in Los Angeles—we can't take things for granted, you know, Matt. And *if* you have enough time after seeing Mama and Papa. That has to come before anything else, don't forget." Matthew was holding his own academically and establishing a good rapport with his fellow students. "Call me if you need anything. Reverse the charges, I'll take care of it on this end."

Jude was careful to ask the operator for the cost of each call, and then left the amount in an envelope on Wade's desk. Wade was not going to accept the money, but he had to acknowledge that was Jude, and that was *exactly* why Jude was so rare. How many others would be that conscientious?

Jude read Wade's new script as soon as it came in. It was a war story about a marine landing in the Pacific—very macho, very dramatic, full of action. Jude liked it and thought the role was perfect for Wade. He hadn't seen any movies recently, but before... He wistfully recalled how Thelma had loved the picture shows, and how she had dragged him to the theater every chance she could. Any Wade Colby film was a must because "My husband knows him personally!" Thelma would have been in seventh heaven. But then she was in heaven, wasn't she? He wouldn't be sharing Hollywood with her just as he wouldn't be building sand castles on the beach with Keane.

Jude was gradually learning how to cope with these lapses of grief and sadness. He would force himself to return to the present, compel his mind to concentrate on the real, submerge the ubiquitous memories and, with effort, move forward.

Because a double would be used extensively in the battle scenes of this new film, Jude plunged into training with Wade. The marine command was very accommodating, and so together they drove to Camp Pendelton near San Diego to participate in the rigorous programs with the young recruits. Every muscle groaned in protest, and although Jude had overcome his limp and had reinstated his balance, these routines were extra hard on his bad foot.

"I'm getting too old for this," lamented Wade. "Look at those kids, even they are showing fatigue."

They learned how to crawl while under attack, how to handle weapons, how to engage in hand-to-hand combat, how to scale a wall, how to run a zigzag protective path, and on and on and on. The full secondary course took six weeks, but their schedule only allowed two weeks, which was ample for their purpose. They also learned the chant and exercise that was used to demonstrate the respect due their rifles.

"This is my rifle!" they sang, hoisting their Mls.

"This is my gun!" they continued, grabbing their crotches.

And it was, like everything else, repeated and repeated and repeated.

On their last day of the grueling drills, Wade and Jude contemplated the burden of their defective bodies. These fine specimens of American youth would be shipping out all too soon to a real war, with real bullets, real explosives and enemy. And Wade and Jude would return to a make-believe arena, the closest they would ever come to an authentic battle. A humbling consciousness for two strongly patriotic souls. Both were determined to do the best damn job possible to portray these boys as the brave heroes they all were. And Jude sent a quiet prayer that the war would end while Matthew was still in school.

Jude adapted to the studio system rapidly. He was always in close range during rehearsal so that he would be familiar with Wade's exact moves when it came time for camera setups. He knew exactly where Wade should be to achieve special lighting effects. He studied Wade's movements—how he walked, ran, turned, moved his head and hands, so he could be effective as a double.

As Wade's middleman, Jude was a natural. No one permeated Jude's protective shield unless invited. The charting of a day's activities was detailed, but spaced comfortably. Jude instigated an itemized cash-expense notebook, which became invaluable to Wade's accountant for tax purposes. He rechecked charge receipts so there could be no chance for duplicity. Jude was determined that Wade would not be shafted again, at least not while he was around.

Work had begun on *Seek and Destroy*. The film was to depict the lessons learned by the Allies during the Solomons campaign, a technique of amphibious warfare involving air, land and sea forces working as a team. Interiors, including those of a ship, were duplicated at the studio. Official footage was used for the comprehensive shots. The landing scenes were to be simulated on San Onofre Beach, near Camp Pendelton, which was the same location the military used for their own practice landings.

For such a massive undertaking as the landings, several cameras were used simultaneously, two for longer shots, two for medium, two for cross vantage points. There wouldn't be a second chance to catch the entire sweep of the action before the scene had to be broken down into smaller, closer angles. Even a complete rehearsal for the landing was impossible. All that could be done was to meticulously map out how the director—with his cameramen—could hope the maneuver would unfold. Everyone, in front of, and behind the cameras, had to be flexible, ready for the unexpected, prepared to improvise.

The special-effects unit had a gigantic responsibility. The water had to churn and splash as if enemy shells were exploding in it. The beach had to be prepped—it had to appear that enemy bullets were spraying the sand. Hundreds of tiny hollow cylinders, called squibs, had been filled with minute amounts of an explosive powder and then buried in the sand and set off. Each M1 rifle, machine gun and hand grenade carried by the actors had to be equipped with realistic blanks, which normally weren't dangerous unless fired point-blank.

The director wisely understood that no words of his could produce the overwhelming sense of passion and emotion this epic scene needed. So, to establish the proper mood, real photographs were shown to the company—horrifying, terrifying, stark examples of war. No one thought of the film as "just another job" after that.

Finally, the director, his numerous assistants and his cameramen felt they were as ready as they could be. Ten script supervisors were strategically placed to watch and record every happening. Ten alert intense pairs of eyes would be held accountable—all subsequent shooting had to strictly match this main master shot, this one-time overall filming of the landing.

The men, including Jude, were loaded into the boats, kept out of camera range. The director roared into a two-way radio, "Remember, keep going no matter what happens. Cameras are rolling—come on in and take this goddamned island!"

A swarm of airplanes swooped from the skies. The legion of packed vessels glided into view. "Shells" commenced hitting the water, causing the boats to rock heavily. A few men got seasick off the side of their boat. Fear registered loud and clear on every face. The boat Jude was in actually capsized as it neared the sand, but nobody stopped. Jude assumed command and herded each man onto the "shell-racked" beachhead. The squibs, as well as shells, began blasting. One went off right where Jude threw himself to the ground, blasting sand in his eyes so that he could barely see. The marines were starting to really get into the scene now—they were mad at this abuse, determined to do away with the enemy. They helped comrades if they stumbled; they supported the wounded, left the designated dead lying there; they fired their rifles and tossed their grenades with a vengeance; they yelled and screamed and cursed; they ran and crawled and fell, and got up again for more, their emotions at a fever pitch. In other words, they were terrific. The din was so loud and intense, it was difficult to hear when the delighted director shouted, "Cut!" The crew spontaneously broke into applause. Each and every actor received bonus pay.

Then the damage was assessed. Nothing serious—some bumps and bruises, some powder burns. All were dirty and grimy and drenched. The force of the sandblast had broken a small blood vessel in Jude's left eye, but the camera didn't pick it up. The powder burn on his right cheek—where a blank had grazed it was noted so that makeup could copy the injury on Wade.

"You really made me look good, old buddy. But are you sure you're all right?" Wade asked, grateful but worried.

"I'm okay. I feel sort of like a dunked doughnut," Jude said, panting. "But I got to tell you, even this kind of war is hell. I just can't—can't imagine—can't believe—what those poor guys are going through. And it's happening all over the damned world!"

Jude, as well as everyone else, was visibly shaken by the experience of the mock battle. Neither he, nor Wade, were aware—until later—that Jude, for the first time, had spoken of death without immediately relating it to Thelma and Keane. The enormity and far-reaching consequences of war had taken precedence over Jude's personal tragedy.

By the time the film wrapped in early October, the company was an extremely close-knit unit. Wade gave a party on one of the studio soundstages. The motif resembled the Academy Awards ball, and Wade handed out miniature statues, somewhat resembling the coveted award, to every member of the cast and crew. The booze and sentimentality flowed generously. Jude's contributions were highly praised, his back slapped, his hand shook—there were even a few embraces—and, inevitably, the phrase "Couldn't have done it without you" was uttered.

Darryl Zanuck made a brief appearance. Jude was feeling mellow, but he wasn't ready to face Zanuck—not yet. His ego wasn't ready to risk a possible face-to-face rejection by the great one this time. The incident at the gate was still too fresh, so he faded into the shadows during the executive's visit.

Wade went to Palm Springs for a short rest before preparing for his next film. Jude declined; it was too soon for "that" kind of socializing. Wade's method of relaxing was wine, women and song.

Moreover, Jude really wanted to concentrate on his mission. He had decided to yield to the spark of his new position with Wade and become as educated and well versed in the motion picture business as he could. And so he read about its origins and the men and women who had created it. He read about the inventions that had progressed the industry and contributed to its history. He read about the courage, the daring, the dedication of all the pioneers, from the earliest to those of the present day. He watched old pictures—made available through Wade—and saw every current release. He studied the evolution of technique, mechanically and artistically. He started to analyze the appeal of performers—why some endured and some swiftly receded into obscurity. The tree of knowledge he wanted would take time to sprout, he conceded ruefully, but he was not dissuaded. Rather, he was fascinated. The more he learned, the more he knew he had to learn. And with this, he realized, as he had realized many years ago in Sun Valley, that he needed to listen to how refined people talked, and watch carefully how they dressed. Every clue to the mystery of knowing was important.

Matthew arrived in Los Angeles on Christmas Day, after spending a week with the family in Ketchum. Jude had finally installed a separate telephone line in his wing and called home a great deal. But it was still too soon to go to Idaho.

As Jude had predicted, Matthew had not been prepared for Hollywood and the opulent home of Wade Colby. He walked around tongue-tied, for a time. Then he chatted like a magpie, full of news about his activities and gossip about the folks: Ethel was pregnant, due next June, and Luke was already a basket case; John, Jr., had taken a few steps on his own and had two teeth; their sister, Revel, at three and a half, was an auburn-haired beauty, a total terror, spoiled and utterly bewitching; Noah and Willamina looked well—of course, they missed the two of them, but their lives were full. Noah, in particular, appeared more stimulated than ever, thanks to his booming business.

In only six months, Matthew had developed remarkable poise. Jude was proud of his little brother and delighted in people's reactions to him. Anna and Eric adopted him completely and catered to him shamelessly. Basa was overjoyed when he saw

Matthew, and even Floozy gave him a warm welcome. And Wade was very impressed.

"When I heard you were going to be able to join us, Matt, I decided to wait until tonight to have our Christmas dinner. I was with my family last night, so tonight is ours," Wade explained. He had been concerned that the holidays would be a difficult time for Jude, sensing a creeping melancholy in Jude's behavior as the season approached.

But Matthew's arrival raised Jude's spirits and Wade was determined to make this a happy occasion. Anna's feast was superb, and Matthew ate three helpings.

After supper, Wade asked Anna and Eric to join them by the tree. "After all, you are our family, too!"

Wade played Santa Claus and handed out the gifts. Every package produced oohs and ahs. Everyone was indulged—two- and four-legged animals alike. Finally, there were two presents left, one small and one large. "Matt, this is a start for you after all this craziness is over and done with." Wade handed Matthew a wrapped envelope, which when opened, revealed a five-hundred-dollar war bond. Matthew was speechless. So was Jude. But Wade hurried on. "Jude, this last present is really a selfish gesture on my part because I've missed hearing you play." Wade opened the big box and pulled out a beautiful guitar. Jude and Matthew gasped. Jude hadn't gone near a guitar since...

Anxiously, almost apologetically, Wade pressed ahead, "I realize it won't have the exact tone of your father's. But I spoke with your mother, who graciously described Noah's in detail, and I came as close as I could to finding that model. A musician at the studio helped me. He also tuned it and assured me this was a top-quality instrument." Wade paused, and then softly asked, "Will you play for us, Jude?"

Wade knew he had taken a risky step, but he had faith that this could mean a giant step forward in Jude's healing.

Jude sat and stared at the guitar on his lap. He heard Noah singing to him. And he could hear himself singing to Keane, and to Wade and his fishing groups. He could see Willamina and the old canvas wagon—Keane and Thelma by a lake. He could see the last picnic campsite. He looked up and suddenly saw Matthew and Wade—the love in their eyes, the apprehension on their faces, the care in their hearts. Jude knew his own heart was aching and that his eyes were reflecting it. But he knew, too, that Matthew and Wade were waiting. He sucked in his breath. He had no choice: he would not, could not, disappoint them.

Silently, he picked up the guitar, fingered it and hesitantly began to sweep the strings. And then he played. The old tunes, Papa's tunes. He couldn't sing because he was crying. Crying because he was playing. Crying for those who couldn't hear. Crying for those who could. Crying for what he had lost. Crying for what he had found. Crying for the past. Crying for the future. He was crying. But he was playing.

There were no dry eyes. The plaintive melodies brought haunting personal memories to each one. Jude's emotional struggle had touched their souls.

There were grateful tears, joyful tears, too. And then there was joyful music. Jude finally was in control; Jude was playing Christmas carols. The voices blended into a chorus of thanksgiving for this very special Christmas Day.

13

New York, Waldorf Towers
March 1944

"I would rather get into the harness for *The Hunchback of Notre Dame* than put on this monkey suit!" grumbled Jude as he struggled with his bow tie.

"Let me help," soothed Wade, and he expertly tied the bow-knot.

"I'm supposed to be here to make things easier for *you*—not the other way round! How did I ever let you talk me into coming on this damn publicity trip? I'm so flustered, I'll probably scratch my watch and wind my ass!"

Wade was constantly amused by Jude's expressions, but he stuck to his guns. "Wasn't the premiere in Los Angeles a pleasant evening? Didn't you have a good time? And didn't you practically save my life—*again*—by rescuing me from that mob? At the very least, you preserved my modesty—they might have disrobed me! Well, there is no difference, this is the same."

"No, it's not!" insisted Jude. "This is here, and I don't know here!"

Wade was becoming adept in coping with Jude's reluctance to attend functions. All he had to say was "I need you, it's important!" and that was the end of the discussion. This approach had worked for the Los Angeles opening and with the journey to New York, and now it would work again. And what Wade said was true. Jude was practically indispensable. In these eight months, their arrangement had exceeded all expectations. Every aspect of Wade's life was running smoother because of Jude's organization and scrutiny. He relied on Jude's intuitive judgment, which was quickly advancing to substantiated judgment. Jude had even started to read the *Wall Street Journal,* and Wade was gleefully awaiting the day when Jude would pose questions to his business manager. Jude's sole intent was to protect Wade's interest—in all fields and at all costs. And Wade knew this unequivocally. What an associate he had picked!

The only problem was Jude's negative attitude about attending social affairs. Wade wasn't sure of the reason, or reasons. Shyness? Perhaps. A feeling of inadequacy or inferiority? Perhaps. But that was ridiculous; Wade was convinced Jude could handle any situation. Fear? More likely, in fact. A fear of involvement outside of business? There certainly was safety in being a loner; one was not as vulnerable. But then, why had he allowed Wade to get so close?

At any rate, Wade had taken on the challenge of drawing Jude out. He believed mixing with others would speed Jude's recovery and be beneficial to his friend's career. And that Jude had begun a career, Wade had no doubt.

Jude, despite his present protestations, had only mildly balked at the traveling. He turned out to be exhilarated by the plane ride after he'd overcome his uneasiness at yet another unknown. The stop in Chicago hadn't given them a chance to see much of the city, but the approach had offered a panoramic view of that untamed town. And then New York! He was convinced that his first glimpse of the city was even more dazzling than his father's had been, for New York had grown in all directions—up, down and sideways—since 1915. And Jude was seeing it as a native-born American *and* in first-class style. A studio representative met them at the airport and was available for their every need. Any whim was indulged, and it was complimentary, to boot. A limousine drove Jude and Wade everywhere they went, except when Wade played hooky and took Jude on the underground train to Brooklyn, and later a hansom cab ride in Central Park.

While trotting around, taking in the magnificent sights, marveling at the relative wilderness of the park in the midst of towering concrete, another buggy passed by in the opposite lane. "Hey," Jude said, nudging Wade. "Isn't that Mr. Walker, the producer of your next picture?"

"I believe you're right," replied Wade. "I wouldn't call out to him, however, I have a feeling he isn't anxious to be recognized.

That young thing he's pawing, you see, is not his wife.'' Wade chuckled. ''He must have felt safe, because the sophisticates never take a hansom cab, only the tourists. Sly old bastard! What a funny coincidence!''

Jude thought for a few minutes. ''Maybe it's a lucky coincidence. I know who that woman is. Her name's Tania Hope. She's round the studio all the time. Talk is, she'd do anything for a good part, if you get my drift. You better check on the casting, or she's liable to be your leading lady. And she's not right for the role.''

Wade was amazed. ''How do you know all this?''

''Oh, I hear things. As a matter of fact, she tried to come on to me—just to get to you, I'm sure. If at first you don't succeed, try try again. She's not as dumb as I thought she was—but Walker is!''

The perks for a star on a publicity tour were plentiful, but Jude soon discovered that every one of them was earned. Wade's schedule was crammed with endless appearances, photo sessions and interviews. The colorful, controversial and powerful commentator, Walter Winchell, most impressed Jude. He remembered how his father had insisted the family listen to Winchell's staccato-delivered broadcasts on their old RCA radio. Jude had always been intrigued by Winchell's opening: the rat-a-tat-tat of a wireless transmitter, and then the ''Good evening, Mr. and Mrs. America, and all the ships at sea.'' He—Jude Abavas—was right there hearing Walter Winchell in person while people all over the world were doing the same by their radio sets.

Wade had been adamant that visits to military hospitals be included in his agenda. When the two friends couldn't get over how the boys thanked them for coming, Jude got the idea to give two hundred free tickets to servicemen for the movie's opening at the Roxy Theater. Wade passed the idea on to the people in charge and it was done.

The always-persuasive and renowned author, Rachel Crothers, had cornered Wade and extracted his promise to show up at the Stage Door Canteen. She was the president of the American Theater Wing, and the prime organizer of this project located in the basement of the 44th Street Theater. A combination nightclub and soup kitchen, the Canteen was staffed with volunteers, and the famous were there consistently, serving food, waiting tables, helping with chores, performing or simply mingling. They had expected to serve about five hundred servicemen a night when the Canteen opened in March 1942, but the number had turned out to be closer to three or four thousand, most of whom had to stand in line on the street before there was room inside.

It was truly the place to be. On one night, for example, the mighty voice of Ethel Merman could be heard blasting "Pistol-Packin' Mama." She was followed by Gracie Fields and then the soulful sound of Ethel Waters. Their music reached out to the lonely boys, while superstar actors and actresses like Helen Hayes, Lynn Fontanne and Alfred Lunt could be seen bustling around the tables, willingly doing KP duty. Wade and Jude fell into the latter category.

Later in the evening, Wade got carried away by the spirit of things, grabbed a guitar from the combo, shoved it at Jude and pushed him onto the stage. If looks could kill, Wade would have been gone. But there was nothing Jude could do. He wanted to sink through the floor, but eager young voices urged him on. So he played. Many of the boys were from small towns and could relate to Jude's folk style, and even the city boys liked the homespun touch. Wade was so delighted with the success of his idea, he had to take it one step further. He forced Jude to follow him outside to the throng waiting to get in and made him entertain while Wade went up and down the long queue, chatting and shaking hands with each GI. They loved it! New York's finest arrived on horseback ready to deal with a riot in progress. But all they found were excited and happy servicemen and two crazy civilians wanting to please them.

"We have to do this at home, at the Hollywood Canteen, when we get back," Wade said to Jude in the car on the way to the hotel. "I was convinced we would be in the way, that they only wanted to be around pretty girls. I had no idea we could be useful there."

"Easy for you! But I'm no professional!"

"They didn't know that, or mind. It was the fact that strangers, like us, cared about them—that's what was important."

Jude had no argument. That, he could understand.

When Wade was on tour, especially in highly visible New York, he usually chose not to squire around local or visiting beauties. He was there to work and he simply didn't want to start the rumor mill churning. So Jude was drafted as his "date." This served Wade's purposes twofold: one, because Jude was then obliged to go places; and two, Wade derived great pleasure from being the one to introduce Jude to so many firsts.

They had one night free to attend the theater, and for this event Wade had an ardent companion—Jude needed no coaxing. He inhaled Times Square. He was intoxicated by the fever of Broadway. He was high on the pulse of the masses.

Jude walked into the theater as if the stage were a shrine and he were treading on hallowed ground. As he watched the exceptional talents of Margaret Sullavan and Elliott Nugent in John Van Druten's *The Voice of the Turtle,* he almost forgot to breathe. He was utterly captivated by the impact of the contact between the performers and audience.

Seeing Jude's absorption, and aware of his own, Wade was reminded again of the power of live theater over film.

"One day I am coming to New York to see every show on Broadway," Jude swore. They were weaving through traffic, en route to the Stork Club and El Morocco. Wade wanted to give Jude a taste of New York's high society, and what better way than to expose Jude to the two most sophisticated, expensive, elite watering holes of the rich and famous. Just a quick introductory visit, though, because Wade knew this aspect of New York would not particularly appeal to Jude.

Later, in their suite, Jude confirmed Wade's suspicions. "It's all very elegant, I guess. But walking in gave me the heebie-jeebies," Jude claimed. "All those people standing and waiting around—herded like two-legged sheep behind that heavy gold cord. Then you walk in and the rope disappears like magic. And then reappears! Creepy, I think. And it seems so boring! I mean, sitting around in those zebra-covered cubicles, all dressed up like mannequins in store windows, everyone looking at everyone else through the smoke. Can't talk cause it's too noisy—trying to drink out of those teeny glasses. Maybe if I knew how to dance or something! Hell, all I know how to do is the Stanley Stomp! You should have stayed with your friends, Wade. Boy, you know everybody!" Jude felt badly, that perhaps he had spoiled Wade's fun.

"Absolutely not! I have no desire to be at either club for any length of time. And you're right, of course. Frankly, it is a little boring... and a little silly, and a little phony. By the way, dancing does help, but—'' Wade stopped to chuckle, impressed by his friend's perception. ''But one does what one is expected or conditioned to do. I just wanted to pop by to say hello so these people wouldn't think I was neglecting them completely. They, too, can have fragile egos, believe it or not. They get insecure.''

Jude puzzled over what he thought was Wade's strangest statement of the night. He simply couldn't imagine that any of the people in those clubs were insecure. But had Wade revealed something to him tonight? Jude decided he was going to watch Wade closely. Maybe he had missed something. Maybe there was something Wade needed.

The climax of the trip was at hand, the movie premiere and the party, toward which their limo was now making its way. Now was Jude's turn to reassure Wade. Because even with Wade's seemingly endless store of composure, Jude knew his friend was nervous. The West Coast opening of *Seek and Destroy* had been extremely successful, but Wade was leery of New York's reaction.

''You never can tell about the critics here, or the public. They're fiercely independent. Sometimes contrary—especially the critics—toward Hollywood,'' Wade explained.

''Bull!'' Jude countered. ''The picture is a winner, and you are *stupendous*—how do you like that word? There's no way they can't like this film. Not unless they got shit for brains and ice water for blood.'' He looked ahead to the brilliant arcs of klieg lights identifying the Roxy. ''Jesus H. Christ! We're three blocks away at least, and we can barely make it through the crowds already. Oh, my God, the people recognize you in here. Keep smiling and waving, Wade. Driver, keep inching forward, don't stop or we're dead. Looks to me like the verdict on the movie is in, Wade.''

When the limo finally made it to the front of the Roxy, the fans stormed the car. The police formed a human chain around Wade and Jude for protection, but when the throngs thought they might be denied a glimpse of their idol, they surged against the human barricade, forcing the police to do a little shoving of their own.

''Don't run—whatever you do—or they'll stampede,'' Jude shouted. ''Officers, let Mr. Colby go toward the mob, *slowly.*

Wade, shake some hands—talk to 'em, calm 'em down. Once they see you're not trying to bolt inside we'll be okay. Just keep moving easy—slow and easy—that's it. No one panic and no one'll get hurt. Goddamn it, I said, don't push!'' This was directed at a frustrated policeman.

"Let 'em get a look at you, Wade, but keep moving toward the entrance." Jude spotted a large decorative urn near the box office and quickly turned it upside down in the doorway. "Wade, stand on this, so the ones in back can see you." A huge roar of approval went up as Wade stepped up and became visible to all. They were safe now, in the doorway of the theater.

The beleaguered police kept muttering and shaking their heads. "Between this guy and Sinatra, we're gonna be driven crazy! Bunch 'a nuts out there! Did ya see that one kid kick me?"

"How did you manage to get me through that?" a disheveled Wade asked his friend, trying to pull himself together.

"Well," drawled Jude, "Papa always said if you run from an animal, they're likely to charge and get you in the back. But if you face 'em, and advance—bit by bit—you challenge 'em, and you'll at least have a better chance head-on. If you show fear, they smell it. Made sense to me. Course, I never tested the theory on human beings before. You were sort of my guinea pig!"

Wade was surrounded by the press and well-wishers before he could retort, and then, at last, the guests were steered to their seats and the film began. Wade and Jude listened intently, alert for any signs of restlessness from the audience, or inappropriate responses to the action unfolding on the screen. There wasn't a single one. They could sense the audience's interest and then gradually their total submersion in the movie. At the conclusion, there was a moment of contemplative silence and then a burst of applause. Wade was clearly relieved, and Jude leaned over and whispered, "Told you so!"

It was an elated group that invaded the posh 21 Club on 52nd Street. The studio had reserved the second floor of the former speakeasy, so popular in the twenties, and there was good reason to celebrate that night. Darryl Zanuck rushed over when Wade and Jude arrived to congratulate his star. "You were stupendous, my boy!"

Wade grinned and said, "Thank you, Darryl. I am flattered. You all are going to spoil me—my colleague here used the same phrase earlier. You remember Jude Abavas, from Sun Valley?"

"Of course, of course! How are you?" Zanuck said effusively. "Nice to see you again. I hear good things about you—my spies keep me posted,you know—ha! ha!" And then he was off, running about the spacious but warm rooms, greeting the newcomers.

Jude understood immediately that Zanuck didn't identify him with Sun Valley at all. On the other hand, he didn't doubt that Zanuck did have, if not spies, then informants who checked out people on the lot, especially those closely connected to Zanuck's major players. Well, at least he had been given a favorable report card. He also recognized, somewhat belatedly, that there was absolutely no reason that Zanuck—or anyone else, for that matter—should have recognized him from the lodge in Sun Valley.

14

Santa Monica, California
Tuesday, April 25, 1944

"Jude," Wade said, "would you please look over these changes in the script and see if they include the things we discussed with 'our producer friend,' Mr. Walker? And would you sift through his casting suggestions—for the *entire* cast, I might add—and jot down your thoughts? Ever since I questioned that so-called actress Tania Hope's ability—thanks to your intuition—Walker feels compelled to run absolutely everything by me. And then—"

"Wade, stop a minute! I know it's April 25. You know it's April 25. And I know that you know it's April 25. I know, too, that you've kept me charging around all day. And I know why. And I appreciate it. But, sooner or later, sometime today or tonight, I'll have to face what date today is and deal with it. There is no need to run yourself ragged trying to keep me busy."

Wade shrugged apologetically, caught in the act. "I had hoped not to give you time to think. Or be alone. And of all nights, I promised Jack Warner I'd go to his screening of *To Have and Have Not*. Why don't you come with Joyce and me? Forget the work! We can do that tomorrow."

"No, my friend. But I thank you, more than I can ever say, believe me. And I'll be fine, honest. I think I need to be by myself for a while. And you need to get dressed and go. I hear the picture is hot stuff—Bogart and this Bacall girl really heat up the screen, they say. Don't forget the juicy parts. I want all the details in the morning."

After Wade had been convinced to go on his way, Jude and Basa and Floozy took a long walk on the beach at sunset. The air was crisp and chilly. The dark, rounded outlines of the cumulus clouds were tinged with an iridescent glow. They revived images in Jude's mind of the mountains—the mountains that had brought him such joy and such pain. He tried to stare beyond the clouds, to see into heaven.

As he neared the house, he realized there was someone he could talk to—someone who would understand, someone who had always understood.

"Hello, Papa? It's me, Jude. No—no—nothing's the matter. I just wanted to talk to you. Mama fine? That's good. And everyone else okay? How about you? Not working too hard, are you? You bought more land? Oh, I see—with the money the government's paying you. Smart—very smart, Papa. You'll own all of Idaho at this rate. If I read anything in the *Journal*—the *Wall Street Journal,* Papa—I'll clip it and send it to you. They have articles about every kind of business, and they're accurate and impartial. Uh, it means that they're fair and just in what they report. Well, thanks—I'm trying to learn. Things are going well. Wade has really been good to me. And good for me, I guess. Well, that's what I wanted to talk to you about. You know what day this is. Yeah, I figured Mama would go to church. Tell her I'm grateful for her prayers. It's just that I'm having some feelings and questions and I hoped maybe you could help me sort them out." And suddenly, Jude was a young boy again, sitting on the ottoman in front of Noah's armchair, by the fire, looking up into Noah's wise eyes, asking for guidance.

When he hung up the phone, Jude walked outside and gazed at the black sky and the bright moon. *Thelma, I will never be able to accept the divine order that the two of you had to go. But Papa said we're created for life—we must grow and move onward. He said you'd be proud of me and what I'm trying to do, that I owe it to you—my wife and my son—to make the most of this life. So, if I was meant to live, then I have to live. I'm gonna try, honey, I'm gonna go for it.*

15

Los Angeles, California
November 5, 1944

"Jude, ah, I've been needing to kick something around with you. But you have to promise not to get mad or laugh at me, either one. Promise?" Matthew asked anxiously.

"Yeah, I promise—I guess. Can it wait until we get Basa dried off at least? Before he ruins the house?"

"Oh, sure," Matthew said, vigorously attacking the squirming Basa with a towel. Basa had met up with some tar in the sand and wasn't happy with this clean-up routine.

Jude eyed Matthew curiously as he emptied soapy water into the patio drain. What could Matthew have on his mind? They had exhausted the subject of Matthew's decision to abandon a pilot's career at Christmas. Jude had hoped Matthew would continue on that path because the length of the flight training program would have kept him away from combat, perhaps for the duration of the war if the U.S. forces sustained their recent advances. But Jude couldn't dictate Matthew's preferences, and Matthew simply could not deal with the tedious math requisites. Nor did he have the patience for the prolonged clinical instructional process. And then there was the fact that the quota for naval aviation personnel had been filled. And so, Matthew had opted to complete the four accelerated terms necessary to qualify as a deck officer. He was on leave now, on his way to midshipman school from which he would graduate next March, commissioned with the rank of ensign. If all went well, Matthew planned to finish his last two years of college after the war.

Jude didn't think Matthew needed to discuss anything family-related; they had covered that ground as soon as he had arrived from Ketchum. Luke and Ethel had expressed their thanks—again—for the war bond Jude had sent when their son, Noah Horace Abavas, came into the world on June 15. Revel was in an uproar, protesting any new bundles of joy who might usurp her as the focus of attention. Misfortune had saved her from having another one to contend with. John's wife, Lila, had suffered a miscarriage with her second baby at the end of October. Jude had sympathized deeply with his bereaved twin and had attempted to console John by stressing the positive—that he did have one healthy son, a wonderful wife, and could try again. But John hadn't been receptive, and Matthew reported that John was still in bad shape. Mama was doing well, actually grateful the restaurant had closed down because of the war—it gave her more time for her grandchildren and Revel. And since Noah was prospering, she had decided not to reopen the restaurant, even when Sun Valley was once again welcoming visitors. There was no longer the need. Papa had shown Matthew all the clippings from the *Wall Street Journal* Jude had mailed, and bragged to everyone about his son, the businessman.

Jude figured something else had to be gnawing at Matthew. "Okay, let's have it," he said as Basa bounded off to find Floozy, probably to complain about a dog's life.

"Uh, you sure you don't have to do work for Wade?"

"Mr. Colby," Jude corrected.

"He said to call him Wade," defended Matthew.

"Okay, okay! No, I have no work to do, and Wade is with, well, a lady friend. So what's eating you?"

"Well, uh, ya see," Matthew stammered, "we had to study a lot at school, you know. And not much time for outside fun. But Denny—my roomy, remember...?" Matthew paused and Jude nodded, suddenly apprehensive, sensing what was coming, worrying how he would react and what he would say.

"Anyway," Matthew continued, "Denny and I did get to a few dances—'cause our grades kept up. And—and I met a girl." Jude flinched, sure his worst fears were confirmed. Matthew rushed on. "Her name's Nancy, Nancy Morris. She's beautiful—and I like her. And she said she'd wait for me and write all the time."

Jude sat quietly, knowing there was more. And there was.

"We—I—" Now he was having trouble. "That is, we were smoochin' in her car my last night in Seattle and getting really fired up. I mean, I hurt so bad I thought I'd burst open. And she...well...she was moaning and groaning and whispering, 'Put it in, put it in.' I wanted to—oh boy, did I want to!—but I was afraid—and, well, shit—I came in my pants.''

Jude was so relieved, he had to struggle not to go over and hug his young brother.

''I was so embarrassed—an' she was still moaning and groaning and whispering, so I—so I put my finger—you know—inside her—so's she could come, too. An' I got hot all over again—and popped off again. After, we were both glad I didn't—we didn't—go all the way. What if she got pregnant? And I'd be gone—what would she have done? What would I have done? But—'' He hesitated. ''But—''

''But what?'' Jude asked gently. ''You did the right thing, Matt. I'm proud of you. You are a gentleman.'' *And a better man than me,* he thought.

''Yeah, but damn it, Jude, I'm a virgin! I've never really screwed anyone! I never got to one of those places on River Street back home. And Papa kept saying how wrong it was to do it with a 'nice' girl. So I didn't.'' It was tumbling out now. ''But what if I get killed? I'd die not knowing what it felt like to...you know, be inside a woman. And I want to know! But at school they showed us these films, how guys caught horrible diseases because they fucked—sorry.''

''No holds barred with us, Matt. You can say anything you want, any way you want. We're two men talking now,'' Jude assured him. ''You were saying?''

''Well, because they fucked whores who weren't clean. Now I'm not sure what to do. How do you know if someone has somethin'? And is it bad to want to get laid? And is Papa right about the 'nice' girls, even if they *want* you to do it? There—I said it, and I'm glad.'' Matthew sighed.

Jude looked at this earnest innocent and he felt his compassion well up. The poor kid had obviously been grappling with this for a while. He realized his response would be crucial. He hoped he could answer truthfully and in today's terms. He was only six years Matthew's senior, but he felt so very much older.

Jude had to walk a tightrope himself, painfully aware of his own history. He didn't want to be hypocritical or sanctimonious, and yet he would not jeopardize Thelma's position in

Matthew's memory, or have him doubt the love Jude eventually felt for her.

"Well, now, Matt, I'm not as good at this as Papa. But I'm gonna do my best with what I know. And I'll be as honest as I can be. First off, it means the world to me that you trust me enough to share your questions.

"I already told you that you did good. Yes, Papa is right about the 'nice' girls. It's our responsibility to keep things in line—you figured out the consequences by yourself. Sometimes, though, we forget—when we're horny or liquored up—and that's—that's too bad. Maybe if you've gone with a girl for a long time and you're not going away and you're going to get married, anyway...well, then maybe it would be all right, if that's what you both want."

"Did you and Thelma— No, it's none of my business. I shouldn't have asked," Matthew said contritely.

Jude looked straight at him. "It's okay. Yes, we did. And I'm not pleased with myself about that, not one bit. I acted like a shit-heel and never forgave myself. But she did, she forgave me, I was lucky." Jude paused, not certain if he should go any further. He decided it wasn't necessary, it wouldn't serve any purpose.

"But, is it *bad* to want to get laid? Hell, no! It's perfectly natural. But you have to go to the right place—you have to use your head, and you have to wear protection. It's damn near impossible to make sure a girl's not infected, so *you* have to take the precaution. Don't let some smart-ass punk tell you that a rubber takes away the sensation. So what if you lose a little of the thrill? That's a hell of a lot better than ending up with some kind of crud!"

Matthew was silent for a short spell, digesting what Jude had said. Then he said tentatively, "Since...since Thelma died, have you...had a girlfriend? Or been with anyone?"

Jude was startled. Could Matthew read his mind? For, as he was explaining the normalcy of a man's sex drive, he'd felt his own starting to stir.

"There hasn't been anyone." Pause. "Funny, I haven't thought about anything like this for a long time—until now. I'm kind of like a dried-up creek—no flowing juices, you might say. Couldn't make it right in my mind. Guilt? Disrespect to Thelma?

I don't know." Jude drifted off into his own introspection. Matthew's guileless inquiries had triggered a revival of buried emotion. He wondered if this sudden surge of awakening was a logical progression from his declaration last April to live. Was he ready to test the waters? Certainly Matthew was prepped and deserved some help. Could he do the same for himself?

"Marco!" a blindfolded Wade called out.

"Polo!" several voices answered, mixed with the sounds of splashing and gurgling laughter. Bodies slithered by him in the pool, but he wasn't fast enough to seize one.

"Marco!" Wade shouted.

"Polo!" came the elusive replies. This time, he concentrated in a particular direction, dived backward and captured his prize.

"Now, who do I have here?" Wade ensnared the wiggling bathing suit-clad body in his arms. He cupped the breasts with his hands. "Let's see—it's not Betty—it's not Tina—it must be Joyce." He ripped off the soggy handkerchief from his head. "You are 'it,' and your other penalty for getting caught is—" And he untied the top of her suit. Her bosoms, their paleness in stark contrast to the tanned skin, floated like two white balloons on top of the water.

"Wow!" Matthew gasped.

This was to be a night of "wows" for Matthew and, in a different way, for Jude.

Jude had gone to Wade for advice on just how to go about organizing Matthew's initiation to sex. Wade had quickly perceived this could be a breakthrough for his friend, too—very welcome news, if true. Of course, there were River Street-type establishments, but Wade suggested a more civilized alternative. His current girlfriend, Joyce, had a few really attractive chums. "We could all go to Palm Springs. You've never even seen the house I rented for the season. It would be relaxed and private there. The six of us would just be going down for a couple of days of fun. We'll let Mother Nature take her course from there. Rest assured, these girls are safe. As long as Matthew understands that once he leaves my friends, caution is the word."

The drive to the Springs had been full of cheerful banter. This was also to be Matthew's farewell party. The house was invitingly cool and comfortable, a large, sprawling structure shaped in a U around a heated pool. Wade assigned Joyce the room nearest his master suite, then Betty and Tina to the next guest room, and Jude and Matthew to the adjacent one. He hoped these sleeping arrangements would prove temporary. Betty, a voluptuous platinum blonde—and Tina, an equally endowed, raven-haired beauty, were not exactly high-priced call girls, but they weren't far off. They modeled some, but belonged to a sect of femininity whose main business was to decorate the arms and beds of important men who were either too occupied or too lazy or too wary or too shy to pursue companionship the regular way. These weren't scatterbrained bimbos. On the contrary, they were entertaining, intelligent young women who had recognized their limitations and capitalized on their assets. They enjoyed their life and insured that enjoyment by being extremely discriminating in their choice of clients. For some, these associations resulted in permanent relationships, including marriage. For others, more traditional careers had been found. And for a few, this road had led downhill to despair.

But on this warm November evening, pleasure was the only priority. Dinner at Don the Beachcomber's had been highly successful. Jude and Matthew had never tasted Cantonese cuisine, and they'd gorged themselves on wonton soup, mandarin duck, egg rolls, dried pork, fried shrimp and fried rice. As it was meant to do, the liberal use of soy sauce had made everyone thirsty, and exotic rum drinks were consumed like lemonade. Winding their way homeward—definitely not walking a straight course—they had appropriately sung—or tried to sing—their rendition of "Rum and Coca-Cola." Sober strollers were amused and tolerant, while the unsober ones had attempted to join in.

A dip in the pool had seemed like a good idea, and the game Marco Polo started soon after. With Wade's introduction of the new penalty rule, it wasn't long before everyone was without suits.

While eluding Jude, who was "it," Betty brushed against Matthew, discovering his arousal. Slipping one hand around his neck, she explored his submerged body with the other, fingering his chest and stomach, stroking his groin, finally reaching his erection. His lips hungrily sought and found hers. Carefully, she guided him into her waiting emptiness and he filled her completely. She clasped both legs around his middle and pushed back and forth only a few times before she felt him peak and go limp.

"Oh, wow!" Matthew gasped.

"Let's go inside," Betty whispered. She swam to the steps, climbed from the pool and wrapped her glistening nakedness in a terry-cloth robe. She brought one for Matthew, and together they ran through the darkness to her room. Matthew didn't give a damn what Jude or Wade or anyone else would think. He knew only that he wanted to spend the night doing more of the same.

Wade and Joyce left the pool shortly after, intent on the same indoor activity.

"Marco!" yelled Jude.

"Polo!" a single voice rang out.

"Where is everybody? It's cheating if you don't answer," complained a frustrated Jude.

"I'm the only one left," Tina explained.

He took off the blindfold. "I guess I don't need this thing anymore then, do I?" Jude was uncertain about what he wanted to do—or what he could do.

"Are you cold? Do you want something?" Jude asked her, suddenly feeling flustered.

Tina came to his rescue. "I know! Why don't I fix us a hot toddy and we can lie out here and enjoy this pretty night?" Without waiting for agreement, she threw on a robe and hurried into the house.

Jude stayed in the safety of the water until she was out of sight, and then pulled himself from the pool, dressed in a robe and settled back on the double chaise lounge. He tried not to think.

A short while later, Tina returned with two steaming mugs. "Not a sign of anyone, they've disappeared." She positioned herself on the chaise—close, but not too close.

Jude could feel the hot brandy working its way through his body, causing a warm flush.

"Oh, would you mind? I brought out some baby oil—the chlorine absolutely dries out my skin and I can't reach my back." Tina rolled over and let the robe fall to her waist.

Jude hesitated, and then said, "Sure." He poured the oil into his left palm and gingerly started to apply it with his right. She was soft to his touch. He slowly followed the curve of her shoulder blades, through the narrow valley of her spine. She was right, the chlorine was drying, and her skin gluttonously soaked up the moisture he provided. His hands moved over her round firm buttocks and he rubbed the lubricant intensely, pushing the robe farther down, to her thighs, her calves, heels and feet.

"Oh, thank you. I can do my front."

"Please—no, let me," Jude uttered hoarsely. He gently turned her over and, using both hands, traced the hollow of her throat, past the collarbone, and lingered at her full breasts. He caressed her midriff with wide circular movements that touched and then included her pubic hair. He knelt on his haunches between her legs, his hands dripping oil, and massaged the long slim limbs. The slippery friction was like an aphrodisiac. He could feel his lust, his flesh tingle, his penis swell. And without hesitancy now, he spread her legs and plunged deep inside her. He was crazy with desire. He drove harder—harder, he tried to go deeper—deeper into her.

"Ah—ah—ahhh," he cried as release flooded his soul.

He collapsed alongside her, breathing heavily, heart pounding, his manhood splayed, spent and soft. He didn't feel guilt. He didn't feel love. But now he remembered how good it felt to be with a woman.

"It's your turn now," Tina said in a sultry voice.

Straddling him, she emptied the bottle of oil on his front, and tantalizingly smeared it with her body. She pressed down and rotated, grinding the slick liquid into his skin. Then, on her hands and knees, she roamed his anatomy with her dangling bosoms, pausing at his mouth so he could feast on first one nipple and then the other. He was rigid again and she eased herself down on him. She controlled the pace, undulating slowly, sensually, savoring each probe, nourishing the mounting passion until it was almost unbearable. Her tempo changed—faster—faster—he grabbed her derriere and clamped her tight to him as they both exploded.

It was, indeed, two days of "wows" for all. The girls had a good time. Matthew was sent on his way to midshipman school, contented and seasoned. Wade was well satisfied with the results of his planned retreat. And Jude returned to Los Angeles a liberated man.

16

Los Angeles, California
February 9, 1945

Jude tossed the script he had been reading on top of the reject pile. He was disappointed. They were all so ordinary. And tired. He didn't feel comfortable recommending any of them to Wade. That book he had finished last weekend, however, still stood out in his mind. He had been entertained, intrigued and carried away from the world's troubles for a short time. *Who Did Done It?* exemplified what Jude believed the public was ready for—a change. As a film buff, he knew he felt saturated with movies about war and death and violence. The newsreels, the newspapers and magazines, the radio kept the horrors before him in detail. He wanted to be an ostrich once in a while, and bury his head in lighthearted diversion. This book combined comedy, mystery and romance and had allowed him escape. Jude knew that musicals would provide that type of escape, but Wade was definitely not a song-and-dance man.

Maybe Jude's judgment was influenced because he was only seeing the scripts that were sent to Wade, and from them had to conclude that a shift in Wade's career direction was due. Maybe he was early. But there were so many steps to a film. The writing, the preproduction, the shooting, the postproduction, the scoring, the advertising, et cetera, et cetera—all of which had to happen before a film was released. Hell, you had to be early to foresee a trend. What was started today would take a minimum of a year to reach the theater. You had to gamble that your guess was right.

Jude decided to bring the book to Wade.

The telephone rang and Jude picked up the receiver, assuming his painstaking practiced manner of speaking. "Mr. Colby's residence, Jude Abavas speaking. No, Mr. Colby is not available. May I help you? Yes, of course I'd be happy to give him a message. Mr. Colby has been nominated—he's been *what?* No shit! Oh, excuse me! Thank you for the call. I—he—I don't know what I'm sayin' here! Mr. Colby will be thrilled with this news."

"Wade! Wade!" Jude yelled, flying at top speed toward Wade's wing of the house. They had a day off from their latest military film, and Wade and a new "friend" were dallying on the protected private beach, soaking up some of the weak rays of the February sun. Jude didn't care if Wade was at the height of an orgasm, he was sure he would be forgiven. Basa and Floozy joined Jude as he burst into Wade's territory. Fortunately, nothing was in progress.

"Sorry to barge in, but this news just couldn't keep." Jude paused dramatically before making his announcement. "Wade Colby has been nominated for an Academy Award as Best Actor in *Seek and Destroy*—along with Charles Boyer, Cary Grant, Bing Crosby—"

Wade jumped up so fast, the deck lounge tipped over and sent the lady sprawling on the sand.

"You're not serious!" said Wade.

"Kid you not!" assured Jude.

"How fantastic! How utterly fantastic!" Wade began pacing. "I never believed it could happen—I never even let myself think about it! I thought the studio was absurd to unleash all that ballyhoo ad campaign. I'll be damned! I don't have a chance in hell of winning, but I don't care—I am nominated!"

In early March, Ensign Matthew Abavas was shipped to Pearl Harbor, Hawaii, without a home leave. Jude attempted to quell Willamina's and Noah's fears. He didn't know if he was successful, because it was difficult to camouflage his own anxieties.

On March 15, 1945, Wade's prophecy proved to be correct. The Academy's Oscar for Best Actor of 1944 went to Bing Crosby for *Going My Way.* But true to his word, Wade harbored little disappointment. He had been genuinely honored by his peers' recognition, and that knowledge was reward enough.

In the first week of April, preproduction began on the movie *Who Did Done It?* Wade had agreed with Jude's choice of the story and his ideas, and so the studio had bought the rights to the book and hired the author to do the screenplay. Wade used his powers of persuasion to have Jude work closely with the credited producer. After all, it was Jude who had been responsible for finding the project and getting it off the ground.

On April 12, 1945, President Franklin Delano Roosevelt died and Harry Truman became the thirty-third president of the United States. The Allied cause had been steered with such expertise by the late president. Would this tragic loss affect America and the Allies' possible victory? Jude kept up a steady stream of communication with Ketchum, trying to reassure Mama and Papa with positive information, garnered from every available source.

At midnight, May 8, 1945, Germany signed the papers for an unconditional surrender. One front down—one more to go!

In July, word came that Matthew was still at Pearl Harbor, Hawaii. But in the hospital! The diagnosis was acute allergic sensitivity to the volcanic dust on the island. Matthew was mortified. There he was, surrounded by the human ravages of war—and he hadn't even seen any action, didn't have a heroic wound. All he suffered was a runny nose, swollen watery eyes, a constant sinus headache, enlarged glands—and a very bruised ego. Matthew was the only member of the Abavas clan upset by this development.

On August 6, 1945, the first atom bomb fell on Hiroshima.

On August 9, 1945, a second atom bomb was dropped on Nagasaki.

* * *

On August 14, 1945, Japan accepted the terms of the Potsdam Proclamation—unconditional surrender. The war in the Pacific was over.

On December 14, 1945, Jude flew to San Francisco, California, to meet the soon-to-be-discharged Ensign Abavas. He wanted to spend some time with Matthew alone, before sending him home to the waiting arms of the family. He needed to assess Matthew's condition—physically and mentally—and assist him, if necessary, in the transition from military to civilian life.

The filming of *Who Did Done It?* had just wrapped, and Jude felt he could spare a few days before editing and postproduction began. He wasn't about to miss any part of the process. He had involved himself from step one, reading page by page as the writer transformed a meandering novel into a concise, tight script, without losing the intent of the story or the development of characters. He sat in on the meetings about set designs and costumes. He participated in the all-important budget and scheduling process, which always raised the question "Why don't they film movies in sequence?" The prohibitive expense of keeping a set intact for the duration of a picture, stage availability and the rental fee charged to the production, and the cost of carrying supporting players past their guarantee, were all issues that helped answer that question. Casting, once the stars were on board, and sometimes even with the luminaries, could be a chess game, Jude discovered, a balancing act between favoritism, nepotism and sexism. Talent was not always the issue.

It was all a giant puzzle that was gradually being solved. Jude noted how the cinematographer and director moved the camera in a scene for dramatic effect; it was quite obvious to him the best results were accomplished when there was a harmonious collaboration. He could tell when the director was not communicating well with his actors and he could see how the resulting performances suffered.

Oh, yes, Jude's learning tree was being watered. And now he would begin the concluding phase of putting the pieces of the puzzle together; that is, finishing the movie. He had already assisted in assembling a rough cut of the footage. The fine-tuning was next. And then there was the music—the dubbing—and he was high as a kite with the expectation of what was to come next.

The producer, on the other hand, seemed to feel his work was practically over. He said he always became bored with these laborious finishing details, believing his creativity was wasted on technicalities.

Jude had been flabbergasted. The fine-tuning was the icing on the cake, the ribbon on the package. Walking away at this point was akin to getting all dressed up in your best suit and shirt and tie and leaving your shoes behind. This is what would make the film whole—a complete offering. This is what would make it special. And Jude could hardly wait.

Treasure Island, which extended into the San Francisco Bay, had been converted to house the 1940 World's Fair. After the start of World War II, it became the embarkation point for the Pacific arena. It was the place where wives and sweethearts and mothers and fathers said goodbye and sent their cherished young men off to serve their country. It was the place from which the ship with its precious cargo would sail but no one would know when, or where it was going, or when it would come back. Or if it would come back. It was the place where the waiting began.

Now, with the end of the conflict, it was the disembarkation and termination depot. And the waiting was over. The ones who had survived were coming home. How they were coming home no one knew. What damage had been done no one knew. And no one cared. The only important fact, the only thing that mattered to anyone was they were coming home.

Jude stood in the midst of this deliriously happy crowd. A cheer went up for every exiting figure, who was immediately encircled and hugged and kissed. Jude could feel tears rising and then flowing freely as he watched these reunions. Such tenderness as they touched. Such love as they embraced. Such wondrous awe was felt as a father returning from war hoisted a child he had never seen. Such humble gratitude was expressed as parents sobbed their thanks for their son's safety.

A tall, handsome young officer snapped a final smart salute and walked to freedom. His eyes scanned the throng and when they focused on the face they sought, he broke into a gallop. Without any self-consciousness, Matthew and Jude clung to each other and wept.

Jude had made reservations at the elegant Fairmont Hotel. Located on top of Nob Hill—opposite another San Francisco landmark The Mark Hopkins Hotel—the Fairmont bordered the homes and clubs of the city's blue book society. Their suite— Wade had called ahead to ensure proper accommodations—offered a magnificent view of the sparkling ocean, with the Bay Bridge on one side and the Golden Gate Bridge on the other.

Matthew seemed somewhat subdued. Jude took his cue and limited the conversation to chitchat. A year had made a marked difference. Gone was the boyish naiveté. What those black eyes had witnessed had obviously left a deep impression.

After settling in and calling Idaho, Matthew appeared restless. Jude suggested wandering around the large lobby of the hotel, and they ended up on the lower level in the Conga Room Bar.

"Well, now, tomorrow we'll hit some stores and take in some of the sights," Jude said. "Whadda you say? Unless you wanna stay in that dress suit. You do look pretty spiffy!"

"No—no, I don't," Matthew answered quickly. "That would be great, just great. Thank you."

"It can be sort of an early Christmas present. Nice you'll be with Mama and Papa for the holidays. They were mighty worried."

"Yeah, that'll be nice, all right."

"You know, Wade said we should go to the Top of the Mark—right across the street. He sends his best, by the way. Wanna give it a try?"

"Sure," Matthew said apathetically.

Seated with a drink, Jude contemplated his young brother. "You look really good—tanned and healthy. Did that allergy problem go away?"

Matthew laughed sarcastically. "Half a day out of Hawaii I was as fit as a fiddle, no sign of anything—eyes, nose, sinus all cleared up." He shifted in his chair. This second cocktail had helped loosen his thoughts and Jude's quiet presence served to give him courage. "You wanna know what ship I came back on? The hospital ship that picked me up at Pearl had come from Guam—where it had taken aboard the survivors of the Bataan Death March."

Matthew took a gulp from his glass before continuing. "Jesus, Jude, you can't believe—can't imagine—what they looked like. And they were better'n when they were released from the

P.O.W. camp. I saw some photos. Oh, God, those poor bastards went through hell—since April of '42, over three years. Just like the people from those concentration camps in Germany. No, maybe not quite as bad, 'cause that destruction started earlier, didn't it? What's the shit difference." He sighed. "No one should have to suffer like that." He took another swig.

Jude let Matthew take his time spitting the poison out, because out is where it had to go.

"They were on Guam for a couple of months—gaining strength. Some started to put on a pound a day. And I was still shocked when I saw them. And I felt so stupid! *Nothing wrong with me!*" This time he drained the glass and Jude signaled for another round.

"They were great to me, though. I was kind of their mascot, I guess. We played poker a lot. They were amazing, they could laugh and joke. Shit, I figure I'd still be bawling like a baby if it were me. There was this guy—Princess, they called him—who clucked over them like a mother hen. And that's what he looked like, a plump hen! He was—you know—a homo. But they all liked him, and they said he never, well, bothered anyone who didn't wanna be bothered. I was scared at first, but then he turned out to be okay. Like the other guys. He even was some kind of hero! Can you believe it?" Matthew needed more alcohol for his next revelation.

"After we docked—did you know we all had to go to Oak Knoll Naval Hospital to get checked out? Before we went to Treasure Island? Most of them had to stay there for a while. Anyway, one of the guys—he'd been one of the quiet ones, and looked the weakest, but was so nice and gentle like. Well, the morning after we got to Oak Knoll he...they found him." Matthew choked as he said, "He'd slit his wrists. He was dead—dead—for Christ's sake."

Matthew started to sob and Jude quickly dropped some bills on the table and supported him back to the shelter of their suite.

"I—I saw him—I was coming in t'say goodbye and—and—"

Jude gathered him close and rocked him back and forth. In a tiny frail voice, Matthew moaned, "There was blood everywhere, blood all over. He was so white—so white—and still. I'll never forget. Never! Why? *Why,* Jude?"

"I don't know, Matt. I wish I knew, but I don't."

"They said maybe he was just tired. That maybe he'd held together for so long that when it was over, when he didn't have to be brave anymore, he just gave up and caved in. Could that be, Jude?"

"Did he look peaceful?" Jude murmured, not ready to talk to his brother of death.

"Kind of, I guess. I don't know."

"Matt, I'm not the best person to ask for answers. There is someone though. Papa. I know 'cause he tried to help me understand. It's tough—it's damn tough—I'm still working at it. Until you talk to Papa, try to think of your friend as resting easy. Don't see the blood." *Just like I try not to see the snow,* Jude thought.

"Think no more pain, no more struggle, just his way to be free," Jude went on.

Jude stretched Matthew out on the couch, threw a cover over him, pulled up a chair and soothingly stroked his forehead.

Matthew kept mumbling, "Don't want no part of the military—no part of war."

"Shh! That's okay. You don't have to anymore."

"I want out. Don't want t'be in reserve even."

"You are out. No one says you have to be anything now, not reserve or anything."

Gradually, Matthew dozed off, then when his mind finally allowed his body to relax, he fell into a deep sleep.

Jude remained by him, alone with his own—and Matthew's—thoughts.

17

Somewhere over Idaho
December 23, 1946

"Are you sure you know what you're doing?" Jude yelled over the roar of the single-engine Piper Cub.

"Absolutely!" replied the undaunted Wade.

"Seems awful bumpy!"

"Not to worry! Just a few updrafts over the valley and now the downdrafts because we've reached the foothills. As Churchill said, 'The only thing we have to fear is fear itself,' and as long as the weather holds, we are in tip-top shape. Keep your eye out for the highway leading to Hailey."

Jude couldn't believe his ears. "Don't you know where we are, for Christ's sake? Oh, shit, I have t'take a leak."

"Use the empty Coke bottle, and be grateful that's all you have to do. And if we should run into a squall and need to go above it, don't be alarmed if you feel drowsy. It's just the lack of oxygen. I'm afraid there's only one oxygen mask on this craft, and it's reserved for the pilot."

Wade flashed Jude one of his shit-eating grins that made the ladies across America swoon. It was lost on Jude, however, who was busy trying to maneuver his stream into the bottle neck, muttering obscenities about anything and everything.

"Damnedest, stupidest thing I ever did! Letting you bamboozle me again. Why can't you do things a regular way? Charter a plane! Prob'ly not even legal."

"What did you say? I can't hear you!" Wade shouted.

"I said, you don't know from your ass about flying! You prob'ly don't even have a license!" screeched Jude.

"How did you guess?" And with that, Wade deliberately executed a modified roll.

"Are you completely off your rocker! You don't have a license? Oh, why didn't I stay home with Basa and Floozy!"

Jude scanned the terrain anxiously, willing the road to immediately appear. He wanted the two of them off this thing—preferably in one piece. The studio heads would raise hell when they found out Wade was piloting a rented airplane. They would assume it was another one of his daredevil antics concocted to torment them. And it frustrated their control-oriented minds that they had no recourse, because their ultimate punishment—suspension without pay—meant absolutely nothing to Wade Colby. Jude knew he would get the blame for not preventing this madness, for not curtailing this wild streak in *their* star and *his* boss. Well—up theirs! What did they want him to do? Lock Wade in his room? Put handcuffs on him? Wade was a big boy—at least until he pulled one of his stunts—and he could do what he damn well pleased.

Besides, Jude was pissed off at the studio bigwigs. When *Who Did Done It?* proved to be a box-office bonanza and was heralded as a trendsetter, not one person other than Wade acknowledged Jude's influence over the picture. He hadn't expected any written credit, but he had thought someone would at least give verbal recognition of his contribution, which would be valuable in establishing his credibility and furthering his career. But no, that cocky runt of a producer had strutted around bragging about how he had known immediately after reading the book that it would make a great movie. And the chief operating executive had declared it was *his* vision that an innovative change of pace was due in the industry, and so he had consequently given the green light to the project. And—oh, hell, no sense in going on and on. Jude knew they had stuck it to him.

Okay, if that's the way they want to play, he could play that way, too. He recognized their weakness! Their insecurity was showing. He *must* have hit a nerve at the studio. Why else would they be acting as if he were invisible all of a sudden? Why else would they pull Wade aside to talk to him alone instead of openly discussing things in front of Jude as they had before the making of the picture? Because Jude Abavas had become a threat to them, and maybe a threat to their positions. Because in just over three years, Jude Abavas had gone from a country bumpkin to a force to be reckoned with. Because Wade Colby trusted him and listened to him. True, he was still inexperienced, but he had learned to think, and had refined his crude natural creativity. Those wily ones sensed danger, and they meant to squelch this bug before it bit them. Not that they would get the chance.

"I see it, I see the road! On the right!" Jude screamed.

"Well done, navigator!" Wade banked to follow the guiding path to Hailey.

A fresh set of worries assaulted Jude. As soon as he had agreed to come with Wade for the reopening of Sun Valley—a decision that surprised himself as much as anyone—he had been plagued by doubts. Should he or shouldn't he go? Was he ready, or even after four years was it still too soon? Back and forth his thoughts swung, like the pendulum on the ancient grandfather clock that used to fascinate him when he visited Mr. Wangler's big house.

A call from Matthew had ended the seesaw battle. In February, Matthew had returned to the University of Washington and resumed the regular two-semester program. Over the summer, he had helped Noah and then gone back to Seattle for the fall term in September. Everything was fine—no problems or anything, Matthew had hastily assured Jude. But Matthew really missed seeing Jude and he hoped Jude could get away for the holidays this year since Matthew couldn't come south this Christmas. Mama and Papa would never say so—might sound too much like complaining—but he knew they would be thrilled to see Jude. It had been a long time. Matthew had awakened a yearning in Jude, a need to see Mama and Papa again. And he had innocently awakened in Jude an awareness of his own selfishness in concentrating so completely on himself. So, ready or not, here he was!

The ground sped by beneath them, each mile bringing him closer and closer and making him more and more tense. Familiar sights began appearing with more frequency, generating more memories. Jude was so locked in reverie, he forgot to be nervous as Wade landed the little plane smoothly on the narrow strip of runway at Hailey Airport. At least the snow had been cleared.

"Whew!" Wade sighed wearily. "Now, that wasn't so bad, was it?"

"Are you shittin' me? You *do* have a license—don't you?"

"Nope! Never got around to it. But mum's the word!" Wade taxied to the lone structure where two figures waited. One was the airport's only service employee and the other was—

"Matt! What'n th'hell are you doing here?" asked a confused Jude. "I never said anything about a time. I didn't even know—"

"I couldn't stand not knowing," Matthew smiled, "so I kept calling. Drove this poor guy crazy. Finally came out 'bout two hours ago. It's so good to see you. You, too, Wade. Mama's having hot flashes, she's so excited. Hopes you're hungry 'cause she's fixed enough for an army. Course, with all of our troops, I guess it *is* an army. Gee, nice plane, I didn't know you were a pilot, too, Wade."

"Neither does anyone else," Jude said wryly.

Matthew enthusiastically unloaded their bags while Wade made arrangements for the airplane's care and maintenance. The plan was for Jude to spend as much time as possible with his family, but Wade and Jude would actually stay at the Inn.

"What do you think of Papa's new truck?" he asked Jude, pointing to it. "Pretty neat, huh? You know, it's better you're at the Inn. It'd be too close for you at the house. Revel, for one thing, would drive you up the wall, waking you up with, 'All I Want For Christmas Is My Two Front Teeth.' Or worse, 'Mairzy Doats'!" Matthew paused, then added hopefully, "But we can ski together some days, can't we?"

"Course, although I don't know if I remember how! And this old foot, well, we'll try. And why don't you bunk with me for a while? Mama won't mind, we'll be seeing them a lot."

"I'd like that—boy, how I'd like that." Matthew's eyes shone. "Thanks!" Matthew looked to make sure Wade was still occupied with the attendant. Then quietly, he said, "I want you to know—I'm okay now, 'bout that matter in San Francisco. The ship and all. You were right—Papa did help. But so did you, Jude, a lot. Thank you." Brightly, he continued, "Remember that girl—Nancy Morris—the one in Seattle? Well, we did date when I first went back to school, but, well, she's just too immature. So I'm footloose and fancy-free. And am I having fun looking around, if you get my drift,'' and Matthew rolled his eyes upward.

"Hey, Wade!'' Jude called. "We've got a real ladies' man here!''

Wade had completed his business and was approaching the two. "Uh-oh—cutting in on my territory, is he? I guess he learned his lesson too well!'' he said sternly, winking at Jude. For a moment, Matthew thought Wade was serious, until he caught that mischievous twinkle.

"Ah—you two! Come on! I'm gonna give you the ride of your life.'' And once they were all in the truck, Matthew careened onto the road, causing Jude and Wade to brace themselves or be jostled to bits.

"Jesus!'' Jude complained. "This is more dangerous than flying with you, Wade!'' Wade could only nod in agreement.

"Prepare yourselves to be smothered!'' Matthew warned, skidding to a stop a while later in front of the weatherworn house.

Jude slowly slipped out of the front seat, squinting through the fading light at the place he had called home for so long. Somehow it seemed, well, smaller than he remembered.

He saw Noah and Willamina standing quietly in the doorway. He saw Revel peeking out from behind Mama's skirt, a trifle unsure about this older brother and his famous friend. Beyond, Jude could see the lights of the Christmas tree and the cheerful flicker of the fireplace.

He wanted to rush to them, but something held him tight. He was rooted to the spot. He looked again toward the door, and the ghosts of the past had joined Noah and Willamina, signaling for him to come—contented ghosts, waving and smiling and laughing. *It's all right,* they seemed to be telling him. *Don't be afraid.*

Instead of lead weights, now his shoes had wings. He bounded up the stairs and tried to pull Mama and Papa and Revel into his arms all at once. The ghosts had melted away, their mission accomplished.

"Mama! Papa!''

"You come home! You come home!''

The flurry of exchanges continued as they made their way to the parlor.

Noah brought wine, and Revel carefully placed the box of gayly wrapped packages around the tree, examining each to see which were hers. The grown-ups settled down for some conversation before the rest of the family arrived. When skiing was mentioned, the subject of Jude's belongings in storage was raised. Jude had already made up his mind to start fresh with new ski clothes and equipment. He hoped that skiing—especially the snow itself—would somehow seem less like the same snow as before. Matthew could take what was there. As a matter of fact, Matthew could have everything. And what didn't suit him could be given to Willamina's church. Jude wanted to leave these things behind him.

Noah, Willamina, Matthew and Wade traded glances. Jude was talking quite calmly and rationally. If he was hurting, he was doing a bang-up job of disguising it. These four disparate individuals, arriving at this moment with such diverse sensibilities, shared a common bond—their love for Jude—and they took heart by what they were hearing.

The serenity was shattered by the arrival of John Abavas, Jr., who burst through the back door yelling, "Gamma—Gamma." John and Lila were right on his heels, full of reprimands for their rambunctious offspring.

"I tol' you, Junior—never bust into Grandma and Grandpa's house without knockin'. They might be restin', or have company—like now..." John's voice trailed off as he faced his twin.

The tot froze in his tracks. Eagerness switched to embarrassment at being scolded, then to apprehension. The tension in the room was almost suffocating. Who were these two strangers? Why was that man—who looked a little like Daddy—staring at him? Why were Grandma and Grandpa staring at the man? Had the man been bad? Why were they all staring at him, too? Had he done something else wrong? The man looked as if he were going to bust open at *any* minute. John, Jr., wanted to retreat to the safety of his mama. But suddenly, the man let out an unearthly sound, and stepped toward him, scooping him up, holding him high in the air—and then very close.

"That's okay—lil—lil fella, we're not company, we're family." Jude gulped, struggling for control. Holding that small body—feeling those soft cuddly arms around him—was to be Jude's toughest test of his homecoming. But he had made it!

Shaking hands with John was like shaking hands with an acquaintance, not his brother and twin. Strange, Jude thought, here was a man who had almost killed him, a man with whom he had fought most of his life, a man who had shared a love for the same woman as he, and he felt completely detached from him. Where was the passion? The hate? The brotherly love? Maybe he should try harder with John now that they had both matured?

John's reserve was evident to Jude. Was some anger, some resentment still smoldering inside that stubborn head? With the distinct feeling that any overture on his part would not be well received, Jude moved on to peck Lila's cheek.

The awkwardness was interrupted by the arrival of Luke, his wife, Ethel, and two-and-a-half-year-old Noah. Another small body was held high and close to Jude—another test was passed.

There were introductions, greetings, chitchat, Noah pouring wine, Willamina bustling in the kitchen, Lila and Ethel running after the children, Revel trying to coax permission to open the presents early, but not getting anywhere with her pleas, Lila and Ethel announcing they were pregnant and both due next July, and then finally, supper.

At the head of the long table, Noah called for quiet. When satisfied he had their attention, he said a prayer.

"Luke, Chapter 12, Verse 48. 'Everyone to whom much is given, of him will much be required.'"

Noah looked at everyone in the room, and continued.

"I think we all be asked to do much. Because we all be given—so much. We got food, shelter, work, love, and—we be together. Our family be together—again. You be family, Wade Colby. I thank our Lord for his many blessings. And Lord, we will do much for you—for all peoples. Amen."

Wade was the center of attention for Lila and Ethel, and even Willamina and Revel to a lesser degree. Enthralled with the kingdom of Hollywood and the alluring web of its movies, they pummeled him with questions. They wanted to know what John Wayne was like in person, and was Lana Turner as beautiful offscreen as on, and did he know Judy Garland, and who was his favorite leading lady, and—

Jude wondered if he should attempt to rescue Wade. But Wade good-naturedly waved Jude off, indicating he was doing just fine. Revel gathered up her courage and asked for an autograph. Noah glowered at his precocious daughter with an enough-is-enough look. But Wade just smiled and said he would rather send her a special photo. Revel beamed triumphantly at her father.

John and Luke launched a discussion about an irrigation problem on a newly acquired piece of property. Should they put in a new system or fix the existing one? Each appeared to be trying to make points with Noah. But neither came forth with a flat-out recommendation.

Jude tried to look at his two brothers objectively. A phrase popped into his mind, something he had read recently, but he couldn't remember where. It didn't matter—the idea expressed seemed so appropriate: "While some people congeal at a certain point in life, some people remain liquid and thus changeable—and those are the only people truly alive." His brothers were still little boys begging for their father's approval.

How peculiar it was for Jude to register at the Inn as a guest and have someone take *his* luggage. Many of the same employees were on hand, but when they saw Jude with Wade Colby, they were hesitant to approach him.

"Hey! It's me—Jude! Aren't you gonna say hello?" Jude understood their reluctance, and he wondered if, in their position, the old Jude would have reacted the same way. He deliberately made the rounds of the spots where he knew the help hung out on their breaks, and they gradually trusted he hadn't turned "stuck up." And then they filled him in on the happenings since he'd left. He was saddened to hear about the boys lost in the war, including his boyhood buddy, Tom McCruger.

Jude declined the invitation to the gala party given by Union Pacific president and Mrs. Ashby in honor of the reopening and tenth anniversary of the resort. He knew he had only been asked because he had arrived with Wade, and while that was okay, he just wasn't up to making small talk with a lot of strangers. Instead, that night, he and Matthew cruised around Sun Valley and Ketchum. They drove by River Street and the cribs, they took in the six blocks of Main Street, and ended up at the Rio Club. Gloria and Pete Battis, Basques from Utah, ran the successful bar, which featured good food, a jukebox and gaming tables. The couple were friends of the Abavas family, and in earlier days, Willamina and Gloria had vied for the title of best cook. The Battises welcomed Jude and Matthew warmly.

"And yes, 'Aunt' Gloria, I am over twenty-one, I am legal, so you can give me a drink!" said Matthew, laughing.

"Oh, where do time go? Babies all big now!" Gloria's strong arms hugged them and then steered them through the crowded room, past the fireplace, to a small table in the back. "Beers come quick!" she promised.

As Jude scanned the noisy jam of people, he was aware that he could differentiate between the locals and the visitors, not necessarily by the clothes they wore, but, strangely, by their skin—especially the ladies. Interesting—he'd never noticed it before. But after living in Los Angeles, he had become accustomed to seeing women with well-cared for, pampered faces. Even those not in show business, like Wade's mother for instance, paid scrupulous attention to their complexions, with creams and makeup and whatever other mysterious potions were available. He figured Mrs. Prickler had to be a little older than Willamina, but she looked years younger. The years of arid air, exposure to the sun and the wind and the dirt and the snow—without the help of protective lotions—had caused his mother's dry wrinkled skin, her early aging. Not that a look had anything to do with character—his mama was the best person in the world—and yes, the most beautiful, as well, wrinkles or no wrinkles. But did this difference bother Mama? Or did Mama know of the difference? When he pictured his mama's serene face, he thought, no, Mama was not bothered, nor did she know. But what about Revel? At six and a half, she was growing up in a changing world, in changing times. Maybe he should ask one of his female "companions" about the best products and when a girl should start using them. He resolved to look into this matter as soon as he returned to Los Angeles.

"Penny for your thoughts," Matthew said.

"You wouldn't believe what I was thinking if I told you." Jude laughed. "I don't know why, but since I've been here, everything I see or hear triggers a chain reaction in my head. All sorts of oddball thoughts. Anyway, enough of that! Now, what about you? You told me about your love life the day we got here, but what about school? Any idea what you want to do when you get through in...when is it? A year this coming February?"

"Yeah, but I've been thinking I'd like to take a few more classes and wait till June to graduate. I had to enroll in a lot of courses just for the V-12 program, and they didn't relate to my major."

"Which is?"

"Well, since the pilot idea went out the window, I kind of thought, business, management, that area. What do you think?"

"I think that's great! But business where?"

"I know Papa would like it if I came back here. I might give it a try. But...I don't really want to. I'd rather go somewhere in California. And I don't mean the movie business necessarily. And I don't mean that I expect you to do anything. I just think there are more business opportunities down there."

"You have plenty of time to make up your mind," Jude reassured him. "You don't have to decide now. Just keep in the back of your head what we talked about way back on our first drive to Seattle in '43, it's *your* life, and you have to answer to *your* calling."

Jude felt good about Matthew. Jude also felt good about Jude. He had met the challenge of coming home. Sure he would still have bad moments—still have that fear of personal involvement, still have spasms of despair, like the ones that had shot through him when he'd made his soulful pilgrimage to pay homage to Thelma and Keane's markers—but having survived this first trip home almost emotionally intact gave him confidence. And he had been able to appreciate his family, and yet analyze them, too—and felt no guilt. He had been able to admit to himself that he would never actually live or work here again— and felt no guilt. He had been able to declare to himself that he had a goal, a purpose to reach that goal—all without guilt. And that felt pretty darn wonderful.

18

Santa Monica, California
Sunday, February 1, 1948

"There were more fireworks last night at Mocambo's than on the beach for the Fourth of July!" The two men were sharing Sunday brunch and Wade was filling Jude in on the details of the previous evening. "And where were you, by the way? You never showed." He paused while Eric poured the coffee. "Oh, thank you, Eric, I need that coffee this morning."

"You know me, I can only take a few of those wingdings, and there have been so many lately. So I took myself to the movies. Like Garbo, I need to be alone once in a while. I even went clear into Hollywood. So, I'm sitting there, the theater's not too crowded, and somebody comes and sits beside me. No problem with that. I'm watching, eating my popcorn, when all of a sudden I feel a hand on my thing. I didn't know what the hell was going on. I look down and the hand belongs to the guy next to me! Then I see his fly's open and his thing is hanging out and his hand is moving toward my zipper. Hell, I jumped up so fast my popcorn went flying every which way!"

Wade was doubled over, laughing convulsively.

"T'aint funny, McGee! I was scared shitless! People were *shh*ing us, I didn't know what to do. I didn't want to cause any more of a ruckus, so I gave this turd's arm a whack with my fist—hurt him, too—and took off."

Wade could hardly speak. "Wh-what did—did he do?" he managed to ask.

"I don't know and I don't care! I just got the hell out of there. I know one thing, no more solo movies for me!"

Wade was now gasping for breath between spasms of laughter. "But other than that, how did you like the film?"

"How do I know? I really wanted to see *The Hucksters,* too, damn it!"

"Maybe you and I can go back—to your favorite theater," Wade kidded.

"Cut it out! Fine cast—Clark Gable, Ava Gardner..."

"What a body on that one!" Wade sighed, his attention mercifully diverted.

"You can say that again! But don't! Anyway, Ava Gardner, Deborah Kerr—classy lady—Gloria Holden, Adolphe Menjou—"

"Please—please don't mention his name!" Wade pleaded. "He is one of the reasons I have this splitting headache!"

"You have a splitting headache because you got plastered!" Jude retorted. "Don't blame poor Adolphe Menjou. Somehow, I doubt he was even there."

"He wasn't! But he's one of the vehement 'friendlies.' And many of his cohorts were there. As were many defenders of the 'unfriendlies.' And as seems to be the case these days, a shouting match resulted. Mary and Charlie Morrison earned their master's degrees in diplomacy last night, trying to maintain some kind of civilized atmosphere in their nightclub. A fight seemed almost unavoidable. How can people be so rude?"

"If you're talking about what I think you're talking about, that's easy to answer. Feelings are running high, emotions on both sides are explosive. And this town is scared!"

On October 20, 1947, the House of Representatives had begun its investigation of alleged Communist influence and subversion in the entertainment industry. Hollywood and New York had been torn asunder since that time. The House Un-American Activities Committee, chaired by Representative J. Parnell Thomas (R-N.J.), had called actors, producers, directors, writers, studio heads, guild leaders to testify. They were asked if there was indeed harmful infiltration by "red" elements, and to answer the question "Are you, or have you ever been, a member of the Communist party?" Some who were called felt their rights as citizens were being violated and refused to respond, taking refuge in the free-speech First Amendment. Among this group were some of the most gifted talents in the film industry—Dalton Trumbo, Lester Cole, Albert Maltz, Herbert Biberman, Eddie Dmytryk and John Howard Lawson, to name a few. In all, they were labeled the Unfriendly Ten, and then the Hollywood Ten, and had subsequently been cited for contempt by Congress. A contingent of prominent Hollywood leaders had flown to Washington to attend a session of the hearings in support of those called to testify. Included in the trip were Humphrey Bogart, Lauren Bacall, John Huston, Evelyn Keyes, Danny Kaye, Sterling Hayden, and June Havoc.

Fears of government action, unfavorable publicity and box-office retaliation had prompted Hollywood studio heads to hold a meeting at the Waldorf-Astoria in New York on November 24. It was here that the Waldorf Statement was prepared. In essence, the adopted policy said that the Hollywood Ten would be discharged and not reemployed until acquitted or purged of contempt by declaring under oath that they were not Communists. At first neutral, the Screen Actor's Guild voted in January 1948 to require non-Communist affidavits of its members, signaling that the guild would not oppose the studios for firing actors who wouldn't say whether or not they were Communists. The stage had been set for suspicion, speculation, innuendo, blacklists, graylists and bitter division in the community.

"What I don't understand," Wade continued, "is why these ten just don't say, 'We are not Communists,' and be done with it?"

"What if they can't? Look, I don't know much, only what I've read, but—" Jude thought a minute. "Okay! Wade, suppose, just suppose, you were poor and coming out of the depression. You're young, looking for work, idealistic, a little wild. And suppose you hung out with other kids in the same boat. And together you joined an organization that, on the surface at least, promised to make things better, more equal, spread money and jobs around more. It sounded good. It's no different to you than the Democratic party or the Republican party, only it's called the Communist party—and then years later, suddenly—"

"Are you...?" Wade broke in.

"I'm not *anything,* I'm just trying to figure this mess out, just like you. So, suppose your lot improved, money was easier, you drifted away from this party and decided to register in the Democratic or Republican or Libertarian party. You still believed in the principle of equality, but maybe the old unit was getting a little pushy, becoming a bit too radical. Anyway, all the parties offered equality—that's America. Then a while later, times changed, attitudes switched. And gradually, because the world shifted, the Communist party was no longer just another party, it's believed to be a destructive force. It is suspect, thought to be undermining your country, determined to overthrow your government.''

Wade was silent, watching Jude, listening intently.

''And suddenly you are subpoenaed to appear before the U.S. Congress. Under oath, you can't lie and say you were never a member of *that* party. But if you say you were, your entire life will be destroyed unless you prove your remorse by naming names of 'fellow conspirators.' So, what do you do? You're damned if you do and you're damned if you don't. In other words—you're fucked!''

''You sound very sympathetic to these ten,'' Wade said, choosing his words carefully. Why had he introduced the bloody topic, anyway? He had always disliked this type of debate.

''Not necessarily, no! If any of them are still Communists, and if there's proof that they are trying, or did try, to sabotage our country by somehow using our industry, then I think they should be tarred and feathered and strung up.''

''I'm glad you—'' Wade didn't have a chance to complete his sentence because Jude was really on a roll now.

''But if there is no evidence of wrongdoing, if these people are only guilty of bad judgment, if this whole stew is some politician's way of getting attention, then I think it's a crock—''

''I'm—''

''And as far as I can tell,'' Jude interrupted again, ''nothing that has been on the screen from this group points to disloyalty. Sure, they talk against prejudice, and for freedom, but how can that be wrong? That's what this country is all about, isn't it? Did you know that they weren't even allowed to make statements, or offer their...'questionable material' to the committee for review? The committee appeared content to just arouse or accuse and not examine. I mean, the Constitution does say, doesn't it, that one is innocent until proven guilty?''

''May I speak now?'' Wade said after a moment.

''I'm sorry, it's just so maddening, so confusing,'' Jude apologized.

"This conversation is beginning to sound like take two of last night! But you are right, of course—it is a serious situation and sentiments are obviously volcanic. Tell me, is there a great deal of discussion around the studio, on the sets? Have *you* been very vocal? Or had many... arguments?"

"That's a funny question." Jude sensed Wade had something more on his mind. "You know damn well it's practically the only topic anyone talks about. And yes, I voice my opinions, raise my questions, hope for information. But no, I don't stand on a street corner spoiling for a fight. What are you driving at?"

Wade sighed. He cared little about politics, but he cared a great deal about Jude, and this "unfriendly" or "friendly" dilemma was getting out of hand.

"Don't get excited—it's nothing. I wasn't even going to mention it because it's so ridiculous."

"What?" Jude demanded.

"Eric!" Wade called. "Would you please bring me an aspirin—my head is pounding!"

"I'll pound your head real good if you don't get to it," Jude threatened.

"All right, all right!" Wade took the pills from Eric who had rushed in with them, and he waited for a moment while Eric left the room. Then he spoke. "At lunch last week, this same subject came up—naturally! I wish we could all move on to something else, expand our horizons just a—"

"Wade!"

"You say I don't have patience! Okay! Someone at the table, a 'friendly,' was expounding on the danger these so-called Commies presented, and put their sympathizers in the same category—" Wade was having difficulty continuing.

"So?" Jude prompted.

"Well, clearly, this person isn't one of your ardent admirers. And, well, he linked your name to the latter group."

"He *what!*" Jude vaulted out of his chair, his face flushed red with anger.

"Calm down! He didn't get very far—now let me finish before you have a fit! He claimed he overheard you and a writer, I think he said, conversing, and both of you were justifying the position of the ten. And with a shake of his head and close to tears, he lamented, "How could a nice boy like that Jude Abavas go so far astray?'' The rest of us almost broke up, he was so transparent. But we managed to contain ourselves, and immediately put him in the hot seat.''

''Who? *Who* said this? I'll haul his ass!'' Jude was stomping back and forth, arms flailing about furiously.

''Now that would really be smart, wouldn't it? Allow me to go on. Where was I? Oh, yes, we began barraging him about specifics. Exactly what had been said? How long did he listen? And so on and so on. He was finally cornered and had to admit he had only heard one phrase, ''Those poor bastards,'' and from that had determined your views. He didn't dare put manufactured words in your mouth, because he couldn't prove them in a lawsuit. So you see, you must have faith in your friends, they will protect you. Unless you do something stupid, of course, like thrashing him.''

Jude was too quiet. He sat down again, hunched forward, his elbows on his knees, hands in his hair. Wade became concerned after a bit.

''Jude, it's all right! This *person's* snide allusions were completely refuted. And he's not dumb enough to continue after having been caught so blatantly. Actually, he isn't a bad sort, just careless in his nationalism. There is nothing to worry about!''

Jude seemed so lost in thought, Wade couldn't be sure his friend had heard him—or if he had, if he believed him. Wade nervously hastened to further reassure him.

''Surely you don't think *I* harbor any such notions about you! You and I have never talked about this muddle until now, except superficially. I know how you feel about our country— we've discussed it many times—especially relating to our inability to serve in the war. Please—*please*—don't let a zealot's babbling upset you!'' Wade implored.

Jude looked up and saw fleeting uncertainty in Wade's eyes. He became aware that their roles had unexpectedly reversed. Wade had definitely been proud of his handling of a delicate situation on behalf of his friend and had felt in control dispersing his subtle advice. But now, Wade showed signs of tentativeness, a crumpled confidence. He showed uneasiness at Jude's withdrawal. He showed a fear, that perhaps he had botched this thing somehow, and in so doing, that he might have damaged a treasured relationship. It reminded Jude of the insecurity he'd sensed in Wade during their trip to New York. It was as if Wade didn't realize that nothing could fuck up their friendship.

"Don't look so anxious, Wade. I apologize. I heard what you said. My mind was going round and round like a merry-go-round, I'm sorry. I'm sorry, too, you had to defend me to that ass-wipe. But I thank you . . . very much . . . and the rest of the table—whoever—I don't even want to know who. You're the only one there I give a shit about."

A twinge of relief was visible on Wade's troubled face.

"But," Jude continued, "if I was confused before, I'm betwattled now! First I was just pissed off, now I don't know what I am. It's not that I'm worried about me—hell, I can sign any paper they want me to without any qualms, I've nothing to hide. I come from a state and a family that are such middle-of-the-roaders, such gung ho Americans, it would be hard to find a more conservative place!"

"With the possible exception of the Pricklers and Hancock Park," interrupted Wade.

"Got me there!" Jude welcomed Wade's interjection, a signal they were getting back on track.

Eric appeared. "May I clear now, Mr. Colby?"

"Absolutely! Why don't we go outside, Jude, it's beautiful today."

The ocean and sky teamed for perfection. The gulls rollicked overhead, screeching and chattering. It was a scene of tranquillity and beauty, disturbed only by Basa and Floozy.

"What boggles my brain, Wade, is where all this is leading. Those waves out there look harmless, don't they? But we don't know what's happening way out there *under* the water—what rumblings are going on that could change those mild breakers into a destructive tidal wave. Okay, so some dickhead said Jude Abavas is almost one of them just because he doesn't like Jude Abavas, or because he's jealous of Jude Abavas, or whatever. Now, it so happened that Jude Abavas had people stand up for him before the 'almost one of them' became 'one of them.' But what about the poor son of a bitch who isn't lucky enough to have friends around at the right time? What happens to him? Or her? A person's career—life, even—is ruined because someone doesn't like them? Now that's scary!"

Wade sank into one of the deck chairs on the patio, rubbing his forehead. "I never really thought about it that way before," he admitted.

"Hey, neither did I! And maybe I'm making a mountain out of a molehill. Like I said, I don't know. Maybe this will all blow over, maybe this hysteria will roll over and die. But right now, these hearings are getting more press than the war crime trials in Nuremberg, or Tojo and his war criminals in Japan. And my gut tells me there is more to come."

Neither spoke for a while. Wade finally broke the silence.

"You know, Jude, I guess I've led what could be called a charmed life. I've never really had to struggle for anything. Even the so-called stardom in this most difficult profession came relatively effortlessly. And I'm not unaware or ungrateful, believe me. And so I'm extremely devoted to, and protective of, a form of government that provided such opportunities for my grandfather, my father, me and every other citizen. Quite frankly, when all of this folly erupted, my naive initial reaction was one of support for the hearings. Because the idea of anyone doing anything detrimental to this country made me see red! Ha! What a choice of words!"

Jude didn't bother to remind Wade that he, too, shared this passion for democracy. After all, he was the son of immigrants, grateful recipients of what America had to offer.

"I'm not one to campaign publicly, align myself with a candidate or pontificate at functions," Wade continued, "it's just not my style. I vote religiously—religion, that's another topic I try to avoid. I keep quiet and enjoy my life. But damn you, Jude, you make me think about things I don't want to think about! Probe where I don't want to probe! Interrogate where I don't want to interrogate!" Wade smiled his winsome smile. "I realize I did my country a service by not going into the diplomatic core. And now, you are trying to make me grow up and be an adult? I'm afraid I'm a lost cause. I'm a modern Peter Pan."

"So what! We should all have a little of Peter Pan in us. I probably don't have enough—maybe you could loan me some!"

"Oh, Jude, why can't we be as uncomplicated as Basa and Floozy! Look at them—zonked—not even the impending birth of puppies concerns them."

Wade looked at Jude, a sudden shadow passing over his face. "Do you think I'm chicken-shit because I didn't go to Washington with Bogey's group? You know he called."

"Hell, no, Wade. I think it would have been hypocritical if you had gone. You can't pretend to be what you're not! It wasn't because you were afraid, you rightfully chose not to go because you weren't dedicated to the cause. You damn well didn't know what it was all about then, and you're still not sure about it, even now. Me, neither, not really. Everyone doesn't have to be an activist, for Christ's sake! Hell, you and me are having a hard enough time trying to make up our minds about what's going on."

"That is true," Wade said in complete sincerity, grateful not to be considered a milksop in Jude's eyes. He buzzed Eric on the intercom. "Would you be kind enough to bring us a large pitcher of strong Bloody Marys? I know I'm ready for fortification."

"Of course, Mr. Colby, right away."

Jude pressed him. "Well, what *do* we believe? We both don't want anyone rear-ending our country."

"Agreed!"

"That kind should be prosecuted!"

"Absolutely!"

"But we also don't want someone who hasn't done anything to be prosecuted."

"Right!" Wade was valiantly attempting to participate with enthusiasm.

"Wade, I just thought of a horrible scenario. With all the attention on this one business and this one group, what if that diversion allowed real die-hard spies to get a foothold—operate here—and—and really do harm?"

A pause. "You see? I never would have thought of that, either," acknowledged Wade.

"What we have to do more of is read, challenge, be more informed."

Eric delivered their refreshments, allowing the two friends a brief respite.

"Jude, I must confess, I am troubled." Wade reopened the conversation after downing half his drink. "My one remaining brain cell is having a problem reconciling all this. What does it honestly matter if I—we—read more and challenge more and think more? We can't alter anything or make a difference. Perhaps that is one reason I never pursued the having-to-know syndrome. Who cares what I know, except me?''

Wade refilled his glass and poured for Jude.

''I don't want to mislead or disappoint you,'' Wade said. ''Actually, you said it. 'I can't pretend to be what I'm not.' And I am not a crusader. I am not qualified to take on all the evils of the world, and I'm not sure that I want to. I do what can be done easily. Does that make me shallow?''

Wade continued before Jude had a chance to answer.

''I cannot be any more direct than I'm being, because I will not be dishonest with you, your opinion is too valuable to me. I just cannot promise that I can be a different sort of person.''

Jude needed time. ''Our cupboard is bare. We need some more to drink—maybe a lot more.'' He escaped to the bar with the pitcher, knowing that Wade was right. They couldn't fix the world, couldn't even undo the wrong that had been done.

A few minutes later, Jude returned with an overflowing pitcher, his determination restored. ''A toast! To you, Wade. Please don't change—you're just the way you ought to be. And I'm luckier than a clap doctor in a cathouse to have you for my friend. Bottom's up!''

They drained their glasses and reloaded. ''And here's to that forever-to-be-unidentified maggot at the studio who doesn't know his ass from a hot rock, but who did manage, through his stupidity, to inspire this afternoon, and for that I toast him!''

''Hear, hear!'' Wade seconded.

A few salutes later, Wade came up with a brilliant idea. ''Let's call Jane and, how about Charlene? And have them come over for an early barbecue and we can watch television. Probably not much to see, but who cares, we'll find *something* to do!''

Jane and Charlene arrived wearing the latest dress craze, Hawaiian muumuus. The loose-fitting, brightly colored garments showed very little of the body's contour. But Wade and Jude had faith they would eventually explore the curves that were concealed underneath.

''Ohhh—when did you get the television set? Not many of these around. Too bad it's not Tuesday—Milton Berle's on then,'' Jane cooed.

Jude fiddled with the dials and suddenly a black-and-white image appeared on the small screen. It was startling to have an instant picture at home without the need of a projectionist and heavy reels of film. Jude had boned up on this innovative medium when Wade decided to purchase a set. The cost was prohibitive, except for people like Wade. Anyway, however intriguing this television might be, the public had motion pictures and radios for their major source of entertainment. The studios were certainly convinced television wouldn't last. Jude wasn't sure he agreed and he did think that a toy like this could bring Willamina a great deal of pleasure. He decided that if television was still accessible at the end of the year, he would splurge and send a set home for Christmas.

Wade was soon bored with the programming. He decided he needed to loosen his muscles, and suggested the four of them hop into his special tub, where strategically placed nozzles jetted steamy water toward any tense part of the anatomy. Charlene declined, so Jane and Wade went alone.

"I hope you don't mind. It's just—not convenient—for me right now," Charlene apologized .

Jude understood. "No problem. Actually, that sweat bath can be too debilitating sometimes."

"Are you strained, or stressed, or something?"

"I guess I'm always a little fidgety, nothing different about that." Jude laughed.

"Well, I'm no expert or anything, but I do have a gizmo here that might help you." Charlene rummaged through her big carryall, finally coming up with a compact hand vibrator. "Let's go to your room and see if it works."

When they got to Jude's bedroom, Charlene took charge in a nurselike manner. "Now, just stretch out on the bed—that's it. I'll take off these cumbersome big old clothes you're wearing— isn't that better? Oh, do you have body lotion?" She went searching in the bathroom before he could answer.

Jude was amused. Charlene was a nice enough kid, never demanding or pushy, always obliging and good-natured, somewhat more homespun than her counterparts. He was curious as to what she had in mind.

She climbed onto the oversize bed and rolled him over onto his stomach. "I can get at you better this way. Lie still and just go blank—be limp—let go of all your thoughts."

With the whirring machine strapped firmly on her hand, Charlene started at Jude's toes. Rubbing and pulling, polishing his ankles and calves. She lifted one of his legs, then the other, kneading the taut tendons, grinding away at the powerful thighs. The instrument churned its way up his spine, dug into his strong shoulders, down his burly arms. Despite himself, Jude gave in to the floating sensation that overtook him and drifted into a twilight zone. The fluid friction dissolved the pressure in his neck, the pressure in his head. Even his scalp felt liberated.

Feeling no resistance from him, Charlene turned Jude on his back and began to massage his face, his chest. When she reached his penis, she seesawed him, to and fro, back and forth, side to side, until she could feel his body start to quake. She shut the oscillator off and gently took him in her mouth, surrounding him, releasing him, surrounding him, releasing him, mercilessly surrounding him and releasing him until he could stand no more. He wildly grabbed at her head and pressed it down tighter on him, spewing forth any and all anxiety.

"I like your cure, little one. You should patent that," Jude murmured. At almost twenty-nine, he thought of himself as carnally sophisticated, but this was a new experience. To be the passive recipient, to not even be near the woman's sexual conduit, to barely touch her—this was different. He fleetingly wondered what else he had missed.

There was no question that the 'friendlies' and the 'unfriendlies' were a million miles away now.

Anna's frantic voice jerked Jude back to reality. "Mr. Colby! Mr. Abavas! Come quickly! Floozy is birthing! Vere are you?" Sometimes when Anna was excited, she reverted to her Scandinavian habit of exchanging *w*'s and *v*'s. And she was definitely excited now.

Jude threw on his pants and rushed across the patio to the living room. He could see through the glass doors that Wade was dashing in from his wing in an equally disheveled state.

Anna was standing near the entrance to the kitchen, wringing her hands. "Floozy started vhining—acting funny. I put blankets in vashroom and I don't know vhat to do. Eric is at store." The two men looked at each other in dismay—what could they do?

"I've seen animals back home deliver, but I've never—I mean, if there's trouble," said Jude. "Well, come on, let's have a look!"

Jude and Wade gingerly approached the laundry room. Basa was on guard duty, but seemed as confused and uncertain as everyone else.

"It's okay, ol' buddy, don't worry," Jude said soothingly. When they peered around the corner, they found that a tired but happy Floozy had everything under control. She was proudly licking two wet balls of fur, a white ball and a black ball.

"Well, I'll be," marveled Wade.

"Me, too," Jude echoed.

"Floozy, girl, you're wonderful!"

Anna fluttered in. "Oh, look at that! How cute they are! My little Floozy—are you all right? I do now the vomen's vork," and she shooed them away.

"Come, Basa, you look as if you could use a drink, so we'll have one for you," Wade said as they tiptoed out of the canine maternity ward and joined Jane and Charlene at the bar. The girls heard the news and hurried to the laundry room to gush over the arrivals.

"Quite a day!" Jude and Wade exclaimed in unison.

19

Baldy Mountain, Idaho
January 1950

A new snowfall the night before had pristinely carpeted the mountain, and the skiing was glorious. Matthew whizzed down Canyon Run and turned into River Run on his way home. As he rounded the corner where the first lift unloaded, someone careened down the incline, screaming in panic, and landed in a crumpled heap right in front of him. He jumped to avoid hitting the person and ended up in a snowbank, ass over teakettle.

"What the hell's the matter with you?" he demanded to know, once he had collected himself and his gear.

The figure uncurled warily. A mittened hand pulled the wool hat off and a mass of blond hair came tumbling down. Blue teary eyes and an angry pert face stared up at him.

"Don't you yell at me, you—you human dynamo! That damn contraption throws me off and then you damn near run over me! My damn friends left me after getting me on this damn high tor and these damn slit-boards, and now I'll sit here and damn well freeze to death because—because—because I don't know what else to do!" And then she lay back down as if waiting for the end to come.

Matthew wasn't sure how to handle this creature or the situation. She was like no female he had ever met.

"Well, miss—or ma'am," Matthew said tentatively, "you can't stay here like that. Are you hurt? Should I go and get the patrol and a sled?"

Silence. Then, bravado and temper subdued somewhat, a quieter, smaller voice answered. "No, I'm not hurt. Except for my pride. I just want to get down off this cliff, please."

Matthew tried not to smile. "This cliff" was the flattest run on Baldy, leveler than some on Dollar, planned expressly for beginners. Clearly, she was not even a beginner.

"Tell you what! Would you be game to try something? I did this a few times with my sister when she was still learning last year, and you don't look a whole lot bigger than she was. I'll put you between my skis, with my arms around your middle—no chance to fall that way, you see—and then I'll guide you down 'this cliff.' It's not far really."

Silence. Then, "Can you do that? For certain?"

"Positive! Come on, I'll help you put on your skis," and Matthew pulled the skeptic to her feet and reattached her equipment. "Now, you hold your poles and mine crossways—relax, will you! It will be easy, even fun."

"For you, maybe!" muttered the still-doubtful girl.

Before he could support her, the skis started to move and she was sliding away.

"Help! Oh, my God—help!"

"Snowplow! Snowplow!" yelled Matthew.

"What's that?" she howled, still clutching the four poles.

"Oh, shit!" Matthew exclaimed as he saw her heading for the trees. He pushed off, but couldn't reach her before she had tumbled into a tree well. At least the hole had prevented a head-on collision with the very sturdy timber.

"Are you all right?" asked an anxious Matthew.

"No, I'm not all right! I'm stuck in some damn pit and will never get out! Oh damn! Damn!" She was spooked and close to hysteria, but still feisty.

"Calm down. Just hand me the end of one of the poles and I'll pull you out. You hold tight now. One, two, three." He was making progress when his skis slipped, and he fell unceremoniously on top of her. From his upside-down position all he could see was a tangle of arms and legs and skis and poles. They were such a mess, it struck his funny bone, and he started to laugh.

"What's so funny?" she demanded. And then she surveyed their entanglement and the ridiculousness of it all hit her, too, and laughter conquered her rising tears. Soon the two of them were laughing uncontrollably.

"Oh—oh, my! I'm going to wet my pants if I don't stop!" she blubbered.

"Th-then, you couldn't get up—yellow snow." Matthew was almost choking.

"Hey! What's goin' on down there? You two crazy or somethin'?" a face peering down at them inquired.

"Maybe so! But could you please—give us a hand here? We seem to be stymied," pleaded a weakened Matthew.

Gradually, their benefactor managed to extricate the two from the hole. "Anythin else I c'n do?"

"No, I think we can manage. Much obliged," Matthew said gratefully, with a firm grip on his charge. "That is, if I still have the strength. Well, miss—ma'am—shall we have another go at it?"

"*Miss* Polly Chandler. And don't take your hands off me to try to shake hands!" she cautioned. "Well, why not! What else could happen? Don't answer that!"

"Matthew Abavas, here. Okay, all you have to do is keep your skis flat. Don't try to direct them, I'll do the rest. Ready? Here we go. Don't fight me."

Her five feet height barely came to his shoulders, and she was as light as a feather. "See, this is a cinch!" He liked the sensation of her body near his and held her closer than was absolutely necessary. Slowly, but surely, Matthew steered his wobbly partner to the bottom without further mishap.

"I told you! Here you are, safe and sound!" Matthew had suddenly realized just how attractive his passenger really was. "Can I give you a ride? In a car this time? The bus isn't here yet. Where are you staying?"

Polly took a good look at her rescuer and liked what she saw. "I owe you an apology, I'm afraid—for acting like a spoiled rotten kid. And a debt of gratitude for not abandoning a crabby stranger and then for saving her hide. And now a second ride! I'd appreciate it. Thank you. I'm at the Challenger."

When they arrived at the Inn, she insisted on rewarding her 'knight on shining skis' with a hot toddy at the Ram Bar.

Matthew had no objection and when she shed the bulky parka, he was additionally impressed. And as the drinks segued to dinner and a tour of the Ketchum pubs, he discovered that the pleasing exterior was augmented by a quality interior.

Polly Chandler was born in San Francisco on July 6, 1925—exactly one day before Matthew. She was a fourth-generation

Californian. Her parents were both professors, and both liberals. She had been suckled on independence, candor and tolerance, and weaned on Franklin Delano Roosevelt's New Deal and Eleanor Roosevelt's fight for women's rights. She had graduated from the University of California at Berkeley. "A liberal arts major usually means you really don't know what you want. And that was me!"

She and a girlfriend first moved to an apartment across the bay in bohemian Sausalito. "A haven for ultraintellectuals and struggling artists and writers. The next obvious destination was Los Angeles, the place most San Franciscans don't recognize as existing."

The two free souls found a compatible atmosphere in a tiny house up Laurel Canyon, north of Hollywood Boulevard. Polly had dabbled in free-lance writing, but her call to adventure didn't nurture concentration. Briefly she'd entertained the thought of becoming a pilot, but the learning curve had proved too lengthy and complicated, so she'd settled for a career as an airline stewardess. Her outgoing personality, sense of humor and innate mental agility served her well. And she was content. "You can't imagine the variety of people I meet, from all walks of life. Some are kooks, some are duds, but they're all interesting. I like the traveling, too. I've seen so much of the States and recently begun international flights. As you may have guessed, though, this is my first venture into your neck of the woods."

Polly had been talked into participating in a "Sun Valley Stewardess Week" package, a promotional incentive used by most resorts during slack periods. "I must have been temporarily insane when I agreed to this madness. Or higher than a kite, which is the same thing. Anyway, that's why I'm here. What's your story?"

Matthew and Polly spent every possible waking hour together during the remaining days of her visit. Matthew even arranged with some key-operator friends for Polly to have a passenger trip on the lifts—up *and* down—to and from the very top, so he could show her the vast and majestic view.

"It's breathtaking, seeing the peaks from this vantage point," Polly marveled.

Matthew drew her to him gently, lifted her dark glasses, tilted that captivating face upward. "Don't drink it all in yet. Save some of that wonder and enjoyment. 'Cause I want to bring you up here many many times in our future. I love you, Miss Chandler.''

"I love you, too, Mr. Abavas," she whispered as their lips and hearts met.

Matthew and Polly were married on Wade's lanai, neutral territory. "Otherwise we'll have a tug-of-war on our hands and five hundred well-meaning but musty guests to worry about," Polly explained. "Thank God Mom and Dad approve of you, and know their headstrong daughter well enough to realize I'll do it my way, regardless. They were pacified when we promised them their big reception in San Francisco on our way to Idaho. Isn't it odd they're so liberal and yet still cling to the traditional?"

Polly had decided they'd get married on July 6, 1950, at the stroke of midnight. "That way, I won't feel like I'm robbing the cradle—we'll practically be the same age."

Jude and Wade had been totally enslaved by Polly when Matthew brought her to see them on the first of his frequent trips to Los Angeles. Matthew bunked with Jude in the beginning, but when Matthew and Polly tentatively explored the subject of marriage, Polly aggressively suggested that Matthew stay with her. "Believe it or not, I am still a virgin—although I've been close to losing it. Not that I'm prudish—anything but—I just never believed in anyone enough. Until you. And you never came on to me. Maybe that's one reason, among many others, that I trust you. But we'd better make sure we're right in every department."

Matthew was thankful he had heeded Jude's advice about "nice" girls, given so many years ago. He had wanted to make love to Polly almost since their initial encounter. But before very long, he had sensed that this relationship could be different, could be much more than a fling. He was glad he had restrained his desire.

Matthew was gentle, slow, with thoughtful caring caresses. She was beautifully responsive and free. Matthew realized the full meaning of love when he experienced the pureness that was given for him to take. And Polly knew true passion.

"There's some religion," Polly said, sighing ecstatically, "I don't remember which—that says when someone saves a life, that someone is henceforth responsible for that life. It must be true—you saved me and what do you know, you're stuck with me forever! I think I finally know what I was waiting for. I was waiting for you. And now we have some catching up to do.''

Jude and Wade clucked over the wedding preparations like two mother hens. This provided a welcome excuse to put aside some troubling thoughts for the moment. Anna and Eric were in their glory—a wedding involving their favorite surrogate son, Matthew, and his sweet Polly! Jude was best man. Sandra Olivia Sawyer, also known as S.O.S. or Polly's soon-to-be ex-roommate, was maid of honor. Wade was to give the bride away, an honor he valued highly.

As they had wished, it was a small gathering. Only a few friends of the young couple and a sprinkling of people they knew through Jude and Wade were invited. But no expense was spared. Wade had a studio set-decorator design an exquisite bower of flowers and candles. An aisle was created with borders of full, luxurious plants alternating with floor candelabra, both graduating in size toward the pinnacle of the altar. A twelve-piece orchestra was camouflaged behind mosaic screens. Polly's gown was white satin, embroidered with beads and seed pearls, fashioned after the dress Elizabeth Taylor wore when she married Nicky Hilton earlier that year. "Can you beat that! Me and Liz! Oh, Wade, you shouldn't have. But I'm so thrilled you did!''

Wade was puffed up like a peacock. "If I'm going to be father of the bride, so to speak, nothing is too good for my baby!''

Jude fussed over Matthew's tuxedo with equal attention. "No rental! No, siree! This is yours, fitted to you. With all the trimmings. You look so handsome—nothing's too good for my little brother. Not so little anymore, though, are you?'' Jude was developing a huge lump in his throat. He hugged Matthew. "Better do this now or I'll get all mushy at the wedding. I'm proud of you, Matthew. You're a fine man, and I'm glad I'm your brother... and friend.''

It was truly a romantic ceremony. Polly glided in on Wade's arm, engulfed in a halo of self-luminous joy. Matthew was stunned by her beauty and overcome by the beacon of love that beamed from her. Indeed, no one in attendance was left untouched by the positive currents coming from the two, sparking through the room, lighting each pair of watching eyes, warming every spirit.

The "I do's" had been said, the photographs had been taken, the bride and groom were on their way to San Ysidro Ranch in Montecito, near Santa Barbara, for their honeymoon week. Wade had arranged the reservations at the exclusive country club through his friend and co-owner, Ronald Colman. But it was Jude's treat. The party was suddenly over. Jude and Wade slumped in armchairs and sipped from brandy snifters. Two weary but satisfied daddies. Basa and even the rambunctious Blackie and Whitey—Floozie's offspring—seemed ready to settle down.

"This was such an inspiring occasion, I'm almost tempted to try it myself. I just don't know who with," exclaimed Wade. "That S.O.S. was a pretty little character, wasn't she? I must give her a jingle. By the way, you handled tonight exceptionally well, old chum. I was a mite apprehensive that it—well, you know, could remind you—damn it, anyway, you know what I mean."

"Yes, I know what you mean." Jude smiled. "I surprised myself, to tell you the truth. I'm not exactly sure why. Maybe because these kids were just so—like you said—inspiring. They were so right, they made everything and everyone right, too. And maybe time itself played a part. It's been over eight years. My God! Do you realize I've been with you *seven years?* I feel like *The Man Who Came To Dinner* and never left!"

"And you had better not entertain any thought of that," warned Wade. "Unless you want me to walk into the ocean à la Fredric March in *A Star Is Born.* I need you, I always have, perhaps now more than ever. You're the only one who knows what is going on and tells me."

"Never fear. For whatever it's worth, I'm always here. Don't worry, we'll get through it," Jude promised.

The Abavas clan in Idaho did not embrace Matthew's decision to marry as readily as the California contingent. The courtship and marriage happened too quickly for them. They were used to the slower-paced, more conventional approach. It wasn't that anyone didn't like Polly, but she was an outsider and they hadn't had enough time to get used to her and her newfangled ways.

And everyone had become accustomed to having Matthew home again; they were concerned his marriage might lure him away. And they were busier than normal now that the Korean mess had begun.

What none of them understood was that Matthew had never intended to stay in Ketchum forever. When he graduated in June 1948, he obligingly entered the Abavas Company on a temporary basis—temporary at least in his mind. Early in 1949, with his professional training in full operation, he had suggested a brave new concept and expansion for the family business.

The accomplishments of J. R. Simplot were legendary in Idaho. From the age of fifteen he had built an empire utilizing the new technology of his own inventions, as well as the expertise of other's knowledge. And at the same time, he had acquired more and more real estate.

Matthew did not propose to challenge the enormity of Mr. Simplot's vision, nothing on such a broad scale. But he saw no reason that the Abavas Company, modestly of course, couldn't use some of Mr. Simplot's innovative and practical ideas. The Abavas Company's assets consisted mainly of livestock and acreage. Matthew proposed that the company branch out into the frozen food market, a step that would take advantage of their holdings. He also suggested the company explore the value of mineral deposits on their land—he knew they could save thousands of dollars by producing their own fertilizers.

John and Luke immediately repudiated Matthew's recommendations; they preferred to follow the well-trodden path. Even Noah had misgivings. It was Willamina who spoke favorably of the idea, in the privacy of their bedroom.

"Why not try? You be afraid because you have fifty-one years? Everything make changes. You say you won't watch Jude's present, you say you stay with radio—hah! Now you sit so I can't see box, hardly! If you go slow, what's problem?"

Willamina never ceased to amaze Noah. Even after all these years. She was right, of course. Growth was healthy, and the Lord knew, Noah Abavas was not lazy or cowardly. His verdict was to go forward.

By degrees, the wheels were set in motion to modernize their whole operation. Noah was the captain, Matthew the administrative supervisor. John and Luke, unenthusiastically at first, were put in charge of the on-site execution of the conversions.

When Matthew fell head over heels for Polly, the company's restructuring was on schedule but not near completion. He realized he couldn't desert Noah midstream. But he also realized he would be asking Polly to forfeit a familiar way of life, to totally shift her environment for him. And that was a great deal to ask, despite the fact that the arrangement wouldn't be permanent.

"But I do understand! Of course you can't just up and leave your father's company," his wife said. "That would be awful. I wouldn't want you to do that, I wouldn't like you if you did! I can handle Idaho, I mean, I *think* I can handle Idaho. As long as I don't have to ski—I draw the line there! Anything else, well, I'll learn. I just will, that's all. Because I love you!"

Ketchum, Idaho
June 7, 1951

"I'm a bride—for one more month, anyway—so I can still plead inexperience," offered a defensive Polly Chandler Abavas.

Matthew chuckled, rose from the table, swept his petite wife into his arms, and carried her into the bedroom. "Then perform your bridely duty," he teased sternly.

"Oh, no, you don't! You're just trying to get out of eating the dinner that I slaved over. And I can't even blame you. It's awful, I know it. And I don't think a month is going to do any good, either. Then what excuse will I use? I'm a flop—a failure," Polly lamented.

Matthew plopped the two of them down on their bed and held her close. "I worship you, my adorable blond vixen. And you are perfect, because you make me a very happy man." He smothered her fears with kisses.

Supper was long-forgotten as they lay entwined, relishing the passion of their togetherness, treasuring the tenderness of their satisfaction.

After a bit, Polly propped herself onto her elbow and leaned over Matthew. "He loves me," she chanted as she pulled a hair from his chest, "he loves me not," and she tweaked again.

"Ouch!"

"He loves me," and out came another.

Matthew retaliated by tickling her.

"I give up—I give up!" Polly laughed. "Oh, Matt, I love you so." She cradled his head to her breasts and her tone became serious. "I want to be all that a good wife should be. But I just don't know how to function here, I don't seem to fit. I've tried so hard, but I guess I'm too much a city girl. Or accustomed to being a career girl. Or something—alien to Idaho certainly!"

"Honey, please," Matthew implored, "you are a good wife for me and that's all that matters. Has anyone said anything to you?"

"No, no! Your mom and dad are dear, they accept me—even though they don't understand me. And the others are... all right. Revel and I are the closest, I think. I'm just ... different. I think differently—my interests are different—I stick out like a sore thumb. I can't cook worth a damn. I cry if I'm in the kitchen when a chicken is cleaned, or a fish, or a poor little duck or pheasant, or, well, I can't even talk about those big-eyed deer."

"If I was marrying for food, I would have married a chef," Matthew told her.

"And I'm such a dumb klutz! I can't ski. I don't hunt. I have a hard time driving in the snow and ice and slush, I can barely walk without slipping. I can't sew. I can't talk about the children because so far I can't even get pregnant. About the only thing I can do is clean and keep your books. Well, I guess I can play tennis with you and I do love to hike and ride the bikes and swim."

"And make me proud that you are my wife," continued Matthew. "There, you see? Just like I said, you're perfect!"

"You are so patient. And kind. And good. And smart. And sexy. And I love you to pieces," and Polly proved to Matthew again just how perfect she could be.

Around the end of July, after Polly was no longer the bride but a wife, and after their twenty-sixth birthdays, Matthew felt comfortable with the progress of the company and determined the time was right to start preparing for a gradual withdrawal. On the pretext of having too much work to do, he recruited both of his brothers' wives, Ethel and Lila, to assist him at the office a few hours a day. That way, Matthew figured, they could become skilled in the various administrative operations and eventually carry on what he had established. Willamina contributed by minding her four grandchildren—John's eight-year-old son, John Jr., and his four-year-old daughter, Roberta, and Luke's seven-year-old son, Noah, and four-year-old son, Luke, Jr. Polly concentrated on helping Revel with her upcoming eleventh birthday party, a task Willamina was glad to be relieved of. Willamina was having trouble coping with her insurgent young daughter; the generation gap was rearing its head in earnest. On top of which, she had never dealt with a girl child before and was embarrassed and flustered when Revel raised any question about intimate matters. At this point, Polly's modern frankness was a bonus, and Willamina pleaded with her to take over Revel's sexual education. Not a moment too soon, either, for Revel turned out to be an early bloomer and began her menstrual cycle ahead of schedule.

"I don't want my hair done like Debbie Reynolds—I want to look like Rita Hayworth!" Revel complained, the afternoon before her big day.

"Don't we all!" exclaimed Polly. "But don't you think at almost eleven that's a little, well, sophisticated? The boys might be scared off."

"This bunch are such goon-heads, who cares!" Revel declared. "Now, if we could invite some eighth-graders, or even freshmen from high school, that would be like wow! Would you ask Mama? Please and pretty please? I'll be your best friend forever."

"Not a chance! I'm barely keeping my head above water around here as it is. I'm not about to make waves. Listen, you're lucky the seventh-graders got to come, so don't push it! Would you settle for the June Allyson-gone-auburn look?" Polly asked diplomatically.

Revel's party was a smash; even Revel had fun. There were none of the usual parlor games. Instead, Polly played all of her newest record albums and coerced the youngsters into actually dancing together. She was the instructor, the motivator and a participant. Her happy energy was contagious and the most bashful and reluctant of the preteeners was infected. Normally, the boys only came to these "dumb parties" for the cake and ice cream and because their mothers said they had to. This one turned out to be different. Heck, everyone got a present—a good one, too—not just the birthday girl. Revel's Aunt Polly was definitely okay in their books.

Polly was still basking in the afterglow of her success the following Sunday, the nineteenth, as she and Matthew relaxed on their breezy front porch.

A strange car stopped abruptly on the street in a cloud of dust and a man quickly got out and hurried toward them. Matthew squinted against the bright glare, and recognized Ethel's father, Horace Wangler, Jr. The habitually well-groomed, fashion-conscious gentleman looked a wreck.

"Mr. Wangler! This is a pleasant surprise. I knew you had come for a visit," Matthew said politely in greeting. The figure stood now in a stupor. "Uh— I thought you were on the river with Luke." Still the figure stood in petrified silence. "Uh, I don't think you've met my wife, Polly."

The glazed eyes didn't see Polly's outstretched hand. "Luke— Luke—" The congested voice was scarcely audible. "Luke is— is dead."

Although shocked by the news, Matthew and Polly were forced to put aside their rising anguish to deal with Mr. Wangler. They supported him inside to a couch and covered him with blankets, trying to quiet his shaking body and stem his hysteria. The facts unfolded, bit by bit.

Horace Wangler, Jr., and three of his closest country-club cohorts had descended upon his daughter and son-in-law with plans to shoot the rapids on the middle fork of the Salmon River. He had given up control of his father's property to Noah soon after the senior Mr. Wangler and wife had passed on, and Ethel and Luke had been settled. The land, and working the land, had never enthralled him. Mr. and Mrs. "Junior" had moved to Boise, where he dabbled in state politics and lived the easy life. But he still owned some percentage of the vast acreage and if Mr. Wangler craved a little adventure, Luke was always ready to act as his guide. John and Luke couldn't be spared simultaneously at this busy time. Nor could Matthew. So Luke had arranged for a professional mountaineer, Chet Stoddard, to man the sweep, the second raft that carried the provisions, camping equipment and supplies. The wooden McKenzie boats had been used for these excursions since the 1930s. They were tapered on both ends, built for the shifty currents, highly maneuverable. But since World War II, the lighter, more accessible and less expensive surplus rubber rafts had become the popular choice.

The two rafts had put in at Boundary Creek—identified by the locals in the know as Dagger Falls—on Tuesday. Day one of the five-and-a-half-day trip had been spectacular—a trifle hairy perhaps for the novices, but exhilarating, all the same. Eagles, ospreys, moose, even a bear with two cubs climbing a tree were seen. Days two and three had been equally rewarding. They had opted to pass up possible rests at Indian Creek and Harrah's Middle Fork Lodge. The white water was potentially hazardous, and this year the low river level made the going more treacherous because of the volume of exposed boulders. But everything had fared so well and everyone was in such high spirits, there hadn't seemed to be a need for extra stops.

On day four, the weather had suddenly turned. A summer mountain storm hit hard. Rain pelted them, lightning flashed close, the wind boiled the already churning waters. Their vessel was tossed about like a cork in a washing machine. Life jackets were always a requisite, and now any grumblers about their bulkiness knew why.

Luke had tried to shout over the turbulence, but only scattered words had come through. "Try—get—camp—jump—say so."

One of the risks feared most on the river was capsizing, primarily because if the boat tipped over on top of someone, he could be trapped underneath. The rule was that if an upset seemed imminent, jump as far away from the craft as possible. And hope for the best.

Luke had navigated with as much control as he could muster, but the elements were formidable. A particularly severe jolt had jetted one of the men to the other side of the raft, instantly lopsiding the balance.

"Can't—keep—*jump!—now!* Fer Christ's sake—*jump!—jump!*"

Desperately, one by one, they had leapt into the icy, wicked water. Luke had stayed until all were clear and then he, too, had sprung over the side. The raft bobbed for a few seconds and then was tossed end over end. Luke lunged and grabbed the cords laced around the underside of the raft, and then he managed to manipulate the floundering men toward the relative stability of the ropes.

"Hold on!—slower—up a ways!" The five miraculously avoided the jutting slabs, averted the peril of the whirlpool hole on the bottom side of rocks, and after what had seemed an eternity, found themselves drifting in calmer waters. The storm had subsided as abruptly as it had begun. They clung as they were. No one had the strength to attempt to right the raft. It was only then that Horace Wangler, Jr., had seen the ugly gash on Luke's temple, spurting blood.

"No matter," Luke gulped hoarsely. "Camp soon—watch for sweep."

In their lives there had never been a more welcome sight than the other raft moored ahead, smoke spiraling up from a fire. Pitched tents were ready and waiting to shelter the battered bodies. From the shore, a dry silhouette beckoned to the bedraggled crew. Chet Stoddard waded in and pulled the boat and men ashore. He first secured the raft and then helped his party.

"That be a nasty-lookin' scrape ya got there, Luke. Better see t' it," Chet drawled.

"I'll jus' sit here a spell. Feel kinda dizzy. Be okay—jus' tired, I guess." Luke spread out as if to nap.

Chet hustled about, making everyone comfortable, doling out hot coffee fortified with good scotch. He brought a cup to Luke, but Luke shook his head weakly.

"Gonna be sick." And then Luke vomited, violently. Chet cleaned up as best he could and tried to cleanse Luke's wound. He practically carried Luke to one of the tents and settled him in his sleeping bag.

"I don't like th' way he's actin'," Chet had said worriedly to the others. "I think we'd better pull inta th' Flying Bee tomorra, mebbe call fer a plane. But we'll see how he be in the mornin'. What th' hell happened, anyways?"

The men all spoke at once, explaining the details. The most logical guess was that Luke had struck the oar when he vaulted overboard. Perhaps he had been a little careless because he had delayed so long.

Chet kept checking on Luke while he fixed supper. "Jus layin' there," he reported to the anxious group. Sleep came easily to the weary campers, but not to Chet. He continued his vigil outside Luke's tent in case he was needed. At dawn, he went in to rouse Luke, but Luke did not respond to Chet's voice or his gentle probing. Luke's pulse was feeble and his color was ashen.

Chet hastily woke the others and barked out orders. "We gotta git goin'. Piss if ya hafta, then shake a leg! Gonna leave th' gear here an' one raft, git it later. Luke's bad. Put all the sleepin' bags on the bottom so he rides easy. Couple of ya take his feet so's I c'n lift 'im in. Com'on, chop chop."

The men were bewildered and frightened, but somehow pulled themselves together. The fire was extinguished, Luke was placed carefully in the raft and the group made its way toward the Flying Bee. Luckily, the river was smooth on this stretch, the white water began again below the Flying Bee.

Once there, Chet radioed for an airplane and a doctor. Then they waited. Two workers volunteered to make the arduous trudge up to the vacated campsite and retrieve everything left behind.

Late in the afternoon, they heard the sound of engines and rushed toward the rustic landing strip. Dr. Bob Seaton was rushed to Luke's bedside. The diagnosis hadn't taken long.

"Under no circumstances can he be moved now," Dr. Seaton had gravely announced. "Far as I can tell, he suffered a contusion with the hematoma—a blood clot—probably going to the brain. I don't know if there is anything I can do to save him. I'm sorry."

Sunday morning, they were told the worst. Luke had died during the early hours, never regaining consciousness. The group had been stunned, demoralized, obviously not fit to act. Chet had been forced to assume leadership, putting his own sorrow on hold.

"This is what we hafta do. Wangler and th' doc 'll take Luke back in th' plane. Ain't room fer us all. Me an th' rest 'll go on down an git out at th' confluence, like Luke set up. One of th' boys here 'll take th' sweep." Everyone had been grateful a plan had been decided for them, and had carried out Chet's instructions, woodenly and with heavy hearts.

Mr. Wangler had gradually stabilized and become more rational during the telling of his story.

"And I came here straight away, I didn't know where else to go. John lives too close to—I just couldn't face Ethel, or your folks, Matthew, alone. I just couldn't. Forgive me for this added burden. I realize Luke's loss is pain enough. But please, help me, I beg you to help me tell them," and Mr. Wangler started to falter again.

"We'll both go with you, you won't be alone," Polly assured the distraught man. "You've had a heartrending ordeal, we know, but try to compose yourself as much as you can—for your daughter's sake. She's going to need your strength." Matthew, who felt he had had the wind knocked from him, glanced at Polly, thankful that she was there.

Pulling himself together, Matthew recommended they see Willamina and Noah first. Perhaps then, the five of them could go break the news to Ethel.

When Matthew pulled up in front of the old house, John's truck was there and so was Ethel's car. Evidently the two families had gathered at Mama's and Papa's after church. So be it. The three bearers of tragedy heaved heavy sighs, prayed for counsel, braced themselves and opened the screen door.

Jude sat next to Matthew and Polly in the church packed with mourners. He drank in every detail, the beautiful floral arrangements, the woeful Basque melodies that dulled the sounds of sorrow, the light dancing and streaming through the stained glass windows, the simple sturdy casket. And the faces! What each one reflected, the degree of grief each showed. His mind began to drift to the day Thelma and Keane had been remembered. He wondered if the sun had shone? What expressions had the faces of those attending worn that day?

Then Jude caught himself. He compelled his thoughts to return to the present. Today he must be strong and in control for his family.

Noah stood straight and tall, a mountain of a man, and looked a long time at the gathering. And then, he spoke clearly, without faltering.

"The Lord giveth and the Lord taketh away. Blessed be the name of the Lord. We cannot question. Each of us, many times, go down river. This time, our Lord chose to take a son, a husband, a father, a brother, a friend." Noah's eyes sought Jude's before going on. "Nine year ago, he bring a daughter and grandchild to live with him. We must trust the Lord's will."

Tears were streaming down Noah's face, unnoticed as he continued. Willamina was valiantly struggling to follow Noah's lead, clinging to her faith, trying not to succumb to profound grief. Even so, she couldn't stop a few audible sobs from escaping.

John and Lila couldn't even try to hide their misery. John looked a broken man, slumped over in the pew, a lost soul.

Ethel was inconsolable, lashing out with all the accusatory yet pathetic questions: *Why? Why?* What saved her from total breakdown was the measure of courage she was compelled to show for the sake of young Noah and Luke, Jr., a veneer which hopefully would one day be the bridge to acceptance and peace.

Matthew, through his sorrow, thought of Polly and their plans. Matthew saw Noah, standing alone, and knew their move would have to wait. He couldn't take himself away from Papa and Mama now, not yet, not for a while. And for Luke—maybe they hadn't been as close as they could have been, but he had loved Luke the best he could—for Luke, he had to be around for Ethel and the kids. He believed the role he had created for Ethel in the business would help her get through this. But it would all take time. How much time, he didn't know. He only hoped Polly could hang on.

Polly watched her husband, watched him looking at Noah, then at Willamina, at John, at Ethel, and she knew what he was thinking. She was thinking the same thing. She felt she could help, too, and she wanted to help. Especially with Revel, who was clutching her arm this very minute, who was confused about death and why it had intruded upon her eleven-year-old world. Polly reached over and clasped Matthew's hand in hers. And squeezed. "Don't worry, we can manage!" the gesture said.

Jude saw it all. And he understood what was in their hearts.

III

20

Beating the air with the manuscript he held, Wade bellowed, "This is insulting! That's what this is! How dare Max submit this—this—"

"Are you trying to tell me you don't like it? That it's cow dung? Just spit it out, loud and clear! Because I couldn't agree with you more. Max is reaming you. I hinted at it last year, but I'll say it today—Max is fucking you around. I'd sure like to clean his plow!"

"You what? That's a new one!"

"Beat the shit out of him!" Jude translated.

"Oh! Well, I'm not exactly thrilled with the man myself. But why? Why after all these years would he turn on me? It doesn't make sense!" Wade paced the floor of his study.

"Sure it makes sense—now. It all started when Max left the Charles Feldman Agency and became Goldbloom Associates, and you loyally followed him."

"Of course I did! What's wrong with that?"

"Not a thing! Then he used you as his in-house star to attract other clients." Jude could see another objection coming and held up his hand to ward off the interruption. "Hear me out! There's nothing so wrong with that, either. But his stable increased as more of the established money-makers returned from the war, and a whole crop of new young faces surfaced, and so you gradually became less important to Mr. Max Goldbloom. So what happened then? He began to use you as a bargaining tool. For instance, he promises the studio to deliver you for picture A,

no matter if it's bad for your career, so long as the studio casts
his client Joe Schmo in picture B, which would be very good for
Mr. Schmo's career. And very good for Mr. Goldbloom's pocketbook.''

Wade stopped marching around and gaped at Jude, dumbfounded. ''Is that possible? Or legal? I do know that such a
practice, if it exists, is certainly not ethical!''

Jude answered gently, for he could see Wade was shaken.
''Yes, it is possible. I don't know if it's actually illegal. And yes,
you are right, it certainly is not ethical. In the past, let's say the
last two or three years, what percentage of the films you made
were ones you had initially turned down? And why did you
change your mind? Be honest now, 'cause I know the answer!''

Wade slumped glumly into an armchair. ''I don't need to take
much time to review. *All of them.* I had refused all of them. And
you had been in absolute agreement. Then, each time, Max persuaded me to reconsider, saying perhaps I had acted hastily,
hadn't realized the high hopes the studio had for the project, the
elaborate budget and plans they had prepared. Hah! And how
they counted on me to come through, as part of their family.
Well, no need to tell you, the family statement always got to me,
as I guess Max knew it would. And so I would relent, telling you
we should rely on Max's experienced judgment. What a stupid
fool I was—am.''

A pause. Jude knew how Wade's mind worked. He knew
Wade could never be the squeaky wheel that gets oiled. He knew
Wade always assumed everyone spoke the truth; he never suspected ulterior motives. He knew it was not in Wade's makeup
to be assertive. And he also knew Wade found rejection dis-
turbing.

''You're not the fool, Wade,'' he responded quietly. ''I am. I
should have fought you harder, told you what my belly was telling me. But I couldn't be downright positive about what was
happening. There's been a lot of funny goings-on, I think, but I
didn't believe I knew enough to start sounding off. I should have
warned you when I had the first inkling something was up.''

Another pause. Wade turned and contemplated Jude.
''Strange. It really doesn't bother me so much about this script,
or that script, or even the status of my career. I would have to be
a complete idiot not to realize box-office receipts on my pictures

were falling. But that is not all-important. No, what troubles me is the treachery, and the reason or reasons behind that treachery, and my damn-fool childish naiveté. Perhaps the time has come for me to pay a little attention. Tell me, what 'funny goings-on' have you noticed?''

"Well, there's this agent double cross we've just talked about. The succession of those mediocre films did cause the audience to lose some interest. But it's not irreversible if we correct it soon," Jude hastened to add. "Then, uh..." Now Jude hesitated.

"Then what, Jude?"

"Hell, Wade, you're going to think I'm paranoid or something."

"I assure you that I won't. Please continue." Wade used his Peter Pan smile.

Jude had to laugh. "You are a rogue, you know that don't you?" A sigh. "Okay, here goes! First. After the success of *Who Did Done It?*, wouldn't you think the studio would have opened more doors to me? Especially when you consistently asked them to do just that? You indicated you wanted me as associate producer on all your pictures, and they explained about their problem with seniority. Bull! So they threw out a few crumbs, and for a while I did sit in on some meetings for the planning of your movies. Laying the foundation, priming me, they said. But any suggestions of mine landed on deaf ears, even if they were good, unless those ideas were later ordered directly through you."

"Didn't we discuss that issue and decide that they felt threatened by your rapid progress? And that we would bide our time? Or am I forgetting something?" Wade asked.

"Yes—I mean, no you're not forgetting—yes, we discussed. But look at the timing—*Who Did Done It?*, end of 1946. The Hollywood Ten, end of 1947. That Communist accusation about me, early 1948. The postponement of upgrading Jude Abavas, 1948. The beginning of the inferior scripts to Wade Colby, 1949."

The room was noisy with the clicking of the two brain machines. Wade leapt from his seat and strode purposefully to the wet bar in the corner of the paneled cabinets.

"I think, I *know* I need a drink! You?" Jude shook his head. Wade swallowed one jigger straight, then mixed a cocktail. He walked slowly back to his chair, savoring the spirits, trying to absorb the implications Jude had raised.

"I believe our joint downward curve is related, Wade, not only to their so-called intimidation of me, or to the unfaithfulness of Max, but to that whole Communist business in '48. You think you stopped that guy from slinging mud at me. What you may have done is given him more ammunition, which he decided to use against you, as well. Guilty by association. Ever heard of that, my friend?"

Wade was stupefied. "It is so preposterous, it could be true. Has everyone gone mad? Me—or you?—a *Communist?* It's ridiculous!"

"Here's something else for the pot. Maybe the studio didn't fully buy that hogwash. Maybe they saw the tittle-tattle as a means to an end. Things are changing around Hollywood. Louis B. Mayer is out, and maybe the other old gray Mayers ain't what they used to be, either. Maybe Twentieth Century Fox grabbed on to this hearsay to ease out of a very expensive contract, losing me at the same time, and paving the way to use less expensive players."

"There's another zinger! Boy, are you working overtime today." Wade felt like a boxer just hit with a combination of punches.

"It seems to fit, Wade. I could be way off base, but my gizzard says I'm not. And we can't square off with a libel suit, even though we signed those damn affidavits saying we're not affiliated with Communists. The bastards can cover themselves. They could argue they never heard any stories, never called anyone a Commie, they only want what's best for the country. They had been so crushed by what came out of the second hearings in 1951, not to mention the sessions in 1947. Why, they had embraced some of those people as family before they knew the shameful truth. No, we're afraid Mr. Colby and Mr. What's-his-name are only trying to excuse the fact that Mr. Colby's popularity has slipped dramatically, despite all our efforts."

Wade rose for a refill. "You would have made one hell of a lawyer—I'm ready to throw our case out of court. You ready yet for a drink?"

"No, thanks."

"Well, providing there is some truth to your allegations—which I'm afraid there might be—what do you propose we do? Or *is* there anything we can do?"

Jude waited until Wade was settled once again before he stood up and paced the room, punctuating his staccato outpourings with clenched knuckles and pounding fists.

"I've been kicking around a lot of ideas trying to sort things out. First, I think we should just ignore the Commie bit, and not play into their hands. Papa always said, 'The fish wouldn't be caught if it didn't open its mouth.' Second, we should dump Max. Pay him off if we have to, or maybe a new agent can split commissions until Max's contract is up, or maybe we have to pay double commissions. I don't know, but either way it's worth the loot 'cause we know Max is not going to change his spots. Third, we need to decide who you want to represent you. From what I've seen, Music Corporation of America is a top contender, one of, if not the best."

Jude stopped for air, and time, before dropping his next bombshell.

"After that, if I were you, I would ask to be released from Twentieth, through my new agent, of course. In the end, that might help them save face, as well as being what's best for you— keep the sort-of-friendly relationship you've held together. I know that's important to you."

Wade wasn't quite as shocked as Jude had anticipated. But he was quiet for a spell. "Hmm. How can I feel sad and scared and revved up all at the same time? I wonder if this is how a little bird feels when it faces leaving the nest. Probably has more courage than I. Hmm. Suppose all of this Part One could happen. Do you have a Part Two?"

"Well, I have an outline, an idea. I'm not sure of the ending, though." Jude leaned toward Wade, took a deep breath and then dived in. "Television didn't go away like everyone thought it would. It's spread faster than weeds. I don't know the exact numbers, but I bet these days, people watch *I Love Lucy* or *The Ed Sullivan Show* or the *Arthur Godfrey* or whatever, more than they go to movies. I don't mean movies are dead, Wade, but I'll kiss your ass at the Brown Derby if television doesn't become as important, or more important, to the public in just a few years."

"Dear Lord, let him be right! The penalty is not a pleasing prospect to me!"

"Just a figure of speech. Trust me, you're not my type. But you do get my drift. I think, too, the big studios are gradually

running out of gas and the future belongs to television and independents." The big finale. "So, the upshot is, I would like to
see you do a television series. Get in while there's still a ground
floor." Jude just passed over Wade's dropped jaw. "And, I
would like to see you own it—produce it, finance it—I mean *own*
it. And, I would like to see it filmed at the studio *we* buy! There,
I've shot my wad. Now you can tell me I'm off my rocker and
there is no beginning or ending to Part One or Part Two." Jude
flopped down, spent from nervousness.

"I'll put my own words in my own mouth, thank you very
much. I'm just not sure what the words are yet. You've dished
out a lot at an alarming rate, and I need time to digest it. Boy, do
I need time!"

Jude nodded, understanding. He was encouraged that Wade
hadn't flat out told him he was out of line and to forget these
pipe dreams. He padded over to the bar, picking Wade's glass up
on the way. A drink definitely seemed in order now. He placed
a full tumbler by Wade and brought his own back to the chair
facing Wade. He waited, his mind racing.

Wade sipped. Shifted. Sipped. Wheezed. Sipped. Sniffled.
Sipped. Shifted. Sipped. Sipped. Sipped. Jude fixed another
round. Wade sipped. Sighed. Sipped. "Well!" Wade's loud ex-
clamation jarred the hushed surroundings. "Well!" he repeated, just a smidge quieter, staring at his drink. "This all boils
down to one question—do I have the balls or not? And the answer is—I don't know." He looked up at Jude. "I want to be
nervy. I want to be bold!"

"But you have nerve! You are bold! Think of all the risks
you've taken—flying airplanes, riding motorcycles, skiing—you
name it, you've done it! And look at the chance you took with
me. I could have been a crook or an ax murderer, or some other
kind of bad guy!"

"Jude, listen to me. Those were toys I was playing with, I
wasn't challenging the status quo. And you! You were never a
chance, you were my one flash of brilliance. Look, I can handle
getting rid of Max, even moving to MCA—if they'll have me."

"Will you stop? Of course they will!"

"We'll see! And Noah is right, we should not dignify garbage
with recognition." Wade averted his eyes briefly and then fixed
them solidly on Jude. "What frightens me is taking those other

giant steps. Leaving, cutting the umbilical cord, plunging into unknown waters—maybe shark-infested waters—presuming the inhabitants of this new world would accept me, then let me compete in a leadership capacity."

Wade laughed. "When I listen and hear your words, Jude, I am really tempted, even excited. But when I talk and hear *my* words, I'm scared shitless."

Jude remained silent. It was Wade's career, Wade's future they were tossing around. It was also his career, but he wouldn't have one if it wasn't for Wade, so Wade came first. He really believed he was on track, but he couldn't give a guarantee. The next move had to be Wade's.

"Why do things have to change, Jude? I like my life, I like my profession. Believe it or not, I try hard to be good at what I do, and I would like to continue doing it. Not for the money, or the quote—fame—unquote. But because it is my job, something I can contribute, no matter what the degree of contribution might be."

Jude wanted to interrupt, wanted to reassure Wade of his value, but thought better of it and kept still.

"I'm almost thirty-eight years old and I've had a good run. What the hell, what difference does it make to anyone if I make a fool of myself? Who else really cares? I can't stop progress, I have to either wither on the vine or join the forward march. If I'm too old to change then I'm too old to live. I say we have a Part One *and* a Part Two. And the ending? To be continued! And if I'm drunk, let's shake hands on the deal before I sober up!"

The two stood, put down their glasses, and solemnly shook hands. And then they both started jumping and hopping around the room, yelling and laughing like schoolboys excused for summer holiday.

Blackie and Whitey heard the commotion and assumed this was their cue to run in and raise a little Cain, too. Both Basa, who was a mite hard-of-hearing now, and Floozy waddled in a bit later, sniffed around and plopped down in a corner to watch the merrymaking.

"I am so high I could fly!" Jude cried, hardly able to get the words out straight he was so happy.

"So am I! So am I!" Wade matched Jude's excitement.

"There's so much to do I don't know where to start. What time is it? Shit, it's too late to do anything now."

"Not too late to have another drinkie. Good God, I think I am drunk—probably the only way I could make this decision!"

"Not true! It's a big day, for Christ's sake, we deserve to celebrate. Now, let's see—don't know what to say first. Well, uh, I have an idea for a story line I want to kick around with you. And we have to go over a list of writers—there's an approach to the networks I'd like to run by you, too, and if you agree, we could suggest it to your new reps. And that's number one on our agenda—new representation."

"I feel wonderful! And free! And wonderful! Wunderbar! Wunderbar!" Wade promenaded around the room singing his best, but not very good, Howard Keel impersonation, at the top of his lungs.

Jude joined him for one or two equally bad bars of music. But his brain was still in high gear. "First chance we get, I'll drive you over for a look at a small studio that's kind of up for grabs now. Needs some work, but it could be good for us." Jude abruptly stopped.

"Wassa matter? Why'd you stop?"

Quietly, Jude said, "I am a complete nincompoop. Here I keep saying 'we' this and 'we' that and 'us,' and we've never even talked about being actual partners. I mean, I *work* for you, and would—and will—do everything and anything I can to make certain these plans happen right."

Jude hesitated, then went on. "But it just dawned on me, you might not *want* a partner. I know you don't need help financing, but I have saved up some, and if—if it's okay, I'd like very much to invest in your new company, whatever percentage it's worth. But if not, I understand—honest—and nothing will change, nothing!"

In an apologetic tone, Jude continued. "Sometimes I get so worked up, my mouth starts spouting before my mind tells it to. So there's no problem. Either way, I—"

"Will you just shut up, please!" Wade had to collect himself. "You are already my partner, there's never been any question, with or without money. But of course, this will be the perfect solution and the perfect combination. Now, enough of that nonsense! Let's get down to important things, like, the name. What shall we call—us?"

Jude tried to cover up the emotion that threatened to overcome him. He felt as close to this man as if they were blood relatives.

Hoarsely, Jude volunteered, "Ah, well, it must be Col something."

Wade took it from there. "Col—Colaba. No, Colbav. No—Colvas. Colvas—*Colvas*—not bad. How do you think that sounds?"

Jude was still having trouble swallowing. "That sounds—that sounds absolutely unbelievable."

"Then Colvas it is! A toast to Colvas Incorporated! And now the president—" Wade gestured to himself "—and the chief executive officer—" pointing to Jude "—of Colvas Inc. will clink and drain their glasses."

The two collapsed into their chairs with that last burst of exertion, heady, debilitated, not just from the considerable amount of alcohol consumed, but from being overwhelmed, weakened by the realization of their bond. And the enormity of their resolutions.

"Many more days like these and I'll end up an alcoholic. Maybe I already am," Wade groaned, looking at Jude like a little boy. "And now I'll bet you are going to make me watch television all the time."

21

Hollywood, California
March 1953

"You may go in now, Miss Pope," announced the gracious and efficient Muriel Brewster, secretary-assistant to Jude Abavas.

Penelope Pope straightened her skirt as she rose, fluffed her long ash blond hair in the conveniently placed mirror, sent a silent prayer toward the heavens and crossed her fingers for luck as she was ushered into the inner office. She didn't know what to expect, her agent didn't have much inside scoop about Jude Abavas or the embryonic Colvas Studios. It was definitely new—the faint smell of paint still lingered in the air! All she had been told was that she had an audition for a role opposite Wade Colby. Wade Colby! Only one of the biggest names in Hollywood! She hoped she had a chance.

She hadn't been prepared for Jude Abavas. He wasn't exactly the stereotypical version of a casting director or a producer. His tall muscular frame was overpowering and the intense black eyes that looked down at her, from the roughly hewn handsome face, were uncharacteristically kind, even gentle.

Jude hadn't been prepared for Penelope Pope, either. It wasn't only that she was beautiful—he had been smothered in pretty girls recently—she radiated a softness, a freshness that matched her dewlike skin. Her brown eyes met his without guile.

"How do you do, Miss—" he looked down at the résumé on his desk "—Miss Pope."

"Please call me Penelope, or Penny, if you like. I think that would make me less nervous. I haven't been on many major auditions and I'm—I'm a little scared."

"That's okay, so am I. I've never been a producer before. Why don't we start with you telling me a bit about yourself. By the way, I like Penelope—sounds nice, kind of old-fashioned." Jude settled into a chair near hers, instead of behind the desk, to make the meeting more informal.

"Dad tells me I was named after an old girlfriend of his."

"He was taken with the name, but not with the lady?"

"I guess so. Mom used to tease him about it a lot. Anyway, he's a sound technician at Metro-Goldwyn-Mayer. Mom is a housewife. Nothing too exciting about us, fairly ordinary, middle-class. Mom did go back to substitute teaching to help out with my college tuition. And I worked at the campus bookstore my first two years, until I became so involved in the drama department. Then my parents decided they could manage. Is this what you want to know, or am I rattling on in the wrong direction?"

"I want to know everything. You're doing just fine. Where did you go to school? And was drama your major?"

"I graduated from UCLA in 1950. I was always inclined toward the arts and I guess I just assumed I would be a teacher, probably of literature, and then—"

"What made you change your mind?"

"Well, this is going to make me sound silly, I think—" Penelope blushed, but valiantly continued. "But it's the truth. The young man I was dating—actually, I really liked him a lot, even thought I was in love for a while—well, he was active in the little theater group and persuaded me to join. We worked together a great deal and it was wonderful—the camaraderie, the challenge, the excitement of the performance, the high afterward— oh, it was wonderful! And intoxicating! And fun! And gratifying! All of it!"

Jude gave her a high score for enthusiasm. And honesty. "So that gave the teaching profession the old heave-ho!"

"Sort of...well, in fact, yes! And eventually the romance, too, I'm afraid," she added ruefully.

"How so?"

"Are you sure this is what you need to hear about?"

"Absolutely! Unless you're uncomfortable telling me."

"No, it's not that. I feel so asinine. I mean, what does my love life have to do with anything here?"

"Nothing! But you see, all this helps me to know the person. And that is what's important—who this person is, what makes this person tick, how this person thinks and feels. It's a shame these interviews can't be done over a period of days or weeks, but unfortunately, time doesn't allow for that, so we have to take shortcuts. Is that okay?"

"Yes. I understand."

Points for intelligence. And frankness.

"Well then, 'Penelope Faces Life,' continues..."

And a sense of humor.

"We had a ball, even spoke of wedding bells—after we were a success, of course. Then, during our last show before graduation, a talent scout from M-G-M—no one my father knew—asked me to come to the studio and talk about a basic contract. Nothing fancy, standard deal, but it was an opportunity. And it was encouraging. He had to have seen something he liked on that stage. The acting bug had struck again, I was hooked."

"What about your friend?"

"That was the problem, or the start of it anyway. The man didn't say anything to Chuck—that was my friend's name—only me. Chuck was very disappointed and frustrated, especially since he felt he was responsible for my being there in the first place, and then for encouraging me to grow as an actress. A bit of the Svengali attitude, but without evil intent. I think he expected me to turn down the offer because he wasn't included. When I didn't, he became angry and announced he was going to New York, where real artistry thrived. And so he did!"

"That's too bad. Were you terribly upset? Excuse me, the intercom—"

Jude quickly rose from his chair and flipped the switch at the desk, "Yes, Muriel? Apologize for me and try to reschedule for tomorrow morning, explain I got tied up, okay? Oh, is Mr. Colby around somewhere? Oh, that's right, I forgot. Leave word with Dolly for him to call me, please. Thanks." Jude returned to his seat.

"I'm sorry, you were saying? This Chuck up and left for New York."

"Mr. Abavas, I feel I'm taking up too much of your time. I can hear that you're busy—"

"But *this* is my business! Look, I'd like to talk more. And I'd like to introduce you to Mr. Colby, but he won't be back for a while. Am I keeping you from an appointment or anything?"

"Gosh, no, Mr. Abavas."

"Good! It's almost lunchtime. I usually take lunch in my office. What if I send out for something for us?"

Two hours later, Jude felt he had a good understanding of Penelope Pope. She had been hurt and bewildered by Chuck's behavior. She had believed they'd both been striving for a chance and that if the situation had been reversed, she would have been thrilled for him and supportive. The disillusionment, the realization of his selfishness and that he had never cared enough about her, and the abrupt dismissal of their relationship, had taken a while to sort out and get over.

M-G-M had kept her on for two years, but last July did not exercise the option on her contract. While there, she had been given some small parts, something between an extra and a featured player. She had studied diligently with Lillian Burns, the best drama coach in the industry. She had made two tests, good ones, for two different films, but the roles had gone to bigger-name players. The environment on the lot had changed after the all-powerful L. B. Mayer had been dethroned by Dore Schary. There was a decided split in the ranks, a civil war between the old guard and the new. Instead of having "more stars than there are in the heavens" in its stable, MGM was allowing contracts to lapse. The studio's remaining names were loaned out to other studios more than ever before. Economy was the order of the day. Realism replaced the lavish escapism as the focus in films. There was tension in the air, and Penelope was now glad to have been released. Her father agreed, bemoaning the fact she hadn't been around to witness "the great years."

A Howard Hughes spokesman had made a few overtures about signing her, but she'd flat out declined. She'd heard enough rumors to know she didn't want any part of that scene, whatever it might be. The directors for whom she had worked evidently liked her performances because they still cast her in their pictures whenever possible. So she was comfortably situated. But she had not made a big splash.

Jude contained his mounting excitement about the possible discovery sitting across from him. He didn't want to send any premature signals that could cause a letdown later; he needed to see Wade and Penelope together, and naturally, he had to get Wade's reaction. But all his years of observing people, all the films he had devoured, all the hours he had spent scrutinizing the silhouettes that peered at him from covers of magazines, had fostered an intuition. He had carefully studied the personalities captured by *Life* and *Look* and *Time, Modern Screen* and *Photoplay. Ladies Home Journal* and *Redbook* and *Vogue* and *Harper's Bazaar.* He had spent hours analyzing why these particular people warranted such visibility, trying to decide what message it was they conveyed to the public. What was their special spark that ignited the public's fire? There was no single explanation, of course—it wasn't only classic beauty, or sensuality, or vivaciousness, or vulnerability—but there was always something or some mixture of somethings that set them apart from the rest. And that *something* was what he was receiving from Penelope Pope.

"Where is everyone?" Wade wanted to know, breezing into the office. "Muriel's gone, Dolly's gone— Oh! excuse me, I didn't mean to barge in." Wade started to make a quick retreat when he saw that Jude had company.

Jude hastened to retrieve him. "The ladies are on a late lunch break and don't you dare go away. You are just the man we've been waiting for! Meet Penelope Pope. Penelope, this is Wade Colby."

Wade looked at Jude with some surprise. He knew Jude had been interviewing actresses for days, but only a couple had made it as far as an introduction to Wade, and even then with a degree of reluctance. But Jude actually seemed eager today, with an unconcealed—to Wade, anyway, it was unconcealed—gleam in his eye.

Then Wade took a good look at the girl and realized that Jude thought he had found a promising candidate.

"Well, hello. May I call you Penelope? And what have you two been chatting about while I was slaving away at an interview? I'm sure it was much more interesting than me telling the boring story of my life again!"

Two hours later, Jude and Wade apologized for having kept Penelope so long and told her they would be in touch.

One hour after that, Muriel Brewster telephoned Penelope Pope to ask if it was convenient for Miss Pope to do a test with

Mr. Colby tomorrow. The script would be delivered by messenger immediately with a scene designated for the test.

One minute after viewing the results of the test, Wade turned to Jude, reverent admiration all over his face. "You son of a gun! You picked the prize one out of a field of roses—she glows with talent! How did you know?"

One week later, the trade papers announced, "Penelope Pope has been signed by Colvas Inc. to costar with Wade Colby in World Broadcasting Systems' new series, *The Wade Colby Show,* debuting this fall."

Wade was astounded at how easily the transitions in his career had occurred. Max Goldbloom and M.C.A. had settled their issue amicably. Max had opted for a ready cash buy out, ten percent based on last year's earnings, rather than split commissions on the remaining time on Wade's contract. It was a move he would later regret because he forfeited any interest in the television revenue.

Twentieth had been "magnanimous" in their desire not to stand in the way of this giant step in Wade's profession.

The WBS Television Network welcomed Wade Colby's defection from movies to television. It was a coup. And they readily agreed to Jude's proposal that Colvas Inc. would own the package, would deliver the acceptable end product and that the network would buy exclusivity rights at a hefty price for each of the guaranteed twenty-six episodes. The rest was up to the audience.

Wade had approved the choice of the modest studio facility Jude had selected, and its purchase was the first order of business once Colvas Inc. was registered as a company. Jude's percentage investment amounted to one-fifth of the total output, but Wade insisted Jude's share be two-fifths. After all, he argued, it was Jude's vision that had conceived the entire plan, and that was worth money in itself.

The Communist innuendos faded to oblivion. Apparently, "they" had bigger fish to fry. Charlie Chaplin had just been barred from the United States as a Communist sympathizer. Julius and Ethel Rosenberg had been executed as spies. So Wade and Jude were small potatoes, not worth the effort, especially when there was no evidence to support such a claim. Although the two men had wisely decided to maintain a low profile in that arena, they discussed their own form of revenge against "them." As soon as their company was in full operation, they would use blacklisted writers, with or without anonymity, whatever the traffic would allow. It would help the displaced and unemployed men and woman, and, hopefully, make a statement.

Wade and Jude followed the lead of *I Love Lucy,* utilizing the three-camera technique in front of a studio audience that had been pioneered in 1951 by Lucille Ball and Desi Arnaz. Wade, and Penelope, as well, were excited about performing "almost live" again, as they had in their theater days.

The format of *The Wade Colby Show* was a slight deviation from the family sitcoms dominating the television screens. Wade played Wade Thornton, a wealthy Los Angeles businessman in his thirties, who inherits the responsibility of a friend's daughter when that gentleman suddenly dies. The gentleman had been like an older brother—he had watched over Wade Thornton as a lad when Wade had been sent to Arizona because of asthma. Wade Thornton had spent four happy years with this man—on the ranch his parents had bought for that purpose—but when he outgrew the asthma and returned to the city, he gradually lost touch with his friend. Until now. Of course he would honor his friend's request, even though he hadn't been aware of any baby and he certainly didn't know a thing about small children. This popular bachelor nervously sets about hiring a nanny and re-decorating the guest room for the arrival of a little girl. Enter the daughter, Penelope Smythe—lovely, twenty-something, a breath of fresh desert air, unsophisticated, naive, but not dumb. The situations, comedic and dramatic, would naturally evolve—from the complications of a beautiful woman living under the same roof with her handsome suave guardian, to their diverse back-grounds—country versus city, to the attitudes of Wade Thornton's social circle and staff.

Jude believed this premise was the perfect vehicle to capture Wade's personality—his humor, compassion, innate breeding, the occasional exposure of frailty, the abundance of passion—and that it would make him more appealing to the public than ever before. That was why the search for the ideal actress had been so vital. She had to be compatible with Wade's qualities, and yet have qualities of her own that would help depict two worlds and two philosophies. And she had to have the talent to bring those qualities to life. Penelope Pope filled the bill and then some. She was a gift from the gods!

Jude chose the other series regulars as meticulously, and even characters appearing on a single episode received the same painstaking attention. His theory was that a show had to function as a whole, as an ensemble—down to a one-line part—in order to achieve a consummate result. Like nature. One misstep would put the entire process out of balance and spoil the product. His view carried over into the technical aspects of the production, and the crew was handpicked carefully, for ability and for an understanding of team spirit. Everything and everyone had to have its own order.

Jude and Wade were mulling over a rough draft of the script for the second episode. Shooting wouldn't begin until July, but Jude insisted on ample preparation time. Fine-tuning made the dialogue sharp, the intent pure and the result tight and crisp.

"What do you think, Wade? Doesn't that line make Wade Thornton sound a little too flip? It's funny, but seems out of character to me. Say it out loud—what do you hear?"

Wade did, and grimaced. "You're right. Good line, though. Maybe there's a better way to phrase it."

"By the way, who are you taking to the Academy Awards?"

"Cripes! I forgot to ask anyone! When are they? Next Monday? We've been so damn busy. You're such a taskmaster, it's your fault. So either I skip this year or you are 'it,' old boy!"

"You can't skip it. This is the first year the Oscars will be televised and it's just too important. The timing is perfect. Why don't you take Penelope? That would be some introduction for her."

Wade seemed uncommonly flustered. "Well, she may be going already... or she may not want to go. Or she may be busy. Anyway, I don't know her well enough to invite her on a date."

"I've never seen you bashful before."

"She isn't exactly like the others!"

"No, she isn't." Jude thought a minute. "Tell you what. I could suggest that escorting her to the Oscars would be good publicity for the show. And that's no crapdip, either. How's that?"

"Except for the crapdip part, it's good. But only if you come, too, then it's really business."

Penelope was delighted at the prospect, but was immediately concerned about what to wear. The wardrobe department wasn't completely organized yet; in fact, the designer had just come on board. Dependable Muriel came through with the solution. She called Western Costume, close by on Melrose Avenue, and they assured her they could find something appropriate for Miss Pope. Muriel hinted that their assistance would not go unnoticed—Colvas Inc. would more than likely utilize the workrooms of Western Costume for *The Wade Colby Show,* which is exactly what they later did.

The roar of approval from the bleacher fans when Wade Colby stepped out of his limousine in front of the Pantages Theater on Hollywood Boulevard had to warm the hearts of the WBS brass. The crowd loved him. "Wade Colby! Wade Colby!" they chanted and yelled from the bleachers. The photographers and media closed in around him. Ronald Reagan, the television announcer, was in full swing on the sidewalk.

"Next year, they'll be calling 'Penelope Pope!' Just you wait and see," Jude whispered to Penelope.

Penelope was positively luminous in an elegant champagne-colored, cut-on-the-bias jersey dress. It had a high neck with long sleeves, and champagne satin collar and cuffs. The material molded softly to her full body. Her hair—almost the same color as her dress—was brushed back slightly, hanging loosely around her face, framing it beautifully. She was a knockout! The cameras had a field day.

Jude tried to melt into the background, but he wasn't allowed to totally escape. As the head of a studio, no matter how unpretentious, he was obliged to be interviewed, a duty he didn't relish.

After the Academy Awards ceremony, they went to Ciro's, a popular nightclub on the Sunset Strip, to have supper and to see the highly acclaimed act Kay Thompson and the Williams Brothers. Wade had the time of his life teasing Jude about Mr. Executive's new profile in Hollywood.

"So, how does it feel to be a celebrity, my shy friend?"

"I felt like a damn—a—a moron," Jude grumbled, catching himself before he used questionable language in front of Penelope.

"Don't worry, Mr. Abavas," Penelope began.

Wade broke in "Come now! I do believe the time has come that he is Jude, and I am Wade. I know we're old, but we're not that old. Or are we?"

"Of course not, Mr.—whoops—Wade. It has nothing to do with age. I guess it's just an expression of my respect and regard for the two of you. And my deep gratitude. I appreciate all you've done—the confidence and trust you've shown me—so very much."

Penelope's sincerity stopped them both. They were touched. Wade recovered first, clearing his throat. "Well, ah, we thank you. But it's what you are going to contribute to the show that's wonderful. But, ah, I interrupted you."

"Oh. What was I going to say? Oh, yes, I remember. I just wanted to assure—Jude—that he doesn't have to worry about me. I've been around enough sets to have heard ample foul language, so he needn't monitor himself that carefully."

Jude found his voice. "Well, I'm glad to hear that . . . in case I slip. But I try not to use those kinds of words, at least not in the presence of ladies."

"There is one problem you may have in dealing with Jude, however, Penelope," Wade said. "You may need an interpreter for some of his Idaho idioms. He can come up with some of the darnedest metaphors I've ever heard."

The evening turned out to set a precedent for times to come. When Jude and Wade worked late, they often grabbed a bite on the way out to the beach rather than try to keep a schedule with Anna and Eric. From the day Penelope became a part of the collaboration, it seemed perfectly logical for the three of them to go from the studio straight to dinner. Sometimes they dined at Lucy's on Melrose—the designated watering hole for VIPs from nearby Columbia Studios, Paramount, R.K.O. and now Colvas Inc.—but they were usually found at the more relaxed Dominick's, farther west on Beverly Boulevard, where the famous and not so famous could wear whatever they wanted and not be nagged by fans or cameras.

As Jude had been on his first visit to Dominick's, Penelope was fascinated by the small eccentric bistro. It was manned by

Dom, the owner and bartender, Peggy, the wife and cook, Addie, the waitress and cousin, and a cleanup person. Dom never expanded and never redecorated, always staying with the same spotless red-and-white checked tablecloths and napkins. He never turned on his neon sign, never altered the menu—except when Peggy decided to whip up a special entrée or dessert—and never allowed anyone in unless he knew and liked them. A pedestrian could walk into the empty restaurant and Dom would say, "Sorry, we're full!" This was his castle, his home, only friends were welcome. He loved music from the forties and would sing along with his favorites on the jukebox. His customers squeezed into the minuscule parking lot in back, entered through the kitchen, chatted with Peggy while she was cooking and headed straight for the bar to greet Dom, who would say, "The usual comin' up!" Then Addie would show them their table. Dominick's was the only spot where a person could come alone and not feel odd. Dom would stand behind the bar and talk for hours to some troubled soul, or just shoot the breeze with a regular. He had to know every secret in Hollywood, but there was never a leak. The natives cherished this retreat and guarded it fanatically.

The pace accelerated as the series start-date drew closer, and the threesome's dinners became more frequent. Humphrey Bogart and Lauren Bacall had their "rat pack" years before, now Jude, Wade and Penelope called themselves the "three comrades," a label borrowed from a 1938 movie classic starring Robert Taylor, Robert Young and Margaret Sullavan.

A comfortable alliance was brewed, a ragout for which all the savory ingredients were thrown in the pot, seasoned well and allowed to simmer for hours and hours. The result—a hearty, tasty, completely satisfying enjoyment of one another.

They were in the midst of a lively exchange one night at Dominick's, when a well-known actor, Timothy Davis, walked by their booth. "How are you, Wade?" he said.

"Hello, Tim. Well, thank you. You know Jude Abavas, of course. And this lovely flower is Penelope Pope. Penelope, the famous and infamous Timothy Davis. Be wary of him, my dear!"

"I've been reading about you, Penelope. Congratulations. We have met, you know. Do you remember?"

Jude could feel his neck muscles tighten. There was something about this guy's attitude that bugged him—a lot. Jude's instinctive animal reflex leapt to the fore, ready to strike. He was about to suggest that Timothy Davis move on or step outside, when Penelope answered.

"Yes, I do. Nice to see you again." And under her breath Jude heard her add, "But not really!"

Fortunately, Mr. Davis chose to saunter on toward his group, whom Addie had seated at the other end of the room. "We'll all have to get together!" was Davis's parting remark.

"Not if I can help it," Jude growled. He turned to Penelope. "What was that all about? What's with this bird?"

"Nothing, really!" Jude and Wade couldn't decide if Penelope was crying or laughing, but she was definitely gasping for breath. "I—just can't—imagine—he—he would want to see—me again." The two were relieved to find out she was desperately trying to throttle giggles.

Finally, she was in control. "Well, oh, it's so ridiculous! Well, anyway, I met him when he did a film for M-G-M. He was pleasant and entertaining on the set and toward the end of my two weeks, he asked me out for dinner. He sent his car to pick me up, first, and then go by his place to get him. His chauffeur expected me to go in, but I said I'd wait in the car, obviously not the usual routine where Tim was concerned because the driver seemed unsure what to do next."

Jude and Wade traded glances, and then sneaked a glower in Davis's direction.

"He did rally, however—" Penelope continued "—and relayed my message to the butler, I guess. It wasn't too long before Tim came out, said sorry he was late and was Perinos all right, or would I prefer La Rue. And was the temperature in the car comfortable and what kind of music would I like to listen to and where should we go afterward and on and on. At Perinos, he started drinking martinis, three or four before we ever saw a menu. Then he had to make a big fuss about the year of the champagne, but we finally did order our meal. He started to come on pretty strong, just talk at first, but then his hand kept landing on my knee...'accidentally,' you know."

Jude and Wade were becoming more disturbed; the glowers toward Davis were burning now.

"After the captain had brought our first course, Tim really became obnoxious. The hand was no longer an accident, it started creeping up my leg. I had had it! So, I don't know what came over me, but I stood up, took my chilled vichyssoise, dumped the bowl over his head and said, 'There, that should cool you off—but just to make sure . . .' Then I pulled the champagne bottle out of the cooler and dumped the ice in his lap." Penelope couldn't hold it in any longer and began to laugh. Jude and Wade burst out with loud guffaws and applause.

"I was so upset! I *adore* vichyssoise. And it seemed such a waste." The three of them were close to rolling on the floor. "He looked so stupid! And to add insult to injury, I started to shriek with laughter and ran out the door, leaving him with the captain and waiters hovering helplessly around him."

"At least—at least he didn't send you a cleaning bill," Wade was barely able to blurt out.

"Or did he?" Jude put in.

The now-unrestrained cackles and glee coming from booth number one must have unnerved Timothy Davis, because suddenly he gathered his flock and fled. The three shared the joke with Dom, who pounded his hand on the bar top, bellowing, "I love it! I love it! Next time he calls to come in, I'll ask Peggy to make vichyssoise the special!"

Jude and Wade were both oddly quiet on the drive home, each absorbed in his own thoughts. Much to Jude's shock, he acknowledged to himself that, for the first time in eleven years, he was thinking of falling in love.

The three comrades sat nervously in front of Wade's television set at the beach house with Anna and Eric. Tonight was the premiere of *The Wade Colby Show* and it was fingernail-biting time. Tomorrow, the overnight ratings would indicate if they had a hit—or a miss.

Seven episodes had been put "in the can"—they had been edited, scored, dubbed, finished. The studio audience's reception had been rampant enthusiasm. Everyone connected sensed a winner. But no one could predict the whims of television viewers.

Glasses in hand, they waited. Even Penelope needed fortification to brave this ordeal. All eyes were glued to the square box.

But six eyes also kept dodging over to Anna and Eric, to watch their responses. The couple had no idea of the importance of their role for the evening. Jude and Wade knew the two were much too honest to fake how they felt about the show; their reactions were a vital barometer of what could be expected on the show's report card. The theme music blared forth, the opening credits rolled, and the announcer introduced the show and cast. There was almost reverent silence in the room during the first commercials. And then...

Jude, Wade and Penelope watched Anna and Eric smile, chuckle, lean forward, sigh, mist a bit, relax and then belly-laugh, never seeing a flicker of disenchantment in their eyes or a waver in their attention.

At the conclusion of the show, Anna and Eric turned to Wade with genuine disappointment. "Is it over? So soon? What nice people. I like those two young people—oh—*you* two nice young people!" They gestured broadly to include Penelope. "What happens now? Do you—"

Wade laughed and hugged them. "Oh, no, you don't! No inside information! You'll see. You'll see next week, and the week after that—same time, same station. Thank you! You helped us very much!"

Anna and Eric looked bewildered. "We did? How? All we do is sit and look."

"Yes, but it's how you looked that was so wonderful!" Jude joyfully explained.

Anna and Eric retired to their apartment, shaking their heads, still not understanding what they had done, but glad everyone seemed happy.

The telephone started to ring. Wade's parents, the Pricklers, the self-appointed representatives of the entertainment industry for their set, called to give their enthusiastic endorsement. Idaho spoke—Matthew, the mouthpiece for the Abavas clan and Ketchum and Hailey and Sun Valley, told them that all of Blaine County must have called him to voice approval. The network officials, friends, peers called with a thumbs-up critique. Jude, Wade and Penelope realized tomorrow would tell more, but for tonight they were pleased with what they had seen on the tube, what they had seen on Anna's and Eric's faces and what they were hearing from all over the country.

"It works! I'll be a son of a bitch, it works!" Jude, usually the pragmatic one, had thrown all caution to the wind. "You two work, the story line works, the cast works! I feel it, I can tell! If it takes a while for the public to find us, that's okay—we'll get them. We'll saturate them with so much promotion there won't be a household in America that won't know about Wade Thornton and his ward Penelope Smythe. Because it *works!* Yahoo!"

"Whatever happens, we know we're a smash in Hancock Park, Blaine County and Santa Monica," Wade said. "But we haven't heard from Culver City yet, Penelope."

"I didn't give my folks your number, I wasn't sure if I should."

"Well, call...right now! Your daddy knows this business— Jude and I would appreciate his opinion. Besides, don't you think it's about time we met? Even if it is on the telephone?"

"Mom and Dad," Penelope was saying moments later. "Mr. Colby and Mr. Abavas want to say hello. Wade and Jude, here are Robert and Helen Pope!"

After the exchanges, Penelope reclaimed the line to talk to her parents. She was beaming when she hung up. "They were as pleased as punch you spoke with them! And Dad said they were very proud. And that the show had quality and taste. That it was too bad it wasn't a full-length feature, because it would have been like 'the good old days.' He said we reminded him of William Powell and Carole Lombard!"

"Now that, I like! Your papa makes good sense. Come, Carole and give Bill Powell here a kiss to celebrate."

Wade and Penelope embraced and he whirled her wildly around the room, falling finally on the couch in a heap.

"Now, Carole, you should give the young genius—shall we call him Thalberg?—over there a kiss, too!"

"No, no, that's all right, you don't have to do that," protested an embarrassed Jude.

"But I want to," Penelope insisted, highly animated and slightly tipsy. Her lips brushed his and her arms squeezed him tight. He was absolutely still.

"Now we're going to have some bubbly," Wade announced. "I know Eric put some bottles on ice."

"Let me get the champagne. I know where it is. I'll bring it to the bar in the living room." Jude had to leave for a minute, collect himself. He felt out of kilter—trying to read the show, allowing himself to believe in it—and then Penelope—he couldn't untangle Penelope yet.

By midnight, not one but two bottles of bubbly had disappeared. The three tried to discuss the dilemma of getting Penelope home; they spoke very slowly and deliberately, clearly intoxicated. Wade led off.

"Now, we know—what do we know?—yes, yes, we know it is out of the question for you—" pointing to Penelope "—or you—" pointing to Jude "—or you—" pointing to himself "—to drive Miss Penelope, Miss Carole, home, right?"

The heads nodded in accord.

"Well, then, we must arrive at another conclusion, right?"

The heads nodded again.

"Good! What is it? I give up!" Wade teetered over sideways.

Penelope was next. "I say, I take a taxi, right?"

"Wrong!" Jude's turn. "I say, I take Wade to his bed. Then I show Miss Penelope to the guest room." He stopped. He was talking to himself. The other two comrades had dozed off.

"Come on, buddy boy," Jude grunted as he raised Wade to his feet and supported him to his wing. He settled Wade, and went back for Penelope. Actually, there wasn't an extra guest room, Jude was the guest who had stayed—permanently. He gently scooped Penelope into his arms and carried her to his side of the house. Carefully he placed her under the sheets, and just as carefully, pulled the blanket up to her chin. He gazed at her for a long time.

Then he quietly grabbed a cover from the linen shelf and went out to the open deck. It was a balmy September night; a Santa Ana wind kept the air warm even at this late hour. His eyes sought the stars, and then he watched moonbeams playing on the water. He was sober now and sleep escaped him.

He was in love with Penelope Pope.

22

Hailey, Idaho
September 1953

"Polly, you just hafta talk to Mama and Papa" was Revel's greeting as the screen banged shut behind her.

"Oh, no! You slammed the door—that'll make my cake fall, won't it?" yelled a fretful Polly.

"How should I know? I hate to cook worse'n you!"

"Damn, damn, damn! Why can't I cook? Why can't I do anything right?" Polly was close to tears.

"What's the matter with you? You gettin' ready for your period or somethin'?" Revel was surprised. She had never seen Polly so undone about such a minor thing.

"No, I'm not getting ready for my period—I got it. Damn it to hell! I had hoped, well, never mind. I'm sorry, honey, I guess I'm a little out of sorts today. Now, what do I have to talk to your mama and papa about?"

"Oh, I get it—you hoped you might be pregnant but you're not." Revel grinned. "It's funny, I know a girl or two who would give anything to get the curse right now—and you're mad cause you did!"

"Oh, you do, do you? Well, one of those girls had better not be you, young lady!" Polly threw an affectionate arm around Revel and led her outside to the porch, muttering to herself, "Let the stupid old door clobber itself. Stupid old cake won't be good anyway."

"Don't you worry about me, I'm not that dumb! Besides, I'm not ready to lose it—*yet!*"

"Aren't you the worldly one! Be sure to tell me when you *are* ready so I can alert the *Wood River Journal.*" Polly tried to keep her scattered nerves in check. "So—okay, what's up?" Polly was more and more amazed at her thirteen-year-old sister-in-law's surging worldliness. Revel read everything she could get her hands on and was way beyond her years in many aspects.

"Well, remember we talked about my going away to a boarding school out East after graduation? And Mama and Papa didn't want to go into it? They kept saying, later! later! Well, it can't get any later! Applications have to go in soon for next September. I'm gonna have a tough enough time being accepted, as it is. I just can't be late on top of it. I have the papers from four schools—the vice principal helped me send for them and he helped me fill them out. But Mama and Papa have to say yes and sign them. Will you help me? I wanna go so bad!" Revel didn't seem very grown-up now as she pleaded with Polly for the freedom she so desperately sought.

Willamina thought she knew why Polly had come to see her alone that September afternoon, and she had already made up her mind. She might have a problem communicating with Revel, but that didn't mean she was oblivious to her daughter's needs and desires. Willamina sighed. Revel was the most challenging of all her children, even of her grandchildren, and she instinctively realized Revel needed something more than she and Noah or Hailey could give her at this time. Willamina sighed again. The world changed so quickly now, the young people didn't stay young long enough, it seemed. This rush must be due to "the bomb," and yet another war. Thank God Korea was over. It puzzled her that the more people learned, the less they were satisfied. She prayed that Revel would know how to handle this different world.

"Oh, Mother Abavas, you are absolutely first-rate!" cried Polly, hugging Willamina. "Revel will be overjoyed! Are you sure Papa Abavas will agree with you?"

"I take care of Noah. He will agree." Willamina leaned toward Polly.

"But I need favor of you. I hope you go with Revel for—these school talks."

"You mean the interviews?"

"Yes, interviews! You be better—you understand things. I know nothing."

"Well, of course, I will if I can help. I'll discuss it with Matthew, if you wish. But wouldn't it be a wonderful adventure for you—you and Revel making the trip together. Almost like a holiday, a vacation—seeing the campuses, the dormitories, the cities! I could call my old pals at the airline, and they would take extra-special care."

"No—no—no!" Willamina was emphatic. "I no go in airplane. I no go. This be where I belong, this be where I stay!"

Polly hastened to reassure Willamina of her support. "Whatever you say, Mother Abavas. I'll talk with Matthew as soon as he comes home. I don't know why he would have any objection to my going with her."

"Good! That be settled, then!"

There was quiet after that. Polly fidgeted, wrestling with indecision. She felt an urge to confide in someone about her own problems, but she wasn't positive Willamina could relate to them.

For a moment, Willamina's eyes searched Polly's face, then she said, in a low-pitched, kindly tone, "This be good for you, to go away, see other peoples, take mind off other things." Willamina opened her arms and Polly gratefully sank into the sanctuary of the older woman's bosom, the bosom that had soothed and fueled her family so many times, for so many years. Neither spoke, there was no reason to verbalize what each already knew. Polly was awed. How could this apparently unsophisticated woman harbor such insight and yet manage to speak so sparingly. How, without hearing a word, could she be so understanding about Polly's private anguish?

"I'm going to call you Little Miss Fix-it!" Matthew teased after Polly had related the day's events, omitting, however, the last part of her time with Willamina. "You are a peach to go to bat for Revel. She worships you, you know. And of course you must go with her."

Polly laughed. "Do you know what that little she-devil was doing when I left her? Naturally, she was excited. And then she immediately started pouring over fashion catalogs—to plan her wardrobe for the trip!"

"This is going to cost Papa a pretty penny! Come over here."
Polly snuggled into the nook of his arm and lay beside him on

the couch. "And what about you? What is this going to cost your papa?"

Polly's face clouded; she wished he was a real papa.

"Nothing, honey, I don't need a thing." Except a baby, she added silently.

"I'll have to put you in the world's record book—the only lady on this planet who doesn't need a new something to go traveling!"

"No—really—I don't. Everything I have for the city is practically new. We hardly ever wear regular clothes here. I mean, it's all so informal and casual. I mean, it's so easy to be just comfy."

Matthew drew her closer to him and whispered, a little sadly, "I know what you mean, sweetheart, I know. You have been more than patient, you've been a saint. Staying this long wasn't our plan, but you pitched right in alongside me with no complaints. Well, I think we're close to the end of the tunnel, I think we can begin the weaning process soon."

This was the second time today Polly had been held in protective arms. It felt good, and gave her the courage to broach the delicate painful subject to her husband.

"Matt—"

"Mmm?"

"What do you think about my going to—a doctor, a specialist in gynecology? When I go East with Revel? Maybe he could examine me, or take tests, and find out why I don't get pregnant. Maybe he could prescribe a treatment or an operation or—"

Matthew sat upright. "Wait a minute! Wait a minute!" He turned Polly so they faced each other squarely. "So that's what's been causing my girl grief. I could tell something was haywire, but I thought it was only country life getting to you. I guess I've been concentrating so hard on us breaking away from here, I didn't see anything else."

Polly traced Matthew's face with her fingers. "Honey—I didn't—and don't—want to burden you with my problem. I probably wouldn't have said anything tonight if this trip hadn't come up. Yes, it has been on my mind." Matthew questioned her with his look. "Okay, it's been on my mind *a lot*. I can't figure out what's wrong! I've read all the information available, I've talked to the doctor here. And I followed all of his instructions—taking my temperature—seducing you when I was supposed to be ripe—''

''Seducing me? Since when did I need any seducing?''

''Will you squish your male ego for a minute and let me finish? You didn't—I just wanted to make sure we took advantage of every opportunity. And nothing has worked.'' Polly's lip started to tremble.

''Polly, dearest one, don't—I'm sorry, I really didn't mean to make light of... I didn't realize how concerned you were.''

''I want so very much to give you a Matthew, Jr., or a Matilda, or both. I feel I'm not fulfilling my part of our bargain. I feel inadequate, deficient. Oh, God, Matt, what if I'm barren?''

Sobs racked Polly's body and Matthew rocked her back and forth. ''Shh—shh—oh my poor little girl, carrying this load all alone. Why didn't you share this with me? It's all blown out of proportion...there, there...'' Matthew reached for his handkerchief. ''Now blow your sweet red nose and listen to me. First. You are never—I repeat—*never* to allow something that's bothering you to fester inside you. You have to tell me—that's what makes a team, and what makes a team work. Okay?''

''B-but—''

''No buts, just say okay!''

''Okay.''

''Second. If we had talked, we might have stumbled upon some plausible answers. For example, did you ever consider the fault could be mine? That maybe my sperm don't know how to swim, or maybe they're just puny and weak? Huh? Did you think of that?''

''No. Th-that's not possible.''

''You know it is possible, but you were assuming all the guilt, weren't you? We both said, 'I do!' my darling—you were cheating me out of my portion of guilt. And that's just not right.''

The weeping had subsided. Matthew believed he was making progress.

''And then, I have heard—I'm obviously no expert—but I have heard that sometimes when a lady tries so hard to get pregnant, her muscles or whatever tense up so tight that a kamikaze sperm couldn't get through.''

Polly allowed a spark of hope in her voice. ''Do you really think that could be why?''

What Matthew had to get across to Polly now was crucial to the discussion, perhaps even to their marriage. "I don't know, sweetheart, I just don't know. Maybe. And maybe one of us has a problem of some sort. We don't know that, either. And if there is a problem, we don't know if it's correctable or not. That's what we don't know. But this is what we do know—we know we love each other! *Nothing* can change that, nothing else matters. If there is a simple answer to why—fine. If the answer is more complicated, we'll deal with it. And if the answer is a definitive 'we can't,' so be it. Would you want me to think—if the reason is me—that you wouldn't love me anymore?"

"Of course not! Don't even say such a thing!"

"I know that, my darling Polly! So please—*please*—trust my love the same way."

"It's—it's not the same!"

"Oh, yes it is! None of this makes any difference between us! It has nothing to do with us! I didn't marry a skier, a cook, a secretary—or a baby! I married you, Polly Chandler Abavas, and I love you, Polly Chandler Abavas, and I want to spend the rest of my life with you, Polly Chandler Abavas! The children we have—and we will have children whether they come from your womb and my sperm or not—will be loved and treasured because we will love and treasure them together. That is the truth. You must believe that!"

Tears had welled up in Matthew's eyes.

Polly sat still, barely able to breathe. She had tears in her eyes, too, but they were of a different nature than before. These were tears of gratitude, and of wonder. What had she done right in her life to be worthy of this man? Whatever it was, she hoped she could keep doing it. She had known from the beginning that Matthew was a gem, but in their three years of marriage, he had widened the separation that set him above all others. Suddenly, she thought of Willamina. Of course! Matthew had been shepherded by the best.

"Thank you for being in my life," she whispered. "Thank you for being my husband." Slowly, she melted into the contour of his body. "My womb and your sperm may malfunction in one department, but they sure tango nicely in another."

For the second time that day, Revel burst into the house. "Guess who I—oh—did I interrupt something?" she asked, grinning wickedly.

Matthew almost spilled Polly onto the floor, he sat up so quickly. "Don't you ever knock?"

"Sorry, but I had to tell Polly. Oh—and you, too, of course. Guess who I just talked to?"

Polly gave Matthew a shrug, resigned, and said, "President Eisenhower? I don't have a clue. Who?"

"Wade Colby!" Revel proudly proclaimed.

"You called Wade? In heaven's name, why? Why would you call Wade?" Polly and Matthew sputtered.

"Because..." A dramatic pause, then, "He is now one of my sponsors!"

Polly and Matthew sat, aghast, at Revel's audacity.

"See, I needed one more reference. An' I thought, who better than the rich and famous Wade Colby? I bet that name'll open those school doors! Isn't that neat?"

Polly was the first to find her voice. "What exactly did he say? And what did *Jude* say about your call?"

"Well, Mr. Colby—"

"Thank God she at least said 'Mr. Colby,'" Matthew muttered to Polly.

"What do you think I am—an ignoramus?" Revel retorted. "Anyway, Mr. Colby answered the phone himself and, well, I just asked him. An' right away he said, 'Why, how flattering you would chose me. It would be my pleasure to sponsor you, Revel, and I will give you a glowing recommendation indeed!'"

"Wade Colby deserves the Medal of Honor!" exclaimed Polly to Matthew. "And then?"

"Well, then Jude got on the phone, an' what could he say? I mean, Mr. Colby had already been so nice an' all, so he just sorta hemmed and hawed and said he'd call tomorrow. I'm gonna ask him if I can get some clothes in Hollywood."

"Don't push your luck!" warned Polly.

"Oh, I can handle Jude—he's a pushover! Anyway, that's my news. You two can go back to—whatever you were doin'. Bye." And Revel flounced out, to go home and dream of the ultraglamorous dress she would wear at graduation and the awesome trunk of duds she would bring to her new school.

"Thanks for your permission!" Matthew called.

"Anytime," came the faint reply.

"Who was that?" a bewildered Matthew asked. "Do you know her?"

"I believe you're related," Polly murmured, "but she did have one good idea."

"What was that?"

"For us to resume what we were doing . . ."

23

Beverly Hills, California
January 1, 1954, 12:01 a.m.

"Happy New Year!"
"Happy New Year!"
"Happy New Year!"

The three comrades formed their own circle in the midst of the revelers. Two hundred or so of Hollywood's "A list" were jammed into a sprawling Beverly Hills mansion to bring in the new year. Charles Lederer, writer and nephew of Marion Davies, and his beautiful wife, actress Anne Shirley, hosted this lavish bash every other year. An invitation cemented one's status among the elite. The ladies dazzled all in haute couture gowns and brilliant jewelry, and the gentlemen held their own in fashionable tuxedos. Photographers were not welcome—this was a private celebration—not a publicity party, which just added to the chicness of the affair. The only mildly disgruntled attendees were the long line of limousine drivers waiting for their clients outside. Mr. and Mrs. Lederer saw to it they were all well dined, but not wined.

"Que estos dias felices de tu pasado vuelvan con fecuencia en tu futuro!" Jude saluted his friends.

"That sounds very nice, but what the hell did you say?" Wade asked.

"Papa always made that toast after he'd had a few schnapps. I wouldn't attempt it in Basque, but I think I came close in Spanish. It means, 'May the happiest days of your past be but the saddest days of your future!'"

"What a dear, warm wish!" Penelope exclaimed. "I know I can't top that—I'll just say, To the two best friends a woman could ever hope for—thank you for the most wonderful year of my life. And may all your dreams come true!'' With that, she gave Jude and Wade each a precious kiss.

"Good heavens! What's left for me to say!'' Wade pondered out loud. But then he smiled. ''I'm afraid I'm going to have to be slobberingly sentimental. I'm not comfortable in this role, but it's about time for me to express myself, and I had better have at it before I get too sloshed. So, to Jude, I never thought I would say I love you to a man. But one should never say never. Because old boy—and don't take offense or get nervous—I do love you. You are the consummate confrere, and you have enriched my life beyond—beyond any possible words I know how to use. I am a very fortunate man.'' He turned to Penelope. ''Now, Penelope, you have been in my life not even a year, but you have already placed your irreplaceable stamp on my heart. I have said I love you to many women, with a completely casual and meaningless intent. But Penelope, I must now say with absolute sincerity, and extreme humbleness, I *love you!*''

Jude stumbled through the ritual of clinking glasses. He automatically mouthed the words to ''Auld Lang Syne'' and when Wade pirouetted Penelope to the dance floor, Jude vaguely waved them on. He couldn't think—didn't want to think—not yet. He only knew he had to get away. Somehow he managed to scribble a note, gave a waiter ten dollars to deliver it to Wade, and threaded a path toward the exit. His vacant eyes didn't see some of the knowing winks exchanged. His muted ears didn't hear the sly remarks, ''Uh-oh! An early casualty!'' He searched for their driver and finally found him having a cigarette in another car. His instructions were to bring Mr. Abavas home, return to wait for Mr. Colby, and please, no conversation. Jude sank into the seat of the car, then leaned forward to pour a full tumbler of scotch from the portable bar, and then lay back into the cushions again, waiting for the numbness to come. Maybe...maybe then...he could perform an autopsy on the dream that had just died.

As Wade read Jude's note, Penelope became concerned. ''What's the matter? Is Jude ill? Should we go after him?''

Wade carefully folded the paper and put it in his pocket. ''No, nothing like that. Sometimes holidays are difficult for him. He just didn't want to spoil our evening. Did he ever tell you about his wife and son? About what happened?''

Penelope shook her head.

''No, he probably wouldn't have. He isn't the sort who burdens others with his problems. I wish he would sometimes, though, it pains me to see him suffer so much alone. But he is his own person, and of course, it's part of the reason he's so special.''

He sighed. ''Since I brought up the subject, let's go over to that quiet little table in the corner, and I'll unfold a story that will tear you apart. But also help you to better understand our third comrade.''

Wade seated Penelope, then himself, and covered her hand with his. ''And then, my exquisite 'ward,' 'Uncle' Wade has another story to tell you, about a vagabond Romeo who has at last found his true love.''

Jude entered the dark, silent house with heavy steps. He went directly to the bar, picked up a bottle, woke Basa, and motioned for the dog to come outside with him. It was a clear night with a chill in the air, but Jude didn't notice the cold. He took off his patent-leather dress shoes and silk socks, looked at them with sudden loathing and heaved them toward the beach.

''Come on, boy, let's walk!'' Bottle in hand, Basa by his side, Jude walked and drank. And walked. And drank. And walked. And finally talked.

''Basa, Basa, your old master's going down the toilet. You see those dumb shoes bobbing at the edge of the water? Well, your daddy's so crazy, he blamed that—that—leather there for his misery—and threw them away. Isn't that something? Talk about drowning your sorrows—I tried to drown my shoes.'' Jude laughed hoarsely but without humor; the sound was closer to a howl.

Basa staggered a bit. ''You okay, lil' guy? Here, I'll carry you.'' Jude hoisted Basa into his arms, weaved his way back to the lanai and flopped onto a deck chair, still cradling his dog. ''I forget—I forget a lot of things, I guess. I forget we're both getting on in years! It's hard for you to walk now, isn't it, lil' guy? Hard for you to jump up on the bed, too, isn't it? Maybe I should build you a ramp. Would you like that, lil' guy?''

Jude took a long swig from the bottle. "You know who I used to call lil' guy, don't you? Yeah that's right—Keane. Our lil' guy, Keane..."

He buried his head in Basa's fur and cried. "Why? Why does everything I touch turn to—? I was just starting to dream again. Hah! You know what she said tonight? She said, 'May all your dreams come true!' Isn't that funny? How could she know that my dream was going to die tonight? Another death!"

Jude hummed a funeral dirge as a lullaby, his torso swaying slightly, still nestling Basa.

"Who would've guessed, Basa? The friend I love, loves the girl I love! We'd make a good soap opera, wouldn't we, boy? The real Prince Charming got Cinderella, all right—'cause I'm sure no Prince Charming, I'm a horse's ass! I should have seen the signs. Just plain stupid. Should I have opened my heart to her? But what good would that have done, anyway? Not a damn bit, right, lil' guy?"

Basa shuddered. "Oh, you cold? Here, I'll put my coat around you."

They sat that way for a while. Jude guzzled, and thought. "The Big Guy upstairs is playing games with me again, isn't he? At least I'm good for something."

Jude contemplated his feet. "Look at those ugly things, they're deformed! Maybe my head is out of order, and my insides too! I'm just one big snafu. I don't think I'm supposed to dream anymore—maybe that's what he's trying to tell me."

Jude looked upward. "Is that it, Big Guy? Is that what you're saying? Okay, okay, I hear you."

His vision was blurring, movement was becoming increasingly hard. Deliberately, with difficulty, Jude raised his right hand. "Whoops, better put the bottle down first. Uh-oh, it's empty—no good anymore, anyways. Okay—now—I promise— see, my hand is up—I promise I won't dream no more—won't dream no more—no—" And Jude fell into the abyss of oblivion.

"Ohhh, I don't feel so good," Jude groaned to the wall near his bed.

"I can't imagine why" came Wade's voice from the other side of the room. "All you did was consume a fifth or more of scotch and go to sleep outdoors barefoot, in damp trousers and without a coat. It's a wonder you don't have pneumonia. Of course, that could come later."

Jude's head was spinning, but some memory was beginning to penetrate the fuzz. "How did I get . . . here?"

"Well, as you've done many a time for me, I put you there. You see, when I came home—about five this morning, I guess— I wanted us to talk and raise one more New Year's glass together. But you weren't in your room or in the house. Your car was still in the garage so I knew you were somewhere about. And so you were. You and Basa were outside shivering in your sleep."

"Basa! Where's Basa?"

"He's all right. Eric roused the vet—I bet he was pissed—and took Basa in for a check. Basa had a shot and has to keep warm and quiet and take some tablets twice a day. Anna and Eric are watching him. I'm afraid his days of dissipation are over—he has to behave."

"It's all my fault! I'm sorry, Wade, I really am. I didn't mean—I—didn't want to cause trouble."

Wade walked over and looked down compassionately. "Don't you think I know that? You don't ever have to explain anything to me. Look, supper will be ready in a while—why don't you take a long hot shower, put on a robe and we'll have a quiet New Year's Day dinner? Just us two old buddies?"

Eric served them in the den in front of the fireplace. Basa curled up at Jude's feet, Floozy endearingly close. Blackie and Whitey had stopped wrestling over the rawhide bones and lay snoozing on the rug.

"I never want to see another drink!" Jude said ruefully in answer to Wade's offer of a cocktail.

"That's what we all say the day after. I know, believe me! But you will—you will!"

There was a lull while Eric passed the entrée. The details of the preceding night had all come back to Jude, with haunting clarity. He felt awkward, unsure if Wade had a suspicion of the reason behind his erratic behavior, uncertain if he had compromised his relationship with either Wade or Penelope in any way.

"Penelope was worried about you when we received your note." Jude winced at the mention of Penelope. "I hope you don't mind, but under the circumstances, I felt I should . . .

confide in her. I realize you don't go around unloading your past on people, but I think you love her as much as I do."

Jude's heart skipped a beat. Could his friend possibly know his true feelings for Penelope?

"Of course, in a different way," Wade continued. "But we'll get to that later. What I'm confessing now is that, without your permission, I told Penelope about your...loss. And why certain times are more difficult for you than others." Wade looked to Jude, hoping for approval.

"I'm glad you told her, Wade," Jude replied, inwardly breathing a sigh of relief. "Of course I don't mind, I'm grateful you did. I would have, sooner or later, but I didn't think it, well, you know me."

"Yes, I do know you, and we have to talk about that, too. About your reluctance to let off steam with those who love you. But I can't scold you now. Because I want to tell you something you will find almost impossible to believe. I can hardly believe it myself."

"If you thought my toast last night was a new approach to get another dolly in the hay, I couldn't blame you, not with my history. But Jude, I meant it. I meant every word. I love her, I adore her, I want to marry her—and I haven't even been to bed with her! Isn't that wonderful!"

Jude called on all of his reserves. "You bet it is! And it's not hard to believe at all!"

"And I think she feels something for me, too. She didn't say she loved me—that way—but she didn't say she didn't, either. We have time, I know. But who cares about time? We have the rest of our lives! I'm like a schoolboy with his first crush, the difference being I'm closing in on forty with my first love."

Jude was able to say easily and earnestly, "No one deserves this happiness more than you. No one!"

Jude broke his promise to himself that very night. He did dream. *He and Penelope were walking hand in hand along the beach of a deserted island. They wore coverings of woven palm leaves. She laughed and darted away, returning with a handful of berries. "Lie down and I'll feed you," she said. The wet sand was cool on his back as he obediently did what he was told. She put a berry in her mouth and lay beside him, raised herself onto one elbow and reached across his chest with her other arm. Her mouth was above his and she slowly closed the gap, giving him her berry. Then another one. And another, until the berries were all gone. But their mouths stayed together. The sea tickled their feet, then their legs. "I'll dry you," he whispered, and he started to lick her dry. But the water wasn't salt water, it was sweet, like lemonade. He licked her all over, beginning at her toes. The leaves disappeared, and he sucked the ocean from her body. He tasted the sweet nectar of her passion and the earth quaked as he released his ecstasy...*

Jude bolted awake—shaken, confused. Where was he? There was no sand. No water. No Penelope. It had seemed so tangible—so real—but he was here, in his bed, and Basa was the only other breathing being in the room. As he settled back into the pillows, he was mortified to discover the only reality of the experience had been his orgasm.

He wasn't safe even in his sleep.

24

En route to Hailey, Idaho
June 1954

Jude had welcomed an excuse to get away from Hollywood. He
assured Revel he wouldn't miss her graduation for anything, and
yes, he would bring her a big present.

He looked out the window of the airplane at the vast empty
sky. He was tired, drained. This had been a tough year so far.
Work had been exacting, albeit successful. The studio was operating efficiently. *The Wade Colby Show* was a huge hit, and
had been renewed for the coming season. His vigilance and demand for excellence had taken its toll. He needed assistance, but
he hadn't found anyone to whom he could delegate authority.

And that's when he thought of Matthew. Jude wondered what
his own status was at home. He had been so damn occupied with
professional—and personal—decisions, he really hadn't taken
the time to think much about the family. The fleeting phone
conversations with Matthew and Polly had been superficial, but
now, in retrospect, he remembered sensing something—perhaps
discontent? He felt guilty he hadn't asked more questions then,
but he would rectify that on this trip.

Matthew and Polly would be perfect. With Matthew's business training and Polly's charm, they would be an ideal duo for
Colvas Studios. He could trust them implicitly, which would free
him to pursue other projects for the company and allow him to
spend more time on *The Wade Colby Show* itself. Wade couldn't
be expected to do more than what he was already doing. The solution was so obvious, he couldn't believe he hadn't thought of
it before. Of course, they might not be interested, or feel they

could leave Papa. Well, he would soon find out. If this idea materialized, it would be the first positive happening in his life this year.

The three comrades were still functioning in name, but as the relationship between Wade and Penelope developed, Jude tried to find reasons that he couldn't make dinner or go with them to some affair. He always had an important meeting, too much work at the office or a "hot date." The two sweethearts hadn't noticed the subtle change that was taking place. It wasn't indifference on their part, just their growing attachment to each other. The workplace, the rehearsals, the conferences, the filming were the same—even fuller and smoother, if that were possible. The chemistry between Wade and Penelope was so compelling, the fans were writing in, urging "Wade Thornton" and "Penelope Smythe" to get together. The network had agreed, and so in March, on the last show of the first season, the two characters had become engaged. Next season, which would start shooting in July, would focus on the betrothal and eventual marriage between the two. Jude had no doubt that real life would soon follow reel life.

After that fateful New Year's Eve, Jude realized he would have to move. When the inevitable night came that Wade and Penelope wanted to be together, Jude knew it would be an embarrassment for them all if he was in the same house. For Jude it would be sheer torture. So, quietly, he commissioned a real-estate broker to find him a suitable place. Jude wanted to rent, but the agent convinced him to rent with an option to buy. He didn't really care either way, but the agent's proposal did seem to make better business sense, so he agreed. Jude didn't particularly like modern architecture, or French provincial, so he settled for a two-story Spanish-style house on Maple Drive in Beverly Hills. The owners had just renovated the entire dwelling, inside and out, tile roof and all—and then their divorce had put the house on the market. The pool and yard were fenced in, and the lot was quite deep, so it would be a good home for Basa and a comfortable one for Jude. There was also a guest cottage in the back of the property, with plenty of room for Matthew and Polly or whoever.

Jude delayed telling Wade of his plans as long as he could, to spare himself more than Wade. Leaving the house, leaving that refuge, leaving behind that remarkable kinship was something he dreaded. He would be alone again. Prosperous, recognized, even respected—but alone. Again. There could not be a stay of execution, however.

Jude waited up for his friend one night after Wade took Penelope home, and then simply broke the news. Wade was silent a long time. Inadvertently, as in the past, Jude had forced Wade to confront his own life transitions. Wade actually disliked change, but now he himself realized life wouldn't allow for that. He, too, knew the time had come—accepting that was traumatic.

It wouldn't be the termination of their bond by any means—neither thought that—but it was an end to a vital era of their lives. How sad to have to say goodbye to that! The future without the other frightened Wade as much as it did Jude, but Wade knew he had to have Penelope in his life. Both he and Jude had challenges to meet and adjustments to make.

They pledged they would help each other, and would always be there, one for the other, no matter what, when or where. And they both believed in this beyond a shadow of a doubt.

But unlike Wade, Jude had to begin his new existence without Penelope. And without Basa—for Basa did not wake up one morning. Jude was, once more, completely alone.

The house on Maple came fully equipped—the owners had not wanted to take any reminders of their failure with them—so all Jude had to do was move in. He had entrusted his secretary, Muriel, with the task of hiring a housekeeper, and after thorough research, she had decided on a daily cleaning woman and an English live-in butler, Oliver Parrish. Jude didn't think he needed all that, but he allowed Muriel to have her way—what did it matter, anyway?

Floozy pined so for Basa, she soon joined him in their final resting place. Wade and Penelope urged Jude to take Blackie, but Jude didn't feel it was fair to separate the two remaining dogs. One of these days, he said, he would go to the pound or an S.P.C.A. shelter and pick up a stray. But not yet, the wound was still too raw.

Jude tried to fill the new emptiness in his life by becoming a man-about-town, by playing as hard as he worked. This new lifestyle gave him an excuse for not joining Wade and Penelope in after-work activities.

"Busy? *Again?*" Wade complained. "We're going to have to make an appointment! How about the first of February, 1956?"

Once, in private, Wade said to Jude, half kidding, half in earnest, "You're going to wear yourself out! Are you sure you're all right?" And when Jude gave a great performance and assured Wade he was having a ball, Wade answered conspiratorially, "Well, in that case, I am going to make the supreme sacrifice and turn over my personal telephone book to you. I hope you appreciate the time and study I invested in these numbers. I can't believe I'm doing this. But, if my hopes are realized, I won't be needing this anymore."

Riding in the fast lane put Jude in contact with most of Hollywood's high fliers. He was not intimidated by celebrity so much anymore, partially because he was now accepted by the ruling class. True, he was a Johnny-come-lately and still a mite rough around the edges, but one thing this group could understand was success and talent, and, however grudgingly, they had to credit him that. So Jude joined the party circuit. He was there, at Ciro's, the night Darryl Zanuck went on stage and brought the place down by doing one-arm chin-ups on a trapeze. "That guy was unbelievable!" he reported to Wade the next day. "They tell me I was about to challenge him, but I could barely walk." He was drinking more than he ever had, and on more than one occasion, he had insisted all the guests at a function continue celebrating at his house until the wee hours. Incredibly, this double life hadn't adversely affected or slowed down his pace at work.

But none of it helped. No matter how many beautiful women ended up in his bed or how many people swarmed the house, he still felt alone. Hollow—and alone.

Willamina's first words after hugging Jude were: "You lose weight—you tired—too much work," and she went straight to the kitchen to begin preparations to fatten him up.

Jude had planned to stay at the Sun Valley Lodge or the little hotel in Hailey, but Noah and Willamina asked if he would stay with them. There was plenty of room and they could all visit more, since Jude didn't make it home very often. Revel wouldn't bother him, they promised, she was too caught up in the festivities of graduation.

Jude experienced a pang of guilt and immediately said of course he'd stay with them. Revel had long since taken over the rooms once occupied by Jude and Thelma and then Keane, but to ensure the least amount of haunting memories, Willamina settled Jude downstairs.

It was comforting to be fussed over, Jude was surprised to discover. Noah and Willamina had wisely not arranged a big family dinner the first night. Revel, ever the Queen Bee, disappeared with her drones right after she had received a beautiful gold wristwatch and a tidy check for her school wardrobe from Jude. Matthew and Polly were coming by after supper, but the whole clan would not gather until the next evening.

So everything was peaceful, relaxed. Jude cleaned his plate and Willamina beamed when he wanted more. They discussed the problems of a shrinking globe, the continuing world conflicts, and wondered if the presence of atomic weapons could deter another world war. They rejoiced over the landmark decision handed down by the Supreme Court outlawing racial segregation in schools; Noah was so proud of "his" United States. They talked about the television show *See It Now,* when Edward R. Murrow challenged Senator Joseph McCarthy's witch-hunt for Communists. They touched on family news: Ethel, Luke's widow, was doing fine, and was actually starting to keep company with Clyde Warhas, who had never married.

"Oh, Jude, I be sorry I no think," Willamina said, covering her mouth, mortified that she had thoughtlessly mentioned Thelma's brother, Clyde.

"Mama, Mama, it's all right." Jude got up and went over to his mother's chair and put his arms around her. "It's all right. It's been over twelve years. Thelma and Keane will always be in my heart, but thanks to help from you and Papa and Thelma— yes, I've sort of 'talked' things over with Thelma over the years—you made me realize I had to go on living." Jude was quiet for a minute. "Maybe it's time I talk to her some more."

Willamina and Noah exchanged looks. What could be troubling Jude now?

Later that evening, Polly greeted Jude with an intensity that bothered him. There was almost a sense of desperation about her, as if she was hoping for something from him. Jude wasn't sure what. Matthew appeared to be all right—quieter, perhaps. Jude felt an underlying current from the two that had him worried.

The conversation progressed normally enough. All the usual probings from both sides. And sitting around the old fireplace brought back a flood of memories. How many times, the boys wondered, had they been hauled on the carpet with Papa standing sternly in front of that very same fireplace. Too many to count!

Noah's guitar still leaned against the wall. "Would you play, Papa?" Jude asked wistfully. It seemed a night for remembering.

Noah hadn't touched the instrument in quite a time, but he sensed a desire, a need from his sons to revisit their days of innocence. So he willingly obliged Jude and turned back the clock with his strumming and chanting. Polly was mesmerized by the haunting ballads; she had never heard Noah play before.

"Tell us some stories, Papa, about the old country." Matthew sounded as if he were a child again. "I always liked the bear stories especially!"

Revel had slipped in during Noah's serenade and was sitting on the floor next to Willamina. "What bear stories? You never tol' me no bear stories! Never sang to me, either!" she accused Noah.

Noah laughed and motioned for her to come and sit on his lap. "So, my grown-up daughter—who wiggle-waggled her way to school away from home—wants Papa to tell her stories now, eh? I think you be a she *artz*."

"That be a bear," Willamina explained.

"Well, let me see," Noah began. Revel snuggled close to him, content for a moment to be his little girl. "There was this man, from my village, who go to America with his trained bear. The bear danced, my papa tell me—I never see—since man leave before I was born. Now this man say he need shoes, not clogs, to go to America. So our village leather man make shoes for him. But this shepherd say he won't pay for shoes until he know they will last. That be all right with the cobbler, so off man and bear go to America. Before I come here, man come back, over twenty years later. He wear shoes, but they all broken. And he mad at cobbler, he won't pay because durn shoes wore out! My papa say—us Basques drive hard bargain!"

Everyone enjoyed a chuckle.

"Can bears really learn to dance? Aren't they too thick-headed?" asked Revel.

"No, my little one!" Noah was quick to respond. "Bears be smart, very smart. I tell your brothers long time ago, never make light of bear—they run faster, they swim faster, they climb faster! One shows respect! I tell you one more true story. And this when I was in my village. A neighbor, a shepherd also, couldn't understand why he keep losing two, three lambs each night. So he hide. Pretty soon he hear what sound like whistle, and sure enough, a couple of little critters wander toward sound. See, shepherds use dogs to gather flock, but they whistle, too. This wise old bear learn to make same sound as shepherd's whistle, close enough anyway to fool the babies. Now what you think about bears, eh?"

"We keep our distance!" they all chimed. Jude added, "And I think I'll name my new dog Artz." He stopped. "That's strange! I don't even have a new dog. I guess—I guess I'm telling myself I should get one."

Noah and Willamina glanced at each other, the same question in their eyes—a good sign, yes?

Jude, meanwhile, was studying his parents. Another thought had popped into his head. "I didn't pay attention, or think about it until just now, but I've heard stories ever since I was a kid about how the Basques who came over to seek the pot of gold always kept longing to go back to the old country, but somehow never got around to it. And they were brokenhearted. Is that true? Because—Papa—Mama—if you would like to take that trip, I would like to give it to you. It would, well, it would mean a lot to me to make you happy."

All eyes turned to Noah and Willamina. None of the children had thought of this before. And to their recollection, Mama and Papa had never mentioned it.

There was a long silence. Finally, Noah turned to Willamina, "Mama? You want to talk?"

Willamina's eyes were misty as she looked from Noah to Jude. "You be good boy. That very nice thought. My life here now, my family here. Our mamas and papas pass to heaven—I not really know sisters or brothers. This be my home. Papa?"

"Mama be right," he said to Jude. "You make us happy because you show you care, you make us very happy! And Mama be right—this be our home. This be our country. We find our pot of gold." Noah examined the faces focused on him. "Our family, our friends, our house, our business. We are very full. Mama and me talk about this before and both feel same way. We think those who be unhappy never really join the new country. They want to take something from it, and when they fail, they want to go back to what is easy, easy because it is what they think they know. We think—yes, we be Basques and proud of it. But we be Americans now—and proud of it. Our country give to us, and we want to give to our country.''

''Well, I'm glad that's settled!'' Revel chirped. ''I like you right here! I'm going to bed now, graduating is very tiring!'' Revel dramatically blew a kiss to all and flew up the stairs.

Jude, Matthew and Polly were still digesting what Noah and Willamina had said. Though his parents had declined the trip, Jude felt good about having offered it. The whole evening had such a harmony about it. Jude wondered if this might be the time to broach the subject of Matthew and Polly's coming to California. The atmosphere seemed right. And he certainly didn't want to go around anyone's back; he wanted everything up front, out in the open. He decided to risk it.

''You know, on the plane coming here, a brainstorm hit me, and I'd sure appreciate your reactions—good or bad. If I'm way off base, please tell me right away and that will be the end of it. Okay?'' Jude paused for a moment, then proceeded to outline his need for a second in command, a chief executive officer, and why he thought Matthew, with Polly at his side, would be the perfect choice. He explained carefully, almost apologetically, that he didn't know the status of Matthew's present function in the family business, nor Matthew's and Polly's personal inclinations. ''But I'm tossing the idea into the family circle for discussion!''

Matthew looked at Polly, then at Noah. Polly looked at Matthew, then at Willamina. Willamina looked at Noah, then at Matthew and Polly. Noah looked at all of them.

But no one said anything. Jude's eyes questioned and hoped. Matthew's eyes showed excitement, and a little apprehension. Polly's eyes glistened with undisguised joy. Willamina's eyes reflected acceptance of the inevitable. Noah's eyes saw the whole tableau.

And then, all at once everyone spoke. Finally, Noah quieted the group. ''I think I understand each of your heads. This be a

big decision, and it belong to Matthew and Polly. They should
take time. Mama and me can speak only for us. I know Mama,
and I say for us—Matthew and Polly must follow their hearts.
Matthew help the business very much, and Polly help him and
all of us. But Matthew fixed things so others can now do what
he started. He must know this. Because I do, and Mama, too. I
think we should all sleep now, it's late. And Jude, my son, welcome home!''

Matthew and Polly didn't close their eyes that night. Jude's
proposal was a godsend. Noah had assuaged Matthew's initial
reservation, that of leaving the family enterprise in the lurch. He
felt gratified that Noah had applauded the backup training program Matthew had put in place. His other concern—whether he
was fully competent to tackle the unknown in Hollywood—was
answered by Polly. She convinced him that Jude would not have
offered him the position if he didn't both need help and believe
wholeheartedly in Matthew's ability. Colvas Inc. was a business, and Jude would never jeopardize his responsibility to Wade
by making a reckless appointment.

Matthew looked at Polly's shining eyes. Those beautiful blue
eyes hadn't sparkled like this since before she had taken the trip
East with Revel. Revel had found her school, but Polly's search
had not ended successfully. The medical tests had shown con-
clusively that her fallopian tubes were defective. She could never
conceive a child. The finality of the doctor's diagnosis had left
her in a deep depression. Besides telling her husband, she had
confided only in Willamina, and through Willamina, in Noah.
She couldn't bear the thought of the rest of the family knowing.
Matthew ached for her, but he didn't suffocate her with his anxiety. He had allowed time and space for her to make peace with
her hurt, but always under the protective umbrella of his love
and devotion. She hadn't yet come to terms with her fate.

But Matthew was confident this new development could be the
solution, and her—*their*—salvation. In a fresh environment, he
thought she might begin to think of adoption. There was no
question in his mind now: he would accept Jude's proposition.
He would accept the job and they would move to California.

Matthew and Polly's decision came as no surprise to Noah and
Willamina. Jude, on the other hand, hadn't known what to ex-

pect and was bowled over with excitement. The announcement to the other family members was made the next evening at the dinner table.

"You're moving *where?* To do *what? When?*" John exclaimed, with an accusatory scowl at Jude that said, *You son of a bitch, every time you stick your nose in something, you cause trouble around here.*

Revel loved the idea. "Can I come to Hollywood to visit on my first break?"

"Oh, my! You mean we—we'll be *alone* in the office?" Ethel and Lila asked worriedly.

The four youngsters couldn't have cared less. "C'n I have another piece of pie, Grandma? Please?" John, Jr., asked.

"Me, too!" came a chorus from the remaining grandchildren.

Noah opened the Bible to a page he and Willamina had marked the night before. "Mark 2:22— 'And no one puts new wine into old wineskins—if he does, the wine will burst the skins, and the wine is lost, and so are the skins—but new wine is for fresh skins.'" He looked up. "Mama and me be thankful Matthew and Polly open themselves to growth. We send them off to new doors to unlock—and send them off with love and prayers. And with their braveness, we all learn to keep belief in what we able to do. I know I speak for whole family."

25

Beverly Hills, California
Saturday, June 18, 1955

A collective sigh escaped from the guests as Penelope Pope, on the arm of her father, walked down the aisle—and to Wade Colby. Penelope sparkled, the setting sun and countless candles catching the reflection of each bead on her gown. The studded satin dress outlined her form, and the yards and yards of diaphanous tulle that flowed from her tiara created an ethereal misty cloud around her.

The Pricklers had hoped to hold the wedding at their home. The Popes had suggested theirs. Jude had offered his house. To appease all, Penelope and Wade had settled for the Presbyterian church in Beverly Hills, with the reception in the elegant Crystal Room of the Beverly Hills Hotel.

Without diverting his gaze from his bride, Wade whispered to his best man, "I must be hallucinating, Jude. Is this actually happening? She is too beautiful to be real."

"It's the real McCoy, all right!" mouthed Jude. His pain had dissipated somewhat over the last year and a half, but seeing Penelope in her wedding gown rekindled smothered desires. Jude forced himself to concentrate on other faces, other thoughts, squeezing Penelope's image from his mind.

Polly Abavas, Penelope's matron of honor, looked lovely and happy. The move to California had done wonders for her, for all, in fact. Matthew's contributions to Colvas Inc. were already having an effect. And Polly had plunged headfirst into making her presence known. She and Penelope had become instant soul mates. Polly and Matthew had spent a number of months in

Jude's guest house—to get acclimatized to Los Angeles—and Jude had once again looked forward to coming home at night. Polly organized Jude's dinner parties and acted as his hostess. On Thanksgiving Day, she had prodded Jude into convincing the man at an animal shelter in Culver City that if he let them in, one of the animals was assured a home.

Jude, Matthew and Polly had gone up and down the corridors between the cages, wishing they could adopt all of the canine waifs. Finally, Jude had said to the keeper, "Let me see that little gal." He pointed to a black Labrador who had followed them along the mesh wire, dancing on her hind legs every time they passed. The tag read: "Black Labrador retriever, approximately one year, female—not spayed, not claimed within seven days." Jude knelt down, and once released, the dog's wiggling buttocks plunked down on their haunches, the two front paws went on Jude's shoulders and a wet tongue licked his face. Jude looked up at Matthew and Polly, and then down at the expressive eyes in front of him. "Well, little *artz,* my little bear, looks like you've found yourself a new home."

Polly was crying when they left, not because she disapproved of Jude's choice, but because of those they had left behind.

"We'll be back—we promise! Just as soon as we get our place, we'll come back!" Polly guaranteed tearfully.

Abruptly, Jude swung back to the gates. "Hey! Don't close up yet! Hell, I have yard enough for another one. Let's find out if that black-and-tan Doberman likes me."

This label read: "Black with tan markings Doberman pinscher, approximately nine months, female—not spayed, not claimed within seven days."

Another caress from a cold nose, and Jude was the proud owner of two dogs. "We'll call you Orey II—I never did have a second Orey. So now I have a bear and deer. Blackie will have a field day—his own harem. Come on you two, let's go home!"

Now, months later, Matthew and Polly had a modest house in the Brentwood section of Los Angeles, and two dogs and two cats of their own.

Revel had come for the wedding and was in her glory. Jude was astonished at the difference one year had made. Gone was the gawky, tall little girl. In her place was a fairly sophisticated, well-developed young lady. And a beauty! Although not quite fifteen, she looked much more mature. Her thick auburn hair hung straight to her shoulders, the pale mint green off-the-shoulder gown complemented her soft fair skin and her large hazel eyes flashed with excitement.

At the reception, one of the male guests sidled up to Jude and asked, "Where did you find *her,* you sly fox?"

Jude silenced him with a steely look. "She's my kid sister, you horny asshole, and don't you forget it!"

Revel had shrugged off inquiries about the past school year. "Oh, it's okay. I'm doing good—whoops—I mean *well* in my studies. The kids are—they're bitches, that's what they are! And they're stuck-up! Right now, I'm kinda in no-man's-land, a curiosity, the one whose brother has something to do with Hollywood and who knows Wade Colby. But I can handle it—it sure beats the hell out of Hailey High!"

Whirling around the dance floor later, first with one and then another handsome partner, Revel decided exactly where she was headed. She was headed for Hollywood—that was a definite! And she would live with Jude. For a while. Until she knew what she wanted. Or she knew *who* she wanted.

She'd show those snobs at school who she was!

Monday, August 4, 1955

"How I wish you'd been there when we went to the bikini shop in the south of France—St. Tropez, to be exact!" Wade started to laugh as he recaptured the scene for Jude. This was the first day back at the studio since the honeymoon, and Wade was trying to recap the whole trip.

"Why, what happened?" Jude asked, pleased at how happy and relaxed Wade appeared.

"Well, we went into this one place—where everything is made to order—and we picked out the materials we liked. Then the salesman told Penelope to go in the tiny cubicle and take everything off so that she could be measured. I was looking at some other patterns when I heard this—this shriek! It turned out that the salesman was also the fitter and he had pulled back the curtain and there was Penelope in her altogether—hence, the shriek. You know the French—they hardly blink at nudity—and he just proceeded merrily on his way, cupping those beautiful breasts and writing down figures, suggesting how much or how little should be covered and how high the cut should be. My poor baby was in shock, just stood there with her mouth open, her eyes begging for help. I went over, winked at her and at least closed the curtains.''

"My God, I'm with Penelope. I would've decked the guy.''

"It's just different there, Jude. It takes some getting used to. I should have warned her, I guess, but I didn't think. Anyway, by the time we got to Paris, she was ready for the naked chorus line at the Lido.'' Wade sighed. "I can't express how much I love her, how much she has brought to my life. It was such a joy to watch her reaction to the marvels of Europe. She was so excited and wondrous, so appreciative. As many times as I've been there, I felt as if I was grasping the significance of what I was seeing for the first time. All because of her, all because she was so open and receptive and eager. We didn't cover nearly enough ground—only England, France and Italy—and those need more attention. The days went so fast—too fast.''

"You have a lifetime, my friend. A lifetime of such trips, such pleasure.''

"You're right—you're always right! Oh, I do love life! I must tell you about going into the House of Dior.'' Wade continued on and on about their travels, warning Jude that photographs—hundreds of photographs—would be forthcoming as soon as they were ready.

Jude could endure Wade's euphoria, because he was genuinely happy for the couple. His feelings for Penelope had been carefully stored in a secluded part of his heart, once reserved for only Thelma and Keane. He would be able to look at their pictures, and to share their lives. This was the way life was; at least, this was the way *his* life was.

"I hate to bring you back to earth, old buddy, but networks won't wait, even for newlyweds.''

"I know, Jude, I know. Well, we're ready, full of more piss and vinegar than ever! I realize we're getting a late start, so let me have it. Tell me all.''

Jude outlined the script ideas that had been prepared for the new season. "Maybe we'll take Wade Thornton and Penelope Smythe to Sun Valley on their honeymoon later. *I Love Lucy* is going to shoot an episode there, and we certainly know the territory better than anyone in their outfit. And our approach would be different anyhow. The brass like that concept and, oh, yes, they also want you to know that they wouldn't mind a bit if Penelope should get pregnant.''

"Oh, they wouldn't? Well, I'm delighted we have their permission. I'm sure Penelope will be, too. Tell them we'll keep on practicing until we find the proper recipe. Anything for the ratings, right?''

"Right!" Jude moved on to more general topics of Colvas Inc. "Now that Matt has assumed a lot of my headaches at the studio, I think it's time to branch out. Dramatic specials are hot now—ever since Paddy Chayefsky's *Marty* was done in '53 and was such a hit. We could bid for some choice properties right along with the big boys, film it—or them—right here at Colvas, and sell the finished product to WBS. You and/or Penelope could star if you were willing to work over hiatus, and I'm confident we could entice other big names. It could be a chance to expose movie stars to a whole new audience, a larger audience, so many more people would see them. It also would give them a showcase for other dimensions of their talents. Whatever bait works, but I'm just sure we could get them. The hitch is gambling money on good material—because *that* is the key, good material with top-notch creative people. And none of that comes cheap. What do you think?''

"Say no more! I agree wholeheartedly. If you're game, so am I. I think you're right on track. Maybe we could eventually even get into producing some spectaculars, like that Mary Martin and Ethel Merman *Ford Anniversary Show!*''

Jude was jubilant. "Yeah, great! Now we're cooking!" Each took a moment to look at the other, realizing just how far their dreams and collaboration had progressed.

"Moving right along," Jude said, not finished discussing plans yet. "Matt has a damn good idea. This is a little in the future, sort of long-range, but something we should kick around. Matt has expressed surprise at how costly some necessary services are, like renting the cars and limos, catering lunches and dinners for the cast and crew, renting equipment, even chartering airplanes—for *licensed* pilots only, Wade—and on and on. His brainstorm is that we form another company, perhaps call it Studio Services Inc., and make that company the supplier for

all special services to any or all studios, starting with and including Colvas. We'd still have to rent, but we'd be renting from
our own company, and it could be very profitable. He has to
look into the legal ramifications, but there's no sense in spending the hours on research if you don't buy the rationale. So?''

"Jesus! You guys have been busy!'' Wade looked at Jude in
admiration. "Of course pursue it! But I think I remember talk
at the dinner table at home that leads me to think we—meaning
Colvas—might not be able to be involved directly for antitrust
reasons. I'm not sure, Matt can check into it thoroughly, but
even if that were so, Matt could leave Colvas, set up the other
business and we could finance it. We'd have to finance it personally, not through Colvas.

"And now, if that's it for work, please tell me what's with
these silly-looking caps everyone's wearing?'' Wade demanded.
"If I see one more kid—or adult, I should add—in a Davy
Crocket outfit, I'm going to throw up.''

"The power of television,'' Jude answered. "Television is not
a passing fancy. The fad is now a reality. Look how the nation
watched a hundred and eighty-seven hours of TV for thirty-six
days last year during the army-McCarthy Communist hearings.
The response from their constituency was so overwhelming, the
Senate just voted unanimously to extend investigation of domestic communism. Thousands of federal employees have been
dismissed as security risks—''

"We seem to have been forgotten,'' Wade observed.

"We'll never know for sure—and I don't want to!'' Jude
thought a bit. "I wonder when we can start hiring those writers
on the blacklist. Other studios and independents are using them,
I know, under pseudonyms, of course. I'd just cream my jeans
if we could be the first to list their real names in the credits.''

"I would, too. Let's test the climate soon. But enough of that,
I want to hear about Jude. What's happening in your life?''

"Nothing, really. Same old thing—eat, drink and make Mary,
or somebody. I've gone through—oh, about a third, I guess, of
your famous black book. Added a few names, even. But nothing special, nothing lasting.''

"There's no rush, Jude. One of these days someone will come
along and you won't want to say 'Who's next on the list?' ever
again. You'll tire of being the stud. Look at me! So you do know

it can happen. Did I ever tell you—no, I'm sure I didn't," Wade began, valiantly attempting to cheer Jude. "I had a date with this gorgeous brunette once. Well, one thing led to another and the magic moment arrived. I hopped into bed and she started to get ready to do the same. She took off her bra and put it on the nightstand—and there went her boobs. Then her panties—now, that part was intact. When I ran my fingers through her hair, though, they got caught in something—so she put her hairpiece on the nightstand. I was kissing her face and something stuck in my mouth—so she took off her false eyelashes and put them on the nightstand. Well, I couldn't help myself, I looked at her and said, 'I don't know whether I should fuck you or the nightstand.' Boy, did she leave in a huff—with her boobs, hair and eyelashes all stuffed in her pocketbook!"

Wade succeeded; Jude howled at this one.

"Do you think you could leave this place behind you for a few hours and take potluck with us tonight? Penelope would be very pleased—both of us would be, and Anna and Eric miss you. Why don't you pick up Artz and Orey and let them romp with Blackie and Whitey on the beach?"

"Why not?" Jude said. "It's a date!"

IV

26

The arrival of Wayland Earle Prickler Colby on October 7, 1956, was only one of the new additions to the Colby/Abavas clan. Jude's brother, John, and wife, Lila, had welcomed their third child, Wilma Harriet Abavas, on August 23, 1956. Ethel had married Clyde Warhas, and their first child, Joseph Abavas Warhas, arrived on September 14, 1956. Dewayne William and Dewana Judith, twins, were born on September 17, 1956, and the proud adoptive parents, Matthew and Polly Abavas, had taken them home three days later.

Only Jude and Revel were not parents, but that did not mean they were not involved. Jude was godfather to Wayland—soon nicknamed Buzz because he was busy as a bee from day one— and to Dewayne. Wade was godfather to Dewana. Revel was named godmother to Dewayne, Penelope to Dewana, and Polly to Buzz.

Jude flew Revel to California for the christenings. She had continued to blossom both physically and mentally, but was clearly not happy. When prodded, she confided to Jude, "I'm still an oddity at school, still not really one of 'them.' No matter how much I try to dress like them, smoke like them, do like them—I'm still the outsider. But I'm studying hard—and I'm smarter'n them, Jude, and prettier and I'll be just fine, believe you me!"

Revel was a bit awkward at the ceremony when it was her turn to hold Dewayne. But Jude gathered his nephew to his bosom with practiced ease. He had tried to forget how good it was to have such a small bundle close to him. He wondered if he would ever again cuddle a child of his own. One thing he vowed for certain, he would be the best damn godfather it was possible to be.

The rest of the world took little note of these new additions; global attention was focused on the wedding of Marilyn Monroe and playwright Arthur Miller, the fairy tale romance and union of Prince Rainier of Monaco and the actress Grace Kelly, the landslide victory of President Eisenhower and Vice President Nixon, the collision of the *Andrea Doria* and the *Stockholm,* and the Soviet crushing of the Hungarian revolt. And closer to home, the government's decision to pay farmers *not* to grow crops was a constant topic of conversation in the Abavas family.

In that fall of 1956, Colvas Studios bought an apartment in the Sherry Netherlands Hotel in Manhattan. Most film companies had located their head offices in New York and most financial transactions were conducted in the East. New York was not a place to be without money, Jude quickly realized. The realestate broker had given him a quick course in judging the quality of New York co-ops. In "not quite the best" places, one could hear every sound from surrounding apartments—toilets flushing, voices, people walking. But in the "classiest," one suffered only occasional intrusions. Jude could barely explain this distinction over the telephone to Wade without breaking up. "Well, by all means, make sure we get the "classiest" apartment available," Wade had agreed.

The Sherry, on Fifth Avenue across from the Plaza Hotel, was the Hollywood of the East. Columbia Studios and M.C.A., among others, already had suites. Jude became a regular visitor, often needing to be there to compete for properties and close the deals.

Revel would occasionally come down from Connecticut, and Jude, in his quest for material, took her to both on- and off-Broadway productions. In truth, Revel's opinion was helpful in evaluating certain productions, since she offered a totally different perspective—the view of the young.

Revel loved those weekends. Jude always took her shopping. And she liked dressing up and going to the chic restaurants in the city. Danny's Hideaway was her favorite, but she also enjoyed the 21 Club, and after-theater spots like the Copacabana and the Village Vanguard. The Versailles Room and the Latin Quarter absolutely thrilled her. Jude was convinced that by the time Revel went to Europe, which he knew she would one day do, *nothing* would shock her.

If Revel wasn't in New York, Jude would drape a gorgeous model on his arm, just so he wouldn't have to walk in anywhere alone. Except for his enthusiasm for his work, this was like everything else in his life—just marking time.

Over the quick visit home to Idaho for the holidays, Jude had impulsively bought a modest house on the east side of Sun Valley's lake and dam, next to Ann Sothern's place. The house would allow him to remain connected to his roots, but maintain his independence. It also would be there for Matthew's and Wade's families if they wanted to be closer to the action. Noah and Willamina were pleased that Jude wished to keep a link to his homeground.

Penelope needed to get her muscles back in shape after Buzz's arrival, so Wade hired a personal trainer to come to the house. "Won't hurt my old bones, either," he ruefully acknowledged. The trainer's name was Thad Thornton, and he knew everybody who was anybody in Hollywood. And he wasn't adverse to dropping little tidbits of gossip during his sessions. He wouldn't exactly name names, but it didn't take a Rhodes scholar to figure out who was doing what.

Penelope and Wade would compare notes with Jude, another of Thad's clients, and between the three of them they would usually come up with the answers to the riddles. Who *was* the wife of a very famous star who had insisted her wandering husband have a vasectomy so his dallyings wouldn't end up in a paternity suit and thus threaten the wife's position? They decided there were too many candidates to narrow the field to just one.

Who was the "in" hairstylist who pretended to be homosexual, or allowed the male population to assume that he was? Men would trust him to escort their wife or girlfriend when they were unavailable, but in reality he was completely straight and ended up screwing most of the ladies in the town. The famous Mr. Felipi, of course!

Yes, Thad Thornton was good for the body—and tonic for the psyche.

Even with a wife and child, Wade hadn't completely curbed his adventuresome spirit, and quietly had purchased another motorcycle. It wasn't as powerful as the first one—the one that had nearly killed him—but still had enough speed to occasionally thrill him. He presented a smaller version to Penelope the Christmas of 1956, and a medium-size one to Jude. He gave each of his pupils a few lessons and the three of them enjoyed some easy rides along the coastline.

On New Year's Eve, after several toasts, the three daredevils thought they would show off their skills to Jude's date, Nina, who wisely declined to participate. They made a couple of runs on the wet sand of the beach, and were wildly applauded by guests at the various parties in the beachfront homes. Abruptly, Penelope's machine stalled, and in trying to kick-start it, her foot slipped off the pedal. The momentum carried the bike forward and the back wheel ran over her foot. Jude tried to stop and help her, but in his nervousness, he maneuvered the throttle instead of the brake and hurtled through the open gate straight into Wade's swimming pool. The lone surviving rider hurriedly parked his cycle and ran to pick up Penelope, whose ego was bruised more than her foot. Then the two of them, with some guests from a nearby party, went to see about Jude. Jude was struggling to get out of the water. Pulling him out was simple— after he'd been helped out, Penelope and Nina wrapped a blanket around him and insisted he go inside and lie down—but pulling the motorcycle out of the pool was another matter. In fact, it was damn near impossible. By this time, more party-goers had made their way to the Colbys', either to help or to watch or to simply keep the refreshments flowing. Eric was busy opening the champagne bottles.

Now there were as many men in the pool as out, and at about eleven-thirty the rescuers succeeded in pulling the motorcycle from the water. Wade went in to check on Jude and found him in the shower.

"You okay, buddy boy?" Wade asked, turning off the spray.

"Yeah, sure, I'm fine!" Jude assured him.

"You sure you're all right?" Wade persisted.

"Yeah, I said I was fine."

"Well, in that case, maybe you could explain why you're taking a shower with your clothes on!"

Jude looked down and, sure enough, he was still completely dressed. His leather jacket was drenched, his red wool sweater was dripping dye onto the tiles, his shoes sloshed as he moved. He sheepishly looked up at Wade. "I guess—I mean—I'm okay now. Maybe I was a little cuckoo for a while there. I thought a hot shower would fix me up. God, I'm sorry, what a mess I made. I'm sorry."

Wade was laughing as he picked out some of his clothes for Jude to change into. "Good thing we're almost the same size. Just shed everything, leave your stuff there on the floor. Come on out, it's almost midnight, and the entire neighborhood is here to celebrate your feat and the motorcycle's recovery. No one has ever provided such entertainment for a New Year's bash. But that doesn't mean that you're both not grounded!"

27

Hailey, Idaho
August 15, 1958

"Happy Birthday, dear Revel! Happy Birthday to you!" Revel blew out the eighteen candles easily, and hoped her wish would come true. The entire family—all eighteen including Revel—had gathered at the old house in Hailey, but unlike previous birthdays, she had invited no friends. There really hadn't been anyone she'd wanted to ask. She had already seen most of her old group, but she couldn't relate to them anymore. There were no mutual interests, no common denominator between them. Jesus, they still thought it was a big deal to try to get someone to say "suck with an F in front of it." She felt ten years older than any of them. She had never been accepted into the inner circle at school back East, and she no longer felt affiliated with the Hailey clique. She knew where she wanted to be, but getting there was another matter. She needed to work on Jude, and then Polly and Matthew.

Jude wanted some answers from Revel, as well, so the two found a quiet spot to talk.

"What's up, little lady? Why didn't you stay for the graduation exercises? I almost had Mama and Papa convinced to make the trip when you called and said you were coming home." Jude wasted no time getting to the crux of his complaint.

Revel had been ready for this. "And what if Mama and Papa had come? First off, they really didn't want to. Then, when they got there, they wouldn't have been comfortable. They wouldn't have known anyone, they wouldn't have understood what was going on, they wouldn't—*couldn't*—be a part of any of the private little socials that took place, even if we had been invited to one, which would have been highly unlikely. They wouldn't have fit in, Jude, just like I never did.''

Jude's voice was solemn. ''Were you ashamed to have your schoolmates meet your parents?''

''No! That wasn't it!'' Revel chose her words carefully, she had to make Jude understand. ''I didn't want them to be hurt— or be disappointed in me. I graduated with honors, I got my diploma—that's what's important to them. I knew that would make them happy, proud even. But they would have been confused by those thickheaded prigs.''

Jude hadn't realized how tough school had been on Revel.

''And I wasn't about to give them the last laugh—or anything! I picked up my papers, said goodbye to my teachers and thumbed my nose at the rest. Believe me, Jude, I made the right choice.''

Jude put his arm around his little sister and drew her close. ''My poor lamb. Thrown to the wolves. I wish I knew why some people have to be so cruel. Maybe it's their only way of feeling important, superior, when all it really shows is their insecurity.''

''I liked my teachers,'' Revel said. ''And they understood, more than they could actually say. You know what my English lit professor said when I left? He quoted James Baldwin, 'The world is before you and you need not take it or leave it as it was when you came in.' Isn't that super?''

''Sounds like a good man. And I don't think there's much chance of your taking or leaving the world as it is. But, what are your plans, Rev? Have you thought about college, or a profession, or—what?''

Now was the perfect opportunity for Revel to set her hook. ''Well, I haven't applied to any university yet, I just wasn't sure what to do or where to go. It's already too late for this term, but with my grade average, I could probably get in somewhere the next semester. I love Mama and Papa, but I don't know if they get the idea that—that I don't want to stay here. There's such a gap between their generation and mine, we don't see eye to eye on, well, almost everything. I'm afraid I might...might be mean to them in my frustration, and I don't want that to happen. I was hoping...well...I thought maybe I could come and stay with you. I could look into USC and UCLA, maybe help out at your studio. Matt and Polly don't have room for me, but they would be close by. And I could help with the new business—or even with the twins—or—oh, I don't know! I just know I don't want to be here and I know I'd like to be there!''

Jude was not surprised by his sister's revelations, in fact, she reminded him of himself, and Matthew too. But he took a while to answer, because he did have some concerns. ''I think I can explain how you feel to Mama and Papa,'' he finally began. ''Believe me, and this is fact, they have more savvy than any of us give them credit for. But honey, how do you or I know that I'd be any better? There's still the difference in ages—my frame of reference isn't going to be the same as yours all the time. And I would have to exercise some control over your life. I couldn't and wouldn't just let you run wild—''

''Oh, Jude, I promise I'll mind you, I promise! I'll listen! I promise, I'll behave! I can smell it, taste it, I feel it in my bones— we'd get along, we're so much alike. Maybe I can talk to you because you haven't been around here all the time and you don't see me as a little girl, as the baby. You treat me like an adult— almost. Please, *please* take me with you!''

Jude knew he couldn't refuse her; he suspected she'd leave on her own in any case. But would this plan work?

''Okay, my big-little sister,'' he said. ''We'll give it a try. I'm not sure what we're letting ourselves in for—we'll see, won't we? But get one thing clear—*I am the boss!* Now, I'll go talk to Mama and Papa.''

28

Los Angeles, California
Sunday, September 16, 1958

Because September 17 fell on Monday, Polly had decided to have the twins' second birthday party on Sunday so the adults could.come and play, too. Revel had arrived in Los Angeles in time for the celebration, but not in time to enter college. She wasn't ready to make that commitment.

Noah and Willamina had not been shocked when Jude broached his—rather, Revel's—idea that Revel move to Los Angeles. In fact, they were actually grateful, because they'd been unable to arrive at any solution to the problem they knew existed. They were well aware of their inability to cope with their daughter's zealous appetite for the modern. They were not even sure what it was she hungered after. But it had been painful for them to acknowledge that Revel could not be satisfied with living in Hailey, that she belonged to a different world. Jude's solution made it easier to accept the inevitable, that they had to let their baby go. And, like Jude fifteen years before, they didn't expect Revel to return to them permanently. They prayed that Jude and Matthew and Polly would safeguard Revel.

So, it was with heavy hearts, but brave words, that Noah and Willamina bid Revel goodbye. Because her parents had agreed without much fuss, Revel left Hailey feeling more in tune with them than she had felt in a long time.

On the other hand, John had been vehemently opposed to letting Revel go. He was suspicious of Hollywood and fearful of its influence on her. Noah had answered John's questions with "A place not be evil. Only people make place evil."

"Yeah, well, Jude's in that place, so that makes it evil," John muttered to himself. His hatred for Jude had been rekindled when, in his judgment, Jude "lured" Matthew and Polly to "that sinful town." Now he had corrupted Revel's mind and wooed her away with God only knows what kind of promises.

Jude had used the weeks before Revel's arrival to redo his guest house under the supervision of the great "General Muriel." Soft greens and blues predominated and Revel was thrilled when she walked into her new home—her own, private little cottage. She had thrown her arms around Jude and then demanded that he tell her how the stereo equipment, the intercom system and the lighting gadgets worked. Oliver, the omnipresent butler, had introduced some aspects of the big and little houses' daily routine. Muriel clued Revel in on a portion of the office's operations.

"I want to help as much as I can. Just ask me to do—oh—*anything!*" Revel bubbled to everyone.

"I forgot, do you know how to drive?" Jude had asked her that first day.

"Of course I do, you ninny! Matt taught me on the qt before I was fourteen, and then Papa showed me when it was time to get my license. Papa just couldn't get over how quickly I learned! Now, how much time do I have before I have to transfer my license from Idaho to California?"

"I think it's six months, we'll check it out." Jude fished in his pockets for something. "Let's see now, that means you might be able to use these." He tossed some keys at Revel.

"What—what are these for?"

"Why don't you look in the garage and find out?" Jude was enjoying his surprise.

Revel's mouth dropped and stayed that way as she bolted for the garage. "How do I open these—damn doors?" she panted, finally taking a breath.

"Just press that button."

The automatic doors slid upward to reveal a shiny yellow Buick convertible with a bow on the hood ornament. And a card that read "Welcome Revel! I belong to you. Drive me carefully and I'll give you much pleasure. Drive me recklessly, and I'll disappear."

Revel's excitement boiled over, and she started to cry. "Oh, Jude, I—I don't know what to say. I'm—so—grateful." She ran and buried her head in Jude's chest.

Jude rocked her back and forth. "You don't have to say anything, baby. It makes me feel good to be able to do something for my family, that's enough for me." He held her away from him and looked at her seriously. "But I'm not kidding about the safety bit! The car is a key to freedom, especially in California—pretty hard to function without one. However, I don't want it to be a key to disaster. Los Angeles and Beverly Hills are a lot different than Hailey or Sun Valley. There can be some crazy galoots behind wheels, even some crackpots just walking around the streets. You have to think differently here, in the car and out. Figure on the other guy making a mistake and you won't be caught with your pants down." Jude blushed at his analogy and Revel giggled.

"Well, that's different here, too, and as long as it came up—" Jude seemed to put his foot in his mouth every time he opened it.

Revel stopped tittering—she wanted to save Jude from further embarrassment. "Just so you know, Jude, *it* has come up, but I wasn't ready. And there have been plenty of boys who tried to get my pants down, but I wasn't ready for them, either. Don't get me wrong, I may still be a virgin, but when I decide it's time, I won't remain one."

Jude stammered, "But—but—these Don Juans are older, sophisticated, smoother, oily—"

"And the boys back on the farms are stronger, stubborn as mules and get fired up on two beers. If I can control *it* and my panties at home, or in the East with their gold-plated erections, I can control the slime-bags here. Don't worry on that score, because they won't score unless I want them to."

Jude was dumbfounded. She was like an older sister talking to a younger brother. He was going to be hard put to keep the upper hand!

Revel backpedaled a bit, realizing that maybe she had come on too hard. "But of course you're absolutely right about the driving, I don't know beans. I'll be very careful and watchful and slow. Heck, I don't even know my way around these parts. Please don't be upset, Jude, I promise I'll be good!"

She gave her big brother another hug and pulled him into the front seat of her new car. "Can we go and show Polly and Matt? And then Penelope and Wade? You give me directions—just let me get used to how this thing works. What's this? Oh, I know, I know, it's one of those things that opens the garage from the car. I saw it in an ad. What do you call it? I know, a genie—wow! Now, which way do I turn? And don't fidget, you look like a prisoner on death row! Whee, here we go!"

Revel had gone over early on that birthday afternoon to help Polly with the decorations.

"I like the new colored stockings—they look great if you have nice legs—but I absolutely detest these so-called chic sack dresses," Revel complained to Polly. "They don't do anything for your figure. Designers either hate women or have fat old clients. Well, I'm not going to fall for that, I have a good body and I intend to show it off!"

"I'm sure the couturiers would have to close their salons without you," Polly answered dryly. "And just how much of that body do you want to be seen?"

"Oh, I don't know—enough!"

"Good! Just be sure enough isn't too much! Now that *that* issue is settled, do you think we could get back to blowing up these balloons? Everything else is ready, and we have to finish before the Terrible Two wake up." The love in Polly's eyes belied the sound of complaint in her voice.

Matthew burst in the back door. "Okay, the clown's ready! What's next? Oh, and he brought the Hula Hoops—are you sure you want to have a Hula Hoop contest for the grown-ups?"

Polly laughed at her husband when she saw his outfit: ragged dungarees, a well-worn T-shirt and old sneakers. "Yes, I'm sure. It'll be a hoot, trust me! But next on your agenda should be a shower and a change of clothes. The guests will be arriving soon and we can't have Daddy looking like a Hollywood beach bum, can we? Rev and I can wrestle with these damn balloons."

"I don't think you should try the Hula Hoop, darling," Wade said protectively to Penelope. "I'll defend the family honor. You keep an eye on Buzz, but don't lift him. You ain't seen nothin' until you've seen the old master!" Wade boasted as he joined the other gyrating bodies.

Penelope smiled fondly at her husband's antics and shook her head in mock exasperation to Polly. "He treats me as if I were going to break in half! You'd think with the second pregnancy he'd be more relaxed, but if anything, he's worse. He doesn't even want the nanny to have a day off, afraid I'll wear myself out. The truth is, I love being alone with the little rascal. I don't get enough of him, what with work and all. I'm glad we finish this season in February, so I'll at least have some time with Buzz before my May first due date."

Polly sensed a wistfulness in Penelope. "Have you ever thought of leaving the show?" she asked quietly.

Penelope looked startled, almost guilty. "My God, you're uncanny! It's been in the back of my mind for weeks." She sat silently for a bit, then said, "This will be the fifth year, and Jude claims that from now on the reruns and syndication are very profitable. But deep inside—" now the words were tumbling out "—I feel I might be letting Wade down. He wouldn't do well if he wasn't working, and I'm not sure the series could continue without the two of us. And it's been a while since he's done a feature. And the studio wouldn't be enough—Jude, and now Matthew, handle everything so well—and Wade needs to act. Of course, he could do specials, but—oh, I don't know, Polly, I really don't know."

Polly didn't want her friend to get upset. "Well, it's not something that has to be decided now. But I bet if you put a subtle bug in Wade's or Jude's ear, one or the other or both would come up with a solution. You know they would do anything to keep you from being unhappy."

"Oh, I know, I know. That's why I'm afraid to even hint at any change," Penelope fretted.

"Change can be good. Look at Matt and me! And a little time off wouldn't hurt Wade. He has so many interests, so many toys..." Polly was her usual forthright self. She took Penelope's hand and said, "You're concerned he would revert to his old ways, aren't you? Too much booze and hanging out because he would be bored. I don't think so. Wade's grown into quite a guy. Oh sure, he's going to tie one on now and then, and play the jock with some of the boys, but that's as far as it would go. He worships you and your life together."

Penelope squeezed Polly's hand. "Thank you. Maybe I will start planting a seed." She contemplated for a bit. "In all honesty, Polly, I'm not sure how I would react in the long run. I've been independent, worked all my life. What if I get antsy? I've never been the lunch-and-shop type."

"Lunch and shop? With two kids, and hubby makes three, and a house to run? No way! Anyhow, when the time comes, I'll ease off work, too, and we'll find plenty of mischief to get into. There are causes galore, and politics, exciting candidates—we'll have lots to keep us busy! Whoops! I see a potential free-for-all brewing. See what I mean? Never a dull moment!"

Polly ran through the crowded yard toward her son. "Dewayne, there are enough hoops for all. Please don't take the one Buzz has. Here's the nice blue one you were playing with."

"Mine! Mine!" Dewayne cried, pulling the red hoop away from Buzz.

"Me—mine!" retorted the offended Buzz.

Wade and Matthew stopped their rotating and scooped up their respective offspring, momentarily restoring peace. Polly called for everyone to gather and sit on the lawn as the clown began his show. Then the cakes—one for each twin—were presented, the ice cream dished out, the donkey piñata broken and, finally, the tired but happy children were bundled home to their beds.

Matthew and Polly flopped down in the middle of the debris after the twins were asleep. Their housekeeper, Ophelia, a wonderful no-nonsense lady, was straightening up.

"Don't bother yourself, Mrs. Polly. Lord knows, you must be done in. You just relax there with Mister—this won't take no time."

"Today was nice, honey," Matthew said, holding her so close she couldn't get up if she wanted to. "You were right about the Hula Hoops. Did you ever see anything funnier than Jude and Wade with those things? They wouldn't let up!"

"Well, you weren't exactly Mr. Coordinated!" Polly teased. "No doubt about it, Revel was the best. She practically made that hoop dance!"

"Speaking of Miss Devil Herself, do you think she and Jude will survive?" Matthew asked, nibbling at Polly's face and throat with his lips.

Polly reflected before voicing her theory, trying to ignore his distractions. "I believe Rev will do just fine, as long as she stays on track. She's bright, witty and, of course, beautiful. She could probably go in almost any direction—back to school, to the studio, our offices—she could even be in front of the cameras. It all depends on where she decides to target her energy. And Jude, I believe, is the only one who can possibly keep her in line. We can help, but Jude is the real authority figure."

Matthew tightened his arms around her, "How can someone so tiny know so much? You're too young to be so wise!"

"Ha!" Polly snorted. "You can never be too young, too thin, or too rich—and I don't claim any of those categories!"

"Shall I get out the violins for your sad story?"

Polly leveled a look at her husband.

"Okay, okay. But it's hard to be serious when you're this close," Matthew mumbled in her ear.

"Be patient, you glutton, Ophelia's still here," she whispered as she felt his arousal. "Now, where were we? Oh, I remember, yes, Jude!"

Matthew struggled to get back into the conversation. "Yes... Jude. Let's forget Jude and concentrate on something else."

"Not now, you sex maniac. Just a few more minutes! About Jude, ah, I think Rev will be good for Jude. Like today, he seemed looser, not so uptight. He'll meet some new people—I'm sure Rev will see to that. Hopefully, some nice women. It would be great if he could settle down—but I get the feeling he's always busy because he's almost afraid to be quiet or to take a breather. It is almost as if—as if he slowed up, someone or something would catch him. Am I making any sense?"

"A lot of sense," Matthew said seriously, concentrating, for the moment anyhow. "It all goes back to Thelma and Keane. My God, do you realize they've been gone over sixteen years? And he still shrinks from involvement because he's wary that a relationship can be plucked away from him again without warning. He doesn't think he could ever survive another loss."

"Did you watch him with all the kids this afternoon? He's wonderful—he *should* have children, he'd be a sensational father!"

"He was," Matthew said soberly.

"Well, he should be again. A gift like that shouldn't be wasted! I think I'll enlist Penelope's help—together we'll start Operation Jude!"

"If anyone can do it, you two can," Matthew agreed. "Isn't Ophelia *ever* going to go?"

"You know who else?" Polly continued, ignoring Matthew's complaint. "Revel! Revel can help us."

"Poor Jude! He doesn't have a chance, but can't we—"

"Did you hear that old Blackie finally got Orey II in the family way?" Polly wasn't going to let Matthew finish. "Pretty good for a ten-year-old dog! Revel gets her pick of the litter. I don't think Rev ever had her own dog, did she?"

"I don't know. What is this, 'Make Matt Suffer' night?"

"I'm done, Mrs. Polly!" called a voice from the kitchen. "Night! See you in the mornin'. I put out the list for the milkman already."

"Thank you so much, Ophelia. You were my right arm as always. Bye now!"

Matthew waited until he heard Ophelia's car start, and then he pounced. "I thought she'd never leave. And now, me proud beauty, prepare to be ravaged by Matt the Rat!"

29

Santa Monica, California
Saturday, November 22, 1958

Operation Jude was progressing. Penelope and Polly came.up with the idea of giving Revel a "Welcome to Hollywood" party, with the subversive intent of inviting as many eligible candidates for Jude as possible. Revel, naturally, approved of the strategy, as long as the guest list also included a number of unattached males. The trick was to find some new faces, because Jude already knew most of the single women in town. They had one thing in their favor—Hollywood was a drawing card for the world's beautiful people.

Although it was Penelope's thirtieth birthday dinner, the conspirators were huddled together discussing their plans. Wade had decided to host an intimate gathering to conserve his expectant wife's energy, because their social calendar was heavily booked starting with Thanksgiving the following Thursday. Revel's black-tie affair was to be held on December 6, to launch the holiday season.

"Is it too late to ask someone else to the party?" Revel was saying.

"Not if it's a footloose 'she' who wouldn't mind a late invitation," Polly answered quickly. "Who do you have in mind?"

"Well . . ." Revel played mysterioso to the hilt. "When I was at Mr. Felipi's yesterday—oh, he sent kisses to you both, by the way—he suddenly dropped everything and rushed over to the entrance to greet someone. It was this knockout lady, and I mean drop-dead *beautiful!* I could hardly wait till he got back to find out who she was. Her name is Madge Moore. Mr. Felipi says that's not her real name, though. She's staying at the Bel-Air Hotel, she just arrived in town for a visit and she travels in 'the jet set' crowd! Isn't that exciting?''

Penelope searched her memory. "I can't recall meeting a Madge Moore, but that doesn't mean a thing. I've met so many people with Wade that it's impossible to remember names—I'm lucky if I remember the faces. But if it is someone none of us knows, isn't it awkward to ask her to a dinner dance?''

"Oh, I know her now!" chirped Revel. "Mr. Felipi brought me over to meet her. Introduced me as the sister of the movie magnate Jude Abavas and friend of *the* Wade Colbys. She was real nice, asked me to call her and that maybe we'd have lunch. I think she liked me. I liked her, too. She's *soooo* pretty—and she has this throaty voice!''

"Ask her then!" Polly exclaimed. "I, for one, am dying to see this female wonder!''

"Me, too! You talk to her, Rev, and explain the invitation is in the mail," Penelope said. "But I guess we're obliged to give her the option of having an escort. It doesn't matter, really, Jude is bringing a date. I couldn't very well suggest he come by himself, even though I wanted to. He would be mortified if he suspected what we're doing. Anyway, if she does come alone, tell her we'll send a car, that's the least we can do.''

"Wow! She'll really think I'm somebody—a chauffeur and a limousine!''

"I have a feeling that's what she would expect," Polly put in.

Penelope sighed. "My, this scheming business gets complicated, doesn't it? I don't think I would have made a very good spy.''

Wade interrupted any further planning, clinking his glass for attention. "Let's raise our bubbly in a toast to my wife on her birthday. Lovely Penelope, your friendship is treasured by everyone here. Your presence makes my life worth living. To our wonderful Penelope!''

With everyone's help, Revel had quickly established herself in Jude's immediate circle. At first, Jude's office staff had invented errands for her, but they soon found that Revel's willingness to work as a gofer was extremely useful. Penelope and Wade had asked her to be their part-time girl Friday. Revel was thrilled! She was needed! She became a familiar sight at the studio, auburn hair blowing in the wind as she drove through the gates. The guard had quickly located a special parking place—who could resist those hazel eyes as she asked naively where she should go?

Matthew and Polly tried to support Revel's transition period, too. But for the moment, they could only ask for her to help with the twins now and then. The new business wasn't quite ready yet. Matthew was just putting the final organizational touches on Studio Services Inc. It had taken a great deal of time to ensure that all procedures were properly initiated, and Matthew insisted on every detail being perfect and legal. And he had personally investigated every potential outlet to make certain there was a market for such a company. He had just established separate headquarters from Colvas Inc., on Sunset Boulevard near Doheny Drive, to further separate the two corporations, providing additional protection for his partners. What Matthew and Polly needed right now was a full-time executive. Matthew had someone in mind, one of the young lawyers who had plodded through the structuring of S.S.I. with him. His name was Vincent Franks and he was about Matthew's age. Although Vincent was associated with a prominent law firm, he was low on their totem pole and Matthew had a hunch Vincent could be swayed to leave. If his colleagues agreed with his choice, Matthew intended to offer Vincent the job.

As for Jude, he willingly allowed Revel to keep him on the go, escorting her to charity functions he normally would have declined, taking her to the previews and premieres of new features, television specials and social business dinners. He actually took great pleasure introducing Revel to the people in his life and was proud of how easily she adapted to these new situations. Revel made it difficult for Jude to just tread water, and since Operation Jude had begun, she was on the lookout for someone for her brother. Meanwhile, Jude was surveying the field for suitable escorts for Revel, which was one of the reasons he had decided to take his standby date, Nina, to Revel's party. It would give him more of a chance to mingle.

"May I speak to Miss Madge Moore, please?" Revel asked the Bel-Air Hotel operator in her most sophisticated tone.

"Who's calling Miss Moore?"

"Miss Revel Abavas!" replied Revel haughtily.

Moments later... "*Ciao,* Revel!" There was that voice! "I am so glad you telephoned! Can you play today? Mondays are always boring here. Everyone is too busy with work, work, work."

"Well, ah, yes, I think so. I have a few errands to run for Penelope—you know, Penelope Colby. And if Muriel—if my brother doesn't need me at his studio, I guess I could meet you. For lunch? Should I pick you up?"

"No, I have my driver. Shall we say the Polo Lounge at one? Then you will come with me, and my chauffeur, Antonio, will take us to some shops in Beverly Hills."

Revel's mind was hopping—the celebrity-packed Polo Lounge! What should she wear? Polly would know! Oh, wait, the party.

"Oh, Madge, Penelope and Wade wanted me to invite you to a soiree on December 6. It's sort of for me, you know, kind of a welcome party, I guess. I've only been here since September. They apologize for not asking sooner—the invitation is in the mail but I thought I'd better call first. It's formal, I mean black-tie and they—we—will send a limo for you if you come alone. But you are more than welcome to bring a guest. Anyway, can you—would you come?"

"It sounds divine! Of course I will come! Now we have a reason to go shopping! I think I will ask my friend Artie to escort me. Yes, he will be in town by then. And he is amusing. You will like him! So, that is settled, see you at one! *Arrivederci,* Revel!"

December 6 was a crisp and clear night. The motif for the Colbys' Santa Monica gala was, of course, the approaching Christmas holidays, but emphasis had also been placed on the glamour of Hollywood. The female population had swallowed the bait, the gauntlet had been thrown—who would wear the most spectacular gown of the evening? The ladies became quite secretive, each knowing *exactly* how they were going to dazzle the crowd. It promised to be quite a show. Even the men were ordering new tuxedos or sprucing up the old with the ruffled dress shirts that were now so popular.

From the moment the guests were greeted by eighteenth-century-clad carolers and ushered through the covered courtyard, it was obvious it would be an elegant evening. Tents extended almost to the water, a floor that continued the lanai was built over the sand. Set designers had lined the sides of the tents with simulated snow-laden fir trees, which also camouflaged portable heaters. The roofs of the canvas tents had been transformed into galaxies of twinkling stars. Gold envelopes, with the guest's table number embossed on the inside, were given to each arrival. Strolling minstrels roamed the rooms along with liveried servants carrying trays of sumptuous hors d'oeuvres. Later, when supper was announced, the guests would be led toward the ocean, where an orchestra and dance floor waited. Gold lace over white tablecloths set off gold place settings and golden goblets. The decorator had created the aura of an ancient mythical palace set in the midst of a forest.

"I'm dreaming!" Revel gasped as she walked in with Jude and Nina. "How did they do this? It's the most beautiful castle I've ever seen—even in movies! I must be Cinderella." She looked at her brother. "So where's my prince?"

"Right here!" Wade spun Revel around. "Give old Uncle Wade a kiss!"

Revel hugged Wade and pecked his cheek. "But you already have a princess," she observed, pointing to Penelope by his side.

"No, I don't have a princess—I have a queen! And I am her loyal subject." Wade bowed ceremoniously to Penelope. "Your Highness, may I be so bold as to tell you what an outstanding masterpiece you have created tonight? It looks as though you waved a magic wand. And if I may also add, you look royally magnificent!" Wade grandly kissed her hand. "Your court is a credit to you, as well!" he announced with a flourish that included everyone present.

It was true, the would-be receiving line was a sight to behold. After much deliberation among the hostesses and guest of honor, the results had proved well worth the effort. Penelope indeed looked regal in an Empire gold-brocade gown. Except for a true glow that enveloped her, the pregnancy barely showed. Polly was ablaze in vivid red satin, her blond hair swept up in a twist topped with a crimson studded comb. The long lines of her dress made her five feet seem taller. Revel had chosen a deep forest green, an almost ebony French velvet. Strapless, form-fitting until it flared out at the knee, the simple austerity of the dress gave Revel the extra dash of sophistication she craved.

Jude gazed at his baby sister, and also his young brother—so lovely, so handsome—and a torrent of emotion overtook him. He had to stifle surfacing tears. *If only Mama and Papa could see us!*

As if she had read his thoughts, Penelope interrupted the procession. "I hope you don't mind, but I asked our studio photographer to cover the evening. We'll have complete say-so on the negatives, of course. I just thought Revel would enjoy having an album of her party. I know I would. And before anyone else comes, I think we should start with our nucleus, so please gather round. Ray!"

The cameraman appeared from the rear tent. "I was taking some shots back there while the room was still empty. Boy, does it look great!" he said excitedly. Then he took a peek at the assembled small group. "Boy, do you all look great! How shall we do this? Let's see, the ladies in front and the men behind—that'll make it tighter."

Nina graciously excused herself from the session so that only the principals would be photographed. Her discreetness was one of the reasons she had lasted with Jude as long as she had. She realized he didn't like publicity in general, and particularly didn't like being romantically linked to any one woman. She was also aware that nothing would ever come from her friendship with Jude. But he was fun and generous, and—who knew—maybe she would wear him down.

The picture of Matthew, Wade, Jude, Polly, Penelope and Revel would hit the social pages of many newspapers, including Hailey's *Wood River Journal.*

The gala was in full swing when Madge Moore made her entrance. A hush didn't exactly fall over the chattering and laughing crowd, but there was definitely a quieting when this stunning creature materialized. Her extremely long raven hair was pulled back, cascading down from a diamond and emerald headband. A white crepe de chine gown clung tenaciously to her ample curves, its deep V cut reaching almost to her waist. A magnificent diamond and emerald brooch securely fastened the opening of the daring neckline. More than one person wondered if it was the key to Pandora's box of mysteries. Translucent skin was the silken background for her impressive green eyes, which seemed to look into and through one's soul.

Revel was the first to gather her wits and rush to greet her friend.

"Oh, Madge, you came! I mean, you're here—I mean, you look great! Hello!"

Madge laughed. "Hello, *ma chérie!* And you—you are smashing!" She turned to the gentleman at her side. "Revel, this is Atherton Sardos, also known as Artie."

The slender dark-haired young man bowed and kissed Revel's extended hand. His black eyes held hers as he said softly with a slight accent, "Charmed. You are enchanting."

Revel was completely undone. Fortunately, Penelope and Polly saved her as they came up to welcome their newest guests. Introductions were exchanged. Wade and Matthew were presented, and finally, Jude.

"Ah, yes, the elusive Jude Abavas," Madge murmured huskily, holding out her hand to be kissed.

"I'm afraid I never got the hang of hand kissin'," Jude said, taking her hand and shaking it. The onlookers were a little surprised—Jude seemed to be deliberately reverting to a country bumpkin. Jude couldn't have explained his reaction himself. But for some reason, he felt challenged, off-balance, and therefore needed to defend or attack.

Madge was unscathed. She dismissed the moment by saying mockingly, "Perhaps then, you need someone to instruct you!"

Penelope and Revel piloted Madge and Artie toward the rest of the waiting multitude, first fortifying them with goblets of champagne. It turned out that Madge and Artie knew quite a few people, so they did not have to be chaperoned for long.

Once the two were out of earshot, Wade said to Jude, "If I were single, she could instruct me anytime!"

"Me, too!" Matthew echoed. "If I were single, that is!"

"She does have—" Wade fished for the words. "What did you use to say? Oh, yes—a pair of jugs, doesn't she?"

Matthew let loose a low whistle. "She sure does! What's the matter, Jude? Didn't you like her? You weren't exactly polite."

"She's okay, I guess. I don't cotton to all that European crap—hand kissing, for Christ's sake. Come on, let's have a drink. I want to keep Revel in sight."

At the appointed supper hour, the minstrels guided everyone to the dining area. Penelope had placed Revel with Madge and

escort, Jude and Nina. A director, an actor and an actress completed their table. Originally, Nina and the actress had been
seated on either side of Jude, but when Penelope came to check
to see if everything was set, she saw that Madge was sitting in the
actress's spot. Someone had switched cards. Penelope glanced at
Revel, who shrugged her shoulders innocently, but Penelope
caught the impish glint in Revel's eye and knew she was the cul-
prit. Penelope smiled to herself, shaking her head. She also noticed that Revel had put herself between Artie and the actor. Oh
well, what difference did it really make? And this Madge Moore
certainly was striking—entertaining, too. Maybe Revel had a
good idea, after all!

Revel soon found out as much as she could about Atherton
Sardos. Artie was the son of a Greek shipping tycoon—named
for his birthplace of Athens. He had been born on April 12, 1931,
which made him twenty-seven, and was educated in Greece and
the United States. He was a playboy being groomed as heir apparent to his father's business. But the best news of all was that
he was a bachelor! She wasn't sure about his relationship with
Madge, but right now she didn't care—she was having fun!

Jude didn't know if he was having fun. Madge Moore disturbed him and he didn't know why. Undeniably she was beautiful, a Venus, in fact. And interesting. But when they conversed,
he felt out of control—she knew the answer before the question
was even asked, and he wasn't comfortable with that. He directed much of his attention to Nina and the others, but he
couldn't ignore Madge. To do so would indicate that she had
won. But won what? What was the contest?

Revel and Artie were dancing. Madge leaned toward Jude.
"They make a handsome couple, don't they? I like your Revel."

Jude glanced at the two. Artie's olive skin was pressed close
against Revel's contrasting fair complexion, his curly black hair
brushing her chestnut strands. Jude frowned, he wasn't sure he
approved. "Yes, they do," he said carefully. "How long have
you known...ah...Artie?"

"We've been friends for years, he's like a brother. Artie is
witty—I enjoy his company—but he's really just a boy. That is
precisely why I wanted him to meet Revel."

"I see. And what does that make you, Grandma Moses?"

Madge gave a throaty laugh. "Not exactly. Actually, he's two
years older than my twenty-five years. You see, I haven't yet

reached the age where I need to lie. But he is still quite immature, at least to me. I think he regards me as a trusted confi-
dante.''

Jude decided to be blunt. ''Why did you describe me as 'elusive' when we met?''

The eyes bore straight into his. ''Because you are. You are the
withdrawn, silent, rough-hewn hero. Yes, you are visible with
'the men.' Yes, you protect yourself with a different 'ornament'
at night. But you draw a curtain when you meet a real woman. I
have been in Los Angeles many times the last four years, and
your reputation is widely known. Now,'' she bantered, ''do your
social graces extend as far as dancing? Or do you need instruc-
tion in that department also?''

Angrily, Jude pulled back her chair and led her to the dance
floor, determined to show her his social graces.

Madge was five foot eight, and in high heels the top of her
head nestled against Jude's mouth. Her body folded easily into
his. Wordlessly they moved to the music.

Nothing escaped the watchful eyes of Matthew and Polly,
Wade and Penelope—or Nina. As the evening wore on Nina saw
any hope of something more with Jude fade. This enigma of a
woman was threatening. Nina started to get edgy and uncharacteristically bottomed-up quite a few glasses of wine.

At one point, Jude excused himself. Nina looked around,
somewhat confused. ''I wonder, does this place have an aspirin
on the menu?''

Madge overheard and asked, ''Do you have a headache?''

Nina nodded. ''The beginning of a lulu!''

''Maybe I can be of help.'' Madge rummaged through her
Tiffany clutch and pulled out a jeweled pillbox. ''I am never
without this. I sometimes have migraines, so I always carry an
assortment of remedies.'' She found what she wanted and
handed the capsule to Nina. ''This should fix you up in no time.
Oh, it works more effectively if you down it with some wine—
trust me!''

Revel had been listening and looked at Madge in astonish-
ment. She was sure people weren't supposed to mix medicine
with alcohol.

Madge caught Revel's questioning gaze—and winked! As
much as to say, ''Our little secret!'' Revel didn't exactly know

what was going on, although she could guess, and she became a willing accomplice, marveling at Madge's nerve and inventiveness. She never would have dared to do this.

Nina obediently swallowed the pill with wine, saying gratefully between gulps, "What a lifesaver you are."

During the parade of desserts, Nina started to swoon.

"Jude, I don't feel right. Can barely...hold my...head...up. Not sure...I can...even walk."

Jude was concerned, also a mite irritated, because he thought she was simply drunk. "I'll take you home. Here, let me help you up."

"What's the matter? Are you all right, Nina?" Madge asked solicitously.

"She's ill, I'm taking her home," Jude explained.

"What a shame! But should you leave Revel's party so early, Jude?" Madge pretended to think a minute. "Perhaps I have a solution. If Nina wouldn't mind, my chauffeur, Antonio, could drive her home and return in plenty of time for me."

"That...would...be...fine," Nina managed to say. "Thank you."

"Only if you're positive, Nina," Jude insisted. "But to be honest, I would feel better if I stayed, because of Revel. That's nice of you to offer, Madge."

"It's...fine...please...must...go..." Nina practically collapsed as Jude half carried her to the entrance. Madge accompanied them, bringing Nina's purse, collecting the young woman's wrap and giving Antonio instructions. Once the car was located and Nina was settled comfortably in the back seat, Jude gave the chauffeur Nina's address. Antonio walked around the front to request a moment with Madge. Jude stepped inside the car to check on Nina, but he could hear a heated conversation taking place outside. He didn't understand it, however, because it was in Italian. Madge must have had the last word, for Antonio bowed and marched back to the driver's seat, his body stiff with resentment.

"Excuse me for asking," Jude said to Madge as the limo sped away, "but what was that all about? He seemed out of line to me, but I didn't want to interfere."

Madge's eyes flashed with fury. "He is an arrogant fool, an insolent servant who doesn't know his place. How dare he tell me what he will or will not do!"

"You should get rid of him, plenty of drivers around here looking for work."

"It's all the doing of my father," Madge complained. "Wherever I go, Antonio—or someone like Antonio—goes. 'It is for your own protection,' my father says. But it makes me crazy. I feel I'm a prisoner, or a child with a nanny."

Jude raised his eyebrows in surprise, curious as to Madge's need for protection.

Madge continued her tirade as they returned to the house. "However, I always manage to have my way, as you saw. All I have to do is swear I'll tell my father they tried to kiss me—they know he will believe me. But it is such a nuisance and embarrassment to go through that scene time and again. This Antonio is fairly new and too eager. I will think of a way to punish him—tonight!"

They found Revel and Artie flushed with laughter when they rejoined the party. "Jude, your sister has the most refreshing personality," Artie called as they approached the table. "Madge, you must hear this—tell her, Revel!"

"Well, I don't know how we got to it, but Artie and I were talking about social mistakes. Lord knows, I've made so many I've lost count. But one in particular struck his funny bone, I guess. Well, ah, when I went to boarding school in the East, my first night in the dining room I saw 'hors d'oeuvres' on the menu. I had no idea what that was, so I asked the girl next to me, 'What are these "horses' ovaries" like?'"

Madge roared, Artie chuckled again and even Jude laughed.

"I thought she was going to bust her girdle. Wish she had, because then she ran all over telling everyone. It's funny now," Revel added, "but it wasn't so funny to me then."

Artie immediately covered her hand with his, "But they were children, probably have remained so, and could not recognize an open honest soul. That is why you are so special." He lifted her hand to his lips.

Jude was starting to like Artie a little more than he had in the beginning, but he still was concerned about Revel's apparent attraction to this young cosmopolitan.

"Come on, Rev," Jude declared. "I'm not Fred Astaire, but I can give you a whirl or two—Ketchum-style at least!" Jude and Revel glided away. "Having a good time, honey?" he asked.

"The best night of my life! Everything is *sooo* perfect! I think I even found my prince."

"Hold on there, my little buckaroo! Not too fast!" cautioned Jude. "Remember what I told you back in September."

"And you remember what I told you! I said I'd mind you, yes, but you have to trust me, too! Believe I can take care of myself." Revel leveled her gaze directly at Jude. "I want him to take me home, Jude."

Jude guided her quietly along for a few bars of music. He knew he didn't want to make her a rebel without a cause—he couldn't go on dates with her, for Christ's sake. "That's okay with me, Rev."

Revel looked up at him with grateful eyes. "Thank you, Jude."

Madge had a triumphant look on her face when they returned. "I know how to torment Antonio! I will leave before he comes back! I'll beg a ride with someone—maybe Jude and Revel—and Artie, you will tell Antonio that you don't know where I am. That will absolutely panic him!" She clapped her hands with delight.

Revel's eyes darted in Jude's direction. *Please,* they implored.

Jude struggled to suppress a rising heat. He felt manipulated, trapped. But he had promised. There was nothing else he could do—he was forced to offer to drive Madge home.

"What a glorious evening! The Colbys are a lovely couple, and they do know how to entertain. Your brother Matthew and his adorable wife—Polly, isn't it?—are sweet, too." Madge leaned her head back on the red leather of Jude's Lincoln Continental coupe. "Oh, how I wish I could see the fear on Antonio's face when Artie comes out without me!" She smiled, savoring the image.

"It's none of my business—and you certainly don't have to answer—but I can't help being a little curious. Why does your father feel the need to post a guard over you?"

Madge's eyes veiled. "You are right, it *is* none of your business!"

They rode in silence for a bit.

Madge broke the quiet. "I am sorry. I did involve you and I do owe you an explanation. Let's just say, my father has...

enemies, and he worries a great deal about... safety. Unnecessarily, I should add. But..." She hesitated before continuing, "My mother died when I was thirteen, and the responsibility for me lies heavy on him. Too heavy! So, am I forgiven? Friends?"

"Of course. My fault, I shouldn't have pried." Jude remained perplexed by the woman—she seemed sympathetic at times and quite cold at others.

As they neared the Bel-Air Hotel, Madge gave directions. "We don't go to the entrance. My bungalow has its own parking area."

"Naturally," Jude remarked sardonically.

Once the engine stopped, the night turned very still. Jude exited quickly and walked to the passenger side to assist Madge. "I'll see you to your door," he said gruffly. They made their way along the moonlit garden path until they reached Madge's cottage. She had her key ready, but before entering, she turned to Jude. "Since I eluded Antonio, perhaps you might do the honors? To preserve the ritual? He always checks the interior for intruders."

Jude felt the surge of adrenaline that the prospect of danger always encouraged. He moved stealthily into the living room, which was illuminated by only a small lamp. He canvassed every suspicious shadow, searched behind each drawn drape and every door before proceeding to the bedroom, bath and dressing rooms. Satisfied, he said, "Clean as a whistle, no one's here."

"Thank you." Madge had a hint of sport in her voice. "You were really quite thorough, more so than the others. It is too bad you have another profession, you would make an excellent bodyguard. I don't usually reward my policemen, but I think you will be the exception. I have some champagne on ice."

Jude stood stubbornly where he was, feeling as though he'd been put in his place yet again.

Madge faced him from behind the bar. "Oh, come now, Mr. Jude Abavas, where is your sense of humor? I am only playing! Do you know how to open this?"

Something snapped in Jude, he'd had enough! He strode purposefully to her, knocked the bottle out of her hands, roughly scooped her in his arms and carried her into the bedroom.

"I know how to do a lot of things and I'm going to show you one thing right now—one thing I'm very good at! This is what you want, isn't it? This is what you've been asking for, isn't it? You're nothing but a cock tease in expensive duds, and I'm calling your bluff, lady!''

He tossed her on the bed. "You better take off that dress before I tear it off," Jude threatened as he shed his own clothes.

There was no resistance from Madge. She pulled the headband from her hair, unleashing the flowing mane, and unclasped her brooch. The crepe de chine shimmied off to reveal a completely nude body. Jude inadvertently sucked in his breath— *my God, she is magnificent.* He pulled her legs down so her feet touched the floor, knelt and then, without ceremony, rammed into her. Again and again, relentlessly—punishing her.

"No—niceties—for—you!" Jude grunted. "Just plain, country-folk fucking—like rattlesnakes!"

With one last vicious thrust, his wrath flowed out of him. Empty now, of words as well, he withdrew, dressed and left.

He didn't see the self-satisfied smirk on Madge's face.

"Boy, Antonio was really upset," Revel whispered in the back seat of the limo. "But you handled him!"

Artie grinned. "He is a peasant and a snob, the worse combination. Enough of him, I want to know more about you. What are your plans? Is there anyone special in your life? When may I see you again?"

They talked until the car pulled up to the house on Maple Drive, Revel nestling peacefully in the crook of his arm.

"Wait!" Artie ordered Antonio.

The two walked hand in hand, past the main house, to Revel's cottage.

"Jude isn't home yet. Maybe he and Madge stopped somewhere. Would you like a drink? Come in and see my place, anyway!"

Revel proudly showed Artie around. "I can run up and get some champagne or wine or something else. I don't have it here, I'm afraid."

"You are all I need, my little one," and Artie gently kissed her. A quiver shot through Revel's body and she returned his kiss ardently.

"What fire you have..." Artie was surprised yet delighted by her response. His tongue explored her mouth and found hers.

Revel gasped, "Is this a French kiss?"

"May I?" Artie's lips were caressing her throat and had reached the top of her gown, ready to sample her supple young breasts.

"Oh, yes—yes!" breathed Revel.

Tenderly, he undid the top of her zipper, took one nipple in his mouth, and then the other. She shuddered with pleasure and desire. She was ready, she had decided—this was the time and this was the man!

"Now I know why I waited," Revel mumbled ecstatically.

Artie pulled back and looked at her with dawning awareness. "My God, of course, you are a virgin! How stupid of me! Please forgive me—I should have realized. I am so sorry!"

Revel was stunned.

"I must go now—while I still can. I will call tomorrow—if you are not too angry to speak with me. I apologize for my impropriety once again." Artie was out the door before Revel could utter a sound.

As Jude rounded the corner in his car, he saw the limousine drive off. He looked at his watch. Good! The timing was proper, they had left a while after he and Madge had. Jude was grateful. At least one thing had ended well tonight!

30

Beverly Hills, California
December 7, 1958

Neither Jude nor Revel slept much that Saturday night after the party. Both were in a foul mood the next morning at breakfast. Jude idly glanced at the paper's headline, Pearl Harbor Day, and morosely thought of his life seventeen years ago, a life that had belonged to a whole different person.

Revel was trying desperately to figure out what she had done wrong. She was positive she would never hear from Atherton Sardos again; he had to think she was a pea-brained child.

Jude knew what he had done wrong and was racked with guilt—and also completely frustrated. What was the matter with him? Was he some kind of bad seed? No one else in the family behaved as he did, like a wild beast. He hadn't learned his lesson, even after what he had done to Thelma. No doubt it was a damn good thing Penelope had fallen for Wade instead of him!

Madge had annoyed and irritated him, true, but he'd had no right to—to practically rape her. Why did he lose control? And why did he still want her? Did he dare call and try to atone for his actions?

The two of them jumped when the telephone rang.

"It is for you, Miss Revel," announced Oliver, "a Mr. Atherton Sardos."

Revel ran to take the call privately in the other room. Jude brooded, how nice to be young and innocent and carefree! She returned shortly, walking on a cloud.

"He wants to see me this evening," Revel said wondrously.

"I don't know why that should surprise you, sweetheart. Of course he would want to see you!"

Revel pecked the top of Jude's head. "See you later. I'm going out back, I need to call Madge. Oh, I forgot, how did you two get along? Isn't she something?"

"Uh—it was—uh—all right," Jude stammered.

"I'll say hello for you—"

"No! I mean, yes, sure." He didn't want Revel to get in the middle of this and he didn't want her to know what had happened. "Ah, better yet, I think I'll call her. Later."

Revel looked at Jude quizzically and nodded. He was acting strange today. But she couldn't be bothered right now, she had other matters on her mind.

"Madge, we are friends, aren't we?" Revel asked in a confidential tone.

"Of course we are! You can always depend on that, my little chum."

"I knew it! I felt it right off!" exclaimed Revel. "I have to know a couple of things. First, are you and Artie, well, romantically involved, or anything?"

Madge replied quickly, "No, no, not at all. Artie and I are almost family!" Then, teasing, "You like him, don't you? And he likes you! I think that is wonderful!"

Relief flooded through Revel. "I just wanted everything to be up-front, that's all." Revel was bashful about the next question, but she swallowed hard and plunged ahead. "I don't exactly know how to say this, but you're the only one I can ask. I can't risk Polly or Penelope—definitely not Jude or Matthew—"

"What is it, Revel? You can trust me."

Revel lowered her voice, even though no one was there to listen. "Do you have a doctor here who could—who would—quietly, fit me for a diaphragm? I can pay him out of my salary—I *can't* have a bill come here! Do you think I'm—bad?" Revel dwindled off into a helpless silence.

It had been so long, mused Madge, since she had worried about such trivialities. The girl was obviously still a virgin who wanted to change that status and didn't know the ropes. She would be just the type to get pregnant, too! Another thought flashed to the forefront—what a delicious way to penalize Jude! While simultaneously accommodating his sister!

"Don't say such words!" Madge was now in command. "You are not *bad*—you are perfectly normal. And smart! Most would not take the trouble for preventatives."

Revel gulped; she had almost been one of those.

"And you can't expect a self-centered man to think of the woman. I know a doctor, he takes care of me when I am in town, and I'm sure he will see you tomorrow. Naturally, I will come with you. And no one will know—it is between you and me— just like my little joke with Nina! Now, what time is good for you?"

"You are the best friend in the world," Revel said, and sighed.

Jude telephoned everyone he could think of: Nina, who was still groggy, Wade and Penelope, and Matthew and Polly, and finally found the gumption to dial the Bel-Air Hotel.

He nearly hung up because he didn't want a record of his name on the books, but at the last minute, he said, "Revel's brother is calling Miss Moore." He waited anxiously, and as the seconds ticked by, he felt certain she was not going to accept his call. Then the velvety tone—

"Hello." No indication of welcome? Or unwelcome?

"It's Jude Abavas."

"I know."

"I wasn't sure you would answer."

"I know."

"Well, I—damn it to hell—you're not making it easy!"

"Should I?" came the sarcastic question.

"I guess not." Jude still couldn't interpret her feelings. "I would like to see you. Maybe start off on the right foot this time, or, at least, a different foot." Jude knew he sounded awkward and hated himself for showing his discomfiture.

Madge allowed him to dangle, she was in no hurry. When she decided he had floundered long enough, she spoke. "I've dismissed Antonio for the evening, I planned a quiet night. Would you like to share some cold cracked crab?"

"Yes, I would. I'll bring the champagne—only this time, I'll open it—as a peace offering." Jude's heart was pounding so hard he was afraid she would hear it; he was astounded by his schoolboy eagerness.

He arrived at seven, laden with bottles of Dom Perignon and flowers. Madge laughed when she saw him. "You look like a thin Santa Claus!"

A waft of her perfume floated toward him, beckoning him, luring him, arousing him as if it were a love potion. She motioned him inside the softly lit room. Debussy's *Claire de lune* played in the background. She wore a Chinese silk robe embroidered with red and green dragons, and the exotic fragrance of incense mingled with her scent.

He did not show the expertise he possessed in opening the bottle. Again he felt a nervous inadequacy.

They raised their glasses in a mock salute.

"Why did you see me?" Jude asked.

Madge walked over and stood in front of the fireplace. With the flames glowing behind her, she gave the illusion of being a pagan goddess. "Confucius said, 'If rape is inevitable, relax and enjoy it.' So I did. But I wondered if you couldn't do better."

Jude drained his glass and crossed to her. "Why don't we find out?" He untied the belt of her robe and the silky garment slithered to the floor, exposing her nakedness. "Do you always dress—ready?"

"Only when I want to. And it would be so much more convenient if you had done the same. Now I have to undress you."

Slowly, she unbuttoned his shirt and tossed it aside. Then she unzipped his trousers and leisurely pulled them down along with his shorts, lingering only slightly at his already full erection. She bent and took off his loafers, and then pants. Reclining on the floor, she looked up at him towering over her, "You're quite impressive from this angle."

Jude gazed down at the vision lying at his feet, "The view isn't so bad from up here. But the altitude is making me dizzy." He lowered himself and their lips met. His need was becoming too powerful.

"Not so soon," she whispered, reaching for something on the coffee table. Gently, she rolled him over and took some white powder from a silver box. Soothingly, she rubbed it on him, murmuring, "This is my private remedy, this will help preserve the time."

He was still wild with desire, but something had calmed the urgency; he felt as if he could go on forever. What a wonderful state to be in for the rest of one's life.

"Now, sip of me, drink of my flavor," she whispered huskily.

Ravenously he feasted—her aroma summoned him as a bee to the flower—and he found the core of her honeycomb.

"Ahhh—yes, yes, ahhh," she moaned maneuvering herself into a position where she could enclose him with the warmth of her mouth.

Just when he thought he couldn't stand anymore, the music segued into Ravel's *Bolero,* and Jude and Madge became involuntary auxiliaries to the orchestra, driven by the hammering passionate tempo.

"Come to me now!" she cried, raising herself on all fours and swaying back and forth like an inflamed lioness. Jude became king of the jungle and claimed his feline, hands clamping her buttocks, propelling her back and forth, the cadence increasing to a maddening velocity.

"Now—now—*now!*" she shrieked, and together they soared, floating on clouds of carnality, unwilling to relinquish their place in Utopia.

Jude stayed locked within her; he leaned forward so his chest brushed her spine, and his face nuzzled the back of her head. He reached underneath and cupped her generous breasts.

"You are a witch, aren't you? And you've cast a spell over me, haven't you? Because I can't get enough of you. I need you again—at this very moment."

He pulled her upper body toward him so she was sitting on him, he resting on his haunches. His head was lost in her shock of hair, tantalizing him, drowning him. She kissed the hands that were stroking her breasts.

"Don't ever disappear," Jude commanded. "Don't ever take your magic and vanish into thin air!"

31

Beverly Hills, California
Saturday, December 13, 1958

"I can't believe we're double-dating!" Revel exclaimed.

"Neither can I," said Jude dryly. "Now, Artie is picking you up, I'm picking up Madge, and we'll meet at Freddy's at eight, right?"

"Right!"

"It's on Melrose—"

"I know, I know!" Revel was impatient. "Don't you two be late! You're walking around in a daze lately. Remember, Artie is leaving tomorrow to be home for Christmas and I don't want to spend all of tonight with you guys!"

"Why not? What other plans do you have?" Jude was immediately suspicious.

"Well, maybe, just maybe, we'd like to go dancing, or have a nightcap—alone!" Revel added pointedly. "Surely, you of all people can understand that."

Jude didn't have an answer, so he gave her a swat on her bottom and went upstairs to dress.

Revel could hardly believe the timing. She knew Jude was so moonstruck over Madge that he wasn't going to keep close tabs on her activities. He hadn't been home before two or three in the morning all week. And that would give her plenty of time.

Driving the now-familiar route to the Bel-Air, Jude switched the radio on. The news blared forth but he wasn't in the mood to take it in. He really didn't give a hoot about the pros and cons of the Brooklyn Dodgers moving to Los Angeles, or why a postage stamp went from three to four cents. He searched for a music station and suddenly *Claire de lune* flowed from the speakers. It was as if he couldn't get away from her—as if he were some kind of addict and she was the drug.

"Good evening, Mr. Abavas. The rest of your party is already seated." The maître d' led Madge and Jude through the maze of tables. Heads turned as they walked, they made such a spectacular couple.

"Hello, Joseph! Any new traumas lately?"

"Not that I know of, Mr. Abavas. Here we are, I hope everything is satisfactory." Joseph snapped his fingers and a waiter appeared. "Bring Mr. Abavas's champagne!"

Jude looked around the table for approval. "I hope it's all right—I took the liberty of ordering earlier. We have to celebrate on Artie's last night in town!"

"That's very thoughtful, Jude. But it's only for a little while, I hope," Artie said, looking at Revel.

"I'll drink to that!" Revel said quickly.

"Not too much!" Jude warned.

"Oh, stop being the older brother, Jude. Revel is quite capable of knowing what to do, or what not to do," Madge chided. "Now, tell me, what trauma has that poor man experienced?"

"Joseph? Well, not him personally. Have you read about the rash of robberies in Beverly Hills and surrounding areas in the past year? On two occasions when I was here, the people who were robbed were also here. Naturally there was a lot of commotion," Jude explained.

"Interesting!" Madge's eyes narrowed. "I wonder if any of the other victims were here on nights you weren't."

"It's certainly possible, but who cares?"

"Not me!" said Revel. "Jude, I spoke with Mama today. Artie gave me the notion—I think I'll fly home for the week over Christmas. I'd be back before New Year's Eve—don't want to miss Matt and Polly's bash. Mama asked if you would be coming."

Jude was not prepared, "Oh, Rev, I—ah—can't get away from the office now. Too much going on, you know."

"I understand," Revel said wisely. "Why don't I tell her you can't make two trips and you want to be there for her sixtieth birthday in February?"

"Honey, that is an absolutely wonderful idea—thank you! You are the best sister!"

"I am your *only* sister and don't you forget it."

"You can pull up in the driveway. Don't worry about blocking Jude—he won't be home for hours," Revel told Artie as they approached Maple Drive in his rented Rolls-Royce.

"I really should be going," he hemmed.

"But you have to see Gigi! I just got her yesterday. The mama—Orey—finally let me take her. Of course, Orey's right in the main house, so she can keep an eye on her baby. Gigi's so cute, such a mixture, a real mutt."

"Just for a minute then." Artie wasn't sure he could trust himself alone with Revel.

Little Gigi waddled over to greet them, and as Revel had said, the puppy was adorable. Artie scooped her up and cuddled her before handing her to Revel.

"You dear little fuzz-ball, I love you. Give me doggie-licks."

It was an endearing scene, and Artie couldn't help himself. He put his arms around the two of them, and kissed Revel. Poor Gigi was squished in between.

"Oh, no!" Revel screeched. "She wet on me! Here, take her outside to show her where she's supposed to pee, and I'll go sponge my dress so it doesn't stain. Little devil!"

Artie dutifully did as he was told, and he was playing with Gigi when Revel emerged from her bedroom. She wore an ivory satin Dior robe that Madge had bought for her after their visit to the doctor. And a diaphragm.

Artie took one look, jumped up and started backing toward the door. "I have to go. Ah, packing to do—errands to run."

"But everything is closed, Artie. And I bet you're all packed already. Besides, tonight I have chilled champagne right here—to wish you bon voyage!"

Artie hedged. He didn't want to leave, but he was wary of staying—his sense of respect could only hold out for so long.

Revel popped the cork and gave him his glass, entwining her arm through his—the way she'd seen a woman do in a Cary Grant movie—before taking a sip. "Satin Doll" was on the record player. "Let's dance," she murmured. He was drawn to her as a magnet, their bodies molded together perfectly. He could feel her flesh through the thin material. "Oh, Revel, don't—don't tempt me, please. I'm human, and I'm a man—I can't."

"Shh. It's all right, it's all right! I want you to make love to me, Artie. I want you to be—the one."

"Are you sure, my sweet? Do you know what you are saying?"

"I'm sure. And I know."

He opened her robe and pressed her close to him.

32

Beverly Hills, California
Wednesday, December 3l, l958

"I've never seen a tuxedo look like *that!*" Jude said admiringly as he held open the car door for Madge.

"This? Oh, I saw it in the winter collection in Paris and thought it would be fun. Polly did say this was casual tonight, didn't she?" Madge seemed a tad subdued.

"Absolutely. Their house isn't big enough for a fancy affair. Maybe I've never seen a tuxedo without a shirt before. Looks good on you, Madge, but I don't think I'll try it!" He succeeded in rousing a small chuckle out of her. "Are you okay? I saw Antonio driving away when I came up. He's not giving you trouble, is he? I'll bust his puss if he is!"

Another chuckle. "You do have unusual expressions, to say the least. No, Antonio is not the problem. He's pouting, that's all, because I only use him during the day. I told him I haven't been feeling well and decided to stay in." After Jude closed her door and got in his side, she looked across at him and said wryly, "It isn't a total lie. I *have* stayed in every evening—not that it hasn't been enjoyable."

"I'm glad you added the last part," Jude said, grinning as he drove. "Maybe I've been too selfish. I just didn't want to share you."

Jude could sense that Madge wasn't ready to discuss what was on her mind. "Hey—did you read the papers today? The police arrested my old friend Joseph. Remember him from Freddy's? Evidently he was part of a sting operation. Customers would make reservations for dinner—especially on Thursdays, the servants' day off—and then he would alert the gang, and while he was smiling, they were stealing. The cops finally traced it to him because, in every single case, the burglarized homeowners had been at Freddy's during the robberies. Now that I think of it, you said something like that the night we were there. How did you come up with that theory?''

"A lucky guess," Madge said vaguely.

"It's sure causing a lot of hoopla—a big Beverly Hills scandal!''

Madge was looking out the window at the passing houses, each still twinkling with Christmas decorations. "Are we in Brentwood? It's quite pretty here, more sedate.''

"You're right, it is less glitzy. I'll tell you who's not sedate, though—Revel! When she heard Artie was coming back in time for tonight, she had enough electricity going to light up the whole city. She's been, well, different lately. I don't know if it was the trip home, or what.''

Madge remained silent, smiling to herself. She knew why Revel was different. Revel was having her maiden *affaire d'amour* and was adoring every passionate minute of it. She remembered well how all-important a first love could be.

Jude and Madge created a stir when they arrived. The insiders were well aware that Jude had been seeing Madge, but this was really their coming out appearance as a couple.

"Another New Year's Eve together!" Wade said. "How many does that make, my friend? My God, it can't be—fifteen!" He slapped Jude on the back and turned to Madge. "Oh, no, not the hand tonight, Madge, the cheek at least!''

Jude thought Penelope was looking a mite wan. "Are we working you too hard?" he asked as he gave her a perfunctory kiss. "Don't let us. Just lay down the law!" He was worried, she really did not look very well.

"No, no! I'm just a little weary, that's all. The holidays can do that," Penelope assured him.

Revel hugged Madge. "It's been so long since I've seen you—clear back to about five o'clock!" The two had plainly formed a strong link.

"Welcome back, Artie," Jude warmly greeted him. "Did you have a good trip?"

"Yes, sir! And I'm happy I could make it back here by tonight. My parents, however, are puzzled as to why I enjoy California so much. I told them there was a very sweet puppy named Gigi that I missed a lot.''

Matthew and Polly were buzzing around, being host and hostess.

''I know Jude and Wade have met Vincent, but the others haven't,'' Polly explained. ''Madge, Penelope, Revel, Artie— meet Vincent Franks. Vincent recently joined S.S.I. as executive director and is my key to freedom. *And* Vincent is responsible for allowing my husband to finally keep somewhat normal working hours.''

''How do you do?'' the tall, thin young man said shyly. Vincent Franks was sandy-haired, brown eyed, with a Roman nose. And brilliant.

Madge was festive, but more like an observer than a participant. Jude noticed her slip outside a few times alone. Around eleven-thirty, he saw her quietly leave, and he decided to join her.

She was leaning against the railing of the back deck, looking out at the blackness, puffing on a cigarette. He came up behind her and put his arms around her small waist. ''I never saw you smoke before.''

She wasn't startled. ''I don't, normally. But when I feel depressed or nervous, sometimes these cigarettes give me a lift.''

''And why is this beautiful woman in my arms depressed?''

Madge sighed. ''I would have to tell you sooner or later, so it might as well be now. My father called, a rarity in itself, and he thinks I should come home for a while. Or go to Greece and then Switzerland, with the Sardos family, when Artie leaves. I am very close to them. Usually I come and go pretty much as I please, but that snitch Antonio must have alerted him that I haven't been behaving in my customary manner.''

Jude was stunned. And then panic set in. He couldn't let Madge go away. Out of his life, maybe forever. He couldn't bear the thought of not seeing her, and holding her, and making love with her every night. Yet what could he do? A zany solution popped into his disordered head.

''You look terrible!'' Madge said when she turned to him. ''Here, try one of these. I know you don't smoke, but you don't have to inhale this cigarette. Just suck in the smoke, shut your mouth so it doesn't escape, hold it as long as you can, and then exhale. Your troubles will be easier to handle, I promise!''

Jude's mind was whirling so fast, he followed her instructions without questioning them.

"Now, give it a minute, and you'll feel much better. See? I'm mellower already," and she gave him a long, amorous kiss to prove it.

Jude's zany solution had become perfectly reasonable. Solemnly, he held Madge's shoulders. "There is a way you won't have to do the bidding of your father anymore. I never thought I would say, or even think, these words again. But, I can't be without you." He fumbled only for a fraction of a second. "Marry me, Madge! Be my wife. And we'll never have to be separated. Ever."

Madge stared at Jude. Now *her* mind was spinning. *Marriage?* She hadn't thought of that. Or had she? Had this been her ultimate goal? To bring the unattainable Jude Abavas to his knees?

What would it be like to be married? For starters, it could get the old man off her back. He might even be relieved to have her settle down with a good man—after the initial shock. She wasn't really worried about him anyway, she could always handle her father. But *settle down?* Of course she wouldn't have to *really* settle down, would she? She could continue her life-style while still being a wife, couldn't she? So, why not? It certainly would be novel—Madge Moore getting married! It would send shock waves around the world, particularly because few of her crowd knew the groom. It would be fun to show off Jude. She could just see some of the bitches drooling. The more she deliberated, the more she liked the idea. But she had to play it smart, be a *little* hard to win.

"Marry you?" she said, sounding astonished. "But Jude, we've only known each other three weeks and four days! We know nothing about each other's backgrounds, or anything."

"That doesn't mean a damn thing. We're not marrying families. It's you and me that matters, Madge. We're adults, we don't need months to know what we feel. What we have together is special, we both know it."

Madge appeared to be torn. "It's—it's just so sudden. I don't know—I don't know. What will people say?"

"To hell with what people say!" Jude cried. "I don't want to waste time anymore. I don't want you to go away. I can't lose you!"

She held his face tenderly between her hands. "Nor I *you!*" She kissed him delicately. "But how? Or where? When?"

Jude picked her up and whirled her around. "Oh Madge, I'm the luckiest man on earth!" He put her down. "It's almost midnight. Let's go in. When everyone else leaves, we'll tell our group, and I know Wade can arrange to charter a plane tomorrow and we'll fly to Las Vegas and you will make me the happiest man on earth."

"Wait a minute, Jude. I'm nervous! I need one more of my cigarettes. Please, share it with me."

Not once had the words *I love you* been spoken!

33

Las Vegas, Nevada
Thursday, January 1, 1959

Wade and Penelope Colby, Matthew and Polly Abavas, Revel Abavas and Atherton Sardos stood with Jude Abavas and Madge Moore in front of the justice of the peace in the 24-hour wedding chapel.

To say that Jude's announcement the night before had rendered them all speechless, would be putting it mildly. They had been stupefied! When, at last, they found their voices, there had been the conventional congratulations and flurry. But no questions. Somehow, they knew there couldn't be any reasonable answers. Everyone, that is, except Revel and Artie, who, after the bombshell proclamation, thought it was just *"sooo"* romantic.

Wade had welcomed the excuse of having to leave so he could get busy organizing transportation for the next day.

"What do you make of it, honey?" he asked Penelope on the drive home.

"I'm not sure yet." Penelope chose her words carefully. "Obviously, they are mad for each other. And, God knows, Madge is gorgeous and Jude handsome. But..." She sighed. "It's so quick to make that kind of commitment. It's such an intense fascination, it frankly makes me uneasy."

"Well, I am just plain worried," Wade announced. "Jude never acts impetuously, he's always been the thinker-outer. Jesus, the night they met at the party, I thought he *disliked* her. Remember?"

"Yes, but I also remember we watched them dancing, and while it may not have been love at first sight, there was certainly an attraction."

"Okay, so have a fling! But *marriage?* I don't like it."

Penelope put her hand on his knee. "Whatever our concerns are, it's because of our love for Jude. And because of that, Wade darling, we have to put aside our feelings, and concentrate on making this the joyful occasion it should be—for Jude's sake. Maybe we're wrong, maybe they will make the perfect pair. Maybe Jude had to act impulsively to get past the ghosts of Thelma and Keane. I don't know and you don't know. But we do know we want to help Jude begin what we pray is a happy new life."

"I would like to stop the car right now and give you a kiss you'd never forget, but I guess I better wait until I get you in bed. Of course, my wonderful wife, you are one hundred percent right."

Meanwhile, Matthew and Polly Abavas were having practically the identical conversation. But Matthew had an added worry. "What about Mama and Papa? Should I call them? Wait till they hear Jude isn't going to be married by a real priest, or a minister, and not even in a church! And that he met her only a little over three weeks ago! Oh boy."

"Calm down, sweetheart." Then Polly said emphatically, "You can't call your folks. Jude has to do that himself. But you should be the one to make sure he does call. You'll deal with it, I know, as you always do with everything. But what if we can't find Ophelia in the morning—I gave her New Year's Day off, too."

Matthew looked at Polly adoringly. "I hope with all my heart that Jude is as lucky as I am."

The flight to Las Vegas was loaded with nervous gaiety. Madge had insulated Jude and herself with a couple of drags from her "medicinal" cigarettes, so they were calmer than anyone else.

Madge had chosen a white gabardine suit from her wardrobe. Her hair was pulled back into one thick braid, interlaced with a strand of long pearls. She looked every inch the bride.

When the time came for the justice of the peace to ask, "If anyone has reason to object to this union, please step forward," there was deadly silence. There may have been doubts in a few minds, but no one stirred. Then came the magic words. "I now pronounce you man and wife. You may kiss the bride."

Wade had reserved a suite at the popular Sands Hotel on the strip, so the wedding party could have a small reception before heading back to Los Angeles. The honeymoon would have to wait awhile.

When the first bottle of champagne popped, the glasses were raised in a toast. "To Mr. and Mrs. Jude Abavas—may their lives be filled with happiness and good health!"

As soon as the second bottle was opened, Matthew went over and whispered in Jude's ear. Jude looked at Matthew, put an arm around him and nodded.

Jude took Madge's hand and guided her toward a telephone, saying to the rest, "Excuse us for a minute, I have a call to make." Madge was as bewildered as the others.

Jude dialed, squeezing her hand in assurance and waited. "Hello, Mama. Is Papa there? Could you both get on the line? Yes, it's Jude. Yes, everything is all right. As a matter of fact, everything is wonderful! Papa? Can you both hear me now? Okay—Mama, Papa—I would like you to welcome someone, someone very special named Madge, someone who just became Mrs. Jude Abavas!"

34

New York City, New York
1933

Mrs. Jude Abavas was a woman of many names. When she had come into the world, on June 4, 1933, her parents, Sophia and Bruno Morellini had christened her Maria—Maria Anne Morellini. She was a much-heralded baby, for her parents had been praying for five years that the Holy Father would bless them with a child.

Sophia was happy she had finally been able to please her husband. Secretly she had feared she was sterile, but with an infant in her arms, that fear had dissolved. The birth had, however, been difficult, and what neither Bruno nor Sophia knew was that there could be no more children.

By the age of three, Maria was the image of her mother, with the same black hair, same limpid skin, same green eyes. They lived in a private compound that boasted a number of luxury homes, an impressive guarded gate, stables, tennis courts, Olympic-size swimming pool, and a boathouse. The complex was located in Riverdale, a borough of New York City situated on the Hudson River. There were many youngsters in the other houses and Maria's life was happy and full. Occasionally, Sophia and Maria made excursions to "the big city," but always with a driver and burly family "friend" in the front seat. Bruno preferred them to stay safely in the confines of their protected grounds.

Maria was openly adored by both parents, and after Sophia and Bruno were told there would be no more children, she became that much more precious. Her daddy worshiped his diminutive princess and spoiled her rotten.

Bruno Morellini held an important position within the syndicate. A variety of businesses were operated by the organization, some perfectly respectable, others less so. Because of competition from other syndicates, the board had decided to build this sheltered sanctuary for their families. At times, the rivalries could and did become dangerous, even deadly.

But none of this penetrated to the children, their world was ideal and normal: picnics and ponies and swimming and boating, and in the winter, even a small pond that froze over for ice skating.

Maria did remember parades of long black cars and strange men in black suits who would gather with her daddy and his friends. She remembered this mainly because their presence had interfered with her fun; the young ones were kept inside on those days.

The summer Maria turned six, an unusual incident happened. Her nanny had taken her to the stables, to sit on a pony and be led around the ring. Sometimes the wrangler would let her go by herself, and she would squeal in fear and delight if the pony trotted instead of walked. The rocking motion of the saddle appealed to her, and she had dared herself to go faster. The small horse jerked when it changed gaits and Maria fell off. She was more surprised than hurt, and when the cowboy reached her, she was actually mad.

"Put me back up on that thing—I'll show it who's boss!"

The man picked her up, saying, "You got spunk, kid, I like that!" When he was lifting her to the seat, his hand slid up her skirt. Whether intentional or not, no one would ever know because at that moment, the nanny came running up to them, yelling, "I saw you—take your hands off her! Come here, my angel. I'll take you down."

Maria was whisked away before she could complain and was brought straight home to Sophia. The nanny made Maria wait while she entered the mistress's room to describe what had taken place.

Sophia called for Maria to come in. "Sweetheart, tell Mommy exactly what happened."

"Well, I wanted to make the pony go faster, and I fell off. And the man picked me up and—"

"Did the man—touch you? Anywhere—different?"

The little girl thought a minute. "Different? Well, I don't know. Hmm, oh, his hand went here," and she pointed to her vagina.

"Mary, Mother of God! What shall we do?" wailed Sophia.

"What's wrong, Mommy? What did I do?"

"You did nothing, precious!" Sophia tried to explain. "But that man—that degenerate—put his hand in a dirty place, a private place."

Maria pulled down her panties and examined herself, "It's not dirty, Mommy. No dirt got there, but my dress is, I think."

"No, no! *You're* not dirty, that *man* is dirty. Oh, dear! Just understand that what *he* did was bad—*bad!* You must run away if anyone tries to do that to you again, and you must tell me immediately. Promise?"

"Yes, Mommy. Can I go play now?"

"Run along! But nowhere near the stables. Keep an eye on her!"

The nanny nodded and hurried to keep up with her charge.

Bruno and Sophia closeted themselves in their master suite as soon as he arrived home. Maria was on the lawn with her friends, when suddenly she heard an anguished howl, followed by the sight of Bruno bursting through the front door and running crazily in the direction of the stables.

Maria had never seen her daddy so wild before, and it frightened her. She flew upstairs to huddle behind Sophia, not certain what was going on.

Bruno returned a while later, acting more rational. He grasped his baby in his thick arms. "Nothing more to worry about, sweetie pie, Daddy took care of the bad man."

None of the children knew or asked about the wrangler who wasn't there anymore. The rumor was, however, that he had met with an accident and wouldn't be able to resume his work load.

Maria learned one important fact from this calamity. There definitely was something quite special about *that* part of her body. Something that could cause a lot of trouble.

As the years passed, it didn't seem to Maria that her mother and father enjoyed each other as much as they once had. This didn't necessarily disturb her, it was just an observation. For her life progressed delightfully. Once or twice a year the three would travel to Europe to see business associates. To Sicily, an island south of Italy. To Athens and the Greek isles, which is where she met the Sardos family. Mr. Nicholas Sardos and Bruno were affiliates in a number of ventures. This was Maria's favorite excursion. Beryl and Nicholas Sardos had three offspring: Galen, a son six years older than Maria; Angela, the daughter, who was four years older; and Atherton, the youngest son, who was only two years older than Maria. The four bonded immediately and became bosom buddies.

Maria hated World War II because it prevented their trips to Greece. But as soon as the hostilities were over, in August 1945, they were off once again. She had just had her twelfth birthday party in June, and she had become "a woman" soon after. How she had developed! Her body had assumed eye-catching proportions and she was even more beautiful than her mother had been.

The Sardos lads were wowed by the change. Maria was their chum, yes, but now all sorts of other possibilities loomed. Galen made the first move when a group of the younger crowd took one of the Sardoses' small yachts for a day's cruise. While swimming off the ship, Galen asked Maria to join him as he headed for shore.

"I want to show you a secret cove I found. It's so beautiful."

Maria followed him enthusiastically, welcoming the chance to be alone with her handsome friend. She'd had a crush on Galen for years and now he was actually singling her out. He led her around some brush and over some rocks until they saw a tiny secluded inlet with a small, inviting beach.

"Come on!" he called, and together they plunged into the warm clear water.

"It is pretty, Galen!"

"Not as pretty as you," he answered and kissed her.

This was not a "daddy" kiss, and Maria didn't react in a "daughterly" fashion. They splashed onto the sand and lay panting in the hot sun. He kissed her again and began to fondle her. She was very quiet, relishing these new sensations, curious about what would come next. He undid the top of her bathing suit, removed the bottoms and then his finger penetrated her warmth. She grimaced with pain but didn't utter a word, determined to discover the so-called joy of such forbidden activity. When Galen's trunks were off, she stared in amazement at his erection. He saw to it that she was sufficiently moistened, and then gently forced his way into her. Despite her discomfort, Maria did not protest, in fact, she was fascinated by Galen's behavior. He was practically foaming at the mouth, his eyes bulging like a madman's eyes as he moaned and groaned and thrashed about. And then, when she was afraid he was going to explode, he suddenly pulled himself out and, with convulsing motions, sprayed hot, creamy liquid all over her stomach.

Maria admitted to herself that the ordeal had been pleasurable, but she didn't quite understand what the big deal was about! Surely there must be something more!

Galen rolled over and propped himself onto one elbow so he could look straight at her.

"Well, my surrogate sister, what did you think of your initiation?"

Maria shrugged noncommittally.

"You probably weren't satisfied," Galen granted. "It's hard the first time. But you were cool as a cucumber, not some giggling whining virgin. As a matter of fact, you were terrific. And I promise you, that before you leave, I'll have you jumping with joy!"

"You know, Galen," Maria said slyly, "my mother once said that I should run and tell her if anyone ever—twiddled—my privates."

He paled. "You're not serious! You wouldn't say anything— would you? My pop would kill me. Your pop, too! Oh, no, Maria, you can't."

"Let's see now, what would it take to keep my mouth shut?" She laughed when she saw his expression. "Oh, relax, will you? I'm just teasing."

"I'll give you a gift right now—some practical advice I have a feeling you're going to need, Maria. Every male is not going to be as considerate as I was, which means they won't bother to withdraw and will come inside you, which means you can get pregnant—which means you could have a baby, *capiche?* So be sure the guy wears a rubber for protection. And, when you can, get yourself something that will make you safe. I don't want you to get hurt. Okay? Now, let's go swim and wash off!"

Maria had solved the puzzle. She knew what she had now: as a woman, her body gave her a distinctive power and control over men. Now she only had to decide when and where to use it.

*   *   *

Sophia had come down with the flu just before Maria's thirteenth birthday gala in June 1946. The elaborate affair was to be held at the Riverdale Country Club. Sophia had planned as much of the event as she was able, and then Bruno handled the rest. She was heartbroken she wouldn't be there to share her daughter's celebration.

"Don't come too close—I don't want you to catch this awful bug," she cautioned as Maria and Bruno entered her room before they left. "My, the two of you look nice. Maria, take care that top doesn't come down any farther off your shoulders. Pull it up a bit, now—it's already too risqué."

"Yes, Mama," Maria said resignedly, knowing she would push it lower as soon as she was in the car.

"Bruno, please watch her closely. You can't be too careful with these boys nowadays! And don't drink too much—you know how you get when you're liquored up, and be sure the young ones don't get any booze. I still think it was a mistake to have an open bar, but you and your cronies just couldn't get through the night without it, could you? And—"

"We have to go, Sophia, or we'll be late," Bruno interrupted, angry she would chastise him in front of Maria.

"Bye, Mama, I love you and I'll miss you!"

Sophia waved them off dejectedly. As soon as she heard the engine start, she turned off her light and brooded. She felt sad and very much alone. Her little girl was growing up, and her husband was growing away from her. He hadn't visited her bed in over a year, and she knew his appetite for sex.

Sophia Morellini was a troubled woman.

Maria sank back into the cushions of the car. "Oh, Daddy," she said, sighing. "Wasn't it a fun night? Thank you!" She leaned over to hug him. Bruno looked down onto her brimming breasts, as had most of the young men dancing with her that evening, and he was excited. He was also intoxicated, but not enough to forget the driver and friend in the front seat.

"Uh, glad you had a good time, sweetheart. That's what life should be—a good time for everyone. Right?" With that, he placed his arm around her, his hand dangling close to the bare skin. "Now, we mustn't forget to tiptoe quietly, so we don't

wake your mother when we get home. Right? Mustn't ever tell
her that you had something to drink, either. Right? As a matter
of fact, let's have a last nightcap now,'' and he reached for two
glasses and a bottle from the portable bar.

Shoes in hand, giddy with the alcohol, father and daughter
made their way up the stairs to their house, and finally to the
second floor and Maria's room.

Bruno closed the door behind them. "Safe!" he whispered.
There was only the moonlight coming through the windows.
"Here, let me help you get to bed. It's hard to see." He guided
her toward the four-poster, helped her get rid of her dress and
stockings and turned back the covers. Maria stretched out on the
cool sheet, and Bruno bent to kiss her good-night. But he
couldn't leave. He sat on the edge, instead, goggling at that perfect body, and finally he capitulated to the burning heat that
threatened to consume him.

His trembling fingers reached out and caressed every inch of
his daughter's loveliness.

Maria was in a twilight sleep when his touches came, and in a
hazy voice asked, "Daddy? You're tickling me." She dozed off,
dreaming of Galen, who had kept his promise last summer and
had indeed "made her jump with joy."

Slowly, Bruno took off his clothes, climbed onto the bed and
rubbed himself against her. "My beautiful baby doll, my rip-
ened little peach." He was in that position when the door opened
and light from the hall illuminated the scene.

"Maria? I thought I heard you. Agh—*aaagh!*" Sophia hurtled toward them, shrieking hysterically, pounding her husband's nakedness, pulling his hair. She grabbed a footstool and
pummeled every exposed part of him she could reach.

Bruno was instantly sober and Maria was jarred into terrifying actuality. Bruno tried to fend off Sophia's attacks and hop
into some state of decency, all the while calming her, "Shut up.
Not what you think. Be quiet, goddamn it, you'll wake up the
whole compound. Just tucking her in. Shut up or I'll smack
you!"

Which he did—hard! Sophia staggered and Bruno, dressed
now, picked up her stunned body.

"Don't worry, honey," he said to Maria. "Your mother is
okay. Must have had a reaction from all that medicine the doc

gave her. Started imagining things, made her a little crazy. You don't worry your pretty head—I'll take care of her, just go back to sleep now."

Sleep was out of the question right then. Maria cowered beneath the quilt, suddenly shivering with cold. She could hear her mother and father going at it, and she caught brief snatches of the diatribe. "Molesting your child." "More of a woman than you!" "All because I couldn't have more babies." "Sick of you and your bellyaching!" And on, and on.

What had happened here? Had her daddy really planned to enter her, as Galen had? Or was he just drunk and unaware of his actions? She figured it was a bit of both. What would it have been like to have her daddy inside her? Would it have felt as good as it had with Galen? She decided she would not have liked it. Galen was a handsome boy she fancied, and Daddy was her father.

But what about her mother? And the hatred she heard in both their voices? Would their lives ever be the same?

A door slammed shut, footsteps clanged down the stairs, another door banged and the sound of sobbing filled the night.

Maria certainly hadn't intended to activate this feminine force of hers, but tonight's experience was further evidence that she commanded a potent weapon. Now she needed to learn more about the mastery of it.

The next morning, Maria awakened to an eerie silence. She looked confusedly about her room. It was a mess. Her dress and hose were over one chair, her daddy's coat and tie were on the floor, their shoes by the door, and her stool upside down and broken. Gradually, she made her way to the bathroom and ran a cold shower. It refreshed her and erased some of the tension. She threw on some shorts and a T-shirt and headed for the kitchen; she was starved. Her mother's door was closed, so Maria noiselessly walked downstairs.

"Where is everybody?" the cook asked. "Ain't heard from nobody yet this morning, and the missus is supposed to take her medicine. What do you want, young lady?"

"I'll go up after I eat. Might as well let her sleep as long as possible. Wow, what a night! And hey, isn't it great? Summer vacation! No dumb school for three months." Maria danced around singing, "Doin' What Comes Natur'lly."

"Jus more work for me, having you and your gang underfoot all day," grumbled the cook.

Bruno swung through the kitchen door, disheveled, still in his tux pants and shirt. "Some coffee!" he barked. "Maria, come into the dining room—Cook, bring her food in here."

They sat there, mute, until the cook had left. Servants knew not to ask questions around these houses.

"Honey," Bruno began haltingly, "I have to go away for a while. On business. Oh, hell, I'm not going to lie to you—I'm leaving because I can't stay in this house with your mother another day. It has nothing to do with you. It's not your fault—it's ours. We don't make each other happy, we make each other miserable—and I can't live like that no more. I won't be far—and I'll see you all the time—I just have to go."

Tears welled in Maria's eyes, but she nodded. She understood. None of their lives were going to be the same again.

"I'll go up and pack a few things, send for the rest later, and then..." Bruno heaved a deep sigh, "I'll tell your mother."

"Why don't I wake her up and help get her together, and then you come in?" Maria suggested.

Bruno thanked her with his eyes. Neither said a word about the night before.

Maria cautiously opened Sophia's door. The lamp on the night table was on, but it was still too dark inside. She opened the drapes and sunshine flooded the room. No movement yet, so Maria went to the bed and gently shook her mother's shoulder. It felt rigid and strange. She peeked over the rounded contour. Still no awareness of her presence.

"Mama, it's time to get up," Maria said in a normal tone.

No response.

"Mama, it's time to rise and shine," a little louder.

Sophia remained motionless.

"Mama, wake up! Mama—*Mama!*"

"Daddy! Daddy!" Maria screamed. "Come quick! Something's wrong with Mama! I can't wake her up! Daddy—hurry!"

Bruno burst into the room and ran to Maria, who was bending over Sophia. "Let me see—get out of the way. Oh, my God!" The minute he touched the cold hard flesh, he knew Sophia was dead. Then he saw what Maria hadn't noticed on the stand, an empty bottle of sleeping pills and a note addressed to

Maria. Hastily, he shoved both into his pocket. Maria was by the window with her face in her hands, crying.

"Call the doc, tell him your mother's had an attack and to get over here, pronto. I'll keep trying to bring her to."

Bruno continued the charade—shaking the lifeless form of his wife, breathing into the wooden mouth, pumping the sphinxian chest—while Maria yelled into the telephone.

The doctor arrived in ten minutes—ten minutes of hell for Bruno and Maria. Cook, and the day-maid had joined them in the bedroom, and there was much confusion with everyone milling about, wanting to help, wailing.

The M.D. straightened up after a brief examination and said gravely, "I'm sorry, Mr. Morellini, but I'm afraid she's gone. It appears to have happened peacefully and painlessly, in her sleep. Her heart must have just given up, perhaps weakened by the flu. This strain has been particularly vicious. I suggest everyone leave now, and let me do what's necessary."

Another parade of long black cars entered the gates, and the same men in black suits gathered with her daddy and his friends. This time, however, Maria stood outside with her daddy.

The doctor and coroner agreed, Sophia had died of natural causes, no need for an inquest or autopsy. But what a tragedy! So young, only thirty-six. And such a beautiful woman! Such a devoted couple! And the poor child—to be deprived of her mother at such a tender age. Sympathy poured in from every direction.

Bruno was the quintessential widower. He mourned, but was strong for his daughter. No expense was spared, no tribute missed in the eulogy, no love or emotion was lacking. In tears, he laid a solitary rose on Sophia's casket and said, simply, "Sleep well, my beloved wife!" His grief was almost honest; he may have been about to leave her, but he'd never wished her dead, and they had had some good years together. His guilt was completely honest, though that was his private misery. The fact that his actions had been the cause of her suicide, was a tribulation he'd have to resolve inwardly and alone. Because no one else knew, not even Maria. He had destroyed the empty pill container, and his wife's note to Maria.

Maria was devastated by her mother's death and was only consoled by the entire Sardos family, who had flown to New

York as soon as the news had reached them in Greece. They were a godsend, and they helped Maria, Bruno too, through the difficult days and nights. Maria couldn't come to grips with how drastically their lives had suddenly flip-flopped. The separation of her parents would have presented a problem, to be sure, but this separation from her mother was more than a problem, it was forever.

The Sardos entourage stayed as long as they could, but the time eventually came when they had to take their leave. Bruno was at his wit's end, he didn't know what to do with Maria. She was constantly depressed and clung to Beryl and Nicholas Sardos. Bruno shared his concerns with his friends.

Beryl Sardos looked at her husband for confirmation, and when he nodded his assent, she tentatively spoke. "Bruno, dear, Nicholas and I have discussed Maria's welfare at great length, because we also are disturbed. Would it relieve some of your burden if Maria came home with us for a while? She feels comfortable with us, I know, and she would be away from all the reminders. She could attend a boarding school in England or Switzerland in the fall, and it could be a wonderful experience for her."

Bruno realized he had just been given his salvation. Of course, he would miss Maria, but he was forced to acknowledge he wasn't capable of raising her alone. Moreover, he harbored an anxiety about his ability to maintain a proper attitude toward his daughter, especially as her maturity developed. One drink too many and who knew what could happen. No, this plan was by far the best for all. He would see to it Maria had anything and everything, including a burly family "friend" at all times. If he was protecting her from himself, he sure as hell was going to protect her from other men, as well.

Maria embraced the arrangement—she loved her daddy, but she knew she would see him often enough. She just didn't want to stay in that house anymore, she didn't want to attempt to reestablish normalcy. That normalcy could never be again, for it was buried in the ground, with Mama.

Maria's choice for school was Switzerland. And she decided to change her name, too, to start afresh with a new identity. Bruno didn't object, he actually endorsed her decision. His reasoning was different than Maria's, though—she would be less recognizable in case his foes ever tried to get at him through his daughter.

Maria remembered that Mama's favorite actress had been Madge Evans—and how disappointed Sophia had been when the woman's star began to fade. "Okay, Mama," Maria said to the mirror. "You can have a Madge again! But Madge what? Let me think. What would suit me?"

Maria suddenly laughed, thinking of something Galen had said at dinner. "You're never content, you always want more."

"That's right, Mama, I do want more. More of everything life has to offer! And I'm going to let everyone know who I am. Goodbye, Maria Morellini, hello, Madge Moore!"

The ensuing years were full and stimulating for Madge Moore. The Sardos address book read like a who's who of the rich and famous. When they traveled, they were entertained in royal fashion. They visited the most stylish resorts at high season, whether it be St. Moritz in February or the south of France in August. Under Beryl's tutelage, Madge had become a regular customer at the couture establishments in Paris.

The Sardoses' residences became home base for Madge, and when school permitted, she accompanied them on their circuit. She also made perfunctory pilgrimages to New York in between Bruno's own visits. Their relationship was loving, but not necessarily filled with love. Intuitively, she recognized that she held the trump card, that Bruno always seemed to be walking on eggshells around her. He seldom exercised parental guidance, and then only if his informants thought she was having a problem. Bruno didn't remarry, he preferred the freedom, without a contract. He had soured on matrimony—one disaster was enough!

Madge's beauty, her sensuousness, her obvious wealth, her unpredictability made her the darling of international society. She graduated from Galen to numerous paramours, but she always controlled the relationship. Instead of dispersing favors to the chosen, she made them feel as if they were paying homage to a goddess.

For, tucked away, lurked the suspicion that her mother's death had some connection to her father's behavior that fateful night of her thirteenth birthday celebration.

And within that grew the knowledge that this gift of womanhood also had a vulnerability—a danger zone. She would make manhood suffer—for her mama, and for her own self-preservation. She was beginning an unconscious vendetta.

35

Beverly Hills, California
January, 1959

The elopement of Jude Abavas and Madge Moore did indeed send shock waves around the world. The Sardos family was happy if Madge was happy. The New York family was happy, but only after Bruno Morellini had Jude checked out and was satisfied his new son-in-law was good enough for his baby. Most of the Abavas clan was thrilled for Jude—John voiced some reservations. But absolutely everywhere, speculation and curiosity ran rampant. Did they *have* to get married? Had they been *high* on something? Was one or both on the *rebound?* He married *who?* She married *who?*

The newlyweds were oblivious to the rumors, there was too much activity. Since his bride knew little about running a house, Jude, or rather, his ever-faithful Muriel, hired a secretary and a maid just for Madge. Possessions had to be transferred, arrangements made. Fortunately for Jude's bank balance, Bruno insisted on paying Madge's personal bills, and supplying her with a car and driver. It was the only way for Bruno to keep an eye on his daughter. Jude knew none of this and was surprised to see a limo outside one Monday morning.

"Daddy thought—a little wedding present—to cart me around when you are slaving at work," Madge explained.

Jude couldn't deny his bride anything right then, so he begrudgingly mumbled, "Okay, if that's what you want. But that S.O.B. driver better not be snooping around when I'm home, or he'll wish he'd never been born."

There was no mention of charge accounts. Madge hadn't a clue how much money she spent, Bruno never told her and never complained, but she guessed—correctly—that Jude would not be as lenient. So why even tell him? Instead of thinking her extravagant, he would see that she was thrifty.

Shifty, yes! Thrifty, no!

The only pets Madge had ever known were the trained attack dogs at the compound, and they hadn't exactly been warm and cuddly. She had always been afraid of them and had kept her distance. When gentle Artz, Orey II and Gigi came wiggle-waggling toward her, tails in constant motion, tongues hanging out, she had frozen in her tracks.

"Put your hand out—palm down. Let them smell you," Jude had urged. Timidly she extended her hand. They sniffed a couple of times, and then started licking her and giving her their paw.

"See? I told you. Nothing to fear."

Very soon the dogs were with Madge constantly, following her from room to room. She liked their company—they never talked back—and she even began taking them in the car with her. She bought them jeweled collars and leashes, and felt quite the married lady walking her groomed canines around Beverly Hills with the limo keeping pace on the street. No store dared refuse their entry, for they would lose one of their most lucrative customers.

There were numerous receptions hosted in Madge and Jude's honor and even more were waiting to be held when the two traveled. Madge enjoyed the attention. It was different than just going to a party, it was all for *her*—well, for them. After five weeks, Madge conceded, marriage wasn't bad at all!

Jude was wallowing in the celebrations, too. He hadn't had a chance yet to even think about what had happened. He only knew he was insane about Madge, and could have lingered with her every hour of the day and night, with a large percentage of the time being in bed.

But he didn't have that luxury. He was swamped at the studio. The most pressing problem was to wrap *The Wade Colby* season as soon as possible. Penelope wasn't feeling well, and a decision was made to rewrite the last few episodes, allowing her character to do as little as possible.

Wade finally delivered an ultimatum to his wife. "This is it! No more! I'm worried sick! You can't be the ideal wife, the ideal mother and the ideal actress—it's too much! You're not strong enough! No one is strong enough!"

"Lucy Ball is!" Penelope protested weakly.

"But she doesn't have to put up with me, not to mention our blond bomber Buzz! Honey, would you really mind giving up your career? I'm concerned, that's all. Because maybe—I hoped, after a while, of course—maybe we'd have another."

Tenderly, Penelope placed her hand on Wade's cheek. "I think I would love to be just a wife and mother. But what about you? Will you be satisfied without the series? Will you have enough to do to keep you happy? That's one of the reasons I don't want to stop."

"Believe me, there is much to do," Wade assured her. "I should get into helping at the studio more, anyway. After all, Jude deserves some time off. There are projects in development, and I can always slip in a special or a 'Movie of the Week' if the old ham in me comes out. Trust me. So it's settled? I'll call Jude so we can make script changes and come to some sort of conclusion for Wade Thornton and Penelope Smythe."

Jude's reaction was instantaneous. "I'm relieved, Wade, I really am! I've been anxious as hell about Penelope. And I totally agree—I know we can come up with an ending that will fulfill the audience. And, after five years, it's better to leave while they still want more instead of less."

But it took a great deal of concentrated work. Jude was at the office early and merrymaking with his bride until late into each night.

One evening, as they were dressing for dinner, Jude admitted, "Whew! I'm bushed. Wish we could stay in tonight."

"My poor Jude! But you know we can't. Edie and Ernie would feel jilted—the Kovacs have planned this for days."

"I know—I know!"

"But not to worry! I have just the thing for you, a perfect pick-me-up." Madge went to her stash of medicines and brought back a pill with some water. Jude obediently swallowed.

"You're just full of magic tricks, aren't you?" he asked her.

"More than you know," she said mysteriously.

He grabbed her waist. "Maybe you'll show me one tonight."

"If you're a good boy, maybe I will. We'll see. Now, hurry up—we're late!"

* * *

Jude kept up the pace until the last week of February. The final episode of the series was completed, and the cast-and-crew party over—just in the nick of time, too. Penelope was ordered to bed for the remainder of her pregnancy, and Jude had to go to Idaho for Willamina's sixtieth birthday on the twenty-eighth. He couldn't renege again. Plus, it was time Madge met the family. Madge was not nervous about the meeting in the slightest; she had confidence she could handle anything, but Jude *was* jittery. There was such a vast difference in their backgrounds, and this was a new wife he was bringing home.

Artie had stayed in California to be with Revel until the first of February, but then had had to return to Greece and tend to business. Nicholas Sardos was becoming increasingly dependent upon his youngest son, since Galen expressed no interest whatsoever in the family business. Revel missed him enormously. Fortunately, she was needed more than ever at the studio and at the Colbys. But Revel was also jittery about the Idaho visit. She repeatedly assured Madge that everything would be just fine, and tried to prepare her for what to expect.

"Will you stop? I'm not worried!" Madge said emphatically. "I even know what to wear!"

Jude, Madge, Matthew and Polly—with the two-and-a-half-year-old twins—and Revel boarded the chartered plane on Friday, February 27th. Matthew and brood would stay at the house so that Noah and Willamina could enjoy the grandchildren, and the rest would stay at the Sun Valley Lodge. Jude had loaned his house to a producer friend. Just as well—the lodge would be simpler for Madge at this point.

Jude called from Hailey Airport when they landed, to let Noah and Willamina know they had arrived safely. Ten minutes later, the oversize rental van pulled up in front of the familiar homestead.

The expanded Abavas tribe stood on the front porch waiting: Noah and Willamina; John and Lila with sixteen-year-old John, Jr., eleven-year-old Roberta, and the almost three-year-old Wilma; Ethel and Clyde Warhas, with fourteen-year-old Noah, eleven-year-old Luke, Jr., and little two-year-old Joseph Warhas.

In a combination of emotion and panic, Jude helped Madge out of the car and led her up the stairs.

"Mama, Papa, this is Madge."

Without hesitation, Willamina opened her arms. "We welcome you—our most new daughter."

Madge went easily into the embrace, the first of many that day. Jude hugged his parents with reverence and relief. By that time, everyone else had piled out of the car, and general chaos reigned. Aunts and uncles and cousins hugged and kissed, talked and laughed. John was adequately congenial, though never completely relaxed.

Finally taking control of the scene, Jude suggested the group check in at the lodge and unpack so they could be back in time for supper.

The older boys helped Matthew and Polly with their luggage, and then Jude, Madge and Revel headed for Sun Valley. As soon as the van was out of sight, Matthew opened the inevitable discussion. "I can see it in your faces—you have questions. So, fire away!"

Noah raised the first. "We fear when Jude bring new wife to old place of memories—Thelma and baby—it be trouble for Jude. What you think?"

"Papa, to tell you the absolute truth, I haven't heard Jude even mention Thelma or Keane in quite a while, way before he met Madge. I honestly don't believe that is a problem, unless *we* make it one. If we find ourselves comparing or judging, or not accepting Madge, then yes, it could be a problem."

John was next. "Well, don't you think it was weird to get hitched after knowin' her for only a little over three weeks?" John asked. "And isn't she a bit high-and-mighty for him?"

Matthew was deliberately patient. "As Polly so skillfully pointed out to me, how can anyone else know a heart's timetable except the owner? Or know its needs and desires? I certainly can't."

Polly chimed in, "As for Madge herself—no, she isn't exactly like us. But is anyone? No one in this room is the same as another. Frankly, Penelope and I—and Revel—had begun a campaign to find Jude a mate. Why should he be denied the fulfillment of a family because of a tragedy that happened almost seventeen years ago? Revel met Madge, she came to Revel's debut party in December, and from that night on, Jude has only had eyes for her. So if there's any blame, blame the three of us—we're the culprits, the instigators. We hated to see Jude keep drifting. And I, for one, am thrilled he's found some happiness!''

Willamina had the last word. "There be no blame, sweet Polly. You—Matthew—speak wisdom. I, too, be happy our son find peace. There be no more such talk!''

Alone in their corner suite at the lodge, Jude turned to his bride and cradled her in his arms. "Thank you. You made my family happy. I can't believe it—you even charmed grumpy old John!''

Madge pulled away slightly. "I did nothing. I liked them, that's all. Your mother and father are . . . originals. Obviously, they still hold each other dear. And their children." She was pensive. "Why don't you take a catnap while I bathe? I'd like some time alone."

Jude's spirits were a little dampened, but as soon as he stretched out, weariness took over and he slept.

Madge closed herself in the bathroom and lit a joint. The afternoon's encounter had provoked nostalgia about her own childhood. Here was such an abundance of love and strength. Maybe John was a bit disconnected, but one person couldn't dissipate that solidity. The reflections saddened her. She'd had that once, she'd felt that love and security, she'd felt she belonged to a family. Now she doubted she could ever have it again. The innocence had been butchered, and faithlessness born in its place.

"It's still early—let's show Madge around Ketchum on our way," Revel suggested to Jude as the three returned to Sun Valley later that night, after Willamina's feast.

"Sure, why not? It won't take long because there's not much of it," grinned Jude.

"Oh, Madge, see that side road? It's called East Fork and leads to the Wood River. That's our local lover's lane!" Revel had no way of knowing that was where Jude had taken Thelma on that night aeons ago.

"There's our cemetery, pretty, isn't it? In the moonlight? Our brother Luke's there and Thel—damn me," she finished lamely.

"That's okay, honey. My first wife and our son have a memorial there. You see, they were never found," Jude explained quietly to Madge.

Madge kept silent, just listening and observing.

Revel nervously tried to continue the sight-seeing. "There's the Pioneer Restaurant—biggest portions in the world. I think they practically put the whole cow on your plate. It can get pretty rowdy sometimes, too! And that's the old Casino Bar. Used to have gambling—all the highfalutin' guests from the lodge dropped a lot of moola there. Wouldn't be surprised if they still don't have a back room where the locals can find a game!"

They wandered around the mall, had a drink at the Ram Bar, passed by the Challenger Inn and checked out the dining room for Willamina's birthday celebration the following evening.

"You'll see the mountain tomorrow and Sunday, and I'll give you all the inside scoop on the building of the lifts and the creation of Sun Valley," Jude told Madge. "But on some trip, when we have more time, I want to show you the back country. It's so beautiful and serene and, well, basic. I just know you'll love it."

Madge wasn't so sure about that, but she didn't say anything. He could keep his dreams for now.

As tired as he was, Jude simply couldn't sleep. The ride had rekindled memories. He hadn't given much thought to his earlier life of late, convinced he was through with his personal Hades. But showing Madge his old stomping grounds had brought the past—complete with its guilt—flooding back.

He slipped out of their bed, threw on some clothes and quietly left their room and the lodge.

It was almost a mile to the cemetery. As Jude came closer, his pace quickened until he was actually running—running toward peace, and what felt like his redemption. He knelt, panting, beside two modest tombstones, and bowed his head.

Finally, after what seemed like hours he unburdened his soul. "Thelma and Keane, I'm married! And I want—I need to know it's okay with you. That you understand and—and that you give us your approval. That you don't hate me for taking another wife. I'm almost forty now, even have a few gray hairs, and I found someone who makes me happy. Not the same happiness I had with you, but happy. I don't have to be alone anymore.

Please tell me you forgive me. I'm desperate to know. Do something—anything, please.''

Jude waited. All he could hear was the hooting of owls and the frequent swishing of bats. Suddenly, something brushed his leg and his heart skipped a beat. It was only a stray kitten, purring and rubbing itself against him.

''Whew! You surprised me!'' Jude petted the animal's skinny little body. ''Are you lost, lil' guy? You look like you could use some food! I wonder—my God—could you? Somehow? Could you be a sign?''

He picked up the little piece of fur and snuggled it inside his jacket for warmth. He stood and gazed at the grave markers. Quietly, he said, ''Thank you. Thank you.''

Jude walked with a lighter step to the lodge.

''Do you think you could scrounge some milk for my new friend?'' Jude asked the desk clerk.

''You bet! Just keep an eye on things for me and I'll be right back!''

Jude smiled. This kid reminded him of the young Jude Abavas—ambitious and willing to do any errand to ingratiate himself and garner the big tip.

''I found a plastic pan and dug some dirt for it,'' the clerk said, coming back. ''Tomorrow I'll bring a regular kitty box and litter. Oh, and some cat food. But this milk should hold—him?—until then.'' They both checked and discovered Lil Guy was an appropriate name.

Madge was sitting up in bed, puffing on a cigarette when Jude came in the room. She didn't say anything, but she sensed a difference in his attitude. Calmer, perhaps?

''Honey, I had to take a little walk—settle something for myself. And look what I found! Isn't he sweet? Do you mind?''

Madge took to the kitten immediately. ''Oh, he is so cute, so little! But too thin! We have to fatten you up. Doesn't the milk have to be warm? I know, I'll set the dish in some hot tap water. And he can curl up in my cashmere sweater. What's that awful-looking box for?''

Jude chuckled. Madge was absolutely adorably impractical. ''Well, for the moment at least, that's his bathroom. I don't think he knows how to use our toilet.'' He was, once more, grateful that Madge had recognized this was not the time to question his mood or his roaming.

                                    *   *   *

After his experience in the cemetery, Jude felt comfortable introducing Madge to Bald Mountain. He was eager to share his stories with her, particularly those dealing with Sun Valley's development.

Wherever Madge went, she seemed to know every visiting celebrity. She spotted Lulu, the ex-Mrs. George Vanderbilt and her husband Ronnie Balcom, the glamorous playboy, while they were waiting to get on the River Run lift.

Lunch at the Roundhouse produced Norma Shearer and Marti Arrougé, J. C. Penney heiress Mignon and husband, William Winans. Tea in the lodge's Redwood Room was a favorite social time, and Madge ran into Anne Ford—the ex-Mrs. Henry Ford and her children.

"Too bad we don't have time for you to see more of your friends," Jude apologized as they were dressing for dinner.

"No matter," Madge said casually. "From what I understood, most of them will be in the dining room tonight, so we can do a little table-hopping then. Besides, when we do the traveling—that you have promised, you know—we'll have ample time to visit everybody."

Willamina and Noah had never been inside the Sun Valley Lodge—they had both reckoned the lodge was not for them. Actually, only Revel, Matthew, Polly and Jude had ever had dinner there. So it was with some trepidation that the rest of the family ventured toward the famous resort. Jude was waiting as the caravan of cars arrived. He had prearranged for the bellboys to valet-park. Only John was reluctant to surrender his keys.

Everyone had primped and preened and all wore new dresses and suits. Even Noah looked very dignified in a navy blue double-breasted suit. Willamina wouldn't forfeit her customary black, but she had found an exquisitely beaded cocktail dress.

"You look beautiful, Mama," Jude exclaimed as he helped her up the few steps. "What a handsome family we are!"

Jude guided his flock to the famed lodge dining room where the maître d' greeted them and led them to a long table, directly bordering the dance floor.

"My, my!" Willamina murmured.

In a few minutes, Madge descended the stairs with a flourish, causing her usual stir, waving to a few chums as she rushed to Willamina.

"So sorry to be late! But I had to feed Lil Guy," and she launched into the story of the rescued kitty.

The children wanted to go right up to see the kitten, but Jude intervened. "Later! Two baby-sitters are coming to our suite soon, so the kids can go to sleep or whatever. And the older ones can go up if they get bored down here and play with Lil Guy and watch TV. Because this is a night for all to enjoy!"

Willamina leaned toward Jude. "You be such a good son. You think of each of us."

"That's what you and Papa have done all your lives, Mama. Now it's time we give back to you. I preordered the first course, but after that, you're on your own. I simply couldn't outguess this group. The waiters will help you select if you have any questions. There is champagne ready to be served, but if anyone cares for something else, just holler."

Jude claimed the first dance with Willamina, gently gliding her around the floor.

"I be worried, Jude. Revel is all right?" she asked a little apprehensively.

"Oh, she's fine, Mama. Just between us, I think she is going through the pangs of a first love."

"Something . . . different. I see in eyes," she confided. "I see Christmastime, too! She tell me nothing."

"No reason to fuss—I swear! I guess girls are just secretive about their boyfriends. Now, forget your worries, that is not allowed tonight," Jude scolded.

Everyone had a turn on the dance floor. Noah with Willamina, then Madge, Polly, on down the line. Revel made sure John, Jr., little Noah and Luke, Jr., dared to join the terpsichorers.

When Jude was holding Madge close during a slow number, he whispered in her ear, "You are dazzling! I am the envy of the whole place—of the whole world!"

"I am really revved up now. The day had been tiring, so I took one of my magic pills."

"I'm not surprised you were beat. You were hell-bent for action on skis! You wore me out. You should have given me one, too."

After the last course had been removed, the lights were dimmed and the band started to play "Happy Birthday." A long table, rimmed with sparklers, was wheeled through the room. Every conceivable dessert was on display, with a huge three-tiered cake as the pivotal point.

"Holy cow!" Jude exclaimed to Madge. "I ordered a cake, not a castle!"

The crowd was likewise impressed. When the glittering table came to a halt in front of Willamina, the orchestra leader announced, "Ladies and gentlemen, Mr. and Mrs. Wade Colby would like to invite everyone present to be their guest for dessert and champagne to help them honor the birthday of their very dear friend, Mrs. Noah Abavas—Willamina. Please join us in wishing her a happy day."

The waiters started popping the champagne bottles, everyone in the room stood up and sang to Willamina, and then burst into applause.

"I'll be damned!" Jude marveled. "Only Wade could do this."

Willamina was absolutely undone. She didn't know what to say, what to do. Finally, with Noah's assistance she acknowledged the tribute. The maître d' handed her a silver knife and with shaking hands, she managed to make the first cut in the cake.

"I no believe—how this—be a dream," she kept saying, happy tears flowing.

36

Los Angeles, California
Friday, May 1, 1959—7:00 a.m.

''It's a girl! I have a girl! And she's beautiful! And Penelope is beautiful! The world is beautiful!'' Wade screamed over the telephone to Jude.

''When? Why didn't you call? I could have helped, maybe— waited with you—done something!'' Jude was startled into alertness.

''I didn't have time! It was so fast. She woke me at three o'clock this morning and said, 'I think it's time, I've called the doctor.' My God, I barely got my pants on, drove like a maniac to St. John's—they whisked her away, and by the time I finished the paperwork, the doc paged me and it was over! I couldn't believe it! With the pregnancy being so difficult, it's a bloody marvel the delivery was so quick and simple.''

''How great! Shall I come over?''

''Not yet. Everybody's sleeping. I think I'll go home and grab a few winks and play with Buzz, so his nose isn't out of joint without Mama there. I saw her, Jude! All pink and soft, no pinched little face. I know she knew it was Daddy when I held her for a minute, because she smiled—I swear! Anyway, Penelope is in great shape, just tired. Why don't I phone you at the office before I come back to the hospital and you meet me there?''

''Perfect! Is there anyone I can call for you, or anything I can do?''

''It's all taken care of, but thanks, old buddy. Talk to you later.''

Jude rolled over and put his arm around Madge. "Are you awake? Did you hear? Isn't it wonderful? Penelope had a girl and with hardly any trouble!"

Madge groaned, "I heard, and yes, it's nice. But why do babies always arrive at such ungodly hours? Why can't they be more civilized?"

Jude laughed. "I don't think they have much to do with it. Boy, that sure woke me up. I was still fuzzy from last night."

"I don't have to go to the hospital, do I? I hate hospitals. They are so depressing and the smell makes me nauseous."

"No, no reason you *have* to go. They'll be disappointed, possibly, that's all."

"Tell them I have a sniffle and didn't want to expose the baby to any germs. That should do it," and Madge turned over and dozed off.

Jude felt a trifle let down by Madge's reaction. But as he looked at his wife lying beside him, so guileless and childlike in her sleep, he couldn't keep any hurt in his heart. Why should she have to endure something that upsets her? Where was the law that said she had to go anywhere that was unpleasant for her? He gave her a kiss and hopped out of bed to get ready for the day.

What could he bring to the hospital? Flowers or books were so unimaginative; he wanted something with a *pow* to it. He mulled over several options until he hit upon something unique. He would stop by Tiffany's and buy a modest, but beautiful, diamond, and each year he would add another diamond of similar size until eventually the baby would have a valuable necklace. Yes, he liked that—an heirloom from Uncle Jude and Aunt Madge!

Later, box in hand, he cautiously opened the door to Penelope's room. He evidently had beaten Wade to the hospital, for she was alone, with the baby at her breast, and so intent she didn't realize Jude was there. He caught his breath in wonder—it felt as if he were in the presence of the Madonna and Child.

Penelope glanced up and welcomed him with a shining smile. "She'll be finished soon. Then you two can meet properly."

Jude just nodded, mute with awe. The act of reproducing was the ultimate miracle to him. How the male fluid and female cell could fuse and create a new human being—with eyelashes and hair and toes and ears—was a never-ending enigma. And having this gift of life in the arms of Penelope once again, struck a deep emotional chord in Jude.

Suddenly, Wade burst through the door. "Sorry I'm late," he said, "but Buzz wouldn't eat his dinner unless we went to the beach together. Hon, the baby nurse—the one we liked best—is all set! Let's see, what else? Your mom is thrilled with the name. Oh, Jude—did I tell you the name this morning? I'm not sure what I said."

"No, but it's okay. You better calm down or I'll have to get you a bed in here, too," Jude told him, laughing.

"Well, it's Priscilla Helena Prickler Colby—how about that? Isn't the little glutton through yet? I want to hold her again! Maybe I'll even allow Jude a second of bliss. Where's Madge?"

"Oh, she didn't dare come—she sneezed a few times and was terrified she'd spread a bug around."

"What a shame! But how sweet. Some people wouldn't bother to worry," Penelope said.

"This is for—Priscilla." Jude thrust the box toward them. "And each year, she'll have another. I—we—I don't know why, we just thought, well, you know the song 'Diamonds Are a Girl's Best Friend'? W-well, we wanted her to have a lot of best friends," Jude stammered.

Wade and Penelope were stunned when they opened the box, and then misty-eyed. After a minute, both expressed identical sentiments, almost in unison, "Priscilla couldn't have a better friend than you, Jude. Nor could we! Thank you. And Madge, too, of course."

Madge didn't particularly cotton to Penelope. It wasn't complete aversion, more a feeling of uneasiness. Penelope was so seemingly perfect in everything, that Madge couldn't exert her customary control. And Madge didn't like not being in control. There was something else—not exactly jealousy—but a suspicion. Jude obviously believed Penelope could do no wrong, and Madge wondered if there had ever been anything between them, and, if so, did he still carry a bit of a torch? Madge wasn't concerned about losing him—she knew she could orchestrate Jude like a maestro, play him like an instrument. But she didn't want to share him with any other hidden skeletons; she already had to overcome the dead wife and child in Sun Valley. She wanted his absolute whole for herself, for as long as she wished. Bad enough that he was so involved with work. But anything or anyone else was totally unacceptable.

In the ensuing weeks, Madge was naturally compelled to see the new addition to the Colby clan. She had to admit, Priscilla was a cute little thing. But still, she felt uncomfortable, fueled by Jude's behavior, because he was as gaga over that pink bundle as Wade. Did Jude wish *he* was the father? Was that it?

Madge decided six months was long enough to wait for a honeymoon, and she needed to get Jude away from these meddlesome influences. Besides, she was ready for some action. Playing mama to their menagerie had worn a little thin and she was bored with most of the ladies she knew in Southern California. Charity organizations never had appealed to her. No, she definitely craved new blood. And Revel and Polly were working steadily so were unavailable to be much company. But Artie was coming in mid-June, and Madge knew Revel would free herself for him, which meant for Madge, as well, so she could last a while longer. But she knew she had better start a program of persuasion soon.

After a particularly inventive evening in bed, Jude utterly subjugated by her wizardry, she began her crusade.

"Remember last February? In Sun Valley? When you said to my friends you were going to take your bride on more trips?"

"Sure," Jude mumbled.

"Well, now that Wade is over the baby trauma and can spend more time working, does that mean we could go soon?"

"I guess so. Is that what you'd like? I'd like to just stay like this—forever."

"I would, too, of course. But we can be—like this—in many different parts of the world. Which could make—like this—even more exciting!"

"Is that possible? Well then, we'll just have to see what we can do about that."

"Oh, Jude, we'll have the most wonderful time. The Sardoses have invited us for a cruise in July, ending in Monaco in time for Princess Grace's International Red Cross Ball in early August. And then we could go to—"

Jude silenced her with a kiss. "Hold it! Let's take one country and one month at a time. You don't want to give me culture shock!'' He saw her disappointment. "I promise I'll work it out, at least for the first part. Maybe we could save the 'and then' for a little later?''

Madge smiled. She had accomplished exactly what she wanted.

37

Los Angeles, California
Saturday, June 27, 1959

Jude arranged a small farewell dinner at their house the night before the departure. "Might as well start living it up early. Truth is, I'm nervous and I need fortification from my amigos. How can I be on a boat with people I don't know, going to places I've never been, eating food I've never eaten, meeting *more* people I don't know! You are going to have to get me plastered and keep me plastered until I get on that damn plane or I just might back out."

Everyone was more than willing to do their part. They planned to keep Jude awake and mellow until they delivered him to the airport. It had been a surprise to them, that Jude had actually agreed to this globe-trotting. Madge, they realized, had a real influence over Jude.

"Gosh, it sounds like a dream." Revel sighed wistfully.

Artie tried to make amends. "I had hoped Mother and Father would ask you, as well, and naturally I would have tagged along. But they wanted the focus to be on the newlyweds. They plan to pick up friends along the way, each for a few days, so their whole circle finally has a chance to fete the happy couple. I think Madge's father, Bruno, is even going over briefly."

A touch of melancholy clouded Revel's eyes. She wondered if Artie's parents simply didn't want her there. Shouldn't they be interested in meeting the girl their son loved?—after all, they'd been together for more than six months. Or had he only told *her* how he felt? Did he even mean what he said? Revel was too proud to press for answers, too aware, also, that she had been the maiden aggressor. Yet, maybe she was just being impetuous. Patience was not one of her virtues, she knew.

Artie saw that flash cross Revel's face. But there was nothing he could do about it. He had tentatively mentioned Revel to his family, but they hadn't given the response he expected.

Beryl and Nicholas Sardos were not blind to Atherton's "infatuation" with this young Hollywood thing. Even though Madge had married the girl's brother, and spoke highly of the girl herself, they were not anxious to have the affair turn serious. It was fine that he should have his "fling," but marriage was another matter. Galen could come on the ship, he would be amusing for Madge and her husband, but better for Atherton to return home soon and oversee the family's business.

Meanwhile, Matthew and Polly were busy talking about the first year's success of Studio Services Inc. and extolling the contributions of Vincent Franks. "Revel, when Jude comes home, and since Wade is involved with the studio now, maybe you could divvy up your time between Colvas and S.S.I. We could use more people."

"What?" Revel was drawn back into the conversation. "Oh, that sounds great." She rapidly pulled herself together. "That is, if they can spare me. I don't know if the studio could run without me—ha! ha!"

Wade quickly pounced in. "Don't you 'ha! ha!' yourself, young lady! We do need you. But I will be available, whatever *that's* worth, and this could be an exciting challenge."

"And I can handle my needs, since I'll be just a hausfrau," Penelope added.

"That's right!" Wade continued. "We could allow you, let's say, two days, to start with. But not until Jude returns. Okay?"

"Done!" Matthew and Polly exclaimed.

"I feel like I've just been auctioned." Revel laughed. "I know—you'll do anything for cheap labor, right?" But deep inside was a well of contentment; they were actually vying for her services, even if they were family.

"Don't forget time for me, my sexy executive," Artie whispered.

"As long as you have time for me!" chaffed Revel.

"Well, Jude," Wade proclaimed, "you have nothing to worry about. The business is in good hands. Revel and I will carry on, with a little help from a few others. So, forget your troubles and just get happy!'' Wade launched into a song and dance.

"Oh, dear, he's in his musical period," Penelope groaned.

"Only trying to provide a little levity," Wade crooned.

Revel joined Wade, and then Polly, and, finally, Artie was coaxed in. Everyone else was hysterical. "Judy Garland, you ain't!" Jude howled.

Madge put on some real music and soon they were all bopping around.

"Oh, Revel, I always have such fun when I'm with you," Artie said in her ear.

"Stay longer then! Try it, you'll like it!" taunted Revel.

Wade slumped into a chair, exhausted, "Darling, I don't think you should overexert yourself. It's only been eight weeks, you know."

Polly was amazed. "I can't believe it's only eight weeks. You look fantastic!"

"How's our baby glamour girl doing?" Jude wanted to know. "I'm going to miss her."

Madge rolled her eyes upward. "Spare me," they pleaded. She couldn't wait to get out of here tomorrow.

Madge exited and returned with Oliver, the butler. A silver tray with strange-looking glasses and a bottle of clear liquid, elaborately encased in ice, was placed on the coffee table.

"Hark, everyone! To launch our honeymoon, we are about to embark on a journey here tonight. Now, these small tumblers, as you can see, have round knobs for a base and are upside down on their little dishes. Which means, when they are filled, you must bottom up. There is no nursing your drink. Everybody ready? Oliver, let the games begin!"

The liquid was akvavit—aquavit—a clear Scandinavian liquor flavored with caraway seeds. Sometimes a shot was followed by a beer at Viking banquets, but not so on this night. Either way, akvavit packed a terrific wallop. They were still sloshed when the limousine arrived at six in the morning to take the travelers to the terminal. The luggage was stored and the pair was poured into the back seat, where coffee and juice and rolls were waiting.

Wade, Penelope, Matthew, Polly, Revel and Artie waved their goodbyes, and Wade gravely announced, "Well done, comrades. We did our duty, bravely and thoroughly. Maybe too thoroughly. Now who is going to take care of *us?* I feel god-awful!''

Jude and Madge were greeted in fine style when they landed at the Athens airport. Both had managed to sober up, rest and refresh themselves on the long flight. The stops had allowed them to stretch their legs and Madge's pills had kept them in the right frame of mind. For weeks, now, Jude had been wondering about those pills. Were they safe? Legal? Where did she get them? But he hadn't asked her about them yet. And every time the capsules worked, he was so glad she had them he conveniently forgot his concern that the damn things might be addictive.

The itinerary had been arranged by Madge and Nicholas and Beryl Sardos. A week in Athens to explore the famed antiquities and then on to the Greek isles where they would be guests of honor at two planned receptions. Then they would all fly to meet the yacht in Naples and begin the cruise.

Madge took Jude to the cove where she had lost her virginity. While they were splashing around in the sea, Madge suddenly reached for Jude and implored him to ''Pretend I'm a young virgin and you want to make love to me.''

Jude didn't understand he was helping to reenact a scene from her past. He thought it was yet another, particularly sweet, innovation of hers.

It was perhaps the most moderate sex they ever shared, but the most sentimental.

''Remember?'' Madge whispered to Jude, ''I told you—'like this'—would be wonderful in different parts of the world!''

38

Beverly Hills, California
Monday, January 4, 1960

"What's up, Madge?" Revel asked. "You look glum."

"You are rather a sourpuss yourself!" retorted Madge.

"I'll tell you, if you tell me," Revel bargained.

"Deal! You first."

Madge and Revel were having cocktails at the house, waiting for Jude to come home from the studio. Actually, Madge had been having cocktails since lunch.

"Well..." Revel hesitated. "I'm still hurt that Artie didn't come here for New Year's or for your first anniversary. He hasn't come to California as often lately. I wanted to be with him, not Vincent, at the party."

"Who?" Madge was a bit hazy.

"Vincent. Vincent Franks. You know, Matt and Polly's CEO? He's nice enough, but it's Artie I want. I'd like to know what's going on." Revel hadn't intended to use Madge's relationship with the Sardoses, but she was getting desperate. "You're so close to Artie and his family, I thought you might—I certainly can't ask him—I thought you might tell me if, well, Madge, do you know something I don't?"

"To tell you the truth, I have not spoken to them at length since our return. I get depressed when I hear about their activities. Just a few short calls to say happy birthday or Happy Thanksgiving or Merry Christmas, something like that. But I will call tomorrow. I'm sure it's nothing more than business demands on his time." Madge wryly added, "Knowing your brother, you should be able to relate to that."

Revel didn't pick up on the dig at Jude. "I hope you're right. I really do miss him...a lot, you know?"

"I do understand. Perhaps you should go out more with—Vincent, is it? Or others, and make Artie jealous."

Revel sighed. "You know, Madge, that Artie was, well, he was the first. He's the only...I mean, I've never been with anyone else. And I don't think I want to be with anyone else—ever!"

"Never is a long time, Revel. You are not even twenty, there is a great deal of living ahead of you. How do you know you wouldn't enjoy the excitement of other men? Enjoy the experience, the exhilaration of the power of your womanhood?" Madge felt herself stirring, just imagining the scene described by her own words.

"Maybe...maybe I'm not the rebel I thought I was. Maybe I'm just an old-fashioned girl, after all. I dream about Artie and—and marriage, babies."

"All in good time! All in good time! But first you must *be!*"

Revel was troubled. This conversation was going in the wrong direction. "This entire dialogue has been about me, Madge, but you're not exactly in top form. What's up?"

Madge looked animated for the first time. "But you have provided the antidote already! I have been moody and blue. I have few friends, even the wedding celebrations have ended and life has become tedious and drab. I much prefer the variety of travel, the color of atypical people. But now I see what must be done. I am going to create a new society, *here!* Mr. Felipi knows everyone in town, including the new arrivals, and I can import anyone else I want. I will brew a Shangri-la right in Beverly Hills. *All* will come. And then you will realize firsthand what *living* is!"

Revel was startled by Madge's intensity. "Uh, that sounds good—fine! But you won't forget to call the Sardoses tomorrow, will you?"

"So you like the Monaco caper better than the Corsica saga?" Jude was asking Wade. They had been kicking around the two movie ideas since Jude's return last August.

"I think so. More potential commercially."

"I know you're right! I just can't get Corsica out of my mind—those cobblestone lanes, the narrow stairway that ran from the street to each stone house, the setting is wonderful. But I realize the logistics of filming there would be mind-boggling. We'd have to buy a fleet to house crew and equipment—like Kirk Douglas did for *The Vikings*. Maybe we'll get to that project another year. But for now, I agree, we go with the Monaco thief.''

''I'm sure we'll have full cooperation from the palace. Tourism and public relations are very important for the principality's economy.'' Wade paused before continuing. ''What do you think about me playing the rogue? Am I—too old?''

''Shit no! Cary Grant is fifty-five and no one, but no one, thinks he's old. You're not even forty-six. What do I think? I think it's just fucking great! The acting bug struck again, huh?''

Wade smiled sheepishly, ''I am simply more comfortable in front of the camera.'' Wade jumped up from his chair and went to the bar.

Jude had a hunch there was more to come, so he waited quietly.

''Frankly, Jude, I've been—what's the word? A trifle disgruntled lately. Maybe it's a mid-life crisis.''

''Nothing wrong with Penelope—or the kids?'' Jude asked anxiously.

''God, no! No, it's me. You know my old bounder friend, Errol Flynn, died last year, and that has bothered me. Life is so short. And I'm not ready for mothballs yet, there is still life in this old boy. Perhaps I need to prove to myself that I still have it, that I can still draw—have appeal. I have no desire to diddle pretty young things, but it would bolster my psyche to believe that those pretty young things would want me to! Am I making any sense? Or am I being utterly preposterous?''

Some thoughts clicked in Jude's head. ''Of course not. You're perfectly normal. Now I know why you started racing those damn speedboats—you just had to have some action. I bet that's the reason you joined Ernie Kovacs's poker sessions, too—more action! Well, what's wrong with that?''

''Talking does help put things in perspective,'' Wade said gratefully. ''At least I don't feel like I'm crazy.''

''One thing, though,'' Jude warned. ''When we start shooting, no racing! And no motorcycles! Can't jeopardize the production! You can gamble with Ernie, but only on the weekends!''

"Yes, sir!" Wade laughed, "That gives me, let's see, how many months of delectable sport?"

"I doubt we can be ready by this summer—maybe September, if we're lucky. We have to choose the writer first and hope he's fast. Once we get a draft, we can start preparations and think about the rest of the cast." Jude took a deep breath. "And then there's all the stuff currently going on at the studio. It'll be a busy time, that's for sure. Madge is going to kill me—she wants to take another trip!" Jude pondered for a moment. "Well, if we can get this project operating by September," he said finally, "maybe I can appease her with the prospect of Monaco. But if you and I are both gone, who's going to mind the store?"

Wade was confident. "Everything will come together. We have time. And don't forget, there's always that wonderful invention called the telephone. And airplanes. Why, I would fly you back here in a flash."

"Oh, no! No way! That's another on my list of don'ts! But you're right, we do have time. We'll work it out."

Wade put down his drink and shook Jude's hand. "Thanks for listening. And believing. I'm going to go home now and take my wife out for a romantic dinner. She's the other person in my life who listens and believes."

Jude looked at his watch. "I have to leave, too. I've been late for dinner too many nights."

When Revel returned from the studio Tuesday, Madge was waiting in her guest house with their entire animal kingdom—Artz, Orey, Gigi and Lil Guy.

"Good tidings! Artie said he was coming here in mid-February and—" Madge gave a conspiratory grin "—he said he has something very important to talk to you about. So there!"

Revel waltzed around the room. "Oh, thank you! Thank you! I'm so happy! Wouldn't it be romantic if he arrived on Valentine Day? To get engaged on Valentine Day?" Her dog Gigi was too big now, so she picked up Lil Guy, the cat, for a partner in her dance.

"And," Madge continued, "Mr. Felipi thinks my idea is perfect. He agrees this place needs some juicing up. We're planning the first party for Wednesday, January 27—oh, I know, we'll hold the second soiree when Artie comes. I've already put in some calls to Europe."

"But Thursday's a workday!" Revel said.

"So, who cares? Weeknights are always the most humdrum, anyway. This new vision will liven up those dreary evenings, you'll see," Madge assured her young protégée.

"I'm not sure Jude will be exactly thrilled," Revel warned.

"Then he can go to bed—alone," Madge replied.

Jude didn't pay much attention to Madge's preparations for her party. He was just relieved that she was so happily occupied, since he was overloaded at the office. A suitable writer had been found for the tentatively titled *The Rogue of Monaco.* If things progressed on schedule, filming *would* begin in September. But it would be a crushing schedule. He had not yet approached Madge about delaying their next trip, he wanted to be positive that September was feasible.

He had been so engrossed in work that he was totally bewildered by the hubbub that greeted him at home the night of the twenty-seventh. Chasen's catering truck was blocking the driveway, Chuck's Parking was setting up shop. The date had never registered in his mind.

One attendant hastily adjusted his uniform and came to take Jude's car. "Good evening, sir! Have a pleasant time, and here is your ticket."

"I *live* here!"

"Oh, you must be Mr. Abavas. Sorry, sir, I'm new. I'll pull the car in—I mean, the truck's about ready to move, and then I'll put it away for you, sir. Sorry, sir!"

Jude tossed the boy his keys and grinned. "That's okay, son," he said. "I was only surprised. Don't tell on me, but I plain forgot about the party."

Things were just as hectic inside. Waiters were setting tables, musicians were tuning instruments, bartenders were arranging bottles. Madge had given their regular staff the night off and had hired personnel whom Mr. Felipi assured were efficient and closemouthed and would return the premises to normal by the next morning.

Jude dodged people and bolted upstairs to find Madge. She was luxuriating in her bubble-filled oversize tub. He could barely see the outline of her nakedness but he was immediately aroused.

"You look comfortable and relaxed . . . and beautiful," Jude said softly as he bent to kiss her.

"Well, you don't! Why don't you join me and then perhaps you will," she invited.

Jude quickly shed his clothes and stepped into the steamy, fragrant water. "Oh, you smell good." He ducked under and when he surfaced, added, "All over!"

"You have bubbles in your hair," Madge laughed. "I'm going to put them everywhere." And she grabbed the elusive foam and began to rub it into his tired frame. "They're going away!" she wailed, so she poured an extra dose and turned the spigot on to create more lather. "There, that's better... because *this* part needs special attention." The two were smothered in suds, sliding back and forth on the smooth tile, thrashing in bathtub waves. Their bodies made contact and the bubbles churned even higher. His mouth was milking her creamy breasts, his muscle of love was pumping deep into her, and both were crescendoing.

The timing had been perfect. Madge had wanted to send Jude off to the party a very satisfied man. She had accomplished her mission.

When Jude descended a while later, he saw an effervescent Madge welcoming early arrivals. She was arresting in a bright yellow, high-necked, Chinese sheath, with a slit on the side to her thigh. Her jet black hair was parted in the middle and hung straight and long.

There was a scattering of vaguely familiar faces, but no one whose name he remembered. Jude concluded they must belong to the legion of folk he had met on their European jaunt. Long way to come for a get-together, he mused. But the majority of guests were strangers to him. He felt somewhat like an outsider.

He spotted Revel, who seemed to be enjoying her new acquaintances. When he finally caught up to Madge at one point, he whispered, "Where are Wade and Penelope and Matt and Polly?"

"Oh darling, we see them *all* the time. I decided tonight would be novelty night. I'm sure they understand, probably delighted *not* to attend. I also believe Revel should broaden her horizons, don't you agree?" and she flitted off before he could answer.

The real frolicking commenced after supper. The newest rage was a dance called the twist. Madge had employed four instructors and the eager pupils lined up for their lessons, Jude valiantly attempted to rally his energy, but as the hour grew late, he knew he'd had enough. "Would you be upset if I called it quits?" he shouted to Madge over the music.

"Would you like a pick-me-up?"

"I don't think so, not tonight."

"Then of course I wouldn't mind. You go right up to beddy-bye."

Jude escaped upstairs unobserved. No one even knew he was gone. As he undressed, he gratefully acknowledged his wife's understanding.

39

Beverly Hills, California

Madge and Revel were in high spirits. The success of the debut of Madge's "new society" and the anticipation of her next function kept her sparkling. Revel lived in expectation of Artie's arrival on Wednesday, February 17, which was also the date for Madge's second wingding. Revel didn't care that Artie hadn't made Valentine Day—that he was coming was enough.

He had not wanted her to pick him up at the airport, but Revel paid no heed and rode out in Madge's limousine. She planned to go to the hotel with him while he changed, so that they could have some time alone before the party. Nervously, with Madge's help, she had chosen a clinging chestnut jersey gown. The color almost matched her auburn hair. The turtleneck collar and long sleeves appeared demure, but the adhering material was quite provocative.

At the airport, when the chauffeur opened the limo door for Artie, Revel called out, "Surprise!" and threw her arms around him. Artie was nonplussed. He returned her kiss, but seemed wary.

"This is a surprise." He may have been rattled, but he couldn't disguise his hunger for her. Nonetheless, he insisted the car drop him first so he could settle in, take Revel home and then return for him.

She was disappointed, but didn't argue. They could always celebrate later.

Dinner was almost ready to be served and still no Artie.

"Maybe he's rehearsing how to propose, or how to approach

Jude,'' teased Madge. That thought brought a new worry to Revel.

She found Jude deep in conversation with a French fashion photographer from *Elle* magazine.

"May I speak to you a moment, Jude?''

The photographer grudgingly excused himself, but not without a look at Revel that conveyed a promise of I'll see you later!

"Jude, you like Artie, right?'' Revel quietly said.

"Of course I do, honey. Why would you even ask?''

"Well, if he were to—I mean, if he mentioned anything about loving me—to you—would you say okay?''

"Okay to what? Okay to love you? Okay to marry you? Okay to sleep with you?''

Revel winced at that last one. "I guess I mean, okay to be engaged.''

"Is that what you want, Rev?''

"Very much!''

Jude slowly let out his breath and shook his head. "I can't believe that time has come already. But since it has, and I have to play Papa here, I imagine I would say okay.'' He hugged her close. "My baby sister, all grown up. Where is that lucky guy?''

Revel shushed him. "Don't say anything! This is just a suppose—so far.''

"Oh, I see, warming me up for the kill, eh? Smart little devil!'' Jude glanced over her head. "Well, guess who just walked in? Your Romeo! Don't worry, I'll be good.''

Madge's entertainment for the night was a hypnotist. Many of the guests were already well on their way to psychedelia, so they were willing guinea pigs. Revel and Artie skipped out before the first experiment, and Jude deserted soon after. If Artie was planning to say anything to him, tomorrow would be good enough.

Once inside her guest house, Revel turned to Artie and held him in her arms with all her strength. "How I have longed for you,'' she whispered.

"And I for you,'' Artie said huskily. They caressed passionately, and then Artie abruptly pulled away. "We have to talk!''

"I know.'' Revel was touched by his nervousness.

"You see, my father—isn't well.''

"Oh, I'm sorry.'' She was immediately sympathetic.

"And he wants me to fully assume the management of our holdings."

"But that's wonderful!"

"But it means I would have to be over there most of the time," Artie explained.

"I don't mind living there, my sweetheart. I'd be with you, and that's all that matters."

Artie looked at her with tormented eyes. "Normally, it would be the oldest son who would assume the responsibility, but my brother, Galen, is just not suited for the business world. My sister, Angela, married the son of one of my father's partners. With my new position, my father and mother have arranged—have arranged for me to become betrothed to the daughter of another partner. That is the custom, to keep the associations integrated."

Revel was standing very still, calm, almost as if she hadn't heard what he'd said.

Tears welled and spilled down Artie's cheeks. He loved her so much; he hadn't realized how much until now. He never fathomed how difficult this would be. She looked so vulnerable, so desirable!

"It's you I love, Revel. It's you I want to be with. But I can't do anything about this! I want to keep seeing you."

"*Stop it!*" Revel's voice was like ice. She lowered herself to the couch, staring at nothing. "It's because I went to bed with you, isn't it?" she finally said. "Now I'm not good enough."

"No! No! I *love* you!" Artie declared desperately.

"But not enough to marry me. What an absolute damn fool I was—*am!* You say you love me—that's bull! You love the sex, not me. You want me to be a—a mistress, a whore. And you call that love?"

"I don't mean anything like that. I can't bear to give you up. I was selfish, and now I'm ashamed."

"What a laugh you must have had! Me talking about living over there with you. Oh, hell, I feel so dumb." She was losing control and could barely hold back the sobs racking her body.

"There was—and is—no laughter in me, Revel. Only sorrow and pain. That you must believe."

Then the floodgates burst open. "Just go away, Artie! I—I—don't know what to believe anymore! Please, go—leave me alone."

Artie walked despondently toward the door. Gigi chose that moment to come bounding in from the bedroom.

"Goodbye, Gigi," he said. "Goodbye, my love. You will always be in my heart." And Artie was gone.

"It's my fault." Madge steamed. "I should never have taken for granted that he meant to tell you something special. I didn't think! I adore the Sardos family, all of them. But it never occurred to me that they would hold their son to some insane tradition—merging marriage and business. My stupidity has hurt you. You, my one true friend."

"No, Madge, it wasn't you," Revel said. "It was me. I believed what I wanted to believe. I gave myself to him because I wanted to. Artie didn't force the affair. Only I was dumb enough to expect the happy ending. Now I've just proved what everyone probably knew, anyway—that I'm a birdbrained juvenile. Damn! Damn me! Damn life!"

"Come now, it is not that bad," comforted Madge. "You learned something very important, something I learned a long time ago. You—me—women—we must be the ones to dole out punishment to men. Not them to us. Use the way you were made for your benefit, for your pleasure, for your dominance, for whatever *you* want, Revel. Use *them*."

Revel was silent a while. Then she looked up at her mentor with determination. "You're right! I am going to start living for *me!*"

Jude felt something was wrong, but he wasn't sure what. Artie hadn't called him. Revel hadn't called him. And Revel had not shown up for work today. He didn't know what to expect when he came home Thursday night. He hardly anticipated what he found.

Revel and Madge were curled up in the den, bent over in convulsions, Oliver, the butler, replacing an empty bottle of champagne in the ice bucket with a full one.

"Oh, hi, Jude—oh, dear—what a crazy—" and Revel was off laughing again.

"What's the joke? I could use a haw-haw myself," he said very good-naturedly.

Madge simmered down enough to explain. "We started to plot our next get-together—"

"Already? You just had one last night!" Jude interrupted.

Madge said coolly, "And I intend to have another in three—no—make it two weeks."

Revel chimed in. "And we came up with the most bizarre entertainment—"

"Don't tell him," Madge cautioned. "Let it be a surprise!"

"I think I'd like some of that stuff—that is, if you can spare it," Jude said dryly. "Madge is right, Rev, don't tell me. A little voice is saying it would be better for me to be . . . surprised."

Jude sipped his drink and waited. He wondered how many bottles they had consumed. This was not like Revel, and he was concerned. He tried to sound casual. "You know, Rev, I didn't hear from Artie today."

"That's funny, neither did I!" Revel was being flippant. "As a matter of fact, I doubt either of us will . . . ever again. I broke up with him. It's over—kaput. Let's toast to freedom!" She drained her glass and Madge quickly filled it.

So that was it. "I'm sorry, honey. Anything you want to talk about? Anything I can do?" Then Jude had a flash. "Did he try something with you? Because if he did, I'll find that Greek prick and bash his face in. I don't care whose friend or whose son he is!"

Both Revel and Madge saw the storm clouds coming.

"Now, Jude, you must not jump to conclusions," Madge soothed.

Revel perched on his chair. "No, dear brother, you don't have to defend my honor. I have no honor! Just kidding, just kidding. I—I changed my mind, that's all. I decided I was too young to be tied down. And that's all there is to it. Artie is a very nice man. But he has to be there and—and I want to be here."

"But last night . . ." Jude began.

"Last night was last night. Today is different." Revel went to fill her glass again.

"You seem very troubled to me, Rev!"

"But I'm not," Revel vowed. "Of course, I'm sorry it didn't work out. And I hope I didn't hurt him...too much. But *c'est la vie!* Upward and onward!"

Jude was not satisfied that he had heard the whole story. In fact, he was quite sure Revel was lying. But he also knew that this was not the time to push for answers.

40

Hollywood, California
Monday, May 30, 1960

"**Y**our wife is on the phone, Mr. Abavas," Muriel's voice announced over the intercom.

"Hi, there! This is a bolt out of the blue—you never call the office. Everything okay?"

"Not exactly." Madge's tone sounded odd.

"What's the matter?" .

"I just received a call from a hospital in New York. They told me—my father died this afternoon, Jude."

"Oh, God, I'm sorry, darling. How awful! I'll be right home."

"That's not necessary. I'm fine. But you could do me a favor."

"Anything."

"Would you book a flight for me tomorrow? I don't feel like coping with details."

"You got it. I'll make two reservations on the noon flight, or would you be more comfortable if I chartered a plane?"

"There's no need for you to come, Jude. You would be uneasy, everyone would be a stranger to you. I'm afraid your nervousness would make it more difficult for me. But, do you think—could you spare Revel for a few days? The funeral is on Thursday, we would be back on Friday."

Jude faltered. But only for a second. "Sure, she can go—if you're positive you don't want me."

"It's not that I don't want you, I believe the ordeal would be easier this way for each of us. Revel wouldn't be uptight with these people. And she always knows how to keep up my spirits. A commercial flight is fine. We'll talk more later, I'm tired now."

Jude wouldn't have hesitated at all to accompany Madge, but he was not disappointed that he wasn't going. She was right, he would have been uncomfortable. However, he was a bit apprehensive about sending Revel and Madge off alone. Since February the two women seemed joined at the hip, sharing some sort of veiled secret. Madge's parties had become wilder and Revel had become a regular participant. But this was obviously not the time to make an issue of it. Madge certainly didn't need any more pressure at this point. He would just have to live with his concern for now.

That night, holding Madge close in their bed, he asked about what had happened to Bruno.

"He had gone in to have a face-lift. Can you believe that? He must not have been getting enough nooky in his old age—thought this would improve his chances, I guess. Whatever, he hemorrhaged on the operating table and the idiotic doctor transfused the wrong type of blood. The whole thing is like a bad farce."

Jude didn't know what to say, so he just held her closer.

"Beryl and Nicholas Sardos can't come—Nick isn't up to it and Beryl doesn't want to leave him. I don't really care. Daddy would have cared, but he's not going to know who is or isn't there, anyway."

Jude stayed quiet. He was glad she was talking, better to let it all out.

"Apparently, I have tons of papers to sign. Daddy's lawyers said he left everything to me. They said I am very wealthy, but I don't know what that means. I don't know about money."

Now Jude spoke assuredly. "Don't worry. I'm sure your father left everything in order. If you have any questions or problems, just call me and I'll have our attorneys go over everything. And if you don't like their attitude, tell them to stick it! Thank God money doesn't have to be a concern here. I have enough for both of us."

"I'll be so glad when this is over." Madge sighed. "And then I can come back here and have fun Saturday night!"

"What's Saturday night?" Jude asked.

"You *are* a bad boy! It's your birthday party, silly! And it's going to be *something.*"

"Oh, hell, I forgot. But don't you think under the circumstances we should cancel? I can't imagine you're going to be in any mood for a lot of people. And trust me, I won't mind at all."

"Absolutely not! And I would *mind*—a great deal. These little affairs are very important to me. They are my mark on life, and I wouldn't give them up for anything." Madge disengaged herself from Jude to face him. "You don't seem to understand. I truly am not stricken by this. I'm sorry, yes, but not devastated. It's the technicalities that upset me, and those won't take long to conclude. And then it'll be done, and Saturday will be wonderful. So, enough of that. Come here..."

After Madge was asleep, Jude lay awake, unable to relate to his wife's response to the death of a loved one.

Jude's forty-first birthday on Saturday, June 4, 1960, was indeed a blast. The tented yard was decorated as a Gypsy camp. Covered wagons, gaily adorned with bold blankets and trinkets, rimmed the perimeter. Each had its own simulated open fire, with stew pans and kettles hung from a crook-shaped iron driven into the ground. Inside the wagons a variety of entertainment was offered: tarot card readings, palm readings, crystal ball readings, magicians. Gypsy melodies filled the air and the staff all wore full multicolored skirts and off-the-shoulder tops with long dangling earrings; or black baggy pants, open loose shirts and blazing bandannas. Shawls covered the rough-hewn tables, and heavy pottery with earthenware mugs served in lieu of china and crystal.

Madge and Revel had returned from New York on Friday. Neither had revealed much about the trip except that Madge did explain to Jude that there had been no difficulty with the estate, and that business matters would be conducted as before. Jude and Revel were to be the beneficiaries of Madge's inheritance, unless Jude and she were divorced, in which case Revel would receive the total estate. "It's all academic, anyway," Madge said laughingly, "because I intend to live a long time and to spend everything!"

This night, Madge had invited Polly and Matthew, Penelope and Wade, and even Vincent Franks. She had also called the

family in Idaho, but they hadn't felt comfortable about coming. Madge had known they wouldn't, but she figured she'd
racked up points for asking.

Jude, Penelope, Wade, Polly and Matthew had gathered together after politely making the rounds.

"Whew! This is exhausting, but enjoyable!" exclaimed Wade.

"I'm afraid three-quarters of the people are complete strangers to me," commented Polly.

"I have to admit," Penelope said hesitantly, "I was surprised
to see my old nemesis here—that actor Timothy Davis!"

"So was I!" agreed Jude. "You see, I've never stayed long at
Madge's parties because they're always in the middle of the
week. They're sort of her thing. So I don't know everyone, either. Must be one of her new friends, but he won't be here for
long. He's not welcome in my house."

"Well, I don't give a hoot about all that—I'm having fun,"
Matthew said. "Polly and I were ready for a night on the town.
Wonder how Vince is doing?"

"I think I saw Revel urging him into the magician's wagon,"
Polly answered. "He's such a nice man, I wish Rev would see
more of him. Is she still going with Artie? I haven't seen hide nor
hair of him for quite a while. Come to think of it, Rev hasn't
been around much, either. What's with her?"

"I don't know, Polly," Jude said, showing his worry.
"Something happened last February. Artie and Rev broke up,
but I'm not sure of the actual reason. She really hasn't been the
same since. She doesn't seem to care about work as much—not
that she's negligent, just not as gung ho. She's distant, unfo-
cused . . . unbridled, if you know what I mean. I hope to God I
haven't messed up with her."

Matthew spoke up. "That's not it, Jude, you've been great!
God knows, Mama and Papa could never have coped with Rev.
I think she's just feeling her oats a bit. We can't expect her to be
as dedicated as we are. She has to live a little. Remember how we
were at her age?"

"I can't remember that far back." Wade sighed. "But I am
inclined to agree with Matt. You're not at fault, Jude. If there
has to be accountability, blame it on youth."

"I have a thought," Polly volunteered. "Penelope and I have
joined a group who are going to work on Senator John Kenne-

dy's campaign for the presidency. It's only in the formative stage at the moment, but there's tremendous enthusiasm. And a lot of the volunteers are surprisingly young, not able to vote yet, like Rev. Maybe Rev would be interested. I think she would be quite taken by Senator Kennedy's idealism.''

Wade groaned, "Oh God, a Democrat! Grandfather Prickler would roll over in his grave!"

"Hush, darling!" Penelope scolded. "I think that's a wonderful idea, Polly! It would be good for Revel to become involved in something like this."

Jude was doubtful. "Now all we have to do is convince the lady in question."

"We'll tackle that," both Penelope and Polly promised.

Further discussion was interrupted by a fanfare. Madge took a hand mike and slithered her way to the center of the tent. "Where is the birthday boy hiding? Come up here! The *coup de théâtre* tonight is especially for you!"

Jude reticently threaded his way to his wife, where Madge kissed him and placed him at one of the ringside tables. She waved her hand, and an orchestra in Spanish costumes appeared with a blast, while chanting flamenco dancers suddenly swirled through the tables to the middle of the floor. The wild rhythm of the music and performers captured the audience, who could barely restrain themselves from joining in the fray. After three numbers, there was suddenly a shift in tempo, and the chorus parted to reveal a shimmering figure draped in golden baubles and glittering plumes. Accompanied only by a drumbeat, the dark-skinned Venus began to gyrate, first her hips, then every part of her body, as if she were awakening, muscle by muscle. Those watching were in a trance. She inched forward, plucking a plume off here, a bauble there. The cadence increased and, in a quivering mass, she ended directly in front of Jude, left wearing only a tassel on each nipple and a spangle over her pubic hair. Thunderous applause broke out as she finished, lying prone at Jude's feet.

Any red-blooded human being—male or female—would have to have been affected. And Jude was no exception. He was conspicuously aroused, extremely embarrassed and not sure what he was supposed to do. Fortunately a cake was wheeled out and he didn't have to do anything except shakily acknowledge his tribute.

*   *   *

Upstairs, much later, Jude knew exactly what to do to satisfy his hunger. But just as he reached for Madge, a light rap on their door startled him. Madge, naked as a jaybird, was not at all surprised and jumping from the bed she hurried to open it. There stood Desiré, the exotic dancer, a cape thrown carelessly around her nudity. Madge drew her inside, removed her cover and proudly announced to Jude, "This is my secret present for you. Meet Desiré—a woman who will make your every dream come true—with my assistance."

Jude had scrambled under the sheets and now glared incredulously at the two of them. "What in the hell is she doing here?"

"I told you—she is my surprise gift to you!"

"Get rid of her!" Jude bellowed. *"Now!"*

Madge had not expected such a response and was flustered. She hesitated.

"Now!" Jude was seething.

Madge made a decision. She ushered Desiré out, whispering, "I'll take care of the arrangements tomorrow." Then she faced Jude. "How dare you humiliate me like that!"

Jude was openmouthed. "How dare I humiliate *you?* Shouldn't it be, how dare you humiliate *me?* Do you think I need help in this department? Is that it? Jesus, I can't believe what just happened! Have you gone bonkers?"

"I was trying to please you. To bring an additional thrill to you!" Madge said indignantly.

"*You* please me. *She* doesn't. I have all I want right here— with you. Bringing her in was an insult! Obviously you crave something more—you must feel I'm not adequate!"

"Maybe I do and maybe I don't!" Madge retorted. "But there was no reason to attack me and spoil everything. How do you know that you wouldn't have liked it? You could at least have experimented—that wouldn't have hurt you—or your stupid male ego!" She flounced toward her dressing room.

"Just a minute!" He grabbed a robe and confronted her. "This is screwy! You don't get what I'm saying! What we do together is kinky enough for me—why a third party? Up to now, you've always seemed content."

"I see no crime in sending up a trial balloon. Who knows what we could have discovered? Now you've squelched all the curiosity."

"Not all! As long as we're...airing our opinions, I'd like to know why that shithead actor Tim Davis was invited tonight. I don't like him and I don't want him in my home."

"My, aren't we forceful," Madge taunted. "I can, and I will, have anyone I choose at my parties. Tim is quite charming, he's funny and witty, everyone adores him."

"No, everyone does *not* adore him. Especially me! I'm telling you, if I see him in this house again, I'll throw him out on his prickly ass—after I smash his face in!"

Jude had worked himself up to a point where, like that first night at the Bel-Air Hotel, something cracked inside. He'd been pushed far enough. He slung Madge over his shoulder and tossed her on their bed.

"You want tryouts? I'll give you a baptism of fire, my pampered independent wife! I saw this in a stag film, and that bitch seemed to like it a lot." He took the sash from his robe and tore it in pieces.

Madge knew he was hotheaded, and her eyes widened in fear. Yet a hint of anticipation also lurked beneath the surface.

Jude tied her wrists to the bedposts, then spread her legs as a butterfly and tied her ankles to the foot of the bed.

"It's called bondage. You can struggle but you can't escape. You are completely at my mercy, I can do anything I want. They say that any restraint upon muscular or emotional activity tends to heighten sexual excitement. We'll find out."

He revolved around her, contemplating where to start. A shark circling its prey. Her head twisted to follow him, not knowing what to expect. Helplessness, not being the one in control, was an unfamiliar state for Madge and she didn't like it. But the sense of imminent danger and the unknown was titilating.

"I think I'll give you a tongue bath first." Jude systematically went over every square inch of her body with long, slow, broad strokes. Madge tried to submerge any reaction, but the act of suppressing made the erotic effect even more acute. Now she wanted to do the same to him, but she couldn't free herself.

"Followed by the rat approach." He gently nibbled her breasts, fingers, ears, lips, clitoris. Biting sometimes, causing her to whimper in pain.

"I've heard in the locker room that this can be a rewarding trick." Jude put his penis way under her right armpit, and began the friction movement, her sensations heightened by the pressure against her breast. Madge moaned, kept almost in continuous orgasm.

"Who would have ever thought?" He applied his big toe to her vulva and clitoris and proved it was a magnificent erotic instrument.

"Oh, please, stop—I can't stand anymore," she pleaded.

"That's what I was waiting for," Jude said wickedly. He rubbed himself all over her, brushing her eyes, her hair, her ears. She desperately lunged for him with her mouth, but he eluded her and doggedly pursued the grazing.

"Say you don't need anybody else—say it!" he demanded.

"I—don't—need—anyone—else," she panted.

"Say I can fulfill you—go on, say it!"

"You can fulfill me."

"Say you will never pull a stunt like that again!"

"I—won't—do—it—again—oh, Jude, *please!*"

"All right then, here I am!" And he was inside her pulsing, saturated opening, sustaining his assault as long as he was able, prolonging the inevitable. Then they both crumbled, in absolute weakness and exhaustion.

As Jude untied her, he remarked, "Quite an ending to our first fight."

41

Santa Monica, California
Monday, August 1, 1960

Wade and Penelope Colby's home had been recruited as one of Senator John F. Kennedy's house headquarters, a network of homes, throughout Los Angeles County, that supplemented the party's regular offices. Additional telephones had been installed in Jude's old digs, the guest cottage, which was empty now that the children's wing had been completed on the other side of the house.

"One of the perks of this volunteer business is that we get to see one another more," Polly said in between sealing envelopes. "The twins think they've gone to heaven—they get to go to the beach every day and play with Buzz."

"Yeah, that's a bonus," Revel interrupted before licking another stamp, "but what gets me are the people we're going to work with. Take this opening rally in September—it's at Janet Leigh and Tony Curtis's place! And, Frank Sinatra, Dean Martin, Sammy Davis, Jr., are going to entertain! And Ted Kennedy is the speaker! I mean, is that neat or what?"

"It's all quite exciting, mostly because Senator Kennedy's so electrifying," Penelope said, looking up from the envelope she was addressing. "I hope Nixon agrees to a debate. That would be something—to see the two candidates face-to-face. Of course, we'd likely miss it because of the picture in Monaco. I've got our absentee ballots, but part of me hopes that the weather turns and the picture has to be finished here in Hollywood. Thank heavens the Screen Actor's Guild strike is settled."

"Who's going to watch Wade race next Sunday?" Revel asked, changing the subject. "Madge won't go, so I'm going with Jude. I might find some new talent for Madge's parties."

Penelope and Polly traded looks. This wasn't exactly what they had had in mind for Revel. They had persuaded her to join the ranks, but they weren't sure if she ever would join in the spirit.

"Matt's all hyped," Polly said. "So we'll be there, kids and all!"

Penelope sighed. "Obviously I'm going, and Buzz, but not the baby. I'm only relieved this will be the last race. You know that Jude laid down the law, don't you? And thank God for that! Those boats have always made me nervous—they go so fast!"

"Speaking of making someone nervous, have you seen the new Hitchcock movie *Psycho?* I make one of the maids come out back to my place to watch at the bathroom door while I shower. But they've all seen it, too, and are as scared as I am!"

"Hey," Revel continued a moment later, her mind hop-scotching again. "Don't the Peter Lawfords live around here? Since we're part of the campaign, can't I mosey on down to meet them? His wife Patricia is a Kennedy, right? So at least I'd get to see one of the Kennedys. And maybe another celebrity would be there, too!"

"They live ten homes away," Polly answered, "but no, you can't go there. You'll have plenty of opportunity in the weeks ahead to make your presence known." She paused, and then smiled. "And I have no doubt, dear Revel, that you'll do just that."

Sunday was not a perfect day for the race. The California sun obliged, but the wind did not. Gusts were blowing up to forty-five miles an hour, and the waters in back of Parker Dam looked angry.

Nevertheless, the mood was cheerful and the air was filled with exhilaration. The racers, mechanics and assistants milled around their crafts, testing this, tightening that. The several hundred spectators, comprising families, friends and sports en-thusiasts, wandered about, looking at the boats, making bets, enjoying the anticipation of a contest.

Wade had chartered a plane for the nine of them. Rental cars were waiting at the landing strip. His crew had made the long drive in the truck that hauled his rig.

Revel didn't waste any time hunting for qualified prospects to increase Madge's guest list. She had read in a sports magazine that quite a few macho playboys took this avocation seriously. They could make interesting fodder—someone like a young Wade Colby perhaps!

Jude was worried about the conditions. "Seems pretty hairy to me, Wade. I don't like those blasts—damn near a gale at times. Why not pass on today?"

"Don't be a nagging nanny, for Christ's sake!" Wade told him cockily. "This will be a piece of cake."

"Well, take it easy," Jude warned.

"It's a race, Jude!" Wade complained.

It was time. Wade jumped into the cockpit and his gang pushed the deep-V hull into the water. He gave a thumbs-up sign and started the powerful motor.

"Good luck!" everyone hollered above the roar.

In moments, the racers were off. The first few laps Wade placed in the front three. Then it looked as though he had nudged into the lead.

Jude and Matthew decided to climb the rungs of the observation tower with their binoculars because they couldn't see the whole course from the ground. The spectators below kept calling for updates. It was on the twelfth lap, when the wind was storming so badly the two men could barely hold on, that Jude cried out, "Oh, no! Way out there, someone just turned ass over teakettle. Looks like the wind caught the bow and flipped it straight up and over. Can you make out which— Oh, my God, I think it's Wade!"

Jude and Matthew shimmied down and dashed to one of the pleasure launches moored at the edge of the lake. Penelope, Polly and Revel couldn't keep up with them, but kept yelling, "What's the matter? What happened? What are you doing?"

Jude shouted on the run, "Get a doctor here! There's been an accident! That one, Matt—the keys are in it." Jude and Matthew hopped into the boat, started it up and took off. It seemed like hours before they reached the wreckage. And once there, they were horrified. Wade was draped over the propeller, bleeding profusely from the upper part of his body. When the boat had been tossed on end, the blades evidently had slashed Wade on the downward plunge.

Jude and Matthew tore their shirts in strips and attempted to stem the torrent of blood with makeshift tourniquets, but without much success. Gingerly they lifted the inert form into their borrowed craft and sped for shore.

Confusion reigned. The owner was livid that someone had stolen his boat; Penelope was hysterical; Buzz was bawling; and Revel was screaming she had found a NASA doctor on vacation.

The doctor immediately took charge. "Name's Stewart Tesse. Get a car down here. We've got to get him to a hospital—*now!*"

Jude ran to his car, which fortunately had a good position in the parking lot. He pushed the accelerator to the floor and broke through the wooden barricades to pull right up to the spot. The doctor and Matthew bundled Wade into the back seat while Jude barked instructions and frantically asked, "Where do we go?"

"Follow my friend," Dr. Tesse ordered.

"Matt," Jude yelled, "you drive Penelope and Buzz. Polly, take your car with the twins and Revel. And follow us. Now!"

Jude shot out of there like a cannonball. He didn't choose the normal lanes, the lot was jammed full. He skirted around and drove over lawns, through hedges and a couple of fences to get to the main highway.

It was not a big hospital, but it was nearby.

Jude screeched to a halt in front of the emergency entrance and bolted out the door, shouting for help. White-coated figures appeared and in no time had Wade on a stretcher, wheeling him to the operating room. Jude was extra baggage at this point. Dr. Tesse was talking to the resident physician. "Show me where to scrub—get a test on his blood type—he needs a transfusion—lost a lot of blood. Do you have a good supply? If not, call Red Cross and fly some down—pronto!—have to tie off—hurry!"

Jude slumped against the hood of his car. He felt so powerless. There was nothing more he could do, it was out of his hands now. He felt drained, weakened. He dragged himself to the wheel and managed to start the car and park it in a proper spot. He found some change and went inside to the pay phone to call Madge. When she didn't answer on the fifth ring, he slammed the receiver down. *Where the hell was she?* He needed her. Probably out with some of her insipid friends! Then he realized how ridiculous he was being—she couldn't have known this was going to happen. He had to get himself together, the others would be here momentarily, and he must be solid for everyone. There *was* something more he could do, he could be their strength and their leader.

Anxiety ran amok in the small waiting room. Everyone had questions and no one had answers. Jude sensed a rising panic, and he had to stop it from overwhelming them. He decided to send all but Penelope back to Los Angeles.

Matthew recognized the wisdom of Jude's move. Although badly shaken, he tried to be Jude's second in command. "Jude's absolutely right. We're only in the way here. Jude and Penelope will call us as soon as they hear anything. Meanwhile, we can do our bit by taking care of things at home."

Polly's eyes were brimming, but she rallied. "I'll stay at your place, Penelope, with the twins and Buzz and baby Priscilla. Don't worry about a thing—I can handle the children and the nannies and the help."

Revel was scared, but she, too, pledged her part. "And I'll be right there for any errands that need to be done, Penelope. Or anything you need done from here."

"We'll take a run by the lake and make any necessary arrangements for Wade's crew," Matthew continued. "I'll go to your house, Jude, and talk to Madge. I can even stay if she's nervous. Just don't concern yourselves about anything outside this hospital. Okay? I'll send the plane back with some clothes and any personal things you want."

Jude and Penelope clutched each of them, fervently showing gratitude for their support and understanding. And then Jude and Penelope were alone. And still. And frightened.

After a long, tension-filled silence, Penelope sought Jude's eyes. She hadn't really allowed herself to express her emotions yet since reaching the hospital, but she was clearly on the verge of exploding. "I guess—I—won't have to worry about—absentee ballots." Suddenly racked with sobs, she buried her head in Jude's comforting embrace.

"Let it all out, honey," he soothed. "Let it go. It's going to be okay, I just know it." Please God, don't let him die. Take me, just don't take Wade away from Penelope and his babies.

Dr. Tesse found them huddled together when he finally emerged hours later. They were stunned by his appearance. Haggard and exhausted, he looked as if he'd come from a slaughterhouse. Dried, clotted blood clung to every inch of his surgical gown, his head covering, his mask.

"I've seen close calls in my time, but never this close. Had a hell of a struggle stopping the flow, there were so many open wounds we didn't know where to start." He quickly halted when he saw their horrified faces staring at him. "Forgive me. First things first, he's going to make it." Penelope swayed in relief, and Jude tightened his grip on her to hold her upright.

"Thank you, doctor. I know—we know—if you hadn't been there—well—you were a miracle," Jude stammered.

"Never mind all that. I'll fill you in, and then I order you to rest, before I have two more patients on my hands. As a matter of fact, the hospital isn't full, so I'm going to check both of you in and prescribe a sedative. I can keep my eye on all of you that way, because there's no way I can leave here for at least twenty-four hours. I just want to be sure Mr. Colby is progressing the way I want him to."

Dr. Tesse continued, "Now, he's very weak. He needed so many stitches, I lost count. His upper torso is literally sewn together. By the time we got to every cut, he had had a complete blood transfusion. We have to watch for infection. He's receiving intravenous antibiotics and nourishment. But despite all this, unless there are unforeseen complications, Mr. Colby will pull through. He is a lucky man. So now why don't we go and get some coffee and food after I clean up? And then we'll get you settled. I don't want you to see him until morning. Honestly, Mrs. Colby, it's what's best for him."

It was two weeks before Wade was able to be flown to Santa Monica. Madge was sorry about the accident, of course, but was a little peeved at the disruption it caused and the fact that Jude was there with Penelope—and not at home with her! She didn't want Matthew to stay with her, but she did ask Revel to move into the big house until Jude got home. And to appease her dark mood, she quickly lined up a party to eat, drink and merry the unpleasantness away.

Jude conducted his business from the hospital. There was much to do. He had to cancel all the arrangements for the Monaco picture, as well as manage the day-to-day functions of the studio. And the reporters drove him crazy. As there had been years ago with the motorcycle debacle, there was never-ending speculation about Wade Colby's condition. And so, once again, a press conference was held. This time with Dr. Stewart Tesse explaining exactly what had occurred, and the extent of Wade's injuries.

Dr. Tesse stayed at the hospital for almost a week, and when he felt certain about Wade's recovery, he resumed his vacation. Penelope and Jude and Stu had become good friends during this harrowing time, and promised to keep in touch. They had bonded in this disaster, and each felt the pang of loss when Stu had to leave.

42

Santa Monica, California
Sunday, September 4, 1960

Jude walked over to the lounge chair on the patio, where Wade lay sunning and watching the activity on the beach.

"Hi!" Wade greeted Jude with a big smile. "Trying to improve my hospital pallor. If I felt as bad as I look, I'd be in deep shit!" With great effort, Wade lifted his head off the cushion. Jude winced in sympathy as he saw the difficulty Wade was having with the simple movement.

"Didn't Madge come with you?" Wade asked.

"She wasn't feeling up to par—her period, I think."

"That's too bad. How are you doing?"

Jude settled himself in an adjoining chair. "All is well, thanks—just fine."

"Penelope will be back in a bit. She took the little ones for a walk on the beach. And then we can have lunch. Why don't you pour yourself a drink? You look as though you could use one—or two. The office has been a bitch, I bet. I really mucked things up good and proper, didn't I?"

"Well, you fucked yourself up pretty bad, that's for sure!" Jude said, pouring himself a daiquiri from the iced container. He took a sip. "Mmm, that does hit the spot. Actually, Wade, it's all under control at the studio. Monaco was disappointed, but will welcome us whenever we're ready to start. Everything else is on hold. We lost some key people, but they'll probably be finished with their new commitments by the time we start next summer, anyway, so I think we're okay. Or we will be, as soon as you're up again."

"Oh, I'm coming along great. I just get impatient. I want to be well *now!*"

"You listen to me, Wade Colby! Your body took quite a beating. Hell, it's a miracle you're even alive! So don't go rushing anything, give it time to heal. This is your producer talking to his star, and that is an order!"

"Yes, sir!" Wade saluted. "Between you and Penelope, I have to behave."

"As it should be!"

"But poor Madge was probably more upset than anyone by the whole thing," Wade said.

Jude was startled by Wade's remark. "What do you mean?"

"Well, didn't you say she wanted to go to Europe even earlier than September? But you thought she would be placated if it was at *least* September? Now that the picture is postponed, she must be perturbed."

"Oh, right. Frankly, I forgot." Jude seemed uneasy at that little white lie. "But she knows what happened. Jesus, no one planned this accident. Of course she understands."

Jude reached for the pitcher again. Wade watched him carefully. "As soon as I am able to work, you two should go on a trip, Jude. You've been hard at it for quite some time now."

"We'll see, we'll see, one step at a time." Jude changed the subject. "Guess next week is the big kickoff affair for Kennedy, huh? Has it been a pain in the ass having the volunteer ladies around?"

"No, actually, I hardly know they're here. They stay out in the guest house. And, they are busy, I'll say that for them!"

"Did you know Polly signed up to be a registrar of voters?" Jude asked him. "She's gung ho—everyone seems to be. What do you think about Kennedy?"

"I like him!" Wade declared. "But Jesus, don't ever mention to my family I'm even contemplating voting for a Democrat."

"Your secret's safe with me. Yeah, I agree. I think Kennedy's a good man. I hope the Catholic issue doesn't present a big problem—surely the nation is beyond that by now."

"I'm looking forward to the debates—the first one is September 26, right?"

"Right! Should be a humdinger." Jude smiled. "I talked to Papa a few days ago, and he and Mama can't get over the fact

they're actually going to see the two presidential candidates together on TV. I forget sometimes how powerful our technological advances have become and the consequences they provoke.
This election could actually be decided by these debates!''

Jude rose and began to pace restlessly. ''It *is* a time of
change—I feel it! Hell, either Russia or the U.S. is about to send
a man into space—probably Russia, the consensus is they're
ahead of us. When I was a kid, that was only Flash Gordon Saturday serial stuff. Now it's for real. Imagine what that could do
to our industry, Wade!''

''No end in sight, either,'' Wade agreed. ''The scientists will
probably have a man on the moon in a few years. It's all happening so quickly—just in our lifetime, we've seen such a meta-
morphosis. Our parents' generation must be reeling with all
this.''

''I know mine are! Arriving as immigrants, developing a successful business. Of course, Noah believes marvels are the norm
for his United States, and that he is living proof of it!''

''Well, he is,'' Wade said. ''But however fast the world is
moving, perhaps you should slow down a bit, Jude. You're edgy.
Why don't you go for a swim, relax a little? Do you good! You
know where the trunks are.''

''Thanks. Maybe I will.''

Jude *was* edgy. The four weeks since Wade's crash had been difficult. Not only because of the scare over Wade's brush with
death, or the added load at the studio—Madge was troubling
him, as well. Her reaction to the crisis had baffled, disappointed and even angered him. She had shown neither awareness of the seriousness of the situation, nor compassion for the
suffering endured. He remembered what she had said when her
father died, and that the loss had had such little effect on her. He
couldn't expect more empathy from her for Wade than for her
own parent. But he hadn't comprehended her attitude then, and
he didn't now. And didn't her husband deserve some consideration? When he had spoken to her every day from the hospital,
he had felt a distance, a lack of interest. In the two weeks he had
been home, she had been warmer, but maintained the apathy
toward Wade. Jude had the weird sensation that she was punishing them, blaming them, for the inconvenience of Wade's accident.

The full focus of Madge's attention was still on entertaining, and since Jude rarely stayed downstairs past dinner, he had begun to wonder what went on at these parties. He recalled their trip last year, how he had marveled at Madge's sustained energy, how he had concluded it was due to her pills. Could Madge be taking too many of those "magic" pills? Would that account for her detached disposition? For her inability to share any kind of problem with him?

Madge had not come with him to Wade's this Sunday because they had quarreled in the morning when he had suggested the visit.

"No!" she had vehemently stated. "My God, you were with them constantly for two weeks and you've seen or spoken to them every day since you returned. Isn't that enough? I'm sick of 'Wade' this and 'Wade' that and 'Penelope' this and 'Penelope' that!" Then she had run into her dressing room and bolted the door.

He shouted to her, "What the hell is the matter with you? Don't you realize how close I came to losing my best friend? Doesn't that mean anything to you? I owe *everything* to Wade and I will see him anytime I damn well please! You hear me?"

"And you're absolutely sure it's not Penelope you want to see?" Madge said through the door.

"You leave her out of this!"

"Oh, *excuse me!* How could I—a mere mortal—dare to speak the name of Saint Penelope?"

Jude swallowed hard, trying not to let his temper get out of control. "Look at us! This is crazy! Madge, come out here so we can talk like adults, instead of yelling like children. Maybe I'm missing something here, or maybe you are, but we won't know until we talk normally, will we?" He walked over to wait by the window.

A click of the lock indicated she was coming out. She left her safe refuge, sat on the chaise lounge and spoke slowly and deliberately to his back, her tone sullen. "In my opinion, I have been quite patient in regard to your obsession with the Colbys. You have put them before me since the beginning. And now they have spoiled our trip, and they continue to completely monopolize your time, body and soul. That's all I have to say."

Jude puzzled over this for a bit. Did she have a core of an argument? *Had* he placed his wife second to his friends? Was his dormant love for Penelope a factor here? No, it wasn't true. Madge had been his priority since they met a year and ten months ago. Definitely. Granted, he hadn't spent every minute with her. He had to—and wanted to—work. He also had to— and wanted to—meet the challenge of any loved one's emergency, whether it be Wade or a family member. His feelings for Penelope had never infringed on his feelings for Madge.

Satisfied in his own mind, Jude turned to Madge. "That just isn't so. Actually, we're lucky enough to have more time together than most married couples. My business is a necessity and is very important to me, as is my loyalty to certain relationships. The only time either of those interfered with us has been in the past month. I realize now you have an unrealistic aversion to any adversity, and I'd spare you from it if I could, but life just doesn't let us do that. Real life *does* happen. No one likes it! But when we're confronted with reality, we can't turn away or hide. I was needed and thank God I was there. And I would be again. Somehow, you have to come to grips with that."

He had moved forward and finished speaking directly in front of her. It was then that he saw the glassy eyes. Softly, he said, "Do you really think you can blot out misfortune with those accursed bottles you have in there? Maybe for the moment you feel free from painful facts, but it won't last, they'll be back. What do you do then, Madge? Take more? One day you're going to have to face being a human being again, with the good and the bad, just like the rest of us. Think about it."

43

Santa Monica, California
Monday, September 26, 1960

"He won!" Polly yelled in delight. "No doubt about it, Kennedy bested Nixon!"

"Nixon didn't look good—and Kennedy looked wonderful!" Revel was jubilant.

"Elections aren't a beauty contest," cautioned Jude. "It's what the candidates say that's important. And how they say it."

"I don't care!" Revel pouted. "J.F.K. has my vote—if I had one."

"She has a point, you know," commented Wade. "The female audience is definitely going to be swayed by his good looks."

Matthew interrupted, "Wait a minute! The plain and simple fact is, Kennedy spoke with assurance and knowledge on every topic, he held his own against a skilled debater and an experienced politician. And he spoke to us—it wasn't an oration."

"That's what I think, too! And Wade," Penelope flared, "you're wrong to insinuate women won't judge on the issues. We're not just swooning bobby-soxers!"

"Hear! Hear!" Polly echoed.

"Oh, boy, did I put my foot in it." Wade chuckled. He turned to include Madge. "Now, here's a lady who really *is* close to the whole Kennedy clan. Why aren't you working for your friend? Do you know something we don't?"

Madge had been quiet and noncommittal during the debate. She seemed surprised by Wade's question. "Me? I know nothing. Politics holds no interest for me, never has. I have seen much of the Kennedys over the years, but it's always been in a social context. They know they can count on me for the celebrations.''

"I can relate to that!" Wade agreed. "What about you, Vince?"

"I was impressed by Senator Kennedy tonight. And his grasp of the country's needs. We'll have to see what happens next, but I think round one went to the senator.'' Vincent Franks's large brown eyes warmed as he continued, "I want to thank you for including me this evening. It was much more powerful to share this event with others.''

Because Wade still couldn't go out yet, Penelope had arranged this small dinner. Revel had brought Vince, more for convenience than anything else. He was pleasant company. Every once in a while she dated him, but she remained absorbed with Madge and her friends, and now with the Kennedy campaign.

Madge and Jude had not continued their heated conversation of three weeks ago. She had given the illusion that she had accepted his warning, and they had gradually eased into normalcy again. He was pleased to note that the vials had disappeared from her shelf, an indication to him that she had seen the light. He was equally delighted when she acquiesced to seeing Wade and Penelope. He reasoned there was no need for further discussion—he had clearly made his point.

What he didn't know was that Madge had simply gone underground. Jude's speech had made an impact, all right, but not quite the way he had intended. She had been jolted into realizing that she had to play it cool for a while, not be so blatant with her amusements and her addictions. No sense making waves at this time. She wanted to remain Mrs. Jude Abavas, at least for now, especially since in her clouded mind she had become the hostess with the mostest.

It was ironic, and sad, that she deceived herself. Granted, Madge held that reputation in the eyes of some sectors of Hollywood society—amongst the users and the takers and the low self-esteemers and the would-be's who never would be. And that unfortunate group who still needed pharmaceutical crutches to assure their place in life. And many of the players of the world did follow her philosophy of pleasure and delusion, but what

Madge couldn't allow herself to see was the legion who would *never* honor her as the hostess.

She was confident she had command of Jude, although he was still the most strong-willed and independent man she had yet encountered. So she had relocated her cache and monitored her indulgences until he was off guard once more. That was why she was here, at this drab debate dinner that bored her to tears.

"How many people have you registered, Polly?" Jude asked.

"Quite a few in the malls. But it's the house-to-house canvassing that's hilarious. I went to ring one doorbell, and I looked up and there was a guy standing in the window stark naked."

"You never told me that!" Matthew objected.

"Don't worry, I made a hasty exit. Then there was a couple having a bang-up fight—another retreat—I didn't want to get in the middle of that! Oh, it is weird! Some people act like I was going to rob them, or serve a subpoena, or ask for a handout. It's quite an experience. You'll have to try it next time, Rev."

"No possible way!"

"Glad you said it, honey," Jude remarked. "Because I would not accept responsibility for that endeavor. Mama and Papa would have my head. Sending you around door-to-door to strangers' houses? Unchaperoned?"

"You wouldn't have anything to say about it because I would be of age then, so there!" Revel declared defiantly.

Madge looked at Revel approvingly. She was coming along just fine. It was nice to have an ally in the house.

44

Sun Valley, Idaho
Saturday, December 24, 1960

"Merry Christmas and Happy Anniversary, darling," Jude whispered to Madge as he slipped a wedding band of solid baguette diamonds on her finger. "I never had the chance to get you the kind of ring you should really have."

"Oh, thank you . . . it's very pretty." Madge seemed far away.

They were sitting in front of the fireplace at Jude's little house in Sun Valley. He thought he knew what was on her mind. "I'm sorry we didn't make it to Switzerland, that I could only swing this week off between Christmas and New Year's. Give me a couple more months and we'll have that vacation, I promise."

No response.

"What is it? Why so forlorn?"

Madge jumped up and paced the room. Finally, she blurted out, "I'm pregnant, goddamn it, that's what's the matter!"

Jude sat perfectly still and held his breath. He wasn't sure he had heard right.

"I don't believe it! Me! Who knows better! Who is always so careful! How could I have slipped up—how could I have been so stupid?"

Quietly, he asked, "Are you sure?"

"Of course I'm sure!"

Jude let out a war whoop, "*Yoaw!* That's wonderful! How great! What a present! Oh, wow!" He scooped her up and danced around the Christmas tree. "I'm so happy! Uh-oh, better take it easy with my little mama, here," and he set her gently on the couch and knelt before her.

"Oh, don't go crazy," she reprimanded. "I knew you'd behave like a damn fool."

Jude didn't take offense. He understood her trepidations. This was something she would have to get used to, something completely new, something that would change her life. It would be especially intimidating for such a free spirit as his wife. He would be patient, he would help her overcome her fears. But he couldn't contain the joy he felt at that very moment.

He put his head in her lap. "I'll go slow, honest. I just want you to know how much this means to me."

Even Madge, in her anger at her carelessness and at this unwanted threat to her way of life, relented a bit at his sincerity. She cursed herself, though, because she realized that if she hadn't been fuzzy from the hit she took earlier, she wouldn't have revealed her condition and would have been able to get rid of the problem later, quietly. Now she was trapped.

Jude couldn't wait. Despite the hour, he called Wade and Penelope immediately with his news. They were still awake, putting the finishing touches on Santa's visit. They were delighted, of course. Madge refused to get on the line; she headed for the bar, instead.

Christmas Day dinner at Willamina and Noah's with the entire family gathered together—Revel, Matthew, Polly and the twins had also journeyed to Sun Valley—gave Jude the perfect opportunity to make his announcement. Madge had to endure the congratulations, the kissing, the hugging, the crying. She thought it was absolutely ridiculous the way everyone carried on. And all the grandchildren screaming and running all over the place nauseated her. To think she was going to contribute to this mayhem! A quick trip to the privacy of the bathroom eased the burden somewhat—a sniff of cocaine always seemed to numb any qualms she might have.

The only one who didn't completely share in the exuberance of this event was, as usual, Jude's unforgiving twin, John. Business success and Lila had partially mellowed him, but he still couldn't resist muttering, "I hope Jude don't expect me to git *this* one to the hospital, too!"

Noah, in saying grace, gave special thanks for this added blessing on the Christ Child's birthday.

*   *   *

"What do you *mean* we can't go to the inauguration? I already had my wardrobe designed and I'm sure it's the last time I'll look decent enough to go anywhere." Madge was furious.

"I'm truly sorry," Jude said. "But it would mean being away just at the wrong time and I can't do it. I don't like to bother you with details, but Colvas Inc. is fighting to get an inside track on pay television and cable television. It's been an ongoing battle and the FCC hasn't ruled yet, probably won't for a few years. But a group of us are holding meetings all that week and they're too important for me to miss. And Wade is just not up to it yet."

"Then I'll go alone!" Madge declared.

"I wish you wouldn't. But if you must, you must."

"Well, I must! And I'll take Revel with me!"

Sunday, January 15, 1961, the day Madge was scheduled to leave for Washington, she woke up sick as a dog. "It must have been something I ate," she moaned in her misery.

"Could be," Jude sympathized. "Or something you drank. Or it could be morning sickness."

"Does that mean it'll go away in the afternoon?"

"Not necessarily. Sometimes it lasts for days, even weeks."

"You did this!" she yelled with as much strength as she could muster. "You deliberately did this to me so I wouldn't go to the inauguration! It's all your f—" She barely made it to her bathroom. She emerged, pale and shaking, but able to finish her diatribe. "It's your fault! I hate this baby—I hate you!" Madge sobbed into the pillow.

Jude consoled her the best he could. "I know you're disappointed. But we'll go to the White House later, you know you'll be invited."

"Just go away!" the muffled voice commanded.

"Okay, I'll go. You rest now. I'll break the bad news to Revel. Boy, am I going to be one unpopular son of a bitch."

He'd called it correctly. Revel was as inconsolable as Madge. "Damn! My big chance! And we found the perfect dress, too! I bet Madge is right—you *did* do this on purpose, to spoil everything." And she ran off, crying.

Jude didn't try to make sense out of either woman's accusations because there wasn't any sense to be made. It would all blow over...soon, he hoped. But for now, he bundled the dogs in his car and escaped to the friendly sanctity of the Colbys' beach house.

In the ensuing days and weeks, Madge became increasingly morose. The morning sickness went away, but the afternoon and evening sickness grew worse. Her resentment toward her condition festered. To make up for the lost galas in Washington, D.C.—and the social whirl that followed in Palm Beach afterward—she supplemented her biweekly social functions with daytime gatherings. She inveigled many of the set who had traveled to the inauguration to continue westward and join her playmates in California.

The rumor mill—fueled by workout king, Thad Thornton, and stylist to the stars, Mr. Felipi—flourished. Penelope and Polly heard rumbles about the "swinging times at Madge's," but dismissed them as sheer gossip.

Fortunately, no hints reached Jude's ears. But some nights he did come home to find the servants scurrying to clean up the remnants from the afternoon and Madge "too tired" to come down for dinner. He hadn't uncovered any evidence to suggest that she was once again using the pills, but his concern was heightened.

On the other side of the ledger, Wade was so improved, he was able to return to work the first of February. After a couple of weeks back on the job, Wade insisted that Jude take a break. "You look like you've been stretched out on stakes, you're so tight. Get out of here! I don't want to see your parched face for at least a week—make it ten days! Take your wife and go away someplace—Santa Barbara or Palm Springs or wherever, but go!"

Jude grinned. "Yes, sir!"

Jude hummed on his way home; he felt better already. This would be perfect for the two of them, just what they needed. He wondered where they should go and determined he'd let Madge choose, it didn't matter to him. He stopped to buy a bouquet from a boy on the street corner; he would be just full of surprises for his "little mama."

Revel's car was in the garage. Maybe she had come home on her lunch hour. Jude let himself in the front door and bounded up the stairs. He heard vague voices coming from their suite, probably the television. Grandly, he threw open the door and cried, "Guess who's going on a vacation?"

Three startled faces focused on him from the bed: Desiré, the exotic dancer, Timothy Davis, the actor—and Madge.

The tableau was ludicrously diabolical—Jude standing with flowers in hand, gazing at the three naked bodies frozen in carnal positions. All held the poses for an interminable interval, no one daring to make a move.

At last, Jude had absorbed enough. He threw the flowers on the floor, crushing the blossoms with the heel of his shoe, whirled and stormed downstairs. Revel bumped into him on her way up.

"What are you doing here?" Jude snarled.

Revel stammered, "I—uh—Madge called—said to come home. Why aren't you at the office?"

"Don't go up there!" he roared.

Revel retreated. "What's the matter, Jude? What did I do? Why are you mad at me?"

Jude couldn't explain, he could barely talk. He hugged her hard, hoarsely whispering, "Just do what I tell you. Get some things—go to Polly's—until I call—understand? I don't want you in this house!"

"But what's happened? Why—"

"Go! Now!"

Revel was too scared not to obey. She ran to the guest house in complete confusion. Something awful had happened, but she had no idea what it could be. Madge had sounded strange on the telephone, maybe she was high and that had upset Jude. But this was too strong a reaction for just that. Jude had to know Madge was on the stuff, didn't he? Revel gulped in panic. What if Madge had confided in Jude that his sister also indulged once in a while? But Madge had promised she would never tell him. Oh, hell, that would positively send him over the edge. Revel decided her best course for the moment was to do what Jude said and wait to see what the trouble was. Meanwhile, she could begin to think about excuses and defenses.

Jude drove fast but well. He couldn't have cared less if something happened to him, but he didn't want to be responsible for hurting any innocent bystander. Enough harm had already been

done this day. Jude concentrated solely on the road, not allowing thoughts or images to penetrate his consciousness. He had to
be alone and far away before he could give vent to the black fury
that was ravaging his insides. Automatically, he headed for the
Pacific Coast Highway, passed Wade's house and continued
north.

In Santa Barbara, he stopped long enough to get gas and call
Polly. Thank God she was home.

"Jude? Doesn't sound like you. Are you all right?"

"Can't talk now, Polly. Listen carefully. When Revel comes—
she's there? Good! Keep her there. Don't let her even go to work,
at least until I speak to you again. And don't you or Rev take any
calls from Madge. I know it sounds weird—it is weird, but it's
got to be this way."

Somewhere between Santa Barbara and San Luis Obispo, he
reached the boiling point. He pulled off the highway, leapt out
of the car and ran, zigzagging crazily across the deserted beach.

"*Aaagh—aaagh—aaagh.*" The anguished animal sounds bellowed loud over the ocean's roar. He was trying to expel the
poison in his system. Finally, he was unable to yell or run anymore. His legs buckled and he fell onto the wet sand. He started
to beat at the ground with his fists. The sand became the three
faces that were etched in his mind, and he pulverized them. Then
he rose and kicked and jumped on them, grinding them deeper
beneath the surface so he would never have to see them again.
Demonically he stumbled to his knees and dug with his hands,
burying them.

And then Jude wept, wrenching and twisting the bowels of his
gut, so much so that he vomited—spewing out the disgust and
shock and shame and wrath and disillusion and sadness that
were his.

Jude groaned and opened his eyes. The beam from a flashlight
played across his face and body. Groggy, he raised himself to his
elbows wondering where he was, and then when it all came back
to him, he fell flat once more.

"Mister! Mister! You okay? What are you doing here, anyway?" The highway patrol officer bent forward for a closer
look. "When I passed your car the second time, I figured I'd
better stop and see what was going on. Good thing, too—you

left your keys in the ignition. That's asking for trouble, you know.''

The policeman helped Jude to his feet. ''First I suspected it was a couple of kids playing hanky-panky on the beach. Get a lot of those! Then when I saw you alone and passed out, I for sure thought it was a drunk. But there's no booze. You don't smell good, but you don't smell of liquor.''

''Uh, thank you, Officer. I was—I was driving along—and—and suddenly I felt ill. I was in a rush—to get some air. Didn't think about the keys, I guess. Sorry. Must be the stomach flu that's going around.''

''You're too wobbly to drive far. There's a motel close by, I'll follow you to make sure you're safe. Do you need a doctor?''

''No—no! Just some rest will do it, I think. Much obliged.''

''I will have to check your driver's license, routine procedure.''

Jude hurriedly produced his wallet, anxious to be alone again. The officer called through for a clearance, and when satisfied that Jude Abavas was a law-abiding citizen, saw to it that his charge was deposited securely at the motel.

45

Beverly Hills, California
Friday, March 24, 1961

Madge was in a venomous rage, a condition quite common for her these days. She screamed in French into the telephone, "What do you mean you can't accommodate me? Are you as stupid as the doctors here in the States? Have you suddenly acquired ethics? I don't know why I waited! Maybe I was busy with more important things and lost track of time! What the hell difference does it make? What if I am five months along, you're the genius—fix it! I want out!" She listened for a minute and then slammed the receiver down. "Idiot! They are all idiots!" she muttered, thumping her way over to the bar in her boudoir. "I hate you, Jude Abavas!" she yelled. "First you get me knocked up, then you come home at the wrong time and then you act like a shocked toad! You were never such a prig when *you* wanted to screw me! Oh, no, but when I want to play in my way, you blow up like a hot-air balloon! I'm glad you're gone—good riddance!"

Madge circled the room, continuing to rant at the empty air. She couldn't talk to her friends about something like this—they wanted amusement. How they had enjoyed it when Madge told them she had kicked her husband out because he was boring her! The participants in the triangle, however, aided by Thad Thornton and Mr. Felipi, had spread the true story. Both accounts provided ample material for even the greediest newsmongers in Hollywood.

Jude refused to discuss the situation except with those already involved, namely Wade, Penelope, Matthew, Polly and Revel.

They had stood aghast during the explanation he'd given for his erratic behavior. It was obvious he was speaking with pain and humiliation, obvious that he blamed himself for the marriage's failure. He touched briefly on the details, only enough to account for his actions. Their hearts ached for Jude in his agony, and they damned who they knew to be the real cause. But they honored their friend's silent plea that there be no further discussion, and made it clear that they were there for him, with help and love.

Penelope and Polly held long soul-searching sessions. Could they have prevented this by warning Jude?

Revel, on the other hand, heaved a huge sigh of relief. She had come close to being implicated in this mess. She wondered what her reaction would have been had she walked up those stairs before Jude came home. Would she have joined in? Well, she would never have to face that dilemma. She understood her brother's pain, but Revel was crushed that Madge had been so reckless. Jude had forbidden her to see or talk to Madge, an order she felt she should comply with for the moment, at least.

Jude rented a place for himself and Revel in Santa Monica. Matthew went to the Maple Drive house when the ever-faithful Oliver assured him Madge was out. They collected Jude's and Revel's necessary things, and the three dogs and Lil Guy, the cat.

Jude withdrew from everything except his work. There, at least, was reason and sanity. He sidetracked any calls from the curious or the media. And he had absolutely no direct communication with Madge. He sent word to her through Matthew that:

A. Their situation would remain status quo until the child was born, at which time he would file for divorce, claiming incompatibility.

B. He would maintain the house and assure her every assistance and care during the pregnancy.

C. He would support the child fully, guarantee legitimacy—even if, as he now suspected, the child wasn't his.

D. He would assume custody of the child if she found motherhood interfered with her life-style. If in an expert's opinion the child was not being properly cared for, he was prepared to take this issue to court.

E. He never wanted to see or talk to her again.

Madge was more determined than ever to kill the one thing that mattered to Jude—his baby. And she was quite certain it was his! The regular doctors in Los Angeles and in the rest of the world would not touch her case, but she knew someone who would!

Madge Moore was put through immediately. "Hello, Dr. Jones.—I'm fine, thank you.—Yes, I could use another order of my usual medicines. Tomorrow would be suitable for delivery. Oh, would you mind coming in person? I have something to discuss, privately.—Ten tomorrow evening, it is, then! *Ciao!*"

Dr. Jones didn't bat an eyelash when Madge made her request the next evening. "I believe I have an acquaintance who might be able to fulfill your wish. But I must warn you, the procedure would be quite expensive."

"I'm sure!" Madge said contemptuously. "And what do you call expensive?"

The doctor didn't respond to her tone outwardly, but inwardly the price had just gone up. "Fifty thousand, plus my fee."

"Which is—?"

"Twenty-five thousand. In advance, of course. All of it."

"Of course." Madge laughed scornfully. "You really are a leech, aren't you? But you do know your customers. Consider it a deal. When?"

"I will confirm the time with you in the morning. Goodbye, Miss Moore."

The visit was set for Monday, April 17, at 11:00 p.m. "I apologize for the delay, but that was the first opening," explained Dr. Jones.

"I don't mind, actually it suits my schedule. Now I won't have to cancel my plans for the fifteenth."

"You will bring the full amount with you in cash. A limousine, with our compliments—"

"I have my own," Madge interrupted.

"We prefer you use ours. As I was saying, a complimentary car will call for you at ten and drive you to the hospital. Discretion is mandatory, I'm sure you understand, so the windows will be blacked out. After your appointment and the required recovery period, you will be taken back to your home and assisted to your quarters. Make sure your staff is excused until the next morning—we don't need prying eyes, do we? The driver will ask for your keys when you are picked up. You see, it is really quite simple.''

On Saturday, April 15, Madge gave the mother of all parties. She named it so because it was her own perverse farewell to motherhood. No one else knew, but the crowd buzzed with excitement over Madge's extravagance. She was wilder and more ravishing than ever. They all agreed this was by far the best bash she had thrown, and most were still consorting when dawn arrived.

Madge slept during what was left of Sunday and into Monday. When she was preparing for the evening appointment, she gazed into the mirror at her slight five-and-a-half-month bulge. ''I won't have to look at you after today. You disgust me. Tomorrow I will be flat and smooth and liberated. And then it's off to Europe, away from this prison.'' She whirled in glee, pleased with the prospect.

Madge was ready when the limo came. She had given the servants time off, had the money stuffed in envelopes in her purse and had zapped herself into an euphoric state. She gave the house keys to the chauffeur and settled back into the soft cushions of the murky interior. The partition between the back and front seats was also obscured, so nothing was visible. It felt as if she were floating along on a magic carpet in the midst of sightless clouds.

At 7:00 a.m. on Tuesday, April 18, Jude's phone rang. ''Mr. Abavas, Oliver here. Sorry to disturb you at this hour, sir, but I'm afraid something might be wrong with Madame. When I arrived this morning—she insisted we all take yesterday off—Madame's house keys were still in the front door. Then as I entered the foyer, I saw spots—I believe it was blood, sir—and they continued up the stairs to your suite. At the risk of being reprimanded, I knocked, but received no response. I attempted to open the door but it was locked. So I decided to call you.—Thank you, sir. I'll await you.''

Jude was there in twenty minutes. He rushed upstairs, Oliver close behind.

"Madge! Madge! Open the door! Can you hear me?" Jude yelled. A faint indiscernible sound came from inside.

"We'll have to break it down!" Jude heaved his body against the solid wood with little result. Then he repeatedly kicked at it, weakening it somewhat. "I think if we both lunge at the same time we may make it," Jude said to Oliver. "One—two—three! Again! One—two—three! Once more should do it! One—two—three!" The battered door gave way and the two men went flying into the room.

It took a second to adjust to the dark. And then they saw the curled figure on the bed, lying in a pool of red.

"Oh, my God!" Jude cried. He thought someone had beaten Madge.

"Mother of Mercy!" exclaimed Oliver, crossing himself.

"Can't wait for an ambulance—I'll carry her to the car—you drive!" Jude ordered as he picked her up.

Madge was ashen and almost comatose. Blood was flowing profusely—Jude was covered with it, the seat of the car was drenched. Her eyes fluttered open and registered recognition. "Ha!" she whispered weakly. "So you did have to see me again."

"Who did it, Madge? What son of a bitch would do this to you?"

"It—was—a—boy," she said, barely getting the words out before lapsing into unconsciousness.

With Madge in his arms, Jude ran into the emergency ward of the hospital. Those on the staff who could, stopped what they were doing to assist.

"Jesus Christ, what happened?" someone asked.

"I'm not exactly sure. I found her like this at the house. She's pregnant." Jude was following alongside the stretcher.

"Not anymore, I'm afraid," the doctor said. "I'm sorry, you can't go any farther—you'll have to go back now and fill out all the forms. We'll let you know how she is as soon as we can."

Jude didn't have an opportunity to think. The paperwork was endless and then he made a call to the office, to explain that he was delayed and to cancel his appointments until tomorrow. As he hung up the receiver, he saw a figure coming toward him.

"Mr. —" the doctor checked the chart he was holding "—Mr. Abavas, why don't you come with me?" Jude was led to a small private office. The doctor closed the door carefully and solemnly faced Jude. "Please sit down, Mr. Abavas. We have some serious talking to do."

Jude eased into a chair. His face was a mask, his body perfectly still. Time seemed suspended.

"I'm terribly sorry, but there was nothing we could do. She slipped away before we could even begin transfusions."

Jude remained transfixed.

"At what stage was her pregnancy?" asked the doctor.

"About five—five and a half months," Jude answered in a trance.

"This was not a miscarriage, Mr. Abavas! This was murder, no different than if someone had slit your wife's throat! Do you have any idea who attempted the operation?"

Jude swallowed hard, trying to hold on to his control. "N-no."

"I don't want to upset you more than I already have. But to be perfectly frank, this—this person—is a criminal of the worst kind. No one but a vicious butcher could have performed such a procedure. At twenty-three weeks, even twenty weeks, the blood supply of the fetus is attached and implanted so strongly with the mother that to forcibly abort the fetus is practically impossible. In the attempt to do so, the uterus was perforated, causing your wife to hemorrhage, and someone simply packed her with gauze just to get her home. They knew what had happened—and they didn't care. Mr. Abavas, they sent your wife home to die."

Jude recoiled with every sentence, each a blow, a hammer pounding a nail in his heart, in his soul.

Jude walked out of the hospital not knowing what emotion to succumb to first. Loss! Anger! Anguish! Vengeance! Bereavement! Hate!

Oliver had not been privy to what the doctor had revealed; he was only aware of the morning's tragic end. "My deepest sympathy, sir. Please, allow me to drive. And please, sir, permit me to help you in any way possible—any way!"

Jude only nodded. The doctor's last words were all he could concentrate on now: "I am bound by the law to hand over to the coroner's jurisdiction the death of a patient I have not been attending for at least twenty-four hours. Regrettably, that means an automatic police investigation, and that usually means the press. I can promise you that nothing will leak from this end, but after that . . . ? Any information you can give will be extremely valuable, Mr. Abavas, if we are to find your wife's murderer.''

Jude was actually thankful that his next move had been decided for him. He went straight back to the house and steeled himself as he walked in. The door opened onto memories of such passion, such treachery, such good, such evil—

"Oliver, I—I can't go up there. But it's important I see Mrs. Abavas's telephone book. I think I remember seeing her put it in a desk drawer."

"Of course, sir. I'll get it right away. The rooms are being tended to—I called from the hospital."

A while later, Jude sat rigidly in the lanai, poring over the contents of Madge's personal address file. Jude was astonished by her index. Who *were* these people? Only a fifth of the names listed were familiar to him. And then there were those he hadn't even realized she'd known. Strange, he was beginning to see how little he knew about this woman he had called his wife.

It took over two hours before he reached the last page. Frustrated, he slammed the book shut. Not one local doctor's name was in there! She had to have called somebody! Where did she get her stuff in Los Angeles? Had she used some sort of code name? Jude started from the beginning again and examined each entry for any hidden clue. Nothing under A—or B—C—D—E— F— Wait a minute! Mr. Fix? But there was also an actor, Paul Fix. Still, wouldn't she have said Mr. Paul Fix instead of *Mr. Fix?* It was worth a try.

Jude dialed the number. "Doctor's office! How may I help you?" a polite voice answered. Jude was so dumbfounded when he heard "doctor's office," he forgot to talk. "Hello! Who's there?" This time the voice was not as polite. Jude stammered, "Oh, excuse me, I—I must have the wrong number," and he hung up.

He called the hospital to relay the incident. The doctor said he would pass the number on to the proper source.

Now what? Jude knew there were arrangements he had to make, people he had to call. But he couldn't stay in the house any longer. Where should he go? The Colbys? The rented house? The studio? Oliver brought Jude a complete change of clothes because even his shoes were ruined, drenched with blood. Jude showered and dressed in the downstairs guest room. He left instructions to ignore any strangers at the door and to say nothing to anyone on the telephone, only to say that no one was in at the moment.

On the way out, Jude saw Madge's chauffeur waiting by her car. Jesus, he had forgotten about him. How to handle this?

"Mrs. Abavas has left—on a long journey. She asked me to thank you, and tell you she won't be needing you again."

"Who are you to give me orders? I am supposed to stay here in case—"

"I am Mr. Abavas and I told you—Mrs. Abavas is away and doesn't know when she'll return!" Jude was getting flustered. "Send your bill to the usual place and here's a termination bonus." He handed the man a hundred-dollar bill. "Now get out!"

Jude decided that until anyone stated differently, he was going to say that Madge died from complications of a late miscarriage. For the moment, that's all anyone had to know. And it was not far from the truth.

Jude was in robot mode as he made his way to the office.

"Mr. Abavas! I didn't expect you!" a surprised Muriel exclaimed.

"Come inside, Muriel. I need your help."

Later that afternoon, Jude sat behind his desk, still not sure what he wanted to do about the details. Was this going to be plastered all over the headlines as the latest Hollywood scandal? Or was it to be treated as a normal death? He kept putting off the dreaded but inevitable telephone calls. What exactly should he say?

"A police officer is on the line, Mr. Abavas. Should I tell him you're not available?" Muriel asked protectively on the intercom.

"No—no—I'll take it, thank you." He pushed a button. "This is Jude Abavas."

"Captain Brine here. I'm very sorry about your wife, Mr. Abavas. Lost mine not too long ago myself...know how you feel. Well, we traced the number you found to an address, but your call must have alarmed them. There was no sign of an office or medical equipment or anything. Or anyone! Rest assured, we'll continue to do what we can to locate 'Mr. Fix,' but unless we—or you—can come up with any new evidence, I wouldn't hold out much hope of finding anything. Meanwhile, because there's nothin' concrete to hang on to, we'll just treat this as a routine case, no sense in alerting those sensation-seeking news hounds. You go ahead with your arrangements and issue the regular statement for the obituary column. This way, you won't be bothered with the damn reporters. Okay by you?''

Jude mumbled, ''Yes, that's fine. Uh, thank you—for your help. And consideration.—Yes, I'll be sure to call if I learn anything new. Goodbye.''

At least he knew what to say now. Only Jude, the hospital doctor and the bastard who did it would really know what had happened. The truth would have destroyed Noah and Willamina, not that this was going to be any easier for them to understand. He shuddered when he thought of Revel's reaction.

Jude slumped in the chair, staring vacantly at the telephone, knowing he should pick up the receiver and dial—someone. But his arms were filled with lead, he couldn't move them. He just stared.

That was how Wade found him. Wade walked to the desk, pulled another chair close. Only then did Jude notice him.

''Want to talk?'' Wade asked softly.

Jude's miserable eyes looked at him, puzzled.

''Muriel told me. Don't be upset with her, she was worried about you, and rightfully so.''

Jude waved his hand. ''Doesn't matter—I was getting ready to call you. I just . . . couldn't make my fingers work.''

''I can understand that. I have difficulty sometimes making my tongue work. Like now. I want to help, but I'm not sure how.''

Jude just sat, still, with no expression. Then, springing up suddenly, he began to savagely pace, finally spitting out, ''My wife is dead! And I can't tell you what I feel! I don't know if I give a damn or not. I'm sorry, yes! I'd be sorry for any human being! But do I really grieve? Or do I still despise her?''

''She was carrying your child, Jude.''

''She was carrying my son! My son! And the bitch killed him! She murdered my son! Do you hear me? Did you hear what I said? She murdered my son!!'' Jude was sobbing uncontrollably, wildly stomping around the room.

Wade was astounded and confused, not sure if Jude spoke knowingly, or if he was just ranting and raving in his wretchedness.

"Oh, no, she wasn't satisfied to only humiliate me—she had to have the ultimate revenge, she had to destroy what she knew I wanted most—a child." Jude was a caged beast, fitfully patrolling his prison back and forth.

"She didn't have a miscarriage, Wade, she had an *abortion*—by some heartless quack! But she didn't figure she would die along with her intended victim."

Wade now believed he was hearing the truth, and the truth was horrendous.

"And there's nothing I can do. Nothing!" Jude stopped in front of Wade. "No one is to know—best that way for everyone since the police can't find the murderer. But I had to tell you—I'd go loony otherwise. That's why I can't function—why I don't know which end is up."

Wade looked at Jude, the massive body crumpled—head in hands—utterly lost, and felt profound compassion. He wasn't a terribly religious man, but he prayed now for the right words to comfort his friend.

"What happened will not go beyond these walls. Our next move is to see to the particulars. And to write the press release. Actually, I can give Muriel the minimal statistics and she can do that. Where are Madge's parents buried?"

"Uh, in New York."

"Then that is where Madge should be laid to rest. That also eliminates the need for a service here. You will take her—"

"I don't want to take her anywhere!" Jude started pacing again. "I don't want to be with her! I can't! I don't want to go!"

Patient, Wade tried to talk sensibly. "I think you have to. You were separated, true, but she was pregnant with your baby, and to all intents and purposes she died from a miscarriage of that baby. You did marry her, Jude."

"I wish I could tell you why I married her, but I don't know why." Jude stopped, frozen in his tracks. "I just realized—Wade, do you know that neither of us ever said—'I love you'?" Jude was dumbfounded by his discovery. "I didn't love her. God help me, I just lusted for her."

"Whatever the reason, she was Mrs. Jude Abavas. And for everyone's sake, yours included, you must do this properly—not overboard, not phony—just simply and appropriately."

Jude's frame sagged even farther, and he slowly lowered himself to a chair. "I hate it—I hate the whole thing—I hate her! But you're right, I know you're right." He expelled a huge sigh. In a small voice, he said, "I'll do it, like you said."

Wade had Muriel write the copy for the media. He organized transportation to the East and plans for the internment, emphasizing the desire for a low-key approach. Then he made a tremendous business decision, not easily and not without trepidation. But he knew it had to be done, no matter how much Jude might object later. He postponed the Monaco picture until September, feeling June would be too soon for Jude to produce it. Wade reached the Los Angelès-based family, and also Penelope. He followed through admirably. But then Wade faltered. If only he could assume the responsibility of informing everyone. But he just couldn't. Wade had to leave the most difficult calls for Jude—to Noah and Willamina, and Revel.

Jude's body was in a cold sweat, his fingers trembling as he dialed the Idaho number. How much more unhappiness could he bring to them? It was early evening there, so both his parents were at home. His mouth was full of cotton balls, but he pushed ahead.

Noah and Willamina listened on separate phones, their eyes begging upward that what they were hearing was not true. Willamina gave one soulful wail, dropped the receiver and ran to Noah. He encircled her with his arms and they rocked back and forth, together fighting for control.

Finally, Noah was able to speak. "Can we help?"

"Yes, Papa. It would mean a lot to me if you told the others. It's so hard...to keep talking about it. You know what I mean?"

"I understand. I tell all here. But you—do you need us there?"

"I always need you, Mama and Papa. But it's not necessary to make this long trip. I'm—she—will be buried in New York, with her mother and father. So I'm taking her. I'll come home as soon as I can, though, I promise."

"We be fine. But we worry about you—inside. We say to you again—no matter how we ache and question, we must trust in our Lord. He knows what we cannot know."

Jude gulped; the Lord would really have his hands full sorting this one out!

"Thank you, Mama and Papa. I'll remember. I love you, both."

Jude mustered what was left of his courage. He had yet to face the toughest call. Where was Revel? Heart palpitating furiously, he was close to nausea as he tried the rented house first. "Revel—ah—you're there! Uh, that's good."

"Why is it good? I was just on my way out. What's up?"

"Well, ah, I want to talk to you. Would you stay until I get home? I'm leaving right now."

"Sure, if I have to. I was only going to Polly and Matt's, anyway. You sound funny—what did I do now?"

"Nothing, honey. Nothing. I'll explain when I see you."

Jude stopped by Wade's office on his way out. "I'm meeting Revel at the house. I—I couldn't do it on the telephone."

"Better," Wade agreed. "Everybody wanted to rush over to your house immediately. I asked them to wait until seven-thirty—to give you time with Revel. Oh, and Muriel ordered some food to be delivered there, everything is covered."

Jude looked at Wade, not knowing how to thank him. Wade read the signs. "Don't say a word, just go! And be careful driving!"

In the car, Jude tried to think of an easy approach with Revel, but couldn't. There just was no easy way, no way to spare her— or him. Their relationship since his split with Madge had been slightly off kilter. Not that Revel didn't acknowledge the reason for the separation, or blame him; it was more disappointment and resentment about the disintegration of a life-style she had enjoyed. Madge and Revel had established a firm bond, beginning with Revel's involvement with Artie, and continuing, perhaps becoming stronger, after the breakup, something Jude had never quite understood. But what now? How to tell her?

"Dead! Madge is dead? You're crazy!" Revel yelled in defiant disbelief. "That can't be—just can't be! I mean, I talked to her yesterday afternoon, yesterday! Yes, I did! I don't care that you told me not to, she's still my friend! And she was as happy as a clam, planning a trip to Europe. It isn't true! You're testing me! You're trying to find out if I like Madge better than you! You don't know whether I'll stay here with you or go off with her! You don't want me to have another life outside of you, do you, Jude? You're—you're tricking me somehow.''

It took all of Jude's control to simply hold on and, as gently as he could, make Revel realize it was true—Madge was dead! And nothing she could say could change that.

Revel finally dissolved into convulsive sobs. Forgetting his pain and ignoring her accusations, Jude took Revel in his arms and did his best to console her. But he couldn't disguise his relief when Polly and Matthew appeared. They had brought Vincent Franks with them, hoping he might have a stabilizing effect on Revel. Polly sized up the situation instantly and stepped in to relieve Jude. Penelope and Wade and Muriel arrived soon after.

Wade was concerned. ''I asked Muriel to join us—actually, she insisted on helping—but I'm afraid this is not going to be as quiet as we'd hoped. Madge Moore was not a person the media will allow to go unnoticed, she was too well known internationally. A few minutes after Muriel gave the necessary information to the obituary column, the press started calling for more details. It won't take them long to snoop out this number.''

''I can handle them,'' Muriel assured them.

''Of course you can,'' Wade said. ''And since this news will soon hit the wires, I suggest, Jude, that you call the Sardos family.''

''What about the Sardos family?'' A red-eyed Revel overheard the name as she returned from her bedroom.

Wade started to explain. ''They were very close to Madge and may want to pay their—''

''I don't want any of them here!'' Revel interrupted. ''They don't—belong with—with us!'' She was becoming hysterical once more.

Jude jumped up and cradled her. ''Don't worry, sweetheart! No one is going to bother you—or us. I am going alone—with—with Madge, and put her with her parents. You see, that way we can avoid all the fuss here.'' Jude threw Wade a thankful glance. ''I know Beryl and Nicholas are not well enough to travel, and I will advise their children that this is private because—because Madge wanted it that way. I'm sure they will accept that. Vince, why don't you fix Rev a drink? Why don't you fix us all a drink?'' Wearily, Jude walked toward the den. ''I'll talk to them from in here.''

Wade hurried after Jude and closed the door. "There's more, I'm afraid. The news hounds are making inquiries about the inheritance, the beneficiaries."

"Who cares?"

"Evidently the media. What should Muriel say?" The phone rang and they both jumped. "Don't pick it up!" Wade instructed. "Muriel will get it."

"Say—I don't give a damn! Say—say the will is in the hands of her lawyers in New York and no one else knows anything about the contents. That's true, by the way—I don't have any idea how it ended up. She could have done anything in the past few weeks. And I sure as hell don't give a damn!"

Jude exhaled dejectedly. "Is this only the beginning? Day one of . . . how many I wonder?"

Wade patted his shoulder. "You'll make it," he said. "I know you will. You have to—you're our leader! I'll leave you and go tell Muriel what to say. Then I'll return to whisk a stiff belt under your nose."

Jude managed to get in touch with the Sardos clan, each in their respective homes. He could hear the pain in every voice, and the new frailty in the older couple's. Each honored the request for seclusion, each offered unlimited sympathy and assistance and support. They couldn't have been more understanding, making Jude's task easier than anticipated. Until Artie tentatively asked if he could express his condolences to Revel personally.

"I don't think so, Artie. I don't know what happened between the two of you, and quite frankly, at this point, I don't wish to know. I do know she was deeply disturbed, and I can't take the chance of upsetting her further. She has enough anguish to deal with for now. I'm sorry, Artie, but the answer is no."

Jude hung up the receiver and remained immobile, fatigue fighting to overcome his body. Both telephone lines were busy, and he could hear the noise from the living room. If only he could stay in this chair, put his head down and drift off to oblivion, never to think again. Grudgingly, he lifted himself and forced his feet toward the door. It was not to be. There was more to do.

The evening dragged on. Finally, the telephone stopped ringing and everyone felt it was safe to leave. Jude clasped them close, one by one, as they departed, drinking deeply from their nourishing love.

Alone, Jude and Revel stared at—nothing. Then he stumbled and almost fell onto the couch. Revel rushed over and stretched his legs out and fluffed up a pillow for his head. Carefully, she sat next to him, timidly stretching her hand to rub his wrinkled forehead.

"Oh, that feels good, honey, but you should get some rest now."

This had been a rough night for Revel in many ways. The shock of Madge's death had initially sent her into a self-indulgent tailspin. How miserable *she* was—how this affected *her* life—what *she* wanted. But during the craziness, she had begun to see what Jude was going through. He was the one who had lost his wife and baby—for the second time! He was the one who had had to break the news to her and Mama and Papa and the Sardos family. He was the one who had tried to protect her and calm their friends and family. She had noticed him fading with each added pressure, and suddenly she was anxious about his well-being. What if something happened to Jude? By degrees she had taken stock of all the gifts he had heaped upon her, all the avenues he had opened to her, all the times he had gone to bat for her, all the unselfish love he had bestowed. And it had slowly crystallized what a remarkable brother she had. Now he was hurting and needing. And *she* wanted to give to him.

"Jude?"

He popped up, "Yes, Rev! You okay?"

She gently put his head back down. "Yes, I'm okay. I'm fine, as a matter of fact. Listen, I don't want you to go alone to New York. I want to go with you."

Jude started to protest. "Not necessary—difficult circumstances—"

But Revel cut him off. "I know all that, and I can do it. I won't be a bother or cause any trouble, I promise! I would like to be there for you—to help you. I would like to stand with you and try to be your support—like the family—like you've been mine all this time. I would like to be your friend as well as your kid sister. It's time, Jude."

Jude looked at Revel's earnest fresh face through brimming eyes. When had this happened? When had this tender sprig become a sturdy tree?

Revel was waiting for Jude's response. He drew her to him. "It would mean the world to me to have you by my side. Thank you."

On Wednesday, there were extensive write-ups of Madge's death in the newspapers and substantial coverage on the television news. But no hint of any stigma. Instead, the reporters lamented the unfortunate loss of someone so young, and gave a full account of Madge Moore Abavas's glamorous past. Baskets of flowers and telegrams flowed to the Maple Drive house. Except for members of Jude's inner circle, no one came to visit. None of Madge's "intimates" appeared. Jude's business associates were kind and considerate, but as they knew of the couple's separation, they felt their presence might be awkward.

The final call Jude took on Wednesday was from Captain Brine. Once again he offered his sympathy before updating Jude on the case. Not that there was anything to update. In fact, without further clues, the captain was afraid the case had dead-ended.

Jude was unable to reconcile the captain's rapid capitulation to failure. Were they really stumped? Or was this simply a humanitarian gesture on the department's part? Or had a deliberate decision been made not to pursue this particular criminal? Jude would never know. And he chose not to explore the answers. What was done was done.

Jude and Revel didn't talk much Thursday on the ride East. A soothing companionship had developed between them. Neither felt they had to make conversation, respecting the other's right to privacy.

Jude chose to think. Wade's practical insight that crucial Tuesday afternoon had spurred some profound self-examination. He knew Wade made sense, that Madge *was* his wife. That marriage was for better, for worse. He knew he couldn't blame her for everything—that he should have seen what was happening. That he should have recognized she wasn't just evil, but driven by a sickness. That he should have somehow prevented the inevitable.

On Friday, Revel held Jude's hand tightly when the flower-laden casket was lowered into the ground, and Madge's family priest intoned the prayers. Revel had been to this spot with Madge before, when they had come for Bruno's burial. But that trip had been as different as, well, life and death. This time, Revel bore the full brunt of mortality, her own and everyone else's. Because in that box lay her bosom buddy, her playmate, someone who had shared such an important step in her life—and now her friend was no more. The starkness of that fact hit Revel hard. She bowed her head, trying to hide her grief and fear from Jude, for she had vowed she would be strong.

"It's all right, honey. Let it out," Jude whispered, putting his arm around her. "Say goodbye."

Jude said his own silent goodbyes—to his wife and to the son he would never know. And to another part of himself, a part that he believed would be sealed forever.

Madge's lawyers were the only other people at the cemetery. They had asked for a meeting after the services since Jude and Revel were returning to Los Angeles the next day. Jude had agreed, only to get it over with.

The attorneys read Madge's will out loud. When they were finished, Jude and Revel sat speechless. Madge had either never thought about it or hadn't had the time to change anything. The will remained intact. Revel was stupefied. She and Jude were each to inherit something in the neighborhood of forty million dollars! And *all* of Madge's personal belongings—clothes, jewelry, furs—were left to Revel, with the exception of one designated diamond brooch, which Beryl Sardos had especially admired.

"How old are you, Miss Abavas?" asked one of the attorneys.

Revel finally found her tongue. "Uh, twenty-one this August."

Turning to Jude, the lawyer continued, "It is our advice, Mr. Abavas, that this young lady's interest would best be served by establishing a trust fund. She would receive a healthy allowance, naturally, and if she had some special need—furthering her education, for example—she could draw from the fund with the trustees' approval. And, say, every five years, she could take out a percentage to make her own investments. This way, the bulk of her estate would remain secure and she would still enjoy every possible comfort. Of course you can handle your portion in any way you choose."

All of this was still incomprehensible to Revel; she remained silent. Jude studied the group before him. He had never been told much about Bruno's business, but now he recognized it must have been something unconventional. For some indefinable reason, Jude had a gut feeling he was about to be graded on his response. He sensed their questions. Had this man married Bruno's daughter for her money? Was he going to take it all and run with it, thus liquidating their prudently structured portfolio? And if so, what method could they use to dissuade him?

Jude settled on his strategy. He didn't believe these people were out to cheat—honor among thieves and all that—they were just a strange breed. He wagered he was not going to give them the answer they expected.

"In regard to my sister, Revel, I agree with you. Naturally, I would insist on being one of the trustees, in addition to our brother, Matthew. And we hope you will continue to represent us." Jude saw that he had indeed surprised them. "I think the amount Revel can withdraw, and the time intervals, should be mutually determined. She may want to buy a house, or start a business, or travel—and those possibilities should be taken into account."

"Absolutely!" the men chorused. "Those conditions are completely acceptable. And we would be honored to have you as clients," the spokesperson added.

Jude went on, "As for me, I want you to set up a charitable foundation which will benefit organizations dealing with children—sick children, orphaned children, disturbed children, any and all children in need. I will be the final judge on the grants given. With your expertise in investments, my dream is that this foundation will go on for many years. Are we settled then? You have my office address and my telephone number."

Jude shook hands with each lawyer and herded Revel out the door. There was some light in his tunnel, after all. If he had to be denied his son, he could at least have the satisfaction of helping to care for other children. Children in need. Children he needed.

46

Beverly Hills, California
Sunday, June 4, 1961

Jude entered the hall from his bedroom and started downstairs for breakfast. "What's this?" he muttered. On every other step there was an envelope marked JUDE in bold letters. "What in hell's name—" He gathered them up and continued his way to the sunlit breakfast room, where there were more cards strewn over the table. As he sat down, Revel burst through the kitchen door, holding a muffin with one lighted candle.

"Happy Birthday!"

"Oh, my God—it *is* my birthday! I forgot. Thank you, Rev."

"Now make a wish and blow out your candle. I'll get you some coffee and then you can open your cards. I called Mama and she told me how to make pancakes and sausage like hers— that's your surprise! Hope I did it right." And she bustled off, intent on her culinary duties.

Jude obediently read all the greetings. He could hear the clatter through the door and smiled—the cook was probably having a fit that Revel was invading her domain. The grin slowly faded when he thought of how his birthday bash had ended last year. What a year this had been. He shuddered, not wanting to even speculate about what was in store for him in the next twelve months. His silent wish as he extinguished the lone flame? Please, God, that the next twelve shouldn't be worse!

A week ago, Jude and Revel had moved back to the Maple Drive house. Oliver had removed every vestige of Madge's presence. The medicines, the make-up, the creams, the perfumes, the toothbrush, the desk contents, even the exclusive soaps—anything that was a reminder of Madge. Revel and Oliver had packed dozens of wardrobe crates, emptying all drawers and closets. Revel couldn't bear to keep Madge's clothes, and had decided to donate them to the Screen Stars Thrift Shop. The shop, which had been instituted by Mary Pickford years ago, was intended to help the extras and young hopefuls of Hollywood. The superstars donated their castoff clothing for a tax benefit, and the have-nots picked up lovely gowns at bargain prices. A nonprofit organization, the net proceeds went to the Motion Picture and Television Fund, also established by a group that included Mary Pickford.

The jewelry was put in the house safe, except for the one brooch left to Beryl Sardos. Revel complied with Madge's wishes, but she asked Jude to write the accompanying letter. She just couldn't. She had never met Beryl and Nicholas Sardos, and she still blamed them for thwarting her romance with Artie.

Revel hadn't yet adjusted to the fact she was a very rich woman. None of it seemed real. She understood that forty million dollars was a great deal of money, but having it hadn't changed her life. There was nothing tangible; it was just paper, really. Her one glimpse of what it actually meant came when the law office in New York called to ask if she would like to have a car and driver at her disposal, as Madge had. She'd refused, but it had helped her understand what having money was all about.

As for Jude, he simply existed. Losing this wife and baby provoked totally different emotions than those he'd suffered nineteen years ago. Life with Madge had been such a reversal of life with Thelma. It had been more exciting at times, but never as basic or substantial. And after her betrayal and ultimate treason, it had been sheer hell. Yet, there still was a void.

With his son, Keane, he had experienced and loved for almost four years. The gap the child had left had never been filled. There would have been a chance to recapture some of that love with this new lil' guy. But he had been deprived of that hope, as well.

Jude, Revel, Matthew, Polly and the twins flew to Idaho for the Fourth of July. It was not an easy trip. Noah and Willamina greeted Jude with wordless embraces, the love exchanged said it all. The rest of the family were oversolicitous, making everyone uncomfortable. They also were very curious about the inheritances. None could relate to the kind of wealth their siblings now had.

"Don't worry!" Revel laughed, trying to relax the atmosphere. "Neither can we! Doesn't mean a damn—oops, sorry, Mama—darn thing. So just forget it, okay?"

It felt good to be in the mountains again. To fish, hike and ride the bicycle trails. The pristine air and peaceful surroundings wiped away some of the cobwebs. Still, the city folk realized just how out of touch they were with rural living. A few days were absolutely great, but any longer and they became restless to get back.

The most gratifying reward of the whole vacation was to see how pleased Willamina and Noah were to have their family together again. Noah and the men sat on the porch after supper each night, while the women did dishes and kept an eye on the children. Jude was keenly aware that he was the only man without children, or even a wife. Once again he was the loner, the odd man out. Noah was cognizant of Jude's thoughts, and directed the conversations away from family life. They exchanged views on a range of topics, including the failure of the Bay of Pigs invasion.

"I admire Kennedy for having the guts to admit he made a mistake," Jude commented. "Anyone else would have tried to put the blame on someone else. He's a real leader."

"Don't matter none!" John rebutted. "He shouldn't have done it! Ike wouldn't have been that stupid!" By chance or by design, John invariably took the side opposing Jude.

The two couldn't even agree on the Berlin Wall. "It's a terrible suppression of freedom." Jude stood firm in his belief that the world would never know real peace with Russia as long as it stood.

"I think it's better to keep Germany divided. Get those Jerrys together and they'll start another war for sure!" countered John.

Noah changed the subject. "What you think, Jude and Matthew? We have an offer for some of our land between Hailey and Ketchum—at big profit. Should we sell?"

"Papa, I thought we already decided to sell," John objected.

"All my children are part of company. We should talk."

"But the others ain't here! They don't live here. What do they know about our business?" John continued.

"We talk!" Noah insisted.

Matthew cleared his throat. "Well, ah, John has a point. We haven't been around. But just by looking at the astonishing growth in this area, it would be my opinion to hold on to any real estate, because it can only rise in value in the future."

"Jude?" Noah asked.

"I have to agree with Matt."

"Naturally!" John snapped.

"Unless you need the cash for some reason," Jude finished. "Otherwise, you'll make a larger gain later, as the demand for property increases. But as John said, we haven't been here, so maybe you know something we don't."

Noah shook his head. "No, and that be why I ask. Strangers come and pay much money—some people here grab for good price. I think you be right. If high now, will be higher later. Makes sense. John?"

John glanced at his buddy Clyde Warhas, who had been quiet during the discussion but who now gave John a nod of approval. "Yes, Papa, sounds good. As long as we don't miss the boat."

"John raises a very important point," Jude said. "You will all have to keep a close watch so you can determine when the market peaks. I've heard rumblings that Union Pacific is becoming disenchanted with its Sun Valley holding, because it brings no return to its shareholders. U.P. could sell, which would be a boon for landowners around here, because a new owner would give Sun Valley a much-needed face-lift. Maybe that's why these buyers have come in now, they've heard rumors, too. But you and John and Clyde know everything that goes on in these parts, I'm sure you'll seize the opportunity at the right time."

It was clear from the look on John's face that he'd never expected support from his twin. Had he misjudged Jude?

The night before they were to leave, Jude made a pilgrimage to the cemetery. He stood for a while, just looking at the tombstones, and then he knelt, brushing away some dirt that had gathered.

Jude spoke aloud. "God, I miss you two so much—more than before, if that's possible. Maybe I'm sadder now because—because each year, I realize just how much I lost. You know what,

Keane? There's a tiny—real tiny—lil' guy that I bet just arrived where you are. Would you look after him? Kind of like a big brother? 'Cause he's got to be a little lonely and confused. And Thelma, could you mother him some? He never had a mama.''

Jude brushed a tear from his cheek and rose to leave. But before he turned, he gently kissed the markers.

47

Hollywood, California
Monday, July 17, 1961

"The third try *has* to be the charm. Jude, it looks as if your film will finally get made!" Wade exclaimed triumphantly. The two were at the studio offices mulling over the preparations for the much-delayed Monaco picture.

Jude leaned back and tossed his pen on top of the papers that were overloading his desk. "Could be. But you know me, never count your chickens before they're hatched. I sure hope so! But right now I have to take a whiz."

When he came back from the bathroom, Wade was by the window, chuckling.

"What's so funny?"

"You reminded me of something that happened over the weekend. Buzz is getting to be quite a character. Do you realize he'll be five in a couple of months? Anyway, we were in the john together and all of a sudden he gives my cock a yank—I mean a good pull! Well, it hurt like hell and I yelled. He was instantly sorry and said 'I kiss your ow to make it better,' like Penny and I do when he gets a bump. I didn't know what to say exactly so I stammered and finally blurted out, 'No no, you can't do that! That's where peepee comes from and it's not clean.' And Buzz smartly answers, 'Can't you wash it?' Now, how am I supposed to explain at this tender age that boys don't kiss other boys' privates?"

Jude laughed. "Don't ask me! What did Penelope say?"

"She has her own problems with Buzz! Didn't I tell you? Well, you know we try to be fairly open around the children. They see us in the raw—better they have a healthy attitude about our bodies—all that jazz. A few days ago, Buzz asked Penny where babies came from. She was getting dressed, so she pointed and said, 'Daddy's penis goes in Mommy's vagina and then a baby grows inside Mommy's tummy and months later a baby comes out here.' Buzz laid down on the floor and looked up. He was disappointed. 'I don't see nothin'!' She was flustered and told him, 'There's nothing to see right now, honey.' He wouldn't let it be. 'When? When can I see somethin' come out?' Poor Penny said, 'Uh, as soon as there is something to see, uh, I'll be sure to call you!' I tell you, Jude, we have our hands full with that one!''

It was easy to laugh with Wade at his family's antics, but Jude actually cherished each and every story—it was as close as he'd get to experiencing family life.

The first week of August, Jude received a call from Penelope. "What a nice surprise! And yes, I can come for dinner anytime you say," he said.

She sounded unsettled. "Sorry, Jude, but it isn't about dinner—you know we would love to see you any night, every night. Actually, I—I was wondering if you and I could have lunch one day soon. Just—just us, at some quiet place?"

Jude immediately sensed that something was wrong. "You name it. Today—tomorrow?"

They met the next day at a grill in Brentwood, a middle ground between Hollywood and Santa Monica. Penelope was hesitant. She smiled nervously.

"I feel like a ninny. I'm not sure I should say anything. I don't know if I'm right, or have the right, to tell you what's troubling me."

Jude could see tears lurking dangerously close. "Penelope," Jude murmured, "if you are distressed in any way, for whatever reason, you know you can confide in me. And trust that the conversation will go no further."

The waiter hovered over them for their order.

"Why don't you bring us some coffee? We're not quite ready yet," Jude said. After the coffee came and they were alone again, he put his hand over hers and asked, "What's wrong?"

She began cautiously. "You are . . . the only one . . . I can turn to. I—I don't think Wade is well, Jude."

Jude was startled. This was the last thing he had expected to hear. He covered his surprise for Penelope's benefit.

"I've noticed several signs lately. Wade, of course, hasn't said a word. But he—he tires easily. You know how much energy he always had, how he always had to be on the go. Now he seems, well, listless."

"Maybe he's just slowing down, getting older like me," Jude offered.

Penelope shook her head. "There are other things. He doesn't eat like he should, like he used to, and he's lost a lot of weight. I mentioned this to him, and he joked about having to keep his figure for the picture. But that's not it. He's never been heavy, you know it and I know it."

Jude nodded in agreement and waited for more.

"His color isn't good, either. And every once in a while, I see him hold his throat—as if he was in pain. Maybe I'm overreacting to all of this, but I don't think so. I'm—I'm scared, Jude."

Jude tried to reconstruct his impression of Wade during the last few months. It was possible that he had been so engrossed in his own problems, he might have missed seeing a change in Wade. Concentrating now, he had to admit that recently Wade had looked thinner and paler than normal, that he didn't have his usual stamina.

Penelope interrupted Jude's thoughts. "I realize that what I'm about to ask is a great deal to expect. But I—I have to."

"Stop it! Nothing is too much, you must understand that."

She took a deep breath. "I have no idea how you can do this, but I—I want you to cancel the Monaco film. I really don't believe Wade is up to it. There, I said it." Penelope sighed, relieved.

There was a long pause while the waiter refilled their cups. Then Jude spoke. "I think you may be right about Wade. So, to hell with the picture. The tough part is how do I cancel it without Wade's knowing why?"

They sipped their coffee, each trying to find the solution. Suddenly, Jude clanked down his cup. "Of course! How stupid can I be? Before any picture starts, the stars have to have a medical examination for the insurance. I'll have it done right away. It's early yet, but I'll tell Wade the rules have changed, that it has to be so many more weeks before shooting starts. He never checks on those kind of details. And this way, we'll know for sure if something is wrong."

"Oh, Jude, thank you! I'm so grateful. What would I do without you?"

"You'll never have to worry about that. I'll always be here for you." Jude found himself strangely embarrassed. "Now, I'm going to make a call to set up the doctor's appointment. Why don't you order something for our lunch. Anything is okay with me."

The physician's report confirmed Penelope's and Jude's suspicions—Wade was not well. His white-cell count was high, indicating infection, and his red count was down, which meant anemia. His lymph nodes were swollen and sore. The doctor had to take a barrage of tests to determine the cause, and there was no way he could approve Wade Colby to the insurance company.

Wade was desolate. He carried on at dinner, the night of the doctor's analysis, complaining to Jude and Penelope, "These damn quacks! They don't know anything! Let's go to another doctor. I'll take some Vitamin B shots, that's all I need. And the guy will pass me. I'll give you ten to one odds. Damn it, I want to do this film!"

Jude and Penelope agonized, as well, but not for the same reason. Each had harbored the hope that the examination would prove them wrong. But now it was there in black and white, it was true. Wade was sick.

Jude tried to persuade Wade to abandon the picture. "It's funny this medical business came up now, Wade, because I was about to go over some thoughts with you concerning the disadvantages of continuing this project. For one—"

"But this is your baby," Wade interrupted. "We've been working on it for over a year—ever since you came back from your trip. I will be fine, I tell you!"

"Wade, I'm sure you will be. I'm sure it's nothing more than a flu bug, but that's not the point. Hear me out." Jude stalled for a moment, forming his arguments to convince Wade. He would approach the area where Wade was least knowledgeable, thus most vulnerable.

"Since our last meeting, I really got into the nitty-gritty of the numbers, and I was astounded. The Monaco film could be the most expensive in Hollywood history. We've been focusing on the creative side—the script, the cast, the locales, the wardrobe, and so on, but when I actually began to prepare a budget and add up the figures—wow, it was mind-boggling! The logistics alone, of transferring that many people and equipment are overwhelming. The studio is doing well now, but if this picture doesn't make its nut, we are ruined. And no one knows how the critics will react, or the public, either, for that matter, once the movie's completed. I would hate to see all we've worked for go down the tube. Maybe we'd be okay, but I don't feel like going into debt and risking everything because of some wild-ass idea I had. I think we'd be smarter to stay within our means. We can write off our expenditures so far, no harm done. An old saying rings true, 'It's not the return *on* your money that counts, it's the return *of* your money.' That's my position, but of course, I'm only one vote.''

Jude and Penelope watched Wade expectantly. Finally, he spoke.

''I don't know if you're shitting me or not. You make sense. But obviously my knowledge is limited when it comes to the budget. The timing of your disclosure nags at me, though. Why did the cost factor elude you for so long? Then I realize that each postponement was due to some calamity—first, my accident, and—and then Madge's death. The bottom line is, I guess, you've always been straight with me and I trust you completely. So why should I change now?'' Wade sighed. ''All right, so scrap this picture. I get over whatever it is I have and we go on-ward and upward to better things.''

''Wade, I don't think we'll regret it,'' Jude said. ''I believe the man upstairs has been trying to tell us something. Mainly that this picture wasn't supposed to be made. Why else would he have put so many obstacles in our way? I'm glad we're out of it. Sort of a hangover from another life!''

Jude had pangs about deceiving his friend, even slightly, and for good reason. But the more he reflected, the more assured he became that he had acted wisely. It was true that the Monaco film would have been an extravagance, but because of his desire and ambition, he would have taken the chance. Since he'd had to come up with deterrents for Wade, he was forced to scrutinize the project objectively. The arguments he'd presented to Wade *were* valid.

But none of these particulars really meant a damn thing. The burning fear in his gut was that Wade was seriously ill.

48

Beverly Hills, California
Sunday, October 1, 1961

Revel was romping in the backyard of Maple Drive with Artz, Orey and Gigi. The cat, Lil Guy, was scampering to avoid being trampled by the random running of the dogs. When they were quiet, he ruled the roost; right now, however, he just wanted to survive.

The noise blotted out the chime of the doorbell. The staff was off for the day, and Jude was at Wade's—he spent most of his free time there these days. A figure walked down the driveway and opened the gate quietly. Atherton Sardos drank in the scene wistfully before making his presence known.

"Hello, Revel." He spoke loudly to make himself heard.

She looked up and gasped, "Artie!"

"I apologize for—"

"Wait a minute!" Revel grasped for time to recover. He wasn't an apparition—he was real.

She was frozen where she stood. "What are you doing here?"

"I apologize. There was no response at the door, but I did hear the activity here in the back."

"Doesn't answer my question. What are you doing here?" she insisted.

"I'm in town on business and—and I wanted to see you."

Revel looked at him long and hard. Softly, she said, "Well you've seen me! So—goodbye!"

"Please, Revel. Please don't send me away. Can't we talk? There's so much I need to tell you—so much I want to say to you—please."

Revel searched his face for any sign of duplicity. And her heart for strength. "All right then," she slowly answered. "I'm due at Polly and Matt's for dinner in an hour, but I guess we could go inside for a few moments." Pulling herself together, she became the hostess. "Would you care for a drink of any kind?"

"Thank you, Revel. A glass of wine would be nice, if it isn't too much trouble." He couldn't take his eyes off her, she had become even more beautiful in the year and seven and a half months since he'd last seen her. And there was something else about her, something deeper. She was more mature, more assured, more desirable certainly. Now he was the one who felt awkward.

"Gigi is so much bigger. She was so tiny—before," he began lamely.

"Time changes everyone—and everything—doesn't it, Artie?" Revel served their wine and sat down. In her usual forthright manner—that trait hadn't changed—she asked him, "So what's up, Artie? What's so important? By the way, how's your wife?"

He was daunted by her directness. "Uh, well, she's in good health. But—but we're not together. We separated a few months ago. It shouldn't have happened—the wedding, I mean. We never really belonged together, we were victims of 'the arrangement.' Thank God we didn't have a child."

Revel instinctively felt sorry for him, but she didn't say anything.

Artie grabbed her hand and passionately went on. "I was weak to permit my family to dictate my life. My father is dying, my mother is totally dependent on him and cannot last long without him. And what have they left me with? The business, yes. But what else? A pending divorce from a woman I never really loved. And—and alienation from the one woman I loved the instant I saw her. You!"

Revel drew in her breath and leaned heavily back in the chair. These were the words she had longed to hear on that February night which seemed so long ago—another life ago. And now she was hearing them. Her head was in a whirl. What did he mean? What was he saying exactly? How did she feel about him today? Was she still in love with him? And if so, could she ever forget his betrayal of their relationship?

Artie saw he had unnerved her. "I'm sorry, dear Revel, for barging back in your life, uninvited, and baring my soul to you so quickly. I—I couldn't help it. I wish I could turn back the clock and relive the night I said goodbye—it would be a different scenario, I promise you. But I can't do that. I wanted to come to you sooner but then—then Madge's death, it wasn't an appropriate time. I'm not expecting any kind of answer from you now. I'm just asking for a little of your time, to give me another chance, to allow me to prove my love for you and perhaps to rekindle our flame. Please, my darling Revel!"

Revel needed to think, to focus. And suddenly she needed to see Vince. Would Vince evoke the same response in her that Artie did? Because, yes, Artie still held a major place in her heart, and she had almost been tempted to rush to him instantly. But she was able to control that urge, she was more in command of herself now. She knew she couldn't be rash, she knew she must use reason to untangle this new twist in her life. She knew she had to be fair—to herself, to Artie, to Vince.

"I'm sorry. You must go now. Call me tomorrow and...we'll talk."

Artie turned her hand over and kissed the palm, looking longingly into her eyes. He would have liked to crush her to him, kiss every inch of her and whisk her away. But he knew he had to be patient. "Thank you for listening to me. Until tomorrow then."

A few minutes later, Revel was on her way to Matthew and Polly's. She had been close to them from the beginning of the couple's marriage. There was a trust and communication between them that she admired. She had drifted away somewhat when Madge became her mentor, but after Madge was gone, Revel had returned to their fold. Studio Services Inc. was functioning extremely well. It had weathered the 1960 Screen Actor's Guild six-week strike and was flourishing again. As executive director of S.S.I., Vincent Franks was an integral part of the organization, and a good friend of Polly and Matthew's, so it was quite natural for Revel and Vince to see each other often. Revel still split her workweek between Colvas Studios and S.S.I., and relished her position with each. College held no appeal for her; she had already learned more from life than they could ever teach her at any university, and professionally speaking she was doing just fine. She was intrigued by the Peace Corps, an innovative concept introduced by President Kennedy and headed by his brother-in-law, Sergeant Shriver. But for now, she would pass, believing that Jude still needed her around.

In the past few months, Revel had become aware that Vince had very serious feelings for her. They had never been intimate, but they had done some easy smooching, and Vince could not disguise his adoration. She hadn't discouraged him, but neither had she encouraged him, except for the fact that she did willingly accept him as her escort. Until today, she had not evaluated her feelings toward Vince. She had been content to allow their relationship to remain as it was. But now Artie's unexpected arrival and declaration of love had changed all that.

Revel's mind was revving faster than her car engine. What should she do? What did she want to do? She was certain only of one thing—she wasn't going to be hurt again, no siree! Did she want to give up the security of Vince? Revel enjoyed being with him—he was considerate, interesting and attractive. There was no pressure from him—so far. But she had to admit, he didn't set off any sparks in her. Maybe she hadn't given him an opening, maybe he could make sparks fly if they actually made love. Should she make herself available to him as she had with Artie? How else was she to know? And what about Artie? Was he sincere, was he suggesting marriage? If so, where would they live? Did she want to move out of the country? Or could he conduct his business from here? Another alternative flashed across her mind—should she play both men along? How far could she go with that?

So many questions, so much to consider! And she had to work it out for herself.

Vince bounded from Polly and Matthew's house to greet Revel as she parked. He helped her out and gave her an innocent peck on the cheek. Abruptly, Revel put her arms around him and kissed him hard on the mouth, her tongue scouting his. Vince was so surprised, it took him a minute to respond, but then very quickly he warmed to the challenge.

"Do you want me?" Revel whispered in his ear.

"Oh, my God, yes!" Vince answered hoarsely.

"Now!" she commanded.

"In the street?"

"In the street—in the car—I don't care where."

Vince pulled back and held her shoulders, his eyes piercing hers. "What is it, Rev? Something is different, something is troubling you! What happened since I spoke to you this afternoon?"

Polly called from the door. "Hey, you two! You won't have time for a cocktail before dinner if you don't come in!"

"Be right there," Vince answered for them.

"I—I just can't tell you, I can't explain right now. I'm sorry—about my behavior."

"Will you meet me for a drink somewhere after?" Vince asked urgently. "I think we need to discuss this."

Revel made a decision. She had to find out a few things tonight—before she spoke to Artie tomorrow. "Why don't you follow me home?"

Only Jude's bedroom light was on in the main house. Revel buzzed to tell him she was home. "How is Wade?" she asked through the intercom.

"About the same. He isn't any worse, but he isn't any better, either." Revel could hear the worry in Jude's voice.

"You get some sleep now—and that is an order!"

"Yes, sir!" he said, laughing.

Revel casually added, "Oh, and Vince is coming by to have a nightcap, so don't be alarmed if you see headlights in the driveway. Ah, I think he just drove up. Night!"

"Say hello for me—I like Vince. Night, sweetheart!"

Revel liked Vince, too. But what else was there? She let him in when he knocked, and moved toward the bar.

"What do you want?" She was a bit nervous how to go about this—this seduction, or discovery, or whatever it was she was trying to do.

"I want you!" Vince declared. "But not now, not until I know what's going on! Level with me, Rev!"

It wasn't going the way she had hoped. And it was her fault. She had convinced herself she was handling everything rationally, and then what did she do but blow it with her unnatural conduct outside by the car this evening. Why couldn't she have been subtle? She felt like a confused little girl again.

"Well, uh, I had a visitor today."

Vince just waited.

"And, uh, it sort of shook me up, I guess."

"Who could shake you up so?"

"Artie—I mean, Atherton Sardos."

Vince sighed. He knew about Atherton Sardos. Polly and Matthew had told him about the wealthy young shipping tycoon who had been Revel's beau. But that was at least a year and a half ago, and he had understood that Sardos had married someone in Greece. Why did seeing him today have such an effect on her? Unhappily, Vince knew the answer to his question. She obviously still cared deeply for Sardos.

"I'm baffled about one thing, Revel. Why did an encounter with Atherton Sardos cause you to come on to me so strongly? Was I a substitute for him?"

"Oh, no, Vince, no," Revel said quickly, still thinking how badly she had messed this up. "I—damn—I don't know what—how to say—" She was wringing her hands, and her mouth began to quiver. "Vince, I didn't mean—or want—tonight to turn out like this. Honest! In my own stupid way, I was trying to, well, I never stopped to think about you and me—you know, together. But when Artie said he wanted to come back to me—" now the words were tumbling out over each other "—I thought I should find out how I feel about you. Now I don't know how I feel about anything!"

Vince stood quietly, understanding her misery, even understanding her dilemma. He walked to her and took her gently in his arms. "Revel, Revel, listen to me. I love you, and I do want you. There is nothing I would like more than to lie with you and caress you and hold you. I have deliberately moved slowly in our relationship, one, because of the difference in our ages—fifteen years can be a lot—and two, because I sensed that was the way you wanted it, that you weren't ready for involvement. Going to bed with me won't help you sort out your emotions. A commitment to someone involves more than the physical, much more. Every ingredient adds up to the whole, no one part is above another. I think you are torn and it will take you time. Take the time, my darling, take the time!"

She clung to his comforting arms and he tenderly rocked her from side to side. He kissed her lightly as if to say good-night.

But the kiss lingered. And became more sensual. She reached inside his coat and drew him tight against her. He ran his fingers through her hair and cupped her tear-stained face in his hands. Their eyes were heavy with desire. She felt his growing firmness pressing against her, and she wedged her body closer to it.

Vince murmured huskily, "So much for my advice to the lovelorn."

Revel laughed giddily. "I did take time just like you said—almost five whole minutes! Why don't you take your coat off now and stay awhile?"

Vince was more aggressive than she could ever have imagined. He seemed to have thrown caution to the wind once they had reached the point of no return. Hungrily, he researched that supple young body, pausing only to sample particular delicacies. His browsing excited her wildly, she was lurching for him and finally he was at her threshold and then inside her. Ecstatically, they established a rhythm, the tempo increasing to a wild finale. They remained sealed together afterward, unwilling to have it over.

"I don't want this to end," Revel murmured.

"We'll just have to continue then," Vince obliged.

Revel agreed to meet Artie at the Polo Lounge in the Beverly Hills Hotel at five for cocktails. All day she had basked in the afterglow of her night with Vincent Franks. One vital fact had been confirmed—Vince definitely ignited spontaneous combustion. And he could be romantic; he had sent exquisite roses in the afternoon.

Artie stood up as she was led to his booth. "You look radiant!" he exclaimed admiringly. There was a slight stir as the rest of the room turned to see her lucky companion.

The waiter ceremoniously brought an ice bucket and showed Artie a bottle for approval. "I hope it's all right, I ordered champagne for our reunion." The cork was expertly removed, with the customary pop, and Artie nodded for the waiter to pour.

"I toast the most beautiful woman in the Polo Lounge—and in the world!" Artie's eyes forced hers to join his.

Revel cursed her accessibility. He still made her heart skip a beat, she couldn't deny it. But she wasn't the moony teenager who thought she had found her prince, either. That prince had allowed his family to turn him into a toad.

"Where are you?" Artie asked. "You were far away."

"I'm sorry. I was thinking about when we met and when we parted. We're very different now."

"We are a bit older, hopefully a bit wiser, but what we experienced together is not different. That is the same." Artie hesitated. He didn't want to push, but he had to know. "Did you think about—us?"

Revel looked at his handsome, eager face, and again felt the throbbing in her chest. "Yes, Artie, I've done a lot of thinking. But I don't know how I should deal with this whole thing." She paused to find the right words. "I'm not sure we can just start where we left off. Maybe you never realized how hurt and—and angry—I was when you dropped your bomb on me. It took me a long time to get over that night."

"But I want to make that up to you, and I can—"

"You must hear what I'm saying, Artie! It was hard for me to trust after that. It still is. I don't know if I can trust you again. And I can't manage that kind of pain again."

His dark eyes showed his torment. "I would die before I caused you another second of unhappiness. Please believe me!"

Revel wasn't having an easy time, but she had to get it all out. "I haven't finished, Artie. You see, there's also someone else."

He was crestfallen. He drained his glass and signaled for more—anything to mask the lump in his throat. "Are you in love with him?" he blurted out at last.

"I don't know. I'm so rattled right now—I just don't know. One day everything is normal, and then you show up and all of a sudden I—I'm in the middle of a mess."

Artie saw a ray of light. This other someone couldn't hold her heart if his appearance caused her to be unsure. "Of course, any man in his right mind would not allow someone like you to be alone for long. But I'm in my right mind now, too, and I hope I can still be a contender. I'm not going to give up easily. Say that you'll let me have a chance!"

Revel remembered Vince's counsel. "You are torn, take the time." He was right, she *was* torn. And she couldn't possibly make any kind of decision this soon. Maybe seeing them both wasn't such a bad idea, after all.

Artie continued. "Why don't we get out of here? Take a ride, find a quiet place for dinner? We have a lot of catching up to do."

The car drove them west on Sunset Boulevard toward the ocean. Revel suddenly said, "I know the perfect place to go. Chez Jay. It's small, has excellent food and shouldn't be too crowded now. You'll love it!"

"I've always loved everything you suggested. You always have brought light to my life. Chez Jay it is!"

49

Hollywood, California
Monday, November 20, 1961

In desperation, Jude finally called Stewart Tesse, the NASA doctor who had saved Wade after the boat disaster.

"Jude! Good to hear from you. How are things?"

"Well, Stu, not so good, I'm afraid," Jude replied glumly.

Dr. Tesse was instantly all business. "What's the matter?"

"In August, Wade's wife—you remember Penelope?"

"Of course!"

"She came to me, very worried about Wade..." Jude filled in the details. "And I'm concerned," he continued, "because he seems to be going downhill slowly, like something's eating at him. The tests haven't been definitive, only that his white count is high and red count low, and his lymph nodes become inflamed in different parts of his system at different times. I just wondered if you could shed any light on all this. Is it possibly related to his accident?"

There was silence on the other end of the line. "Anything is possible," Dr. Tesse finally said. "I don't want to attempt any answers with so little information. I happen to be coming to California next week, and if it wouldn't ruffle Wade's doctor's feathers, I would like to see all the files on Wade and examine him myself."

"Never mind his doctor," Jude cried, relieved. "Everything will be at your disposal. I know Wade and Penelope will welcome your input. And we'll all be overjoyed to see you again!"

The Thanksgiving of 1961 wasn't one of the most festive occasions.

Jude spent the afternoon at Matthew and Polly's house with Revel and Vince. Revel had told Jude a little of her current love triangle, how Artie had surfaced again and why, but she'd added that she was also very interested in Vince. Both Artie and Vince were well aware of the other, had seemed to accept and respect Revel's need for time. Jude marveled at how these young people could act so sophisticated in such a delicate situation. He probably would have punched the other guy in the face.

Revel and Artie had fun together during his visit, but she had set conditions: friends only, as they tried to reestablish a base. Vince saw that she was taking his advice and admired her stand. He had no desire to pursue their romance if she was pining for Sardos. She was the one who had to define her emotions. He was willing to bide his time, because if he should emerge victorious, the prize was well worth the wait.

Early Thanksgiving evening, Jude went to have dinner with Wade and Penelope and the children. They all put on a happy face, but there was a barely disguised undercurrent of nervousness. Wade was getting testy with his prolonged bout of illness. He wanted someone to find out what was wrong and fix it— hanging around the house due to his lack of strength was far too frustrating. Penelope did everything she could to keep his mind occupied, but she was running out of ideas. Jude's daily visits were a godsend because the two men could talk business, or yell at the officials during sporting events on TV. It was the uncertainty that was constantly gnawing on all of their souls.

Dr. Tesse scarcely managed to hide his dismay when he and Jude arrived at the Colbys' home the following week. Wade looked bad, almost as bad as he had after the accident.

Penelope and Wade greeted Dr. Tesse warmly. "So nice of you to drop by. Wonderful to see you, Stu! Belated Happy Thanksgiving." Penelope settled him in a chair, brought him tea and then sat next to her husband.

Stu looked at the lovely surroundings and attempted to cover his unease. "Beautiful place you have here—beautiful. Where are the kids? Like to meet those two."

Penelope laughed. "Oh, you will soon enough. Then you won't be able to get rid of them! Do you have children?"

"No. My wife works, I work—I guess we never got around to it. Kind of sorry about that now, though." He hesitated before continuing. "What's this I hear about you, Wade? I can't leave you alone for a year without you getting in trouble?"

A wave of pain crossed Wade's face. Then he jokingly answered, "My two wardens here won't let me out on parole. I think some damn bug got hold of me and won't let go. You wouldn't happen to have any miracle shots that would get me out of here, would you?"

"Well, first we have to find out what kind of bug has hold of you. Would you mind if we went into another room and I took a look at you?"

"My body is becoming public domain," Wade muttered. "But for you, I'll expose myself yet again. Come on!" And he led the doctor toward the master bedroom.

Dr. Tesse was up-to-date on Wade's condition. Jude had taken him to Wade's physician's offices where Stu had studied all the records. He had conferred with him briefly before coming to see Wade.

Jude and Penelope waited expectantly. At one point, a cry echoed from behind the closed doors. They both jumped spontaneously. Their bodies were taut with the tension.

At long last, Dr. Tesse emerged, alone. "I gave him an injection to sedate him. I'm afraid my probing may have hurt." He was obviously disturbed. "May I have a drink, a real drink? Scotch on the rocks would be much appreciated." Jude hurried to the bar and poured for the three of them. Something told him they were going to need it.

Dr. Tesse gulped a taste from his glass. Then he swirled the liquid around and swallowed again. Jude and Penelope sat as if made of stone.

"This is the part of my job I hate most." He looked at them mournfully, wishing he didn't have to continue, but knowing he must. "Okay, let me tell you what I think. Wade has tenderness at every important lymph tissue center. His charts all point to the same conclusion, and I concur with his doctors." Dr. Tesse paused, drank again, wanting to delay his next words. "We believe that Wade has lymphatic cancer. It's possible that he was exposed to something in the environment, or, that the transfusion he received at the time of the accident was tainted. We just don't know—the how—for sure."

Jude and Penelope were dumbstruck. Jude stared at the doctor—through the doctor—and beyond into another world. Penelope's hands clutched the tumbler so tightly her knuckles turned white.

After a long minute, Penelope broke the hush. In a small, feeble voice she asked, "What—what does that mean?"

"The swelling began in his throat, but as you are aware, has moved to numerous areas. The lymph network flows through the entire system, so it's just a matter of time before the first vital organ is completely infected, starts to malfunction and then finally deteriorates. The other organs will follow soon after."

"But isn't there something you can do to stop it? Some drug—or treatment?" Jude pleaded.

"Not that we are aware of. Not yet. Our knowledge is limited, and admittedly we deal in an inexact science. Believe me, if I knew of someone in this country—in this world—who had discovered a gleam of a cure, I would have Wade on a plane right now." Dr. Tesse heaved his big shoulders. "I'm so sorry. I am so damn sorry!"

Jude rasped through clenched teeth, "You're telling us that he's going to die—is that what you're telling us, Stu?"

"I'm afraid so," Dr. Tesse replied gently.

Jude's body seemed to shrink, his head snapped forward, dangling.

Penelope still sat sphinxlike; only her lips moved. "How—how long does—does he have?"

"No way to say—but a guess would be, four months at the most."

Again the frozen silence. Again Penelope spoke. "Why didn't his doctor tell us?"

"He suspected, as did his colleagues, but they kept trying to find a different cause for his symptoms, as they should have. But they ran out of possibilities just before I arrived. I'm afraid we all agree."

Penelope made one last try at keeping herself under control. "Should we—what should we do? I mean, does Wade have to—know?"

"In my opinion? I would say nothing for now. Only that we're still attempting to discover a reason for his soreness and weakness. I will prescribe vitamin shots and iron—and sedatives. When the real pain comes, he'll have every available painkiller for relief, and by then, he himself will know."

Penelope's mind couldn't take any more. The glass slipped from her fingers clattering to the terrazzo floor; she was suddenly slithering down to the marble in a heap.

Jude was jerked out of his own stupor and, with Dr. Tesse's help, he picked her up and laid her tenderly on the couch.

"Get some ice," the doctor ordered as he broke a vial of smelling salts under her nose. "She'll be all right," he assured Jude, who looked as if he was close to swooning himself. "Hang on, Jude! They are going to need your strength, more than ever before. I know it's tough on you, but it's tougher for Penelope—and for Wade."

Jude started as if he'd been slapped. Dr. Tesse's words cut a swath straight to his heart. He would be strong—he couldn't fail them now. Jude brought some ice cubes in a towel and knelt beside Penelope. "Don't worry, Stu—I can handle it."

Penelope was coming to. "One quick question, Stu," Jude said hurriedly. "Are we in accord? We say nothing to nobody?"

"Absolutely! Otherwise, you'll have all the ghouls picking around. Wade and Penelope should have a degree of normalcy as long as they can. I'm confident you'll see to that."

"You can count on it." Jude nodded in determination.

50

Beverly Hills, California
Sunday, December 3, 1961

"Are you sure my going away isn't a problem, Jude?" Revel asked solicitously.

"I am positive! I won't be home much anyway, I'll be splitting my hours between work and Wade's house."

"Is he any better?"

Jude hedged, "Ah, well, he's holding his own. These things take time to get over, you know. The doctors are on the right track." Shifting the subject, he added, "Besides, you're going to be doing some studio business for us, and you and Vince will be representing S.S.I. as well, so it's important you go."

"I'm just worried about my big brother, that's all. You seem so uptight. But I guess with Wade out, you're carrying a lot on your shoulders. Maybe you should hire another assistant until Wade gets back."

"Perhaps, we'll see."

Jude and Revel were having coffee, waiting for the limo to come. Jude wanted to steer conversation away from Wade, it was getting more difficult each day to act out the charade. "Tell me—I assume you've spoken to Artie in Greece—what did he think about you and Vince going off to New York?"

Revel smiled with a trace of smugness. "What can he say? Neither one has any reins on me—I am a free agent. It's kind of a nice position to be in." She sighed. "But I'm soon going to have to make a move. And I don't know which way! I thought it would be good to see Vince in a contrasting environment—you know, more exciting and glamorous. And then Artie is coming the week before Christmas and my idea is to go see Mama and Papa and put him in a more down-to-earth setting. What do you think?''

"I think my smart sister has everything under control. You are a package, all right!"

The door chimes indicated the car had arrived. Vince had been picked up first and he and the driver carried Revel's Louis Vuitton luggage out. She wore a royal blue jersey dress and matching wool coat and hat. One aspect of being an heiress she particularly enjoyed was the unlimited budget for clothes and accessories.

Jude spun her around. "You look spectacular, very sophisticated and very grown-up. Have fun, honey! You too, Vince!" He hugged her and sent them on their trip.

Jude envied Revel's carefree life. Of course, her anxieties probably loomed as formidable to her as his did to him. But his anxiety, once again was life and death. However, by his own imposed rules, he was not permitted to dwell on the weight he carried. His purpose in life now was to help his friends through this crisis.

On the way to the beach, he picked up some Häagen-Dazs ice cream—a favorite with Wade and the children.

"Wow! What a performance!" Revel exclaimed to Vince, as they exited the theater. *The Caretaker* starring Donald Pleasance had been a treat for their last night in New York.

"He was magnificent," Vince agreed.

"But the play was a little too somber," Revel confessed. "Harold Pinter, no doubt, is a genius, but I couldn't find a theme or a conviction—I don't think I understand this kind of theater. Too deep, I guess, for my bourgeois brain."

Inside the plush interior of the limousine, Vince leaned over and whispered, "Make that two bourgeois brains. I much preferred Robert Morse in *How to Succeed in Business Without Really Trying.*"

"Why are you whispering?"

"Because I don't want anyone to know I'm not worldly-wise! It's our secret." He put his finger to his lips.

Revel laughed and kissed him. It had been a delightful week. The business appointments had gone off without a hitch, and the recreational menu had been full of highlights. She hadn't realized how witty and charming Vince could be—and adventuresome.

Vince didn't want the evening to stop. "Let's go to the Peppermint Lounge and Ye Little Club and see if we can master Chubby Checker's twist. There are no meetings tomorrow, and I don't have to drive, so we can even get a little smashed if we want!"

The two danced and drank with abandon. They were the last to leave the nightclub and when the car deposited them at the Sherry Netherlands Hotel, they walked unsteadily to their rooms. Revel had trouble fitting the key in the lock, Vince wasn't much better, but he did at last manage to open her door.

Revel giggled, and said, "Did you say a little smashed? I'd say we're a lot smashed! Bet you can't open yours!"

Vince pulled himself up to his full height and said grandly, "We'll just see about that." He zigzagged down the hall toward the studio's recently-acquired second apartment and, with a flourish, attempted to insert his key. No luck. The more he struggled, the harder Revel howled, until finally Vince gave up and joined in.

"Oh, dear—you—are—funny—" she gasped in the midst of guffaws.

"We're going—to—wake up—the whole place," he sputtered.

"You better—sleep—in my room—we can't stay—out here—"

"You're right." Vince carefully made his way back to her. "How do you know you can trust me?"

"How do you know I want to trust you?" Revel retorted.

"You are a little vixen, you know that, don't you? But I know how to deal with little vixens!" Vince said as he led Revel inside and closed her door.

Before Christmas, Wade knew the secret Penelope and Jude were trying so valiantly to hide. The meandering infection appeared to have settled in his liver, the first vital organ. The spasms of pain were excruciating. His need for relief accelerated, but he gave his doctor explicit instructions not to tell his wife of the added injections, or to disclose that he was aware of his condition. Wade wanted to spare her that pain as long as possible. He was still in control of his body and he was mobile, so he was determined to make this last Christmas as joyful as it could be for his family. To help him accomplish this he had to enlist Jude's help. Ah, Jude! Wade was convinced he and Jude must have been related in another life, how else could they have formed such a bond?

"Jude, I need your help." It was Monday, December 18, before dinner.

"Shoot," Jude said. He recognized there was something different about Wade lately, but couldn't identify what exactly.

"First, let's get this over with—don't say a word, let me talk! I understand what is wrong with me. Please keep this between us. I realize how hard these weeks, months, I guess, have been for Penelope and you. But if I can feel good about anything tonight, it is the knowledge that you will be here to watch over her and the children. I—I can't sum up almost twenty years of a relationship in one sentence. I just hope you know how beholden I am for—your friendship."

Jude's determination to remain strong had its severest test at this moment. He tried to stifle the tide of emotion that was threatening to drown him. He managed to keep it all in, except for the silent tears that escaped and ran shamelessly down his face.

"Now!" Wade continued. "This has to be a bang-up holiday! Can you find a large sled with runners that could work in the sand? With horses to pull it? Unless, of course, you know some reindeer breeders. And a full Santa outfit, complete with sack. Then, somewhere—Tiffany's or Harry Winston's or Beverly Hills Jewelers—someone has to have a diamond heart. I want—I want to give Penelope my heart, so to speak. And for Buzz—"

Jude listened to Wade in complete wonder and reverence as he enthusiastically continued with his list of preparations. What a man he was seeing! Jude buried the powerful sentiments surging within, and joined Wade's plans wholeheartedly. If Wade could rise so far above adversity, so could he.

S.S.I. hired the Clydesdale horses and wrangler, the studio located a sled and Jude arranged for grips to lay tracks—as they did for cameras on a moving shot—so the sled runners could glide smoothly on the beach. Western Costume had the full Santa regalia. He discovered an exquisite heart-shaped diamond pin at Cartier's. And the ultimate children's store, F.A.O. Schwarz in New York, air-expressed the special items Wade had requested for Buzz and Prissy.

Jude had regimented the program meticulously. He spent Christmas Eve day at the Colbys' house. At about two o'clock, he came from Wade's room and told Penelope that Wade wanted to nap and he suggested he take her, Buzz and Prissy for a ride to look at all the dazzling decorations in Beverly Hills, adding how quiet it would therefore be for Wade. The ploy worked. While they were gone, everything was briskly and efficiently put in place. By the time they returned, all was ready.

The adults and children were sitting in front of the fireplace when the door chimes sounded, and twenty carolers were ushered in to sing Christmas songs for the assembled group. The little ones clapped with glee. Wade consumed the peaceful scene as a starving peasant would gulp offered nourishment. He took Penelope's hand and Jude's hand and said softly, "How happy I am! Here we are—the three comrades! I love you so much. Am I a lucky guy or what?"

Jude and Penelope could only cling to his hands, they couldn't talk.

Soon the door chimes rang again, and Wade's parents arrived, laden with gaily wrapped gifts. Mr. and Mrs. Prickler did not know the exact nature or extent of their son's disease; they only knew he had been ailing since Thanksgiving.

"Ganny! Bunka!" Those were Buzz and Prissy's interpretations of Grandma and Grandpa. And right behind the Pricklers, Penelope's mother and father appeared.

"Oh, my!" Penelope exclaimed, "I didn't know we were having a party—what a wonderful surprise!"

Jude and Wade exchanged sly glances—so far so good!

The singers continued in the background during the jubilant greetings, and then when everyone was settled, they asked their audience to join in. Amateur voices zealously blended with those of the professionals and the house reverberated with the season's classics.

When the carolers were finished and the music was still in the air, hot hors d'ouevres and eggnogs were served. Wade excused himself. Jude noiselessly followed a few minutes later.

"The cowboy will get the sled started and then run like hell to the end of the tracks to stop and hold the horses while you get down," Jude explained hurriedly as he helped Wade into the Santa suit. "He'll keep out of sight—the bag is packed—and you be careful. Are you okay?" he asked, concerned when he saw Wade grimace.

"Never been better!" Wade assured him. "Well, let me amend that statement somewhat. I'm fine—now go back or they'll start to wonder!"

The children were playing, the grown-ups were chatting, the tree lights were twinkling, when all of a sudden, sleigh bells interrupted, and began tinkling.

"Where are they coming from?" Penelope asked.

"I think from the beach," Jude answered helpfully. Everyone ran to the big glass doors just as the sleigh came into view. Buzz and Prissy, even the adults, were stupefied.

"It's—it's Santa Claus!" Buzz yelled and slid the doors open.

"Ho! Ho! Ho!" Wade bellowed in his best Santa imitation. "Had to give my reindeer a rest, you know, so my horse friends here helped me out!" He lowered himself to the ground with the huge sack slung over his shoulder. "Why so quiet? Cat got your tongues? Ho! Ho! Ho!"

Buzz and Prissy quickly lost their fear and awe and climbed all over him, clamoring for attention. The adults now recognized who Santa was and were reveling in the reactions of the youngsters.

"Can Santa come in, Mommy?" Buzz and Prissy chorused.

"Of course! Welcome, Mr. Claus! Would you like an eggnog?" Penelope immediately became a member of the cast of players.

"That's mighty nice of you. I could use some refreshment!"

Wade gathered the tots on his lap—with slight difficulty, since the pillow in his suit kept slipping. "I better get down to business. Let's see—ladies first—you must be Priscilla." He reached in the bag and pulled out a Barbie doll, then a trunk filled with every conceivable outfit Barbie could ever wear, from riding habit to ball gown. Priscilla's face beamed and she squealed with delight.

"You have to be Wayland Earle Prickler Colby, better known as Buzz! I had to leave something in my sleigh, Would you—" pointing to Jude "—be my elf and fetch it for me?"

"Absolutely, Mr. Claus, I'd be honored!" Jude was already on his way, and returned wheeling a miniature fully equipped electric car. Buzz's mouth fell open, his eyes popping. "Wow!"

"You must have been a very good boy and girl because there's lots more in here for you. But I think Santa should tend to the other folks, too. Here's a package for Robert Pope—Elizabeth Prickler—Earle Prickler—Helen Pope—oh, here's something for a Mr. Jude Abavas." Jude was startled; that clever fox Wade had put one over on him.

"Another present for Buzz—Priscilla—Priscilla—Buzz. What's this? A box for Penelope Pope Colby."

"It's for you, Mommy, it's for you!" Wade gave the gift to the children to deliver to Penelope.

"Well, I believe my work is done, you turn around now and don't look, so I can be on my way. *Merry Christmas to all, and to all a good night!*"

Wade hustled out the door, the cowboy sounded the sleigh bells and led the horses away.

When Wade emerged from the master suite, the two little ones rushed to him, "Daddy! Daddy! You missed Santa Claus! He was here!"

"No, really?"

"Honest and truly! Look what he brought us! And Mommy, too—and Uncle Jude—and Ganny—and Bunka—and—"

"Whoa, calm down, I'll look at everything."

Penelope hugged him tightly and whispered, "Thank you, Santa, for making this Christmas the best ever. I love you. And my note and pin will be my treasures always."

Wade held her at arm's length and drank in every inch of her beauty. "You are my heart. You know that, don't you?"

She nodded and drew close to him again, savoring the feel of him, holding on to the man she worshipped, clinging to every second she had left with him. For now she knew that he was also aware of how little time they had.

The rest of the family gathered around to thank him for such a special evening. Wade spotted Jude standing alone by the bar and sauntered over to him.

"We did it! We did it!" he said excitedly, but quietly.

"No, *you* did it," Jude responded, also in an undertone. His voice faltered, choked with emotion. "You—you did me in. You

are a—a Titan! Do you have any idea what these mean to me?''
Jude shakily held up the pair of solid gold cuff links—shaped
like a heart!

"I hope they mean to you what they signify to me. You
also...hold a part of my heart.''

The two men stood tall, gazing at each other, their eyes bur-
rowing to the intrinsic core of each other's souls. And then they
embraced.

No more words were necessary.

Jude was the only Abavas absent from the Christmas Eve gathering in Hailey at Noah and Willamina's. It had been a wonderful, happy day—skiing, last-minute shopping, the traditional
torchlight parade, all ending with one of Willamina's sumptuous dinners.

"You have more, Mr. Sardos?'' urged Willamina.

Artie laughed. "Please don't tempt me! I don't think I'll be
able to fit into my ski pants as it is. And please, please call me
Artie.''

Revel was pleased with the way Artie fit in. The family seemed
to like him and he appeared comfortable in this humbler milieu.
Matthew, Polly and the twins stayed with Noah and Willamina,
while Revel and Artie stayed at Jude's house in Sun Valley.
Matthew and Polly liked Artie, but were naturally pulling for
Vince to be the victor. Wisely, they didn't interfere or attempt to
influence Revel.

"Yes, Mama, we have separate rooms,'' Revel had patiently
assured Willamina. "Everything is proper.''

And it had been! But as each lovely day passed, it was becoming more difficult for Revel to shut her door at night. No
doubt—Artie still caused rumblings in her.

Revel and Artie drove back to Sun Valley still singing the carols that had started after supper. Light snow was falling and the
lights from all the Christmas decorations lined their enchanted
path. Jude's house was cozy, the fireplace crackled with inviting
warmth, a small tree illuminated the living room. Artie van-
ished to the kitchen, returning with chilled champagne and two
glasses. He put on a record, opened the bottle and poured. When
the music began, Revel looked at Artie incredulously. The melody was "Satin Doll.''

"You remembered!"

"How could I forget one moment of that night? 'Satin Doll'—your ivory satin robe—you opening the champagne. And then you, unbelievable breathtaking you, with all your innocence and sensualism. That night is solidly etched in my mind. Shall we dance?"

They drifted slowly with the beat. Revel put her arms around his neck and Artie tightened his grip around her waist. They no longer took steps, instead their hips gyrated to the cadence. Soon her breasts were in motion against his chest. Two writhing shadows. Mutely they shed their clothing. Gradually, he lifted her body so she could straddle his middle. Now her breasts were near his face. He took her in his mouth, sucking thirstily. She reached down and guided him into her and then held his head firmly as he inhaled. Their need was strong. He lowered them both to the sofa, still entwined. At their peak, Artie cried, "Oh, Revel—I have—waited—such a long time to be—with—you!"

Christmas morning, Revel and Artie opened their private presents before leaving for the festivities at Noah and Willamina's. Revel had saved a huge box tagged "To my satin doll with all my love" until last. When she unfolded the tissue paper, there was another smaller box. And inside that was an even smaller wrapped package. This one was real. She tore off the paper and lifted the cover to reveal a blue velvet covered jewelry case, bearing the unmistakable trademark of Tiffany's. Revel looked at Artie, almost fearful to go further.

"Go on, open it!" he urged.

Gingerly, she raised the lid and drew in her breath sharply. A perfect solitaire diamond ring sparkled up at her.

"Oh my—oh my—" She was completely nonplussed.

"Do you like it?" Artie was like a little child, eager for approval. "Let's see if it fits. We can have it sized if I guessed wrong."

Revel was still speechless. She allowed him to slip it on her finger—her engagement and wedding-band finger! That realization brought a response at last.

"Oh, Artie, it's gorgeous, it's—it's stupendous. But I—I didn't say—I mean, I can't accept it. I mean, I don't think I'm ready yet."

"It's all right, I realize this is not a commitment. You can wear it on the other hand if you want." He grinned contritely. "It's practice, combined with wishful thinking, I guess."

He was so endearing, Revel reached over and gently stroked his face. "Thank you, Artie. I will wear it on my right hand, proudly! And who knows, maybe this harebrained kid will make some sense one day soon."

"Remember, Matthew—last July? We talk about selling our land?" Noah and the other men were relaxing, having coffee in the living room after the day's full agenda.

"Of course, Papa. You decided at that time to wait."

Artie rose. "Would you like to be alone to discuss business with your sons? I completely understand. I can help the ladies."

Noah, along with everyone else, was impressed by Artie. And just then, he approved of Artie's sensitivity.

"No—no! We appreciate if you stay. And give to us what in your head."

Artie sat, grateful for their trust.

"I tell you my thoughts. This be where your mama and me come over forty-six year ago. With nothing. Children all born here, their children all born here. Some of us buried here. This be our heritage! Our country been good to us. We have plenty— we want for nothing. So, Mama and me—we no sell—anytime! When we go, you can make your rules. Until then—we no sell! Now, what you think?"

The room was silent, each deliberating in his own thoughts.

"John?" Noah asked.

"Well, when ya put it that way, guess it's right. Hate to miss out on that big money, though."

Matthew spoke. "But you're not, John! We're not going to grow any more land in this universe, just more people. So that makes all ground increasingly valuable."

"I know how John feels, but I think Matt has the right idea," Clyde chimed in.

"Artie?" Noah prompted.

"I think it is inappropriate for me to comment on your personal situation. But I can tell you about my family. My father began as a poor seaman. He worked very hard to buy his first small fishing craft. Since then, he has never sold any of his holdings, he only acquired and expanded. At present, he owns one of the largest shipping companies in the world, and has branched out in many other directions. And you know what? He still has that first boat in a warehouse—to remind us how it started. So I believe in one's heritage. That is what I think!''

Noah surveyed the younger men. He was pleased with their reasoning. ''Thank you. I be glad we share our thoughts.''

51

Beverly Hills, California
Saturday, January 13, 1962

"We interrupt this program for a news bulletin. Ernie Kovacs was killed early this morning, apparently losing control of his Corvair automobile on the rain-slicked streets in Beverly Hills. He—"

Jude angrily turned off the television. He was alone in his bedroom upstairs and he shouted at the empty air and silent walls. "What is happening, God? I'm sick of death! Sweet, funny Ernie—why him? Hemingway! Why did he get so fucked up he had to do it to himself? Luke? My babies—my wife—*wives? Why Wade?* Life doesn't make sense to me anymore. I can't handle it—" and Jude gave way to muzzled sobs.

This was the first time Jude had been home in three days. He hadn't dared leave Penelope's side because Wade was so much worse. But the doctors had at last persuaded Penelope to move Wade to the hospital. Jude had called Dr. Tesse, who agreed it was time. It wasn't healthy for the children to see their daddy deteriorate, and the hospital had the facilities and the equipment to meet Wade's every need. There would be a room adjoining Wade's for Penelope and Jude, in which to rest or freshen up. Penelope had gone on to the hospital with Wade in the ambulance. Jude had dashed to Maple Drive to shower and throw some changes of clothing in a bag. That was when he had heard the newscast about Ernie Kovacs's death.

"Jude!" Revel pounded on the door. "Jude! I saw your car in the driveway—open up!"

Jude attempted to get control before he answered. "It's—it's open, Rev. Come in."

Revel swung the hinge, took one look at Jude and rushed to soothe him. "My poor darling brother! You must know about Ernie. And Matt called me—he and Polly and the twins are at the Colbys' to take care of things there. He and Vince said for me not to go into S.S.I. for now. That way, I can cover for you at the studio—well, not cover, exactly, but I can do what I can and at least keep everybody off your back. We'll handle the press— Matt told me they were already showing up at the beach—probably will be at the hospital, too. Just ignore them, push right through the bastards." Revel was talking as fast as she could to pull him together, holding him at the same time.

"I know, I know, they're just doing their job, Jude, but sometimes people need to be left alone, even celebrities. Artie's timing isn't too good—he had to go home. But Vince is coming over, so I won't be by myself. I'm sure you don't want any of us at the hospital yet. Call and tell me if Penelope wants me to call Wade's folks, or hers. Or if either of you need anything done, just give us a holler. Here, let me put some stuff in your suitcase." She competently packed while Jude just kind of sat there, staring blankly ahead.

"There, you're all ready. It's good you had a chance to let off some steam because now you'll be able to rally for Penelope and Wade." Revel picked up the suitcase and led Jude downstairs to his car.

"Drive carefully! I love you, Jude. Please tell Wade and Penelope how much I love them, too."

Jude drove off, and just in time. Revel's bravado collapsed as his car pulled away. Vince found her later curled into a forlorn ball, crying her heart out.

"Wade—is—Wade is—*dying*."

"I know, honey, I know. It's all right to cry, sweetheart, it's all right to cry for a friend!" Vince promised her.

The days became a week, then two weeks. Jude and Penelope never left Wade's bedside. Mr. and Mrs. Prickler, Mr. and Mrs. Pope, Matthew and Polly, Revel and Vince came to visit, but none could endure seeing Wade in such a state of deterioration for any length of time. And it was so frustrating, knowing there was nothing they could do to alter the course of the disease. The malignancy galloped through his body at its own pace, leaving waste, destruction, and, at last, on Sunday, January 28, merciful death. Jude held one hand, Penelope the other, and they saw the last flicker of recognition directed at them, almost a smile of relief, the eyes declaring the devotion in his heart. And then he was gone.

Jude and Penelope kept clutching his hands, not willing or able to accept this finality. Neither had ever seen anyone die—before. The final peace that flooded his face, at last conquering the torment and pain.

Jude wished he could have died for his friend. If only he could have! And again there was that ravaging sense of helplessness, of having no control in his life. Having to marry Thelma. Not foreseeing the avalanche. Not finding Thelma and Keane. Not recognizing Madge's turmoil and not knowing how to deal with it when it did surface. Not being able to prevent the abortion. And now, not able to thwart this plague from taking his strong, lovable, loyal, kind, fun, supreme friend.

As Jude stared at the cold hand and lifeless face, he realized what he could do—*must* do. He would provide Buzz and Prissy with as much support and love as was his to give. Not that he could completely fill their loss. But Uncle Jude would do his best. And he would be there for Penelope—he'd provide the shoulder to lean upon, the hand to guide her, the mouth with the words to comfort her and the heart to strengthen her. He would pay tribute to Wade by making Wade's family his *raison d'être,* his reason to be.

"I can't believe what I'm hearing, Artie!" Revel's voice was feverishly shrill. "First, you leave, knowing how upset I was about Wade's condition and how worried I was about Jude. And—"

She listened for a minute while Artie interrupted. Then, she yelled into the phone, "I know you called a lot, but that doesn't help me here! I don't understand how a stupid business meeting—and I don't care how important it was—can take precedence over being with someone you say you love, especially when that someone needs you. I just don't get it!"

Again she paid attention while he talked. "Okay, so you're sorry. But now, three weeks later, you still can't come to be with me? To be by my side at the funeral Tuesday? That hurts me, Artie—hurts me a lot."

Revel's pitch lowered and became more contemplative. "I've had time to do a lot of thinking, a lot of soul-searching, a lot of crying in the past three weeks. And I have to know something. Is this the way it would be, Artie? Would I always come after your business and your family? I believe you do care for me, but I'm beginning to realize how different we are, how different our worlds are, how different our backgrounds are . . . and how different our priorities are. You see, if you asked me to come and stand by you, I would drop everything and leave on the next plane. That's what I think people who love each other should do."

Artie spoke again. Revel was quiet and took a long beat before responding. "No, Artie, I would rather you didn't try to 'work it out.' And no, I'm not angry now, not anymore. Let's just say I grew up a little since Wade died. If you could have been here, you'd understand what I'm talking about. I was witness to a love, a friendship, an allegiance so strong it defied description. Between Wade and Penelope and between Wade and Jude. I know how far they would go for each other—there would be no limit! No, Artie, please—let me finish! I want that kind of bond, too! I'm positive I don't want to be in third position, I want to be number one. Maybe it's selfish, but I can't help it. I need a full-time, on-the-scene partner. And dear Artie, I know you can't be that to me.—No, you couldn't! Oh, Artie—it's—it's not your fault—it's not my fault, it's just the way we are. I will always remember what we've had together, but I'm certain we would destroy those memories were we to marry. No—no—don't—*please* don't say anything more, Artie. It's hard for me to be a big girl, please don't make it harder." Just before she returned the receiver to the cradle, she whispered, *"Au revoir, mon chéri!"*

Sadly, tearfully, Revel twirled the diamond ring she wore on the second finger of her right hand. At last, with a heavy sigh, she removed it and placed it back in the Tiffany box. Tomorrow she would return it.

Revel felt a wet nose nuzzling her leg. She bent over and buried her face in Gigi's fur. "Oh, Gigi," Revel confided dolefully, "it's so difficult to grow up!"

The days and weeks that followed Wade's burial on Tuesday, January 30, 1962, were a blur of mechanical reactions and rote duties for Jude and Penelope. Protocol had been observed in all the arrangements. The etiquette of the mourners' visits had been borne. The tremendous outpouring of sympathy from all over the country, the world, had been acknowledged. The endless legalities had been tolerated.

One Saturday, in late March, the two remaining comrades sat quietly in Penelope's living room. They watched the surfers, the runners, the ongoing volleyball game, the bustling activity of the beach. They heard Buzz and his friends laughing while building a sand castle. Jude and Penelope, however, were content to be passive observers of the life surrounding them. For they were completely drained, their bodies in neutral, appreciative of the absence, for the first time, of any other people. Neither felt the need to speak, they'd had enough of making small talk with well-meaning visitors. Now it was good just to sit. And think their private thoughts. Finally, Penelope broke the silence.

"I've been thinking, Jude. There must be a reason for all the pageantry and obligations that go along with a death. It gives those left behind so much to do, they don't have time to face reality right away."

"That's probably true."

Penelope lifted her pain-filled eyes and asked, simply, "But the time has come, hasn't it? So now what do we do?"

"We take a day at a time."

"It doesn't seem to get much easier, does it?"

Jude slowly shook his head.

"Oh, Jude, sometimes at night I reach over to touch him—but he's not there. And when I pass his empty closet and barren dressing room, I think I'm going to burst. I look at his picture—that wonderful warm laughing face—and I almost can't bear it. I try to be as normal as I can around the children... Did I tell you? The psychiatrist I called said it was all right to show a degree of grief, that the children should understand Mommy's sad because Daddy went to heaven, but naturally not to go overboard. I just worry I might blow it and—and not be able to stay within his guidelines."

Jude studied Penelope closely. She was quite a person. Her courage during the past seven months, from that ominous lunch in August to the present had been incredible. He must make her understand that.

"I have to tell you something, Penelope. I thought I had set myself up to be the strong sturdy tower for you. But you surprised me and more and more over the past months I found myself following your strength."

"How can you say that? Why, you've been everything to us! Like a brother to Wade, to me, to all of us! You're our family, Jude! You *were* that tower! None of us could have gone through this without you!" Her voice broke. "I know—Wade would say the same thing. And he would be glad if . . . in some small way, I offered any support for you, because it would be giving back a bit of what you've given to us."

She started to add something but then stopped, not sure if she should go any further. Jude could see her struggle, but didn't say anything. He just waited.

Then hesitantly, almost shyly, she went on, "There is something—something I've always read. I'm not—not overly religious, but I do believe there is a source greater than us. And I—I have to believe that our spirit endures, because otherwise Wade would be lost forever. It's a small publication, sort of a thought-for-the-day booklet."

She faltered again, and then regained her composure. "The morning of the funeral, the lesson for that day seemed like it was written just for me—for all of us. It said that we need never feel alone for He is always with us. That He is our comfort and strength through any challenge or change. That if a dear one is no longer a—a part of our lives, we must remind ourselves that all the good we experienced together is still a part of us—as warm memories, as goals achieved, as challenges met and overcome, as love felt. This dear one is an eternal part of us."

She searched his face for any sign of skepticism, but saw only his earnest attention. Encouraged she said, "It helped me so much, Jude. I wanted to share this with you. If I had any strength at all, this is where it came from. And I'm grateful you're not looking at me like I'm some kind of nut."

"On the contrary, I envy you!" he said, wondering if he could ever find strength in such a faith. Because Penelope had confided something so personal, Jude felt he could discuss something that had been on his mind since Wade's death.

"I've been kicking around an idea, and now seems as good a time as any to run it by you. I've talked to Revel already. You see, I really want out of the Maple Drive house—too many ghosts. So I've decided to sell it. Rev is old enough to want her own place, can't say I blame her. And, thank God, she's got the money. I—ah—thought maybe I'd look for something out here, in Santa Monica, on the beach. That way, I'd be closer to the kids and you. I don't mean I'd be a pest or anything, and I know no one can take the place of their daddy. But I figured it might be good for them to have familiar old Uncle Jude close by. And then you'd have someone near, too, to help handle any kind of problem." Jude was anxious for her approval. "Wade and I talked about this, Penelope. And I know he would be pleased if I was handy for all of you. So, how does the idea strike you?"

"Well, it strikes me as absolutely marvelous!" Although she wholeheartedly welcomed the prospect, she wondered if she was being selfish. "But are you sure this isn't too much? I mean, I don't want you to change your life because of us—we don't want to be a burden to you. You've given so much of yourself already, I feel guilty. Jude, you have to live your life, too, you know."

"I know! And this will help me do exactly that."

52

Santa Monica, California
Sunday, August 5, 1962

"Will you calm down?" Jude yelled to Artz and Orey. "I can't hear myself think around here!" The dogs were running wild and barking like crazy. "I'm sorry," he said to Matthew and Polly. "The animals have been so excited since we moved, I can't control them. They really like it here, there's so much going on all the time. Now, what did you say?"

"I said, I think this was one of your best ideas," Polly answered. "I love the house, there's a happy aura here."

"I'll second that," agreed Matthew. "I feel it, too. And you look more relaxed, Jude."

Revel and Vince and Gigi burst in from the street side. Revel toted a small pillow-lined basket. "Are Penelope and the kids here yet?" she asked anxiously.

"No. Why? And hello!" Jude said, smiling at Revel's high energy arrival.

"Oh—hi! And what's all the commotion down the street? Lots of people, police, newsmen and even helicopters—near the Lawfords, I think!"

"I don't have a clue, honey. Maybe President Kennedy is visiting. Now that you mention it, I have heard quite a few choppers this morning. Anyway, what do you have there?" Jude pointed to the basket.

"Didn't you remind him?" Revel asked Polly. "I knew he wasn't paying attention when I mentioned it weeks ago."

"Haven't had a chance yet!"

"*This* is a surprise for Buzz and Prissy. It's one of Gigi's puppies—Gigi and Tom Dooley's, that is. Isn't he sweet? Matt and Polly took the other one to be with his dad. Thank gosh because I couldn't keep it—I'm barely getting by with Gigi—the manager at the apartment building isn't too keen on pets. That's why I'm glad I'm just renting for now. Next year, I think I'll buy a lot and build. I want a yard!''

The gathering marked Jude's housewarming. The home, which was only eight houses north of the Colbys' was a large rambling mediterranean-style beach house. The front door faced the sidewalk, servants quarters were above the garage, an enclosed patio led to ample guest rooms and large sliding glass doors opened onto a walled terrace that overlooked the beach. A walkway from the patio led to the main house; two large master suites were on the left, kitchen and utility rooms on the right.

"Why didn't you bring along your menagerie?" Jude asked Matthew and Polly, referring to their pets.

Matthew laughed. "We figured the twins would be enough trouble for you today."

Just then, Dewayne and Dewana galloped in from the beach shouting, "Buzz is here—Buzz is here!"

"See what I mean?" Matthew said to Jude in an aside.

Buzz raced in, followed shortly by Penelope who was holding three-year-old Prissy. "The sand was too hot for her feet, so I had to carry her. Boy, she's getting heavy! Buzz, did you wash the sand off before you came in?"

"Dee and Dee, you, too! March right back out there and hose off. All three of you—now!" commanded Polly.

Revel and Vince took a quick tour while the little ones cleaned up. "This is really nice, Jude," Vince exclaimed.

"I like the changes you made, big brother!" Revel gushed.

"I'm afraid I can't take much credit. Muriel and a decorator did most of it, and Penelope was kind enough to oversee the workmen and deliveries. All I did was say, 'Yes, those are nice colors.' And sign the checks."

"I sympathize with you," Matthew said ruefully. "Polly's decided to do our place. Ooouch! I think it would probably be cheaper to buy another house. How did you make out with the exchanges?"

"I don't have exact figures, but about even, I would guess. I got more than I paid for Maple Drive, furnished. But prices are up everywhere now, beachfront especially, so the buy and sell probably balanced out. Maybe I'll come out a little ahead."

"What do you think, Polly?" Matthew asked.

"I know what!" Revel exclaimed. "Matt, why don't you move to Santa Monica? And I'll buy out here! And we'll have an Abavas Compound, just like the Kennedys in Hyannis Port."

"Would a foreigner be allowed inside?" Vince wanted to know.

"We'd have to take a vote!" Revel teased.

The subject of real estate took a back seat when the now-clean-footed young ones reentered.

"Now!" Revel whispered to Vince. He fetched the basket and brought it to Penelope and her children.

"We hope this meets with your approval, Penelope. Because we all have a present for Buzz and Prissy." Revel lifted the tiny thing out of its bed and handed it to Penelope.

"Oh, look, Mommy! It's a puppy! Can we keep it? Please—please?" Buzz pleaded.

"Puppy!" echoed Prissy.

"Of course we can, darlings! How dear of you all! Here, hold—him?" She checked it out. "Yes, him, gently. He's very young, so you must be very careful! Do you understand?"

Buzz nodded solemnly. He cuddled the puppy close. "Tiddlywinks! His name is Tiddlywinks!"

All the children huddled with the pup, Polly said to Penelope, "The twins absolutely adore Tiddlywinks's sister. But where on earth did Buzz come up with that name?"

"I think he heard it on television," Penelope explained. "It's a new fad of the college crowd—I believe they even have intercollegiate meets. I remember playing it as a child."

"Speaking of TV, I want to find out how the Dodgers are doing!" Matthew opened the cabinet doors that concealed the set.

"Oh, why? It's such a beautiful day, we should be outside," Revel said.

"Go ahead! I'll just check out the scene and join you in a minute!"

Before anyone could move away, the image of Marilyn Monroe flashed acoss the screen, followed by shots of a residence surrounded by police. Then an aerial view of a sprawling Santa Monica beach mansion with a mob of people pushing against roughly constructed barriers.

"That's Pat and Peter Lawford's!" Jude exclaimed. "Turn up the sound, Matthew."

"—unofficial time of death was sometime between 11:00 p.m. and 1:00 a.m. No one seems to have any concrete answers about anything. Who found Marilyn Monroe's body? Was it suicide or was there foul play? Was there a note or any form of evidence? Why was there a delay in summoning the authorities? In other words, ladies and gentlemen, we have little information. Mr. Lawford is understandably in seclusion. Miss Monroe was quite close to the Lawfords and to the Kennedy family. Indeed, there have been rumors for some time that Monroe was *very* close to the Kennedy family."

The pall of death settled once again on the group. Not that Marilyn Monroe had been an intimate friend, but she *was* a household name and the thought that such a beautiful, talented, vibrant young person had died renewed their sense of loss.

"That poor girl." Polly sighed.

"What a waste!" exclaimed Matthew.

Buzz had heard enough of the conversation to know someone had died. "Mommy, does that mean that lady there is in heaven with Daddy?" he asked plaintively.

Penelope went to him and hugged him hard. "Y-Yes, sweetheart, that's what it means."

"Does it hurt to go to heaven? 'Cause maybe I could go visit Daddy—I miss him."

Penelope had a tough time handling that one. Jude saw she was about to crumble, so he jumped in. "You see Buzz," Jude said as he reached down and lifted Buzz high in the air, "we all miss your daddy. A lot. And someday we'll see him. But we just can't hop up there on our own, we have to be invited. Daddy is probably looking down on us right now, wondering why we're not in the water on this hot day. What do you say? How about a swim? The dog—I mean Tiddlywinks—needs to rest. I bet he's tired after his trip and meeting you and Prissy."

"Yeah, let's go!" yelled the twins.

"I'll—I'll—be out shortly," Penelope said, taking Prissy's hand. "She should stop by the ladies' room."

Jude nodded. He understood Penelope needed some time alone. Revel and Vince pitched in along with Polly and Matthew.

"Okay, last one in is a rotten egg!" shouted Revel, and she led the pack out the door toward the beach.

"Put puppy to bed!" Prissy insisted. Penelope let her place Tiddlywinks back in the basket. She covered him with her doll's blanket and nestled her head against him. "I love you. Now don't you go away. Don't want no one to go to heaven no more!"

This was the first time Penelope realized how much her children understood. And she was shocked and frightened how much the loss of Wade had affected them. She hadn't allowed herself to believe that they could be that aware, she had underestimated their sensitivity. "Oh, God, please help me to help them," she prayed.

v

53

Santa Monica, California
Wednesday, January 30, 1963

"Thank you for being with me tonight," Penelope said. "All of you have been such a—such a solid base for the three of us. I realized something today. This is the last of the 'firsts.' We have weathered through Priscilla's first birthday without Wade here. Then Wade's birthday. The first wedding anniversary. Buzz's first birthday. My first birthday. The first Thanksgiving, Christmas, and New Year's. And now the ending of the first year since he...left us. Together—and it has been together—we've faced each one of these delicate occasions. I hope now our path becomes a bit smoother, slightly less rocky. I just...wanted you all to know how much you mean to us, how special you are to us, and to tell you your friendship is not taken for granted—it is treasured." Penelope sat down after her little speech, tearful and emotional.

Penelope had asked Jude, Matthew and Polly, Revel and Vince to come for dinner on the anniversary of Wade's burial. They would not have left her alone this night in any case, but she had initiated the invitation. A good sign.

They were very moved by Penelope's simple, but sincere words, and each one of them wished he or she could have done more to ease their friend's pain. But they, knowingly or unknowingly, recognized the fine line that separated assistance from interference. Noah and Willamina had lent their support, too, insisting that no one should even think of coming home for the holidays, that their place was with Penelope and her children.

"Penelope, I hope you can stand this, but it looks as if we also might be invading your territory soon," Polly announced while they were having coffee in the living room afterward. "Matt has convinced me it would be better to buy another house than renovate, and we like the beach a lot—"

Penelope interrupted, "Stand it? I think it would be sensational! The children will love having the twins so close."

"I was joking last summer about an Abavas Compound," Revel exclaimed. "But, I just made an offer on a house about half a mile north of here."

Jude was startled. "Rev, you never said a word."

"I wanted to surprise you, big brother. Believe me, you will be the first to know if it goes through, because I'll need a check from the boys back East. It's so funny, isn't it? I spent most of my teens wanting to get away from family ties, and here I am, right in the middle of them. I must be getting wacko in my old age."

"Some old age!" Vince teased. "You're barely dry behind the ears."

"That'll cost you, old man!" Revel retorted. "I'll think of a particularly grim revenge."

"Uh-oh, Vince, better watch out! Rev is good at that!" Matthew warned. Turning to Penelope, he said, "We wanted to ask you about schools in the area, Penelope. We think we'd like to enroll the twins in private versus public."

"There are several excellent schools to consider. Wade and I looked at all of them. We narrowed it down to Montessori, and John Thomas Dye. John Thomas Dye was our choice—it's a little more conservative, but a somewhat longer drive."

"Do the kids like it?" questioned Polly.

"Jude can answer that. He went to the 'Christmas Carol' night and saw them in action," Penelope replied.

Jude was somewhat flustered. He didn't know why, exactly, but he hadn't mentioned this to anyone. "Ah, well, I'm not too sharp on these kind of things. But yes, I'd have to say that Buzz and Prissy were happy. They seemed to enjoy their friends, and teachers and the program. The place had a nice atmosphere."

When Penelope had asked him if he would mind going with her, he had readily agreed. He would do anything for her, for them. But as the time approached, he had become increasingly apprehensive. He'd worried that outsiders might not understand their relationship, wouldn't know about the "three comrades" and might misconstrue his presence. The last thing he wanted was to give the gossip mongers any fodder.

And there was something else. He was afraid some observant eyes might unmask what he had so scrupulously secreted away over nine years ago. His love for Penelope. Upholding his promise to Wade, and his vow to himself, had put him in constant contact with Penelope. And there were times, recently, when he couldn't stifle his thoughts, couldn't handcuff his imagination. So he would dream that they could build a life together. And then would come the guilt, the judgment. What kind of person would betray his brother, for he felt Wade had been his brother! And then would come more guilt, more blame, because *he* was that kind of person. Hadn't he already seduced one brother's girl? But how could he carry out his mission and *not* be near Penelope? And so the vicious cycle would begin anew.

Sunday, May 5, 1963

"Now, remember, you two, we are guests! You have to be quiet and watch and listen. Next year, maybe you can be in it, too. Promise?"

"Promise, Mommy!"

Polly Abavas was lecturing the twins on the drive to the John Thomas Dye School's traditional May Day celebration.

"We were really fortunate, Matt," she said, turning to her husband. "Penelope told me she found out they rarely accept new students for the second grade. You have to start in nursery class at three, like Prissy and Buzz did. I bet the Pricklers' reference helped a lot."

"That was nice of them," Matthew said. "Well, are you excited? One more month and we'll be in the new place." He leaned over to kiss her.

"Watch where you're going, you devil!" she warned. Nonetheless, Polly moved closer to her husband and put her hand on his leg.

"Be careful! I might have to pull over, kids or no kids!"

"You wouldn't dare!"

He started to turn toward the curb and Polly laughed, and took her hand away. "Okay, okay, you win!"

"I'll collect my prize later," Matthew promised.

"Why are you getting a prize, Daddy? Can I have one, too?" piped Dewayne.

"Mommy and Daddy were only clowning around, sweetheart," Polly explained. "What he meant to say was—" she threw him a see-what-you-did! look "—we all have a prize, with our wonderful new home and your wonderful new school. We're so lucky!"

Dewayne and Dewana nodded, and once more became engrossed in their latest picture book.

Polly spoke in a soft tone. "Honey, since we're moving to a much larger house, and there's plenty of room, maybe—what would you think about adopting again?"

This time, Matthew signaled properly and did stop the car at the curb. He took Polly in his arms. "Do you know how much I love you? And if it's possible, which it isn't, that right now I love you even more? That would make me very happy, my darling Polly."

"Daddy, you're all mushy!" complained Dewayne.

"Are we there yet?" Dewana asked.

"Thank you, Matt! I love you, too!" Polly whispered. "I guess we'd better get this show on the road or we'll be late. We were to meet Penelope and Jude and Revel and Vince before 2:00 p.m. so we could all sit together. Prissy's group is first and we don't want to miss that!"

Matthew guided the station wagon back into the flow of traffic. "How do you think Penelope is managing?"

Polly took her time answering. "Not bad, but I think she needs to get out more, mix with people, develop new interests. Jude, too! He's comfortable when he's with our crowd, and at the studio, I imagine. But he seems so uptight when there are strangers around us."

"Well, when you stop to think about it, Jude has suffered one tragedy after another in the last two years. And I'm sure they rekindled memories of Thelma and Keane. Maybe he just needs time."

"Well, as soon as we're settled, I'm going to go to work on both of them. I'll get them out of their doldrums!" Polly sounded determined.

"I'll put my money on you any day. Here we are. You get out, I'll find a space."

"They were so adorable, all of them!" cooed Revel. "And the audience! I had almost as much fun stargazing. That Kirk Douglas is a real hunk. And Janet Leigh's new husband is *soooo* handsome. And—"

"You are a piece, Rev! You've been in Los Angeles five years this September, you work in this industry and you still are celebrity crazy!" Jude exclaimed, shaking his head in wonderment.

"So what?" defended Polly. "I am, too! I don't think one has to become jaded just because one lives in Los Angeles. I'll be a movie fan forever."

"Me, too!" other voices echoed, in Penelope's lanai, where everyone had collected to cool off after the afternoon's performance.

Jude laughed and threw up his hands in a gesture of surrender. "I didn't mean to stir up a hornet's nest. I give up. You're right. And to tell the truth? Thank God you all are, and I hope there are many more like you out there. Otherwise, we would be out of business!"

"Our business is sure in transition, though," Vince said. "The majors are losing ground to the television networks, and pay TV and cable TV are beginning to erode the foundation of the networks. Would you have ever thought, Jude, that Twentieth Century Fox's back lot would be razed for a shopping center? Century City? What kind of name is that?"

"Hell, no!" Jude declared emphatically. "All of M-G-M's back lots will follow soon, I bet. The fat cats are moving in. We're sitting pretty, however. What stages we don't use for our own product are snapped up immediately for rentals. Independent production companies are springing up like weeds."

"Tell you something else," Matthew offered. "I don't think it will be too long before the Production Code, or should I say the censor's office, will be replaced. Remember how Otto Preminger's *The Moon Is Blue* defied the restraints back in the mid-fifties? I'm just not sure if this is a good or a bad move!"

Penelope and Polly both agreed the Production Code was needed. If you allowed the producers or directors free rein, children would be seeing pornography and violence in everything, they argued.

Revel voted with the "no censor" contingency. "I believe the freedom-of-speech rule applies here. No one is forcing a person to go see a film that they may object to, it's their choice!"

"But you know darn well, Rev, that if young people think it's something they're not supposed to see, they'll want to see it all the more," Penelope rebutted.

"Then don't let them in the theaters!" Revel answered.

"But why make those kinds of pictures at all?" Polly said.

"Because maybe some moviegoers would enjoy more provocative entertainment," Revel concluded.

"Why, Rev," Matthew teased, "I didn't know you were into erotica."

"Oh, buzz off, Matt!" Revel said, exasperated and slightly embarrassed.

Vince broke in. "Change is inevitable, we all know that. And some of it will be for the good and some of it won't, we know that, too. On the plus side, think about the millions of people who were able to see Judy Garland and Barbra Streisand appear together on television. Very few of the viewers would have ever had the opportunity to see either one of these talents live."

"Don't forget Frank Sinatra and Elvis Presley," Jude added. "No doubt about it, the technological advances have been tremendous and will continue to amaze us, I'm sure. But there are definitely troubling signs in other areas. The average feature in 1949 cost about one million. Elizabeth Taylor alone was paid one million dollars to do *Cleopatra*, and the picture itself is rumored to have cost roughly forty-four million to make. That's a sum of money that could actually bury Fox. God knows what the average film will cost in 1969. If expenses keep spiraling upward, companies are bound to go under. And television prices are rising proportionally, too. It's worrisome."

"Vince and I need to ask your advice about something, Jude," Matthew said. "Because of the outstanding importance of television, we were wondering if we should rename Studio Services Inc. to something more all-encompassing?"

Jude considered this for a moment. "Not necessarily. Networks have studios, cable has studios, I think the company's name covers all arenas. Penelope, what do you think? What would Wade say?"

"I believe he would agree." She looked at Jude, surprised yet again, how far his thoughtfulness stretched.

"Well, boys, there you have it! That is, unless you're having problems getting television people to use you."

"It was slow in the beginning because we were identified with the big studios," Vince began, "but it has picked up, and you're right—every medium uses a studio."

"Well, I'm glad we've settled the industry's problems, the morality question and the question of the S.S.I. name...because we have to be on our way," Polly said, standing up. "Look at those two, I should say those four. They were so clean and proper, and now look—a complete mess! But happy! Oh, so happy! Tiddlywinks is wearing them out. They'll be ready for bed tonight."

Revel glanced at her watch. "I have to scoot and finish packing. The movers are coming at eight in the morning and you'd be surprised at how much stuff I have. Can you believe I am actually moving into my own house with my own brand-new furniture. I am beside myself! And I'm going to have a big housewarming party!"

"I wish I could get Revel to cheer up," Vince said dryly. "But in the meantime, thank you for a lovely day."

"Come here, Rev, and give your brother a kiss. Am I forgiven?" Matthew held out his arms.

"For what?" Revel asked. She kissed Matthew and Polly and the twins goodbye.

"Goodbye, everyone. I am so glad you came today," Penelope called after them. She turned back to Jude. "Quite a wonderful batch, Willamina and Noah cooked up," she said fondly. "Are you busy or could you stay for an early dinner? I feel I should at least feed you after a day of putting up with children and parents and Maypoles. Buzz and Prissy were so happy all of you were there!"

"It was wonderful for us, too. And yes, thank you, I would like to stay for dinner."

54

Hailey, Idaho
Saturday, July 13, 1963

The chartered Gulfstream landed smoothly at Hailey Airport. A row of four-wheel-drive vehicles were waiting, one with a driver. Jude jumped out first and turned to assist Prissy, Buzz and Penelope. Then Matthew helped the twins and Polly from the plane. And, finally Vince lifted Revel out, holding her a mite longer than was absolutely necessary.

Jude assumed the role of tour director. "All right now, here's the plan. We will all meet at Mama and Papa's. After a bite of lunch—knowing Mama, it will be many big bites—the Pricklers' caretaker, over there in the red Jeep, will take Penelope and children to the Prickler estate. Matt, why don't you take the blue car for your group? And, of course, you know you're staying at Mama and Papa's. Now—"

"Can Vince and I have the green one?" Revel asked.

"Why not? And you two are staying with me at my place. Okay, let's get the luggage sorted out, guys. What color do I have? Oh, yeah, the white baby."

On the short ride into town, Jude realized with a sting of remorse, it had been two years since he'd been home. When he saw Willamina and Noah waiting on the porch, with the rest of the folks—twelve in all—tears came to his eyes. Jude focused his attention on the others. John and Lila, Ethel and Clyde looked fine, a little older. But who wasn't? It was the young ones, the children, who surprised him. He quickly calculated—my God, John, Jr., was over twenty already. His calculations carried him further back and he suddenly realized that his own son would have been twenty-five in October.

By now, everyone had arrived, and the Abavas clan was busy exchanging hugs and kisses. Jude tried to quiet everyone down as he introduced Penelope and Buzz and Prissy to the rest of his family.

"Mr. and Mrs. Abavas," Penelope said, smiling warmly, "you have been such a part of our lives for so long, it doesn't seem possible that we've never actually met. I feel I know you so well—all of you." She included everyone on the porch with her gaze. Then she leaned closer and circled her arms around Willamina and Noah.

"I be Mama, and he be Papa, because Wade be our son, too," Willamina said, and she and Noah held her tightly and said everything that needed saying with their touch.

"Mommy!" Prissy tugged at Penelope's skirt. "If Daddy is their son, then we have one more Bunka and Ganny, don't we?"

Willamina and Noah were confused. "Bun? Gan?"

Jude chuckled. "That's their way of saying Grandma and Grandpa."

"Oh! Then yes! We be Bu—Bu—we be what you say!" Willamina and Noah took the two by the hand and led them to meet the other grandchildren.

Revel, with Vince, had held back, waiting for Penelope's introduction to be over. Now Revel whistled for attention.

"Mama, Papa, everybody. Please welcome my friend, Matthew and Polly's friend and business partner, and someone who has heard a lot about the family—Vincent Franks!"

Willamina and Noah were flustered. "Oh, Mr. Franks, so sorry, not mean to be inhospitable."

Vince waved their worries away. "I am really happy to meet you. And, like Penelope, I, too, feel I know all of you already."

Noah looked at Vince keenly as they shook hands. This was a nice person. Very understanding person. Very open and honest person.

There was much to talk about at lunch. And Jude was right, it was a marathon of one tasty dish after another. The new home owners had brought Polaroid shots of their spiffy beach houses so everyone in Idaho could get a feel for how the California branch lived.

Idaho was impressed. "Wow!" exclaimed John, Jr. "And the ocean is right in your backyard?" The envy in his voice was apparent to all.

"Yep!" Revel answered. "Why don't you come visit your auntie? You can see there's plenty of room."

"Oh boy! I—" John, Jr., started to say something, but John, Sr., interrupted. "Hold on, don't go getting no fancy ideas, son. We need you here now, and come fall, you go back to school. Maybe in a year or two you can go see them, but not yet." Plainly, John did not intend to lose any more members of the family to heathenish Hollywood.

Polly piped up. "Well, whenever, you know you're all welcome. Jude has room, Rev has room and we have room. So, come on down!"

"Don't forget us!" Penelope added. "We have room, too!"

Willamina was studying Revel's photos. "My baby—this be my baby's own house! Hard to believe." She looked at Polly and Matthew's again. And Jude's. Still shaking her head with amazement.

Jude said softly, "I really wish you and Papa would take a little vacation and stay with one, or all, of us."

She looked up. "We come...one day. You will see...one day."

All the women stood up to start clearing the table, but Willamina stopped them. "Not today. I ask someone to help me. You go get settled, begin to enjoy your time here. We keep pictures awhile?"

"They're yours, Mama and Papa. That's why we brought them," Matthew assured them.

"Jude, could I talk to you a minute?" Revel was making the breakfast coffee the following morning and Jude had just emerged from his bedroom.

"Sure, Rev. Where's Vince?"

"He said he was going for a run."

"Good for him! I should probably start doing that before breakfast, instead of waiting until the afternoon. Sometimes I'm too tired by then. Anyway, what's up?"

"Should I marry Vince?" Revel blurted out.

Jude was caught off guard and fumbled for a reply. "Ah— Rev—I don't know. For starters, the obvious question is—do you love him?"

"I think so. I can't imagine him not being in my life."

"Well, that says a lot. Are you sure you don't want to see other people, though, for a while longer? Play the field before settling down?"

"I've dated a few guys. But it's funny, I get a feeling they're hitting on me because of...you know...the money. They come on so strong, they just seem like phonies to me."

"Well, we all know how Vince has felt about you for a long time, so no worry in that department. I like him a lot, and I like the way he is with you." Jude walked to her and put his arms around her. "But sweetheart, it's your call."

"Oh, I know. I think I just needed to hear what you had to say. I feel so close to you." Revel hugged him.

Jude and Revel were eager to show Penelope and Vince the sights of Sun Valley and the surrounding country. They drove north on Trail Creek Road to Copper Basin in the Pioneer Mountains, where Jude had guided in his early teens. Then they continued northeast, to the Lost River Range, toward the valleys that had fed Noah's sheep so many years before.

"I've never seen anything like this," Vince marveled. "I was born and raised in Los Angeles, and it seems our family was so busy, we never had much time to travel. When you just fly over this land of ours, there is no way you can judge the vastness, or imagine the size, or really see its beauty."

"Mom and Dad and I went to Lake Arrowhead once," Penelope said. "And it was lovely. But we couldn't explore the back country like now. This is magnificent!"

It was more than the scenery that was tugging at Penelope's heart. This was where Wade had spent many happy days, where Wade and Jude had become friends and shared their mutual love of the country, where the mountains and the dales and the rivers had bonded their comradeship. Now this was a very special place for Penelope, too.

"Idaho has so many different faces. If you go east from Sun Valley, you go through what's called the Craters of the Moon, because of the black lava rock," Jude explained. "It's eerie! And, further east, you come to the Idaho side of the Tetons, really spectacular. Remember the movie M-G-M made in the early fifties about the good old U.S.A., *It's A Big Country?* It sure as hell is!"

On the return trip, the group marveled at the terrifying drop that bordered the outside lane of the road. "Hate to make a fast turn and miss on this road!" Vince said, glancing out the window down to the Big Wood River. The mountain was so steep and the river so far below them, it looked like a silver thread.

"Yeah, it's kind of hairy sometimes!" Jude agreed. "And...there are always small slides that leave big rocks on the road."

About halfway down the last long descent toward Sun Valley, there was a scenic turnout, and Penelope asked if they could stop for a photo session.

They were engrossed in the view, the sun sending out a rainbow of colors as, in a leisurely fashion, it began to sink behind the tallest peak. Vince pulled Jude aside. "Is it all right to go behind that tree?" He pointed to a cottonwood that was a couple of yards lower than their spot.

"It looks safe enough. I think I'll join you. Don't turn around, ladies!"

Penelope and Revel laughed and promised. Gingerly, the two men stepped to the tree and relieved themselves. As they started back, a woodpecker dove from the branches, angry at being disturbed. Vince was startled, lost his footing, stumbled and started rolling down the side of the hill. Jude made a lunge for him, but the sudden movement threw him off-balance and he tumbled down behind Vince.

"Keep your arms over your head! Protect against rocks—" Jude yelled.

Over and over they rolled, their bodies bumping against tree trunks, stirring up dirt and leaves, brushing against boulders. About two-thirds of the way to the bottom, they were stopped— with a hard thump—by a large fallen tree. As the noise of their plummet subsided, the screams from Penelope and Revel could be heard above.

When Jude recovered his equilibrium, he checked to see if he was in one piece. His body ached from the abuse, but the only severe pain was in his left wrist.

"Vince, how are you?" Jude asked hoarsely.

Vince had the wind knocked out of him completely and was just coming to his senses. "I—don't—know—yet," he answered weakly. "Ow—it hurts—when I breathe." He spoke in short staccato spurts, so he didn't have to take deep breaths.

"Probably bruised your ribs. Don't talk. Let me move your limbs."

Vince winced when Jude probed his friend's right leg. "Well, I'm not sure, you could have a broken leg or ankle. Keep it immobile. I don't want to fool around and make it worse, just in case."

Penelope and Revel were still shrieking bloody murder.

"Penelope! Revel! We're all right! Stop hollering and listen to me! Can you hear me?"

"Faintly, but yes!" Penelope said shakily, straining forward to see him.

"Good! Now, just be calm. Everything is going to be just fine—understand?"

"Y-yes." The women didn't sound too confident.

"First! Get all the jackets from the car and toss them down as far as you can. Can you see us?"

"No!"

"Throw them in the direction of my voice, then. Put the flashlight from the glove compartment in a pocket. And the canteen of water in another."

Penelope and Revel rushed to obey. They tied the sleeves of each coat together to make a tighter package and protect what was inside. There was some fruit left from their picnic lunch, so they added that to other pockets.

"Okay!" they called.

"Fire away! As far as you can!"

They heaved with all their might. Nothing reached Jude and Vince, but Jude thought they were close enough that he could crawl and retrieve them.

"Now! Revel should drive, since she knows the road better. I want you two to carefully—I repeat *carefully*—go back to town, and call Matt. He'll know exactly what to do, and when he's ready, lead him back here."

"Can't I stay here, Jude?" Penelope pleaded. "I don't want to leave you alone. Please!"

"Penelope, you can't stand out in the road by yourself. It's going to get cold as soon as dark comes, and it's too dangerous—you'd be a sitting duck for cars or animals. No! You'll be back in an hour or so, anyway."

Jude knew it would take longer, but he couldn't allow her to stay.

"Why isn't Vince talking?" Revel demanded to know, almost afraid of the answer.

"Ah...well, honey, he may have hurt a rib. I told him to keep quiet."

"Are you sure that's it?" Revel was skeptical and scared. Because she now knew without a doubt that she would just up and die if anything happened to Vince.

"Yes! Now, will you go?"

Jude couldn't see their faces to understand how upset both women were. Or hear Penelope say almost under her breath, "Dear God, please don't let me lose someone else I love so much."

As soon as he heard the car pull away, Jude cautiously wormed his way toward the bundles. He could only use his right arm to climb, and as he pulled himself upward, his whole right side grated against the pebbles and underbrush, aggravating his already bruised body. Fortunately, the stuff was nearer than he'd thought. Probably rolled a bit after it landed.

Jude wrapped the jackets around Vince and then himself. They had some water and the fruit and settled down to wait.

"I won't use the flashlight until we hear them come. Never know how fresh the batteries are. Does the darkness bother you?"

Vince shrugged and muttered, "Doesn't thrill me, but it's okay, I guess. Not much choice. Hey, hardly hurts if I whisper."

"Good!"

"Are you all right? You never said how you fared."

Jude leaned back against a tree, and grinned. "I've been better. But yeah, I'm fine. Sore as hell and my wrist is twisted or something, but that's nothing. We are two lucky hombres. Revel could have been a widow before she was a wife." Jude slapped his head with his good hand. "The fall must have knocked out what sense I had. I don't know why I said that."

"Well, it isn't exactly a secret how much and how long I've loved Revel. So it was a natural crack for you to make. However, if what you said is an indication of her feelings for me, I'd be the happiest guy alive."

"Hold it, Vince! I don't know anything for sure. Honest! We talked a bit. But that's all."

"We'll leave it as a play on words then," Vince said, smiling happily, because he knew Jude couldn't see his face.

They were thoughtful for a while. Vince spoke again. "Suppose, just suppose, Revel and I did end up together. The only worry I have is that damn money she inherited. Forgive me, Jude, but it didn't bring Madge much joy. I wouldn't want it to interfere or come between Revel and me."

Jude sighed. He would rather not think about matters relating to Madge. But sometimes, like now, he was forced to. "Revel is not Madge. And I don't believe the money was Madge's problem anyway. Rest assured, Revel is not driven by the dough. Think of it as a nice security blanket for the two of you. That is, if it should be you two. Oh, hell, you know what I mean!"

"Don't make me laugh—it'll hurt again! Yes, I know what you mean."

Penelope and Revel screeched to a stop at the Prickler ranch—Revel had not heeded Jude's advice about driving slowly—and called Matthew in Hailey. He was alarmed, to be sure, but not panicked. "Easy, Rev, easy! I'll alert everyone and we'll be at the ranch as soon as we can. I won't even come in, I'll just honk. What? No, don't wait in the car—it's going to take me a little while. Just relax, will you?"

Matthew called the forest service and an ambulance while Noah called the police and John. Willamina and Polly gathered blankets, ropes, gloves and anything else they thought might be useful. Matthew, Noah and John led the caravan to Penelope and Revel who *were* in the car and ready to lead the way.

Vince was shivering. "You were right, Jude, it sure does get cold quick!"

Jude was concerned that Vince might be going into shock. He took a coat from his legs and put it over Vince. "Try not to think about it. Let's talk about something else. Like how I can't keep my big mouth shut."

"How about I open my big mouth? Rev and I think you should get married."

"Are you *crazy?*"

"No, just delirious! Seriously, we think you should marry Penelope."

Before that statement could completely traumatize Jude, a parade of headlights appeared.

"They're here!" Jude said excitedly, grateful to be spared any more of this conversation. He flicked on their flashlight.

"There they are!" Matthew exclaimed. "Jesus, they really traveled. Jude! Can you manage a mountain-climbing belt and cable? With someone helping you?"

"I think I can, but Vince can't. His leg is hurt!"

The rescuers conferred. It was decided that the two forest rangers and Matthew would rappel down the slope to the pair, the rangers bringing a portable stretcher and Matthew an extra harness and anchored rope for Jude. The four lines were attached to pulley devices, so the group on top were in control. The descent was relatively simple, going up would be tricky.

"Boy, are we glad to see you!" Jude said when the three reached them.

"Ditto," Vince echoed weakly.

One of the rangers checked out the battered men and announced, "You are a mess!" He took a flask out of his pocket. "Here, take a swig of this, that'll warm you up."

They gently wrapped Vince in blankets and strapped him to the stretcher. Vince moaned in pain when they lifted him.

"Careful of that right leg, and his ribs!" Jude warned. The gloved rangers each grabbed an end, and Matthew tied their hands to the handles so there was no danger of them letting go.

"Okay, start pulling them—slowly. Slowly!" hollered Matthew. "Have a good ride, Vince, and don't move!"

"Don't worry. See ya."

Matthew put blankets around Jude. "We'll have to wait. They need all the manpower to haul those two guys and the stretcher."

The powerful searchlights above were trained on the ascending men, and anxious eyes watched as they made the painstaking journey upward. Noah and John were on one apparatus, the two policemen on the other. Intensely and in sync, they turned the wheels, smoothly, so as not to throw the carriers off-balance. Inch by inch, foot by foot, they progressed. Until, at last, they reached the top and safety.

Revel beat the medics to Vince's side, crying wildly. "Oh, I was so scared! I thought I would never have a chance to tell you—"

The doctor interrupted. "You can tell him later, miss. Let me take a look and let's get the other one up here, pronto, so we can get them both to the hospital."

Vince squeezed Revel's hand weakly and, barely audible, whispered, "Can you believe it took a minute to fall down, and sixty... to get back up? I'm such a klutz. Sorry honey."

Now it was Jude's and Matthew's turn to come up. Jude could walk, so this was a simpler procedure, but still not a piece of cake. Matthew supported Jude's left side, to protect the injured wrist, and as the wheels turned, they wound their precarious way to the summit.

Noah and John and Penelope rushed to Jude. "Thank God!" "Where are you hurt?" "Are you cold?"

Again the doctor interrupted, "Put this man in the ambulance immediately! Later with the questions! We'll see you all at the hospital." With that order, he hopped into the ambulance himself and, siren wailing, red lights flashing, Jude and Vince were whisked away.

Revel and Penelope stood numbly, staring after the disappearing vehicle. Matthew spoke to them kindly, "He's right. They're in the proper hands now." Then he thanked everyone profusely for their incredible and prompt assistance, and promised to fill out any needed reports tomorrow.

"I think I better drive the ladies, Papa. We'll meet you and John at the hospital."

Hailey, Idaho
Friday, July 19, 1963

Jude gazed at the memorial markers solemnly. Never would he leave Idaho without seeing Thelma and Keane. But he hadn't come tonight with the torturous thoughts of anguish and remorse that he'd carried with him on past visits. He came to express, again, his undying love for them. And to talk to them, maybe ask for their guidance and direction.

"Thelma, I cling to the hope you can hear me, that's why I like talking out loud here. If you're wondering why I look like I just went a couple of rounds with Sugar Ray Robinson, it's because Vince—that's Revel's new boyfriend—Vince Franks and I took a bad fall. He got the worst of it—I just broke my wrist and got scratched up. But he broke his leg and a couple of ribs, poor guy.''

Jude sat down with difficulty; he was still stiff and tender. ''I guess you can tell something is bothering me. I don't know what to do about it. It's kind of hard to explain. You see, when Penelope—that's my friend Wade's wife—first came into our lives, it was the three of us, as buddies. And, after a while, I found myself falling in love with her. I just wanted you to know she's our kind of people, like Wade. Well, before I could say anything to her, Wade declared his love for her, so naturally I backed off. They married, and then, eventually, there was my fiasco with Madge. Wade and Penelope were always my support system through everything.

''When he became ill—oh, honey, he was so brave and strong and caring. Before he died, he asked me to watch over Penelope and the children. And I have, but it's become more complicated. I love them. And because I spend so much time with them, it's hard to hide my feelings. Vince even said he thought me and Penelope should get married, so now I'm wondering how many other people are noticing and what they are saying. Maybe my presence is preventing her from seeing others, I want to do what's right, I just don't know.''

Jude hugged his knees with his good arm and looked upward—so many loved ones there. He took a deep breath and exhaled slowly, allowing a little of the worry to escape into the air.

''See, I'm afraid someone will think that, well, that I'm betraying Wade's memory. I'd die if anyone, especially Penelope, thought that! You know, I've never mentioned this to her. Do you think I should? Should I ask her if I'm interfering with a social life she could be having? Yeah, that's what I should do. She'd level with me.''

He glanced up again and shook his head in amazement.

''I can't get over it, you never fail to make me think clearer. Thank you.''

Jude stood up and softly kissed his fingers and touched the markers.

Saturday morning, the group met in Vince's hospital room. Jude had been released after two days, but Vince was there until Monday and wouldn't be able to travel until the next Saturday.

Revel was going to stay with him; the rest were heading home in an hour.

"Don't worry, Vince," Matthew was assuring his partner. "We can manage for a week. Not that you and Rev won't be missed, but we can handle it."

Polly laughed. "I'll probably have to go in and bail him out but—" she heaved a martyred sigh "—I've done *that* before."

Matthew gave her bottom a swap. "She lies, you know, not a word of truth in her."

"I'll take care of Gigi for you, Rev, while Polly's taking care of Matt," Penelope offered.

"Oh, thank you, Penelope," Revel said gratefully.

"I don't know who I'll be taking care of," Jude broke in, "but I do know we'd best be off or the plane will leave without us! Sorry your trip ended this way, Vince. At least you get another week of R and R. Rev, just give the key to the housekeeper when you go, she'll take care of everything."

"I really appreciate all your help and thoughtfulness," Vince said, raising himself as much as possible. "I apologize for putting a damper on our holiday. But I still had a wonderful time!"

"Don't give it another thought. You and Jude just added a little drama," Polly said. "Papa and John and the rest will be by to see you. And Mama doesn't trust the hospital food or Revel's cooking, so she will be bringing you two dinners each night. Lucky you!"

Goodbyes and embraces were exchanged and the group left. The three cars stopped in Hailey to bid farewell to Noah and Willamina, and then continued to the airport.

Penelope looked long and hard out the window of the airplane and said softly, audibly, but to no one in particular, "Now when I fly over this country, I'll really know what's down there. And know about the people who live there. This has been such an important time for me, such a meaningful time."

Penelope, Buzz, Priscilla, the nanny and an equally excited Jude checked into the Disneyland Hotel the weekend of August 10. As soon as they were registered, Penelope, Jude and the children headed to the monorail and to the park. The nanny was left behind to unpack.

"Wow, it's fast." Buzz pressed his face against the window as the electric train whizzed along. A special representative met them when they disembarked, a VIP arrangement courtesy of the studio.

"The Matterhorn. The Matterhorn!" Buzz insisted.

The nice young girl who was their guide smiled. "He's very normal—that's usually the first request," she said. She led them to the front of the line and they boarded the next car. Jude held Priscilla, who was already frightened, and Penelope sat in the front seat with Buzz, whose eyes were blazing with excitement. They raced through the caverns of the "snow"-covered mountain, chugged to the highest peak and then plunged downward, defying the law of gravity. Buzz was yelling his approval, Penelope and Priscilla were screaming and Jude was hanging on to his charge for dear life.

"Again! Again!" Buzz chanted as they dizzily made their way out.

"Tomorrow, Buzz, tomorrow! There's so much more to see!" Jude was gentle, but firm. And Buzz had no problem with that. He was on to his next thought in a flash. "Pirates! Priates of the—of the—" He was stuck.

"Pirates of the Caribbean," the guide finished for him.

"Yeah, that's it!" Buzz agreed.

The Pirates of the Caribbean was another thriller ride, with figures lurching toward the passengers, huge swords in their "hands," ships "firing" on the intruders, ending in another steep slide into water. Buzz was ecstatic. Priscilla hung close to Jude.

"How about a ride through It's A Small World," their hostess suggested. "Something charming and a bit quieter."

Penelope and Jude traded looks of relief. From the captivating It's A Small World, they went for one more ride before lunch. Priscilla chose the twirling teacups, somewhat tamer, but still challenging enough for Buzz. In the afternoon, they covered Tom Sawyer's Island, the Jungle Cruise, the Swiss Family Robinson's Tree House, and ended with Mr. Toad's Wild Ride.

"This place is absolutely amazing," Penelope marveled on the train ride back to the hotel. "How can they come up with such concepts, not to mention the engineering and execution?"

Jude was equally impressed. "Disney is a genius! What imagination—what vision!"

"I don't think these two are going to be up to going out for dinner. Look at them, they're exhausted," Penelope said quietly to Jude.

"Why don't you order a bite for them in your suite, and when they're ready for bed, give me a call and I'll come say good-night and take you downstairs? I'll make a reservation. Would eight be safe?"

"That's perfect!"

The dining room was designed for the grown-up crowd—elegant, dimly lit, offering a fine cuisine. Penelope and Jude relaxed over cocktails and then ordered, Jude asking for the wine list, as well. When all was done, they leaned back contentedly, enjoying the calm.

"I haven't felt this peaceful—well, in a long time," she said, almost with wonder. "But while I think of it, was today's activity and carrying Prissy hard on your wrist?"

"Hell, no! I can't feel a thing through this dumb cast, except that it's driving me nuts. One more week! At least today I forgot about it. So, no. And I'm glad you're feeling comfortable."

Jude debated. Was this the time to talk to Penelope? "You know, Penelope, I had a couple of thoughts, too," he began, deciding it was the time to forge ahead. "One, you're so young and beautiful, did you ever entertain the idea of returning to work?"

She didn't hesitate a second with her reply. "Absolutely not! I want to be a full-time mother, not part-time. And later, when the kids are grown, I can find plenty of activities to keep me occupied. There's an abundance of worthwhile causes, both civic and charitable. And, who knows? I've always wanted to write, I may become a writer! But I thank you for your kind words."

She sipped from her drink and then asked, "You said a couple of thoughts, what was the other?"

Now Jude *did* hesitate; he needed to form his words carefully. "Well, the second is partially related to the first. I mean—I just thought that—on the set you could, you know, meet new people..." His voice dwindled.

The waiter's presence halted the discussion. The man displayed the bottle for Jude's approval and then poured a bit of the wine into a glass for Jude to sample.

"That's fine."

When they were once again alone, Penelope looked at Jude with some confusion. "Why is it so necessary for me to meet new people?"

"It's not! That is, it's not necessary, it just might be fun for you." Jude was frustrated. Why was he phrasing this so awkwardly?

She studied him for a moment. "What is it, Jude? You're saying something else, aren't you?"

"No! Well, in a way, I guess—yes." He identified the source of his floundering. He didn't really want her to see other men. Jude forced himself to go on with it. "I'm worried that my...so obvious visibility with you might obstruct you from making new friends. Especially male friends. Me—my family—we've sort of monopolized your time. Perhaps you need to branch out, see different people, and not just us."

Penelope sat quietly. Finally she said, "Of course! How selfish I've been! I have not allowed you any privacy at all, have I? We all fit in so naturally, I just didn't stop to think. Of course you should have more freedom. Why, you've been at our side since that luncheon in August two years ago."

"Wait a minute!" Jude burst out. "You've got it all wrong! It's not me—it's *you* I'm concerned about. I'm afraid I'm in the way, preventing another man from getting to know you and the kids. Hell, if I had my way, I'd never leave. I mean, well, I just want you to have a full life, that's all."

Penelope gazed at him with an unidentifiable look in those huge brown eyes, and replied softly, "Please don't be troubled, Jude. I have as full a life as I want right now. Maybe what we both should do is get out a little more, not be so insulated, socialize a bit. I think I've been so focused on the children that I've forgotten an adult's needs. Like tonight. It's so pleasant having dinner alone, for a change, away from the house. I believe Wade would be disappointed if I—and definitely you—become grouchy old stick-in-the-muds, don't you?"

55

Santa Monica, California
Saturday, August 17, 1963

"Gather round everybody, I'm going to make a speech!" Revel announced from her perch atop a dining room chair. A murmur of anticipation went through the crowd attending her housewarming party.

"First, welcome to my new home! I should say *our* new home, because, second, Vince and I are engaged!"

Words of approval filled the air and a few cheers echoed loudly.

"We spoke to Mama and Papa, and they are very happy. And we called Vince's parents, who are on vacation in Europe, and they seemed pleased, too. Naturally, what we didn't tell them was that we are going to live together for a year to see if it works before we get married. I mean, he might not like the way I squeeze my toothpaste tube or something. Of course, he hasn't complained so far."

Some chuckles and ohs on that tidbit.

"So we're bringing out the heavy artillery—champagne!"

The waiters circulated with trays of glasses and when all were served, Vince rose from his seat to speak. "I couldn't join Revel on that chair—" he waved one crutch "—for obvious reasons. But I can toast my bride-to-be. I hope I pass the test of time, my darling Revel, because I love you so very much, and I will be the happiest man on earth next August if you become my wife." He raised his glass to Revel and drank, along with the guests.

Jude was not very surprised, but he was well pleased. Penelope was misty-eyed and equally joyous. Matthew and Polly *were* surprised, so they really let out a war whoop.

Revel and Vince were surrounded by well-wishers. The family waited until the crowd thinned out around them, and then made their way to congratulate the couple.

"It didn't take you long to make up your mind," Jude whispered as he hugged Revel.

"If you two hadn't fallen down a mountain, it would have taken longer," she teased.

After extending the happy couple their congratulations, Jude and Penelope wandered throughout the house. "She did a wonderful job decorating," Penelope noted. "It reflects her personality beautifully. Young, vital, attractive, joyful! And the colors are a perfect background for her auburn hair, the greens and blues and yellows against the cream. Stunning!"

"I think so, too," he concurred. He took a deep breath. "You know what you said last week in the restaurant? Well, I received an invitation Friday to the charity premiere of *Tom Jones*. It's in October. Would you—ah—would you like to go?"

"I'd love to!" she replied quickly. "That sounds like fun. I've heard wonderful comments about the picture, and Albert Finney is a favorite of mine. Is it black-tie?"

"Afraid so."

"Good! That will be festive!"

Polly and Matthew sauntered by. "How about our little sister?" Matthew asked, shaking his head. "Could you imagine Mama's face if *we* had said anything like that?"

"Times are changing," Penelope said. "God knows what will be acceptable by the time Buzz and Prissy are Revel's age."

Polly laughed. "They'll probably have children before they get married—*if* they get married at all! Sometimes that can work to someone else's benefit, however."

Jude looked at Polly. "Now, why are you looking like the cat who ate the canary? You have that smug smile that says, 'I know something you don't!' "

"I have to tell someone or I'll burst!" Polly cried. "The adoption lawyer called yesterday and thinks he's found the perfect young girl. She's a college student, nice Catholic family. The boy wants to marry her, but she isn't ready, wants to go for her master's degree. But she doesn't want an abortion, she'll carry the baby to term. She just wants to be sure of a proper home and she needs to have her expenses paid. Isn't that wonderful?"

"Honey, don't get all worked up," Matthew warned. "Wait until it's settled—you know how people can change their minds."

"It *is* great news, Polly. But Matt's right—you don't want to be disappointed if this girl decides to keep the child," Jude advised.

"I don't believe she will," Polly said stubbornly, her tone bordering on agitation. "The attorney was impressed with her levelheaded attitude. I just know she won't be wishy-washy!"

The night of the *Tom Jones* premiere was a perfect fall evening, not too hot and not too cold. Penelope wore a fitted pale lavender satin gown with spaghetti straps. A diagonal pattern of hand-sewn beads went from the right top to the left hem. The matching short-sleeved coat swung loosely and full, framing her silhouette. Her long ash blond hair was held back by a lavender satin headband, sprinkled with the identical beads on her dress. A glow of excitement radiated from her face. She was a beautiful vision indeed. And Jude, at forty-four, looked very handsome in his tuxedo. His tall frame remained strong and trim, his rugged good looks had only improved with age.

When Penelope and Jude alighted from the limousine, a hush fell over the fans in the bleachers and behind the ropes. The photographers, media people, guests reacted, as well. This was the first real public appearance Penelope Pope Colby had made since Wade's death. *The Wade Colby Show* had been off the air for four years, however the reruns were extremely popular. And Wade had done a couple of television movies before his sickness, so his visibility had never diminished. These loyal followers had not been at the services or paid visits to the house, had not had a chance to say goodbye or express their devotion, so this was their moment. As one, they stood and cheered for Penelope, cried out her name, cried out their love for her and their lost hero. Penelope cried, too, as she moved along the guardrails to shake the outstretched hands, reaching as far as she was able into the wooden tiers, touching as many as she could, thanking them, showing her appreciation.

The photographers were scrambling all over themselves to capture this moment on film. Jude forgot he was uncomfortable in the spotlight, and stayed right by Penelope's side; the enthusiasts knew him as Wade's partner and friend, and wanted him to participate, as well.

When Penelope and Jude finally made their way into the theater lobby, they found themselves at the center of more personal attention—from their chums and colleagues. Wade, and then Jude, and then Penelope, were beloved in the Hollywood community and everyone was delighted to see these two friends out in public again. They knew it was a healthy sign, and they crowded around the two, eager to show their joy at seeing them.

The evening was a gigantic success. Penelope had been right. Both had needed to be entertained and to mix with their peers. Neither would enjoy this on a daily basis, but it had been so long since they'd felt unburdened that this was most welcome.

She leaned back on the cushion of the limousine. "Oh, what a good movie! What a good time! Weren't those people absolutely dear? And sweet? And wonderful?" She paused. "Do you have an early appointment tomorrow?" Penelope asked suddenly.

"Not too bad. Why, would you like to have a nightcap?"

"Yes!"

"So would I! Driver, please stop at the Beverly Hills Hotel. We'll catch the late action at the Polo Lounge."

56

Children's Hospital, Los Angeles, California
Friday, November 22, 1963

Penelope paced back and forth in the hospital room, waiting for the pediatric surgeon to report the completion of the tonsillectomies. Jude was sitting, hoping to calm her by presenting outward tranquillity.

"I know it's nothing serious," Penelope said to the walls and to Jude and to herself. "I know as long as Buzz had to have it done, it made sense to do Prissy, too. I know all that. What I don't know is why we have stupid tonsils in the first place! They serve no purpose and just get infected, and cause little ones to get sick and mothers to worry! God, I hate hospitals!"

Jude understood her lashing out at—well—anything. He wasn't thrilled about being in a hospital room again, either. His eyes surveyed the room—two maneuverable beds with side guards, two television sets mounted high on the wall, two armchairs, two steel bed stands, two sterile movable tables for the patients, a closet, an antiseptic bathroom—hospital rooms all looked the same didn't they? Whatever city. Whatever country. Bland, faceless, anonymous. And threatening. Frightening.

Just then, the family pediatrician made his appearance. "The surgery is finished and the children are both fine, absolutely nothing to worry about, they'll be coming down in about twenty minutes. As we discussed, they will stay here for today and can go home tomorrow. Their throats will be a little sore, but they'll have ice packs around their necks, and we're putting them on baby aspirin and an antibiotic. And don't forget, they can have all the ice cream they can eat! I'll give you the instructions and medications when I discharge them tomorrow. Were you planning to spend the night, Mrs. Colby?''

''Of course!''

''I'm afraid we don't have an adjoining room available, but I could have a cot brought in for you.''

''That won't be necessary, the chair will be fine. Perhaps a blanket?''

''The nurse will see to everything. There is—'' He stopped.

''Yes?''

''No, ah, I had best be off now. I'll come by in a while.''

''Thank you, Doctor.''

''I think I'll call the office before they get here,'' Jude said as he crossed to the phone and dialed. ''Muriel? Didn't sound like you! Is everything okay?—*What?*—When?—My God, the world's gone mad!''

''What's wrong? What happened?'' Penelope cried.

Jude's face was ashen when he looked at her. ''The president has been shot! In Dallas! Turn on the television! Muriel—Muriel! Calm down. Why don't you go home? No work will be done today by anyone, I guarantee you. I'll talk to you later. Drive carefully, hear me?''

Penelope and Jude stood, mesmerized by the television set, hypnotized like the intended victim of a cobra, as the networks pieced together the events around the shooting. Constant news bulletins from the Dallas hospital disrupted the telecast, but there was still no news as to the president's condition.

A few minutes later, Buzz and Prissy were wheeled in the room by their nurses. Immediately, Penelope turned off the set; the children didn't need to see violence today. She tried to put on a normal face.

''Mommy, Uncle Jude, they made me go to sleep right after I just wakened up!'' complained Prissy softly.

''That's what happens when you have an operation, you ninny!'' quietly explained worldly-wise seven-year-old Buzz. ''Do I have to keep this dumb thing around my neck?''

The nurse answered, ''Yes, you do, Mr. Tough Guy!'' And to the adults, ''Don't be alarmed if they seem to need to sleep. Even though they had small amounts of the anesthetic, children are more strongly affected.'' As the nurses settled Prissy and Buzz into their beds, one whispered, ''Look! They're already nodding off. Your private nurse is at the desk, I'll send her in straight away. You could go to the waiting room and have some coffee, if you wish. She'll call you.''

Penelope and Jude decided to follow her advice. On the way, they were stopped by the pediatrician who motioned them into an empty room.

"I'm sorry, Mrs. Colby, Mr. Abavas. I hesitated before, wanting to say something, but fearful of distressing you. But I know now I must. The drug used is sometimes called truth serum, because people tend to blurt out hidden thoughts while under its influence. Both Buzz and Prissy at one time or another called for—'Mommy.' But they also cried for 'Daddy.'''
He broke off; Penelope had started to cry softly.

Jude put his arm around Penelope and said, "I guess they miss not having their daddy more than we realized."

Penelope sighed. "I'm grateful you told me, Doctor. I—I just don't know—what to do."

"I realize how difficult it has been for you, Mrs. Colby, having to raise them alone. Even with faithful and caring friends, the brunt of the responsibility still falls on you. You're a wonderful mother, and they're going to be just fine. Now that we both know what's in their hearts, I'm confident we will be able to work this out. It just takes time." He glanced at his watch. "And speaking of time, I really do have to run. It's going to be fine, Mrs. Colby, please believe me. In a way, the tonsillectomies proved a blessing. Better we are aware that this need has not disappeared so we can help them. Now, Mr. Abavas, why don't you take Mrs. Colby to get a Coke, or something?"

"We were on our way to the waiting room," Jude explained.

"Good. I'll see you tomorrow."

Penelope and Jude followed the doctor out. Their nerves were frayed to the breaking point again. How many challenges could they handle in one day? When they walked into the vestibule, the set was on and the people present were sitting, numbly, staring at it in shocked silence.

"Here is a bulletin from CBS News." Walter Cronkite, looking stricken, came into view. Jude instinctively reached for Penelope in an attempt to shield her, protect her from what they might hear next.

"President Kennedy died at 1:00 p.m. central time in Dallas."

There was a collective intake of breath. No one in that room, or anywhere in the world, would ever forget where they were the fateful moment they had learned of the president's death.

Not a word was spoken. It was as if there was a conspiracy of denial. If they didn't talk, then they didn't have to accept the news, therefore it could not be true. Walter Cronkite had to be speaking of someone else, not President Kennedy. Not the young, charismatic, brilliant, caring, humorous, beloved, loving President Kennedy!

Penelope buried her face in Jude's chest, and they just rocked back and forth, not willing to break this spell of silence. These were complete strangers in the room, but at this moment there' was an unbreakable bond among them.

The private nurse found them in that same mode of muteness, spiritlessly watching the television—not that they could make sense of the images and words projected.

"The children are awake now, Mrs. Colby," the nurse whispered.

Penelope and Jude jumped, as if they were snapped out of a trance. They walked toward the children's room, hastily striving to assume a happy mask.

"Why aren't you at work, Uncle Jude?" Buzz wanted to know.

"Well, I thought I'd take the day off and sort of hang out with you and your mom. After all, it isn't every day one gets one's tonsils out, you know."

"Goodie!" Prissy said. "Can we play games now?"

"As long as they're not talking games," Penelope warned. "Would you like some ice cream first?"

"Chocolate pwease." Prissy's choice.

"Vanilla—uh—please! Why don't we turn on TV? Maybe there's a football game on," Buzz suggested.

Jude intervened. "Not until tomorrow, Buzz. It's only Friday, and don't you remember? College football is on Saturdays and pro games on Sunday." Then he leaned over and, in an undertone of confidentiality, "Unless you want to watch some kid cartoons!"

"Yuk!" was Buzz's response.

"Maybe you and Uncle Jude could play checkers, and I'll read the new book to Prissy," Penelope said.

Somehow, they managed to get through the afternoon and evening until both little ones were ready to go to sleep for the night. During their prayers, Prissy said, "God bless Mommy, God bless Daddy, God bless Daddy Jude, God—"

"*Uncle* Jude, you ninny, not Daddy Jude!" corrected Buzz.

"Oh, God bless Mommy, God bless Daddy, God bless Uncle Jude—" And soon after, the two drifted off.

Penelope and Jude slipped out to grab a bite at the hospital cafeteria. As they were forcing down some food, Penelope suddenly dropped her fork and lifted her hand to her mouth to smother a scream.

Alarmed, Jude started to get up, but she waved him away. "I'm—I'm okay. It's just—just that the details, the similarities—it's incredible..." She trailed off, still catching her breath.

Jude waited, but not patiently. He was concerned, confused.

"I'm sorry. Only now it is sinking in—what we had heard on TV, I mean. Do you realize that—that the president was forty-six and Wade—Wade was forty-eight? And their oldest child, Caroline, is five and a half, and Buzz was five and a half? And their youngest, John, is almost three, and Prissy was close to three. It's—it's uncanny."

Jude hadn't put that together yet, and she was right—the parallels were startling. The loss of each was such a staggering blow. And today's disaster meant sharing the pain of bereavement again. With heavy hearts they returned to the prisonlike atmosphere of the waiting room. They were alone and holding hands for support; they sat on the sofa, magnetized spectators, as the tragic chronicle of events unfolded before them.

Fatigue finally prevailed. Penelope's head drooped on Jude's shoulder. Gently, he eased himself away, and slid a cushion under her. He turned off the television, tiptoed out, walked to the children's room, told the night nurse where they were and tracked down two blankets. Tenderly, he covered Penelope and settled near, close if she should wake. But sleep would not come for Jude. Sleep that would mercifully block out the happenings of this day—the president's death, the children's need of a father, his own desire to fulfill that role.

Jude watched Penelope a while longer, and just before he left for his house, Penelope awoke, took his hand and looked into his eyes. "A few months ago, you suggested that perhaps I would want to go back to work, to meet new people, to make new friends. What you don't seem to understand is, how could I possibly have gone through the past week, the past year, the past two and a half years with anyone else but you? You must know how special you are to me. It's difficult to say thank you each day, because your giving is endless. But, I don't want to appear that I'm taking your kindness for granted. So every now and then—like now—I have to remind you that I am aware of how much you do, how much support you offer, how much—well— of everything you bring to us. And to refresh your memory, to tell you how much we love you.''

Penelope stretched up and kissed him gently on the lips. ''Good night,'' she whispered softly.

Jude rode home in a daze. Such shivers had gone through his body when her lips had touched his, he was surprised he hadn't given her an electric shock. It had taken every ounce of resolve he possessed not to smother her in his arms and unleash the passion held prisoner for so long. Many times he had fought off the temptation to allow his caring for her to spill over into de- sire. But tonight was the most difficult. Because there was a trace, just a trace, from her kiss and touch, of something else. Or was he reading more into a simple declaration of her gratitude? One of these days he was going to have to find out.

It was Friday, November 29, a week after the president's death. A week of unparalleled drama. The presumed slayer, Lee Harvey Oswald, attempted to hide in a movie theater, and another fa- tality resulted. Police Officer Tibbett was killed in the line of duty. Vice President Lyndon B. Johnson—while a stricken Jac- queline Kennedy, still in her blood-spattered suit, looked sto- ically on—took the oath of office aboard Air Force One before leaving for Washington with the body of the slain president. The television audience saw a local Dallas man, Jack Ruby, level his gun at the accused assassin and fire the shot that killed Oswald. The world grieved as it watched the mournful Kennedy family, and an unprecedented number of reigning monarchs and heads of state, follow the horse-drawn casket to St. Matthew's Cathe- dral in Washington, D.C. And who would ever forget the pic- ture in *Life* magazine of three-year-old John Fitzgerald Kennedy, Jr., saluting his father's coffin.

Penelope wept. Jude wept. Mankind wept.

57

Santa Monica, California
Monday, February 3, 1964

"Penelope, I need your help!" cried a frantic Polly into the telephone.

"What is it, Polly? What can I do?"

"Gloria—Gloria is the young girl who's having our baby—the one we're going to adopt—"

"Relax, honey, take it easy," Penelope urged.

Polly swallowed and tried again. "Gloria was due around the middle of March. But her mother just called and the baby came early—a boy—and he only weighs four and a half pounds and he's in an incubator and I want to go and see him, but I'm so afraid—"

"Go! You must! I'll pick up the twins from school and they can stay here. What about Matt?"

"He's out of the office. I told his secretary. I'll call again just before I leave. I'm on a one o'clock flight."

"To where?"

"Oh, I forgot, to Chicago."

"Do you need a ride to the airport?"

"No, thanks. Ophelia can drop me off, since you're taking the little ones. Oh, dear, I hope they won't be upset. I started preparing them a little bit for the baby."

"Not to worry, Polly. When your two get with my two, I really don't think they miss anyone very much. If Matt doesn't join you in Chicago, he can have dinner here, even stay here if he wants. And I'll tell Rev and Vince and Jude. Jude is coming over tonight, actually. So nothing to fret about on this front."

"Oh, thank you, Penelope. If I had a sister, I'd want her to be you!"

"That makes me very happy, Polly. You know I feel the same way. Now go! Call when you get a chance. Have a safe trip!"

Polly didn't reach Matthew before she left. She kept questioning herself on the plane—was she acting irrationally? But she wanted so desperately to see the baby, help nurse it to health, God willing. Stop it! She couldn't allow herself to even think he wasn't going to make it. She was going to will him to live when she saw him, that's what she would do. That's why she just had to be there!

Polly followed the directions given at the reception desk and stood in front of room 309. Suddenly, she was very nervous about seeing Gloria Peters. They had spoken on the phone, of course, but the adoption lawyer believed the most prudent policy was to keep the relationship between the biological and the adoptive parents impersonal. Too close contact could cause complications. Polly knew all this when she'd made the decision to come to Chicago, but she had felt the circumstances justified going against his advice. She hadn't even discussed the trip or the new development with him. But now she had knots in her stomach.

Timidly she opened the door. The hospital room was fairly dark except for the reading light over the bed. Gloria Peters looked up and Polly inhaled sharply. The blond hair, the animated face—and, as she drew closer—yes, even the blue eyes— this girl could be her sister, or her daughter.

"Gloria?" Polly asked hesitantly.

"Yes?"

"I'm—I'm Polly Abavas."

Gloria put down her book and stared at Polly for a long while. Then she sighed sadly, and nodded. "Mom said she called you. Somehow I had a feeling you'd come."

"How—how are you? And how's—how's the baby?"

"I'm okay, a little tired and weak maybe, but okay." Then Gloria brightened. "And the baby is doing really well."

Polly's body sagged in relief. She pulled a chair over so she could sit next to the bed.

"He's small, but healthy, so I can even feed him—he doesn't have to stay in the incubator all the time. The doctor said he'll catch up real fast. He is so beautiful and so sweet."

"Oh, thank God!" Polly exclaimed gratefully.

"Mrs. Abavas—"

"Please call me Polly."

"Uh—Polly—why are you adopting?"

"Because I am unable to have children," Polly said simply. "A faulty tube, nothing I can do."

Gloria was quiet. Finally, she took a deep breath. "Mrs. A— Polly—I have to tell you something. I've been doing a lot of thinking about, well, many things. The past few months when— when he was very active, I realized for the first time there was a person in there. My person. Before, I hadn't thought much about what was there. I just thought about the best way to deal with the situation. Then, when the pains started and I knew something wasn't right, I panicked, 'cause I didn't want to lose my—my baby. They performed a cesarean so he wouldn't have to struggle, and when I came to, I saw this perfect little being . . . and my heart was so full of love and joy and wonder—"

Polly was absolutely still, her eyes glued to Gloria's face. She was barely breathing.

"I told my Mom I—I just couldn't give him up."

Gloria wasn't looking, so she didn't see the tiny, dewy beads rolling down Polly's cheeks.

"Mom said I couldn't do that, that I'd made a contract and it was wrong to renege now. That you had paid for all the expenses, that you and your husband would be devastated. I think that's why she called you right away. I told her that I would pay everything back, though it would take me a while. I told her I would marry Ted, he's the father, and get a job—" Gloria started to cry. "But I know, deep down, I'm doing a bad thing to you, and you seem so nice and you came all this way 'cause you were worried—so—so—I will—I will—go through with it." She broke down completely, sobs raking through her body.

Polly was riveted to her chair for a long moment, then moved heavily toward Gloria and sat on the bed. She took the shaking girl in her arms. "There, there, it's not good for you to cry, little mama. You'll break your stitches or something. And then you won't be able to care for your—your son." Polly was weepy and heartbreakingly disappointed, but strangely in control—and resolved. She knew exactly what she must do.

"You know, Gloria, it's almost spooky how much alike we are, outside and inside. I'm sure I would have reacted the very same way as you, if I'd had to face this problem at your age. You're a good person, honey, your instincts are solid."

Gloria looked at Polly, confusion appearing behind the tears. Polly smiled encouragingly. "I couldn't possibly adopt your baby now. He belongs to you. You've been through a great deal together, the bonding has already begun."

The young girl stared, afraid to believe what she was hearing. But Polly nodded. Gloria threw her arms around Polly and hugged her tight. "Oh, thank you, thank you! Thank you! You really mean it?"

"I really mean it. Maybe Matthew and I could be the godparents?"

"Oh, yes—absolutely—that would be wonderful!"

Polly pulled back a bit, so she could talk to her. "It's not going to be easy, Gloria, I hope you realize that. But you won't have to pay us back. Consider it our welcoming gift to our godchild."

Gloria started to object, but Polly overrode her. "No! Done deal! You won't be getting the lump sum that was coming at the time of delivery, but at least you won't start your life together in debt. It'll be hard enough as it is. Does—Ted, is it?—does he have a job? And do you love him?"

"Ted, it's Ted Brown, is going into his father's company, a small insurance agency. And yes—yes, I do love him...very much. I, oh, I was just being—trying to be independent, I guess. I don't need a master's to be a teacher. I'm not sure what I was thinking. Maybe I was just scared of baby and marriage both coming at me at once."

"But you're not scared now?" Polly asked softly.

"No, I'm not scared now. You are a remarkable lady, Polly Abavas. Can we be friends? I mean, real friends?"

"I think we already are, Gloria. As a matter of fact, aren't we almost related?"

A nurse came in carrying a tiny bundle. "Feeding time, Mrs. Peters."

"Oh, thank you. This is—this is my friend, from California, Mrs. Abavas. Could she hold him for a minute first? And would you ask the doctor if I could start nursing him? And he has a name now. Matthew Peters Brown—you see, Peters is my maiden name.'' All at once Gloria was in command.

Polly held the blue bundle close to her. So—so—tiny! The twins had not been huge, but the difference between four and a half and six pounds was surprising. She carefully handed her precious cargo to his mama, and drank in his every move. The way he pursed his lips around the bottle nipple, the way his little fist clenched and unclenched in satisfaction, the slight gas smile when he was being burped.

''My Matthew will be touched you named your son as you did, that was very thoughtful. But what about his daddy? He may not be too pleased.''

''Believe me, he will be so thrilled about what happened to-day, he won't mind anything. He's been in a complete funk since my decision. You'll be his fairy godmother, as well as Matthew's.''

The two new friends talked until both were exhausted. Polly planned to come back in the morning on her way to the airport. And promised, too, that Matthew and she would fly to Chicago for the christening and wedding. Polly had a lot to explain to her Matthew that evening, but she was confident he would support her judgment. On the way out, she stopped by to look through the window into the nursery. She waved, even though she knew little Matthew couldn't see her. ''Bye, sweet baby!''

58

Santa Monica, California
Wednesday, August 12,1964

"Another silver place setting! From the Pricklers! Wow, we are cleaning up!" Revel whooped as she unwrapped the last gift box of the day. "Now, we're supposed to display the gifts in some room, right? Isn't that what the etiquette book said?" she asked Polly and Penelope. The three ladies were finalizing the arrangements for the wedding and reception on Sunday.

"That's what it says," Polly answered, checking the page in the wedding book.

"It's a lot of work, this getting married," complained Revel. "I never could have done it alone. Maybe we should just go to Las Vegas instead."

"Oh, no, you don't!" Penelope warned. "No cold feet now! The guests have already accepted, you've had your showers, the rentals have been arranged, and the caterers and decorators are ready to start work Friday, and your whole family is about to arrive from Sun Valley. So you are, shall we say, trapped."

"Oh, I know, I was just kidding. But it *is* a lot of trouble. Are you sure you still want to have the wedding at your house, Penelope?"

"Positive! Eric and Anna are so excited. This will be their big finale because they're retiring at the end of the year, you know. I don't know what I'll do without them, but they deserve to relax now. Anyway, they would be crushed, as I would, if you changed your mind."

"Matt and I were married in that house. It was so beautiful," Polly said, smiling at the memory.

"I'm just afraid I'm causing everyone so much inconvenience," Revel worried.

"Will you hush up? You're just getting nervous," Penelope cautioned.

Polly continued, "Now, let's go down the checklist and make sure everything is covered. All the details of the entire three days."

They worked for another hour or so and found all was in order. Polly was matron of honor, Penelope the bridesmaid. Matthew was best man, Jude the usher. Dewayne and Buzz were ring bearers and Dewana and Prissy the flower girls. The reception would be at Revel's, with dune buggies transferring the guests from Penelope's house after the ceremony. The wedding rehearsal was scheduled for Saturday afternoon, and the traditional family dinner would be at Jude's home that evening.

"I am still in shock that Mama and Papa and all the rest are actually flying to California! Mama must be in some kind of tizzy," Revel exclaimed. "What's funny is, Vince just gave up his apartment, which his parents think he's been using, but now that everyone is coming, he'll have to stay at his folks' place until Sunday—it's like musical beds!"

Polly laughed. "Wait until John and Lila and Ethel and Clyde see their suites at the Shangri-La Beach Hotel. They will be treated like movie stars. The kids will think they've died and gone to heaven—they won't want to go home!"

"I know," Penelope chimed in, "and Willamina and Noah will be so thrilled to be at Jude's, and to see all their children's homes. What a happy time this is!"

"You're right," Revel agreed. "To have everyone here—and for *my* wedding—it *is* a very special time. Thank you, Polly. Thank you, Penelope. I love you so!" Impulsively, she got up and gave each woman a hug and kiss. "I'm anxious to meet Gloria and Ted and Matthew, Polly. That was really nice of you to bring them in from Chicago."

"They're good young people and I'm sure they will enjoy being a part of our family. And since they are staying with us, we'll get to see our godchild a lot. See? A method to my madness."

"Matt must be very proud of you, Polly. You behaved so unselfishly," Penelope said with admiration.

"Oh, I didn't do anything." Polly was slightly embarrassed. "It was Gloria. She was so—so damned noble, I had to rise up to her standards. Anyway, it's all worked out and the attorney thinks he has another possibility. Do you know he didn't charge us anything when the circumstances changed? I almost fainted—very unlawyerlike, if you get my drift!''

The jet Jude chartered touched down at Clay Lacy, a private terminal adjacent to Burbank Airport. Jude, Penelope, Matthew, Polly, Revel and Vince rushed forward to meet the Idaho contingent. The younger family members departed quickly, eager for their first venture into California. Then John and Lila and Ethel and Clyde, who were clearly as curious, appeared. And, finally, Noah helped Willamina from the plane, their eyes bright with excitement and a touch of bewilderment. In less than two and a half hours they had been thrust into another world. The vast disparity between locales had registered keenly during the approach for landing. It seemed to the observers that there had been a sea of buildings for at least twenty minutes. When they left Hailey, they'd flown beyond the developed area in twenty seconds—no, not even that long, more like ten.

Confusion reigned for a while with the greetings, the questions, the luggage. Jude had ordered two stretch limousines for the two families of five. Noah and Willamina rode in his car with Penelope. Matthew and Polly went to the hotel in John's limo; Revel and Vince in the other, to help with the checking-in process. Everything was so different, so new, so unfamiliar, they wanted to ease the transition as much as possible. After everyone was oriented, the limos would take them to Polly and Matthew's house, where the Friday night dinner would be held.

"Now, this is the city of Burbank," Jude explained to Noah and Willamina, probably echoing the dialogue in the other cars. "We'll travel southwest on Sepulveda Boulevard until Wilshire Boulevard, and then turn west to the beach."

Noah found his voice. Neither he nor Willamina had spoken much on the trip, nor upon their deplaning, there was just too much to absorb. "Then this be Los Angeles? Or Bur—bank? But you live in Santa Monica! And your work be in Hollywood! What is?"

Penelope helped Jude out. "All the names you mentioned are cities in the county of Los Angeles. Because there is also the city of Los Angeles, things can get confusing."

"So many peoples! So many automobiles! So many noises!" exclaimed Willamina. "You must have to go much hours, maybe days, to see open spaces and mountains."

"Actually," Penelope said gently, "when we get to the section where we live, the Santa Monica mountains are actually very close. Now, let me hasten to add, they do not compare to what you have in your backyard. But there are mountains and trees and some raw land. California is really unique, there is such a variety of climates and types of ground within relatively short distances. In Southern California, for instance, a person can travel for an hour and a half or two and be skiing in the winter. Or surfing in the Pacific Ocean. Or lounging in the sun in the desert, like Palm Springs."

"That is," Jude said, laughing, "unless the traffic is backed up and it takes an hour and a half just to get out of downtown! You're right, Mama, there are too many people."

"I think you'll be more comfortable as we approach our homes. Jude, why don't we turn off on Sunset Boulevard? It's more picturesque, less commercial than Wilshire."

"Good idea! Unless you're too tired, Mama and Papa, and want to rest right away, because Sunset does take longer."

"We be sixty-five and sixty-six, not a hundred and five and a hundred and six!" Willamina said indignantly. "We see everything—now!"

Penelope laughed. "Bully for you! It's a good thing you two are so sturdy, because the seamstress for your dress, Willamina, and the tailor for Noah's suit will be coming to Jude's later this afternoon. The measurements you sent were so complete, they think it will only be a matter of a few minor alterations. You must sew yourself?"

"I do little bit." Willamina beamed at Penelope's second-hand compliment.

Sepulveda was not wall-to-wall houses, and Willamina and Noah enjoyed that. When they turned on Sunset, they saw some of the grander estates.

"Look at that!" exclaimed Noah. "You say that be a home? Not hotel?"

"That's right, Papa!"

"All relatives live with family?"

"I doubt it, Papa. For instance, that place there might have just a husband and wife. Or just a guy and his, well, ah, a guy and his—uh—date."

"Plus an army of servants," Penelope added quickly to get Jude off the hook.

"My, my!" Willamina mumbled.

"You've heard of Will Rogers?" Penelope asked.

"I think so. He was nice man said he never met man he no like? Then plane crashed?"

"That's right! Well, just ahead on our right, is the entrance to the Will Rogers State Historic Park. The grounds were left to the state after his widow died. I hope you decide to stay this next week, I would love to take you through the park and to so many other interesting and beautiful spots!"

"Depend what Papa say." Willamina leaned over and whispered, "I tink maybe so."

The weather cooperated fully on Sunday, bright and sunny, with a slight breeze that cooled the hot summer air somewhat. The tent area at Penelope's looked like an oasis rising from the sand. The canvas was completely covered with greenery and white orchids, the floor paved with luxurious green carpet, the aisle bordered with arrangements of white ribbon and white gardenias at the end of each row. At the altar, huge candelabra were intertwined with giant gardenia plants. An organ and a choir were on risers in the back, entertaining the guests until all were seated. Finally Matthew escorted Mrs. Franks to her chair, and Jude guided Willamina to hers. The family had been flabbergasted when their mother appeared in her new dress. They had never thought that Willamina was actually beautiful—she was Mama. But they did that day. Willamina looked stunning in the pale yellow crepe Penelope had selected. Simple classic design, her long black and gray hair fashioned into a French twist, held by a pearl clasp. And a face that sparkled with happiness.

Prissy and Dewana captured everyone's attention as they toddled along, leading the wedding party, strewing flowers from their decorated baskets, thoroughly enjoying their duties. Buzz and Dewayne looked properly important, each charged with the responsibility of carrying a ring on a velvet cushion. Both were more worried about making a mistake than anything else. Jude and Penelope came next, followed by Matthew and Polly. The ladies wore a sheer chiffon print, the colors of canary yellow, white and beige blending together as in a finger painting. Off-the-shoulder, tight waist, with a full willowy ankle-length skirt. They carried nosegays of yellow and white flowers, and their hair was pulled back by a matching headband.

When they were positioned by the altar, Vincent joined the men, and all eyes were then focused on the archway where the bride would enter. The wedding march began and Revel and Noah appeared. Noah looked extremely dignified, his back straight, head held high and oh so proud. So proud of being there, so proud of his whole family, so proud and thankful for his God who had led his loved ones to such glory.

Revel had chosen, because of the new see-through-look fad, lace appliquéd to thin nude-colored silk jersey. The gown had a sweetheart neckline, long sleeves and a formfitting skirt that flared at the knees and flowed into a long train in the back—almost like a Spanish dancer's costume. Continuing that theme, a high mantilla adorned her head and yards of lace flowed over her long auburn hair. It was a spectacular offering and created just the effect Revel had hoped for. When she had been deciding on the lace, she had shocked Polly and Penelope with her matter-of-fact rationale behind her color selection. "I can't very well have pure white, you know. After all, I'm not exactly a virgin." So the lace was off-white, almost an ecru. Revel wore a fabulous pearl and diamond necklace and matching earrings from Madge's inheritance. She was a knockout! If it were proper to do so, the guests would have applauded. But their murmurings expressed their approval. Revel was thrilled and pleased with the obvious impact.

Tears of rejoicing and gratefulness flowed freely during the ceremony. Couples' hands unobtrusively reached for and found each other, wanting to share this celebration of love, silently declaring again their own vows in the presence of this newest union. Caught in the magic of the moment, Penelope and Jude were unaware that their hands were linked tightly together, too. It wasn't until everyone rose, as the bride and groom turned to walk back down the aisle, that they realized it and then self-consciously pulled away.

The second part of the wedding photo session was a cameraman's nightmare. The bride and groom and immediate wedding party were a dream. But trying to round up all the younger and older members of the families at the same time—twenty-seven in all—proved an almost impossible task. Finally, the perspiring, rotund photographer succeeded. And it was a treasure to behold, a certified miracle. Everyone was captured in an attractive pose—no closed eyes, no open mouths, no sneers, only pleasant expressions! And cheerful faces! Even John's!

The picture made the front page of the Ketchum and Hailey newspapers, and the society page of the other Idaho press. It paid such homage to Willamina and Noah's legacy that Jude later commissioned an artist to do a painting of the photograph. He would present this prize to his parents on their next anniversary, and it would be a continual source of blessedness to them from that day forward.

The moment arrived for the bride to throw her bouquet and Revel didn't even attempt to camouflage the direction. She turned and tossed it straight to a startled Penelope, who in turn blushed scarlet.

"Okay," Revel crowed, "you know what that means! You're next, my fair lady!"

Penelope tried to pass it off, mumbling something like, "It should have gone to one of your young friends, no sense wasting it on me."

But Revel and Polly wouldn't let her off the hook. "Who's the lucky guy?"

"If you don't know, better start looking, Penelope. Can't renege on this age-old custom—bad luck, you know!"

Willamina had been close by and observed the whole scene. She decided it was time to lend a hand to Penelope. "Revel, I take one last look at my baby in her wedding dress before you must change."

Revel obligingly assumed a pose and then went into her mother's arms. "Oh, Mama, I love you. Even though I'm a grown-up married lady, can I still be your little girl once in a while?"

"You always be my little girl, even when your hair be gray." Willamina rocked her, treasuring the moment, holding on to it as long as she dared. "Now, you must hurry, or you be late for husband."

59

Beverly Hills, California
Wednesday August 19, 1964

"Now we're in Beverly Hills, and this is The Bistro, a very popular spot for lunch. Tomorrow I'll take you to Ma Maison, another favorite hangout of the 'beautiful people.' That's in West Hollywood on Melrose Avenue. Have I completely confused you?" Penelope laughingly asked Willamina.

"You be so kind. And patient. I have such good time all week and I be so very happy. Thank you."

"I have had great fun. I really don't go out that much normally, so this is a real treat for me."

"I be so fortunate. Have opportunity to see and live in children's beautiful homes—Noah and me be so prideful and indebtful for His blessings on our family. And the wedding. And now you take me everywhere—you make me feel like queen."

"Well, you are! Queen Willamina! And what would my lady desire for lunch? I could suggest—"

Later, over coffee, Willamina suddenly said, "Forgive my boldness, I don't mean to mess in your life, but my heart be close to you. I watch your eyes, I hear way you talk—you love my Jude, don't you?"

This was a totally unexpected development. Penelope was shocked into speechlessness. She studied the older woman carefully for a long long moment, and found nothing but sincerity and compassion in her face. Penelope knew she could trust this wonderful, remarkable woman. She answered simply, "Yes," relieved to at last be able to acknowledge her feelings to someone.

"And he loves you. I know. I see his eyes follow your every move. I see the look in them. I listen and when he speaks of you, his voice changes. Why you two be afraid?"

"I'm not sure. I've thought so much about it, all I get is more bewildered."

"Tell me, I talk to no one. Sometime better to think out loud."

She sent Willamina a grateful look, then spoke, "You see, I've always loved Jude as a friend. And the bond between Wade and Jude was immense. We were always there for each other. After Wade died, Jude took full responsibility for me and the children. He was—he is, an incredible human being. I don't exactly know when my love for Jude came to mean that I was *in* love with Jude. The change was very subtle. But once I identified the difference, the guilt began. The widow falls for her husband's best friend—what could be worse? And what would the best friend think? He devotes his life to caring for the helpless family, and the wife betrays the memory of the beloved husband! But then, there are times when I believe Jude does have feelings toward me other than just ones of friendship. Oh, Willamina, I'm all mixed-up. I loved Wade with all my heart, and I would die before I would damage the relationship Wade and I had, or Wade and Jude had, or the three of us had. Am I a bad person for loving Jude now?"

Willamina covered the clenched hand with her own calm, strong, well-worn hand. "No, my child, you not be bad. You be normal—and good. You worry about everyone but you. Wade leave us over two and half year ago. He know you love him, and he know you be too young not to ever love again. I think ... I think he would be so happy that two people he loved most would be together. He would feel complete and comfortable with that thought. Now you or Jude must make move."

While the ladies were sightseeing, Noah visited Matthew's company and was impressed with what his youngest son had created. Another day, he went with Jude to spend a day at the studio and observe his oldest son in action. He recognized some of the character traits that had surfaced in Jude as a boy: that desire to constantly challenge himself, and consequently others, to go that one step further toward perfection; that lack of fear, actually welcoming competition; that doggedness in pursuing what he believed was right. Most of the time, these qualities had served him well, evidenced by his business achievements. Sometimes, more often personally, Noah mused, they had invited trouble.

Noah wandered around the office, examining the leather-framed photographs that were the room's main decor. All of the family were represented, as were many of Hollywood's leading stars, Wade and Penelope alone and with the children, and an early picture of Jude and Wade and Penelope. Noah peered closely; Jude was looking at Penelope while Wade and Penelope were smiling into the lens. With a sharp pang, Noah realized a saddening fact. He and Willamina had both recognized Jude's love for Penelope a year ago when everyone had come to Idaho in July. But now he knew just how long Jude had loved Penelope. And his heart ached for his son. It must have been so difficult for him all these years, he must have suffered so. Because Noah also understood the deep affection and love Jude had for Wade. He was filled with appreciation for his son, for Jude had behaved honorably. And Noah remembered the time, so long ago, when Jude and another brother had not deserved Noah's respect.

Noah had also noticed Penelope's feelings for Jude this trip, and he wondered why neither had ventured toward each other. They deserved to be happy and together, for both had conducted themselves with loyalty and dignity. Noah resolved he would talk to Jude.

"I'm going to miss them a lot," Penelope said wistfully on the return ride from the airport.

"I think we all will," Polly agreed.

"I'm so glad they stayed over. That decision sure surprised John and the others—they couldn't believe it when Mama and Papa didn't leave with them last Monday." Jude chuckled.

"I know," Matthew said. "I can't remember ever seeing Mama and Papa enjoy themselves for this length of time. They really cut loose."

"I wish they lived closer," Polly said. "Now that they've come once, though, maybe it won't be so hard to get them here more often. Oh, driver, you can let us off first, please. Right here is fine, thank you."

Matthew and Polly said their goodbyes and left Jude and Penelope to settle back into the comfort of the limousine.

"I feel such a letdown," Penelope said moodily.

"Me, too." Jude thought a minute. "Tell you what—let's go to my place, jump in the car and drive to Santa Barbara for lunch. What do you say?"

"I say great! Why don't we grab a blanket and a couple of swimsuits and some towels, and maybe we could bring the lunch to a beach and have a picnic?"

It was a lovely drive. Jude put the top down on his Lincoln Continental convertible and the wind blew away their sagging spirits. They didn't say much, just listened to music and took pleasure in the view. And thought!

Jude thought about his conversation with Noah. Penelope thought about her conversation with Willamina. Each wondered if their feelings were as obvious to everyone else as they apparently were to Noah and Willamina. And horrors—as obvious to each other? Each had struggled so valiantly to keep the proper mask in place, Jude for ever so long. And now were they completely exposed? And if so, was that good or bad? It was terribly terribly difficult to just wipe away these deeply ingrained misgivings. And what if Noah and Willamina were wrong about the other one's supposed affection? Then whoever said something first would be in a dreadful position. Neither could bring themselves to take the risk.

"There's a MacDonald's!" Penelope exclaimed. "Let's order from the drive-thru and bring it back to that pretty little beach we passed about fifteen minutes ago. Remember?"

"Sure do! Tell me what you want, then you can use their rest room to change. It's easy for me to slip into my trunks in the car."

They spread the blanket and never had a real gourmet luncheon tasted as delicious. The cheeseburgers and chocolate milk shakes hit the spot.

"The water looks too tempting—I'm off!" Penelope said after a while, and raced away. Jude waited a bit, watching her lithe, supple body run gracefully toward the surf before she plunged into a wave. He wondered why everything had to be so complicated? Why couldn't he tell her he loved her?

He noticed she was getting a little too far out and yelled, "Hey! Come back in." And then realized of course she couldn't hear him, not with the sound of the ocean. He bolted over the sand and dove in, swimming rapidly in her direction. She wasn't floundering or panic-stricken, but she was glad he was there.

"I—can't—seem to—make any headway—to shore," she managed to say between strokes.

"Pretty strong undercurrent pulling you out! Straddle my back—hold on around my middle. Keep low. I think I can breaststroke us back."

Jude struggled against the strength of the riptide. With a final burst of effort, he was relieved to feel sandy ground beneath his feet and the two wearily flopped down in the shallow water. Penelope was still clasping his waist, their bodies now lightly brushing from head to toe. They became aware of their nearness at the same time, and simultaneously reached for the other. Neither had to make the first move or say the first word, it was spontaneous. They kissed, they touched, almost in slow motion, in wonderment, their minds not able to believe this wasn't a dream, but the electricity confirming reality. There was no undue urgency; they both instinctively knew they had the rest of their lives.

They were alone in the little cove, it was as if the outside world had ceased to exist for these two. They lay in the wet sand, partly submerged by the lapping waves, holding each other. They wouldn't let go, even when they shed their suits, unwilling to be apart for a second. His hands stroked her hair, then wandered over her face, as a blind person committed a loved one's features to memory. He examined her arms, clear to her fingertips, and followed her outline all the way to her toes. Jude had suppressed his Penelope fantasies for so many years, he yearned to inspect and become an expert on every single part of her body. And he expected his study to take a very long time.

When they had reviewed each other until every nerve of their bodies was stretched to the limit, his swollen pulsating manhood found its home in her. The sheer beauty of this moment, the love that was power in the air, was almost too much to bear. They climbed to a dizzying height. And then sobbed happily in each other's arms.

60

Forest Lawn Memorial Park, Hollywood Hills, California
Monday, August 24, 1964

Jude stood in front of the simple but elegant headstone that marked the grave of Wayland Colby Prickler. A lovely bouquet of colorful flowers had been placed there; Penelope had arranged for a fresh basket every day from the beginning. It was a beautiful, restful spot and Jude felt at peace. Yesterday had launched the first day of the rest of his life with Penelope, and he needed to share this new life with his comrade. Just as he had been guided by his talks with Thelma over the years, he firmly believed he would be shown the way by Wade too.

He knelt so he would be even closer, and quietly spoke aloud to his friend. "Well, old buddy, how are you doing? I really miss you, Wade—everybody does! There isn't a day goes by that I don't wish you were here. But damn it, you're not! I'm not sure how it works up there, I have a hunch you know everything that's going on down here. Is that true? I have to think it is. Because—because then you would know that our hearts, Penelope's and mine, were always loyal to you. What has happened—what happened yesterday—grew a long time after you left us. At least Penelope's feelings for me came after.

"You see, I loved her—the same time you did. But, but she never knew. And when you told me you loved her, I just buried my feelings. So no one ever knew. And after you were gone, my only thought was to watch over your family for you. Penelope and Buzz and Prissy loved and needed you so much. So did I.

"I can never take your place in their hearts—I wouldn't want to. What I hope is that we will start a new and different life, and yours would always be just like it was in their memories. Am I making any sense?''

Jude had been so intent, he hadn't heard the footsteps, but suddenly he felt a presence.

"You are making perfect sense," Penelope said softly.

Jude stood up, startled.

"How did I know you would be here?" she wondered for him. "It's uncanny how our minds think so much alike, how in tune we are. Come!" And together they knelt again. "Wade, my love, I have faith that you understand the truth. We come before you, for your blessing."

Jude and Penelope looked upward, praying for some sign. And then they heard the chapel bells start ringing joyfully in the distance. That was it. That was their sign. That was their blessing.

Jude and Penelope talked a long time. They knew each other so well, yet they hardly knew each other at all. And always they touched, always made contact, reassuring themselves this was reality.

Their main concern was the children. How would they react to Mommy's marrying again? And to Uncle Jude? In the days that followed, Penelope had discussions with the psychiatrist who had helped her after Wade's death. His suggestions were invaluable: he reminded her that if she was comfortable, the children would be comfortable. That it would be reassuring for them to have a father figure in the house. Their daddy would always be their daddy, but Jude would become the new head of the house.

By Friday, Penelope and Jude decided it was time. They had an early dinner with Buzz and Prissy, and afterward the whole family played with Tiddlywinks on the patio.

"I have a surprise for you two," Penelope announced.

"Goodie, I like 'spises," squealed Prissy.

"*Surprises,* you ninny!" Buzz corrected. "What is it, Mom?"

"Uncle Jude is going to live with us and be here all the time. Isn't that wonderful?"

"Goodie! Goodie! Will you put me on your shoulders every night so I'm the biggest one?" Prissy asked.

"I don't see why not." Jude laughed.

"Why?" Buzz wanted to know. "Why is Uncle Jude moving here?"

"Because—because Mommy and Uncle Jude are going to get married. Uncle Jude will be the head of our house now."

Buzz and Prissy thought about that for a minute.

Prissy spoke first. "Does that mean you're our daddy?"

"Your daddy—my friend—was and will always be your daddy. But since he was called to heaven, I'll be his substitute. So Mommy and you will have someone here to look after you, and love you," Jude gently explained.

Now it was Buzz's turn. "Do we have to call you Daddy?"

"Not at all! You can call me whatever you want."

"Are our names going to be different?" Buzz continued. "And do we have to mind him?" he asked his mother.

"Of course your names will be the same—Wayland Earle Prickler Colby and Priscilla Helena Prickler Colby," Penelope assured him. "Your father is your father! However, my last name would be Abavas—Penelope Colby Abavas." Now she became resolute. "And yes, you both will mind Uncle Jude. But that's nothing different—you mind him now!"

Penelope sat down and drew the two into the circle of her arms. "I want you to understand some things. I loved your daddy so much, and you know how sad we were when he had to leave us. Mommy has been very lonely. Uncle Jude and your father were like brothers, and he promised your father he would care for us through a difficult time. And you know he did. Gradually, over the last almost three years, Uncle Jude and Mommy fell in love. And I am very happy. And I want you to be happy with me. With us."

Jude joined hands with Penelope, the children in the center. "I promise I will try hard to make this a joyful and solid family. We'll all have to help—it may be strange at first, but I know we can do it. Because we love one another." Jude looked lovingly at Penelope and the children. And silently he thanked God for granting him this destiny.

EPILOGUE

Friday, March 16, 1990

Armed policemen pulled open the heavy metal doors. This was it! No reprieve now!

Jude Abavas blinked rapidly, trying to adjust from the relative darkness of the kitchen corridor he had just left to the dazzling array of spotlights that awaited him in the massive International Ballroom of the Beverly Hilton Hotel. As he walked, escorted by his honor guard, each table of ten rose to pay him tribute. He made his way through the crowd, stopping here and there briefly to shake a hand. In the distance, he saw the slightly elevated dais where his family awaited him. Their presence always made his heart beat faster, but tonight he was even more affected.

My family! My precious family, he thought. My beautiful Penelope. My sons—my children—my treasured children. Even now I still get chills when I think of how close I was to losing the two of you—maybe even the three of you. Will I ever forget the call, the terror that Penelope was in the hospital, that she'd collapsed? I prayed so hard to you, Lord. And you heard—you heard! It was all right. Penelope stayed in bed for the last three months of her pregnancy, but then the miracle. I can feel it as if it were yesterday, that indescribable thrill of holding my babies in my arms for the first time, looking at my radiant wife. I thought I was going to be denied that after Keane was lost, and the other lil' guy. But you spared me, God, and even gave us twin sons, in addition to Buzz and Prissy. And there they all are— strong and healthy and loving. How blessed I am . . .

Jude finally reached the dais. Penelope's eyes were full and her lips were quivering. He kissed the wetness and nervousness away.

He went around to embrace his sons, Jude Noah and William Robert, now almost twenty-two; his stepson Buzz, who at thirty-four preferred to be called Wade; his stepdaughter who didn't mind Prissy, even at thirty; Matthew and Polly and the twins, Dewayne and Dewana, and their youngest child, Darryl; Revel and Vince and their three redheaded children; John and Lila and their offspring; and Ethel and Clyde and theirs.

This night of nights was the Cinema Institute of America's annual gala presentation of its Life Achievement Award. And tonight it was to be given to Jude William Abavas.

Jude surveyed the plush, newly decorated room and shook his head in disbelief. There wasn't extra space for one more chair. He saw the heads of each studio, each major talent agency, independent producers, directors, writers, and as the old M-G-M slogan used to say, "More stars than there are in heaven." And they were all there for him! It didn't seem possible. He pressed Penelope's hand so hard, she pulled it away in pain.

"I'm sorry, honey. I was trying to hold on to some kind of reality."

"I know," she whispered. "I understand. But this big ring you gave me digs into my flesh. I'll put it on the other hand, then you can squeeze as hard as you want."

Well-wishers kept coming by their table. Everyone wanted to be a part, however small, of this special evening. Eating was impossible, even sipping a drink was difficult.

Jude leaned toward Penelope and said quietly, "I promise you one thing, I'm going to have one stiff belt before I have to go up there."

"I'll join you," she agreed.

Finally, the program began. First came some film clips of Jude's television shows, television specials and feature pictures, starting with *Who Did Done It?*

The president of the Cinema Institute of America came to the lecturn. He introduced a number of celebrities in the audience and a few industry leaders who offered brief tributes to Jude. He then explained he was turning the remainder of the evening over to Mr. Matthew Abavas.

Matthew stepped briskly to the platform amidst loud fanfare from the orchestra and welcoming applause from the audience.

"We are going to do something a little different tonight. Because my brother came from such a large family, and because we were always very close, I thought it would be appropriate to let them tell you a bit about the man you are honoring tonight.''

Jude sunk low in the chair. ''Oh, no!'' he moaned to Penelope.

''Shhh!'' she scolded.

Matthew had talked to each family member privately and had helped them write their tribute. Some stories were to be funny, some poignant, all were to end with a greeting of love.

Matthew had been sure that John's would be the most difficult to compose. He felt John should go first because he was Jude's twin and the oldest child. Matthew had always been aware that John and Jude weren't as close as they could have been. But it was John himself who wrote his speech.

Jude was apprehensive when John rose, wondering what his twin brother would say.

John took the microphone and began. ''He always made me so mad 'cause he bested me every time. We'd be neck and neck in a race and then a dog would come outta nowhere and bite my—well, bite my fanny—an' I'd fall. And he'd win! Always somethin' like that would happen. Bet I can beat ya now, though, you've gotten city-soft, I reckon.''

That was rewarded with a big laugh. John stared at Jude for a long time. Matthew was ready to move on because he knew that was all John had to say, but John didn't sit down. Finally, he said, haltingly, ''But I guess you were a—okay brother. You were always good to Mama and Papa, and that was good.'' He walked over to Jude and held out his hand. Jude stood and took John's hand and then embraced him. No one else knew exactly what this exchange meant. But the emotion was felt by everyone in the room.

It was a night of touching moments. As, one by one, the family stood, it became clear the impressive number of lives that had been positively affected by Jude Abavas. Ethel and Clyde were a mite uncomfortable in this unfamiliar role, but were very sincere and sweet. Vincent spoke candidly and eloquently. Revel was her usual outrageous and captivating self. The children were endearing and so proud. Polly was, as always, honest and straightforward, all with her charming brand of humor.

Penelope. Well, Penelope was magical. Her voice soared with passion. ''Fifty-four years ago, Wade Colby and Jude Abavas met in Sun Valley, Idaho. And that was the beginning of a friendship, a kinship, that knew no equal. Seventeen years later,

I was privileged to meet them, work with them and be their friend. And better friends you couldn't find. They would have died for each other and for their loved ones. When Wade left us, I knew without a doubt Jude would have begged to take his place had that been possible. I know, too, that Wade is watching this, lauding your choice of honoree, wishing he could add his words. But don't worry, sweetheart, you are being heard tonight. And your pride in your comrade is coming through loud and clear.''

She turned to Jude. ''Congratulations, comrade, from your loving wife.'' He stood as the entire room stood, in absolute silence, in awe of what they were experiencing.

Finally, Jude lifted her hand to his lips and kissed it. He couldn't talk; he didn't have to.

Matthew cleared his throat, the audience settled back in their seats. ''My brothers and sister and I were the product of two remarkable people, Willamina and Noah Abavas. They were immigrants from the Basque Spanish Pyrenees, Papa arrived in 1915 and Mama in 1918. They raised five children, became citizens, and worked long and hard. And well. Well enough to establish a very successful business. They taught us well, too. By example. They taught us values, loyalty, faith, love. They were aware of this evening, and had hoped to attend. But Papa knew Mama wasn't feeling well, so he wrote a note for Jude from them, just in case she wasn't up to the trip. We lost—we lost Mama first. And Papa—well—Papa—joined her soon after. They were together seventy-one years, and now they are together for eternity. I—I hope I can get through this.''

Matthew took a single sheet of paper from his vest pocket and began. '' 'To our beloved Jude. We be so proud for you this great night. We know whole family be there and be happy, too. You bring honor to all of us. Mama and me thank our Lord for each of our children. Your—a—award—is right?' ''

Matthew lowered the paper for a second. ''Yes, Papa, award is right.'' He needed that break to get a hold of himself.

Then he said, '' 'Your award be like—like respect to all of us family. Mama and me content to be with our Lord. He bless us many many ways. We be full of love for you all. Mama and Papa.' ''

Again, the absolute silence. Again, the awe of being privy to such simple, pure devotion.

Matthew continued, ''Jude, I myself can't add much, it's all been said. I am grateful I was born into this family, and that you are my brother and my friend. I have learned from you, we all have learned from you, this industry has learned from you. And everyone is in a better place because you were here. Thank you.''

Matthew looked out at the sea of faces, and, in a strong voice said, "Ladies and gentlemen, Mr. Jude William Abavas!''

There was a roar of approval and thunderous applause as Jude rose. The audience felt they had been allowed to view the inner sanctum of an extraordinary family; they felt part of that force; they felt part of Jude.

At last he was up the few steps and in front of the microphone. Matthew handed the heavy crystal statue to Jude, hugged him and backed away, with tears in his eyes.

Jude just stood there and stared at his prize. Stared at the standing assembly. Stared at Penelope and his loved ones. Stared upward to his God. His heart and eyes were so full, he didn't think he could breathe, let alone speak.

But gradually he raised his hand for quiet, kissed the trophy and placed it on the stand. Then, with both hands, he subdued the banquet room, motioning for everyone to sit and be comfortable. And then he found his voice.

"I—I had planned to be clever—very clever and funny tonight. But you knocked me out—clear out of the ballpark. And now I don't know what I'm going to say. Thank you, of course— oh, my God, do I thank you! God and you and so many others. One thing I know I have to do is use the Kiss Method, Keep it Simple Stupid, or I'll be preaching to the choir.''

Jude stopped, smiling in remembrance. "Right now, Wade would be shaking his head in disbelief. 'He is *still* using those corny Idaho expressions!' And he's absolutely right, I am. I guess it's really true—you can take the boy out of the country, but you can't take the country out of the boy!''

He paused. "But, you know, that's okay. Wade liked to tease me, but I don't believe for a second he wanted to change me to what I wasn't. Learn? Definitely! Grow? Definitely! He knew my family and loved them dearly. You met them tonight—and you heard from Mama and Papa. He didn't—and I don't—ever want to lose what they all taught me. Especially Mama and Papa. It's been a long road to this podium, personally and professionally. From Idaho to California, a road lined with failures and tragedies, but also a road filled with happiness, successes and progress. And I hope it's not the end of the road. I hope the gold watch or this award doesn't mean it's over. I hope it marks the launching of the next step of my development. Because I think there's life in this old boy yet. I think there's something I can still bring to this business I love, and which has been so good to me. I try not to live in the past—I live for today and the future. But I will not deny the past. Inevitable change does not automatically negate what preceded it. Lessons learned should be carried forward to enhance the new.

"I've been thinking about this for quite a while. I guess now is as good a time as any to get it off my chest. I believe the industry's direction should be toward the return of a chain of command closer to the core of creativity. I understand the need for corporate takeovers financially, bigger companies compete better against foreign markets. But creatively, we've dropped the ball in many cases. In huge conglomerates, very often the entertainment branch is the lowest on the totem pole. A company too diversified can cause havoc and confusion. And dilution of purpose—in ours, the goal of entertainment. I'm afraid I've been guilty, as well. But I'm not going to continue to be. Film reflects the moods of the times, turmoil and churning and unrest and violence provoke a similar output in the product produced. I remember when I went to the movies as a kid in Idaho, when I could scrape up the ten cents for the ticket. Hope, dreams, miracles, beauty, glamour, exciting sagas of times gone by were offered. And realism. Then the trend started to shift, swinging to the ugly, to graphic violence and sex, to appealing to the lowest common denominator of the public's psyche.

"I have noticed lately, not just with my contemporaries, but with our children and their peers, a searching and longing for roots. With all the wandering exploration, perhaps we need to return to some of those basics I mentioned from my childhood. Maybe the pendulum is swinging back, at least somewhat, to the need for escapism. Everyday events are shown so thoroughly and tragically on television news and programs, it isn't too difficult to understand why this is so. Violence and sex are so explicitly depicted, it becomes almost ordinary, even the most brutal forms of it.

"*Where* is our imagination? There are some brave and adventuresome and independent souls out there—but far too few. We have to be inventive and sharp so we can allow the *audience* the joy of imagination. I do not propose to return mentally to our origins, but to bring back the simplicity and honesty and continuity our origins gave us. To bring back strength. And we must never forget our purpose—*entertainment!* We can't turn back the clock to tent shows or nickelodeons or silents, but we can and should go back to what those creators always tried to give us—*entertainment!* And they did it under primitive conditions, but they did it. They made us laugh and cry and feel good and feel sad and that is *entertainment!* No one learns a profession overnight. The founders *loved* the movies—a key word *loved*—and worked and learned and worked and learned and worked some more. We have to learn the evolution so we can create it anew. An artist explained it clearly, 'To paint free-form, you have to learn the form before you become free.' Hell, just when I thought I knew it all, I produced a picture that Wade and I had always wanted to make. And damn near sunk the studio. The costs had skyrocketed so fast and I hadn't kept up. Fortunately for me, the audience wanted to see it—it was done with *love* and it was *entertaining*—and they, the people, bailed me out. But I sure learned!

"Hearing Mama and Papa's words and feeling their inner peace tonight reminded me of some thoughts I would like to put before you in closing.

"It wasn't always wrong to be normal.

"It isn't 'square' to care about a job and fulfill obligations.

"Values are valid and respected if one has the courage to show them.

"With those important characteristics of yesterday, today is assured. We need them today, or tomorrow is in jeopardy."

Jude picked up the crystal award and held it high. He looked to his family and then his eyes included every person in the immense room. "Each and every one of you deserves one of these, whatever your role in life. Because you *did* it! I'm just the momentary custodian. Thank you from the bottom of my heart, for the honor you bestowed on me tonight.

"Wade Colby is the one who made this night—and my career—possible. He took me into his home, his profession, his heart. He trusted me and shared his soul. And he opened the doors to a new life for me. I salute him with deep love and respect.

"I am grateful to everyone for the privilege of being in this business, for the opportunities I was given, for the guidance and acceptance I received. The heavens have smiled on me and I will never stop trying to be worthy. Papa said it best, 'I be full of love for you all!'"

The applause was deafening.